Dear Reader:

The book you are a[...]r from St. Martin's True [...] *York Times* calls ''the [...] we offer you a fascinat[...] sational crime that has captured the national attention. *The Milwaukee Murders* delves into the twisted world of Jeffrey Dahmer, one of the most savage serial killers of our time; *Lethal Lolita* gives you the *real* scoop on the deadly love affair between Amy Fisher and Joey Buttafuoco; *Whoever Fights Monsters* takes you inside the special FBI team that tracks serial killers; *Garden of Graves* reveals how police uncovered the bloody human harvest of mass murderer Joel Rifkin; *Unanswered Cries* is the story of a detective who tracked a killer for a year, only to discover it was someone he knew and trusted; *Bad Blood* is the story of the notorious Menendez brothers and their sensational trials; *Sins of the Mother* details the sad account of Susan Smith and her two drowned children; *Fallen Hero* details the riveting tragedy of O. J. Simpson and the case that stunned a nation.

St. Martin's True Crime Library gives you the stories *behind* the headlines. Our authors take you right to the scene of the crime and into the minds of the most notorious murderers to show you what really makes them tick. St. Martin's True Crime Library paperbacks are better than the most terrifying thriller, because it's all true! The next time you want a crackling good read, make sure it's got the St. Martin's True Crime Library logo on the spine—you'll be up all night!

Charles E. Spicer, Jr.

Charles E. Spicer, Jr.
Senior Editor, St. Martin's True Crime Library

"And he promised to kill more?"

Finally Major Kramer waved his arms and restored quiet.

"The morning of the 12th," he began, "some crazy bastard called the sheriff's office saying he killed three people and begged to be arrested before he killed more tonight."

The police officers were transfixed as they stared at the major.

"You mean there's a crazy killer on the loose?" asked Goetz.

"And he promised to kill more?" exploded Melrose. Cox remained silent. He was afraid that a serial killer was loose and dreaded the impact on the women of the community when the news was released that an insane murderer was stalking his next victim.

"Excuse me, Major, but are there any clues of who this person is who called, or any idea of where he could be found? Any idea at all of where to start?" asked Detective Cox.

"Only his voice," replied Kramer sadly. "Only his voice captured on tape."

THE CATCH-ME KILLER

JOSEPH A. VARON

(Published in hardcover as *A Matter of Judgment*)

St. Martin's Paperbacks

This publication is designed to provide accurate and authoritative information in regard to the subject matter covered. It is sold with the understanding that the publisher is not engaged in rendering legal, accounting, or other professional service. If legal advice or other assistance is required, the services of a competent professional person should be sought. *From A Declaration of Principles jointly adopted by a Committee of the American Bar Association and a Committee of Publishers.*

Published in hardcover as *A Matter of Judgment*

Published by arrangement with Lifetime Books

THE CATCH-ME KILLER

Copyright © 1994 by Joseph A. Varon.

Cover photograph courtesy of the *Miami Herald.*

Library of Congress Catalog Card Number: 94-15368

ISBN: 0-312-95934-6

Printed in the United States of America

Lifetime Books hardcover edition published in 1994
St. Martin's Paperbacks edition/June 1996

St. Martin's Paperbacks are published by St. Martin's Press, 175 Fifth Avenue, New York, NY 10010.

10 9 8 7 6 5 4 3 2 1

DEDICATION

To Helen—who wanted
this story to be told.

CONTENTS

CONTENTS

PREFACE

"... there is no such thing as justice either in or out of court. In fact, the word cannot be defined."
Clarence S. Darrow

At the very core of the American justice system a strong voice screams out for fundamental fairness and preservation of human rights, but the true course of justice is thwarted in many ways. For more than a half century I've defended hundreds of murder cases, with painful awareness of the haunting specter that an innocent man or woman may be convicted for a crime he or she did not commit. The traumatic effect of such eventuality is unbearable. There are many instances where providence intervened to reveal the innocence of the wrongfully convicted person, most likely after he or she has served a long, grueling prison term. The prosecution officials apologize. The ex-convict is free to pick up the pieces of his or her broken life.

The story of Florida's *Catch Me Killer* puts the criminal justice system on trial impelling the reader to share my fears and frustrations as ex-policeman Robert Erler's trial attorney. The result is strictly a matter of judgment.

The real names of the individuals in this book have been used wherever possible. Some names have been altered to protect those individuals from embarrassing exposure, but the details of the murder trial were faithfully and accurately recorded.

I want to thank H. Allen Etling, of Lawyer's Literary Agency, Inc. in Fort Lauderdale for his invaluable assistance in molding and restructuring the story that had to be told. For that, and more, I am truly grateful.

JOSEPH A. VARON

THE CATCH-ME KILLER

I
CRIME AND VICTIMS

AROUND 2:30 A.M., on August 12, Patrolman Larry Livingston of the Hollywood Police Department was routinely patrolling the city's expanse of warm sandy beaches. The night was unusually dark. There was practically no light from the August moon, but there was a cool breeze floating in from the quiet, rippling Atlantic. This was a welcome respite from the ever-present and oppressive summer heat.

No bathers or picnickers were allowed on the beach after sundown, but some teenagers would park their cars, drink beer, eat junk food and then litter the idyllic spot with their discarded trash. After their repast they would more likely than not culminate the evening with a common, sought-after reward: sex.

Officer Livingston relished sneaking up on these parked cars, to see what he would "discover." His oft-rewards were sights that would make a porno film seem tame. He once arrested a county commissioner who he caught in a parked car, on his knees with his head buried between a girl's legs.

On this particular morning, Livingston parked his police cruiser at Sheridan Street to make his hourly sweep and spotted a small car parked on the beach. Leaving his cruiser and trudging through the sand, he approached a dark green Ford Falcon with Georgia plates. The officer crept up to the car with caution; not so much for his safety but on the off-chance that he could witness another romantic episode to liven up an otherwise dreary chore.

Peeking into the darkened car, he detected a matronly woman in hair curlers sleeping on the front seat. In the rear, where he usually found all the sexual action taking place, was the sleeping figure of a teenage girl. Livingston knocked on the window and roused the occupant on the front seat. She rolled the window down, releasing a billow of smoke that hit him in the face, making him gag and cough.

"What do you want?" the woman sleepily inquired.

"I'm a police officer," responded Livingston, fanning the smoke away so he could have a clearer view of the two occupants, and raked the car with his flashlight awakening the young girl. "You can't park on the beach at this hour."

"We have no place to stay. We're out of money and have been sleeping in our car for the past few days," whined the puffy eyed woman.

The officer's nose wrinkled with distaste as he continued to explore the car with his light, viewing the filthy unkempt interior that reeked from a combination of urine and burnt fabric.

"Where did all that smoke come from? Did you have a fire in your car?"

"No," replied the woman, "I just burned some sanitary napkins to keep the mosquitoes away."

"Let me see some identification."

The woman reached into the glove compartment extracting a wallet and while fumbling for her driver's license explained, nodding her head to the rear, "This is my daughter Merilyn. She's twelve years old. My name is Dorothy Clark and I'm from Clarkston, Georgia. We came down here looking for work and had to sleep where we could."

Officer Livingston examined the wallet's meager contents which contained a driver's license, Georgia automobile registration and a snapshot of the teenager in the rear seat. Satisfied that the minimum police routine was adequately accomplished, he backed away from the unsightly mess, saying, "Sorry lady, but you have to get out of here. I suggest you find some other place that's better illuminated and safer."

"Gee, Mom," came a voice from the rear, "do we have to move again?"

"Now that your daughter is awake, I suggest you both go north of here. The next town is Dania. They have a nice beach and no one will bother you there."

"Thanks, officer," replied Mrs. Clark. "We will leave immediately."

The disgruntled visitors settled in the car and proceeded in a northerly direction toward Dania. The officer looked on to make certain they cleared the area, and lumbered back to his police car to make an Incident Report, which was unobtrusively filed as a routine report of police activities for his shift commander to peruse.

Dorothy Clark and her teenage daughter, Merilyn, dutifully headed north in the wee hours of the morning and found another resting place on Dania's sandy beach. Before retiring for the remainder of the night they burned another sanitary napkin to discourage the horde of mosquitoes that attacked her and Merilyn. Suddenly a uniformed figure loomed through the waves of smoke.

"Is your car on fire?" asked the stranger.

"No," Dorothy replied and explained her object in burning the rags.

The stranger brandished a gun, levelling it to her head, snarling, "Hand me your dough!"

"I'm dead broke," she nervously laughed, trying to conceal her fear, and turning to daughter in the rear remarked, "Boy, I sure can pick them."

"And how," ventured her streetwise daughter.

That was all Dorothy Clark remembered.

2

DAWN WAS BREAKING over the pale, turquoise-hued, three-story brick courthouse in Fort Lauderdale with the promise of another steamy day. There were no overnight prisoners in the county jail. The sheriff saw to that because he wanted to spare A. G. Whitman, the aging jailer, from night duty, and all prisoners would be released upon their respective promises to return the following morning. Any prisoner who was a stranger or visitor from out-of-town could arrange bail with Chief Deputy Bob Clark, who also acted as bondsman. The sheriff's office was deserted with the exception of two new deputies who manned the split shifts until the following 8:00 A.M.

Business was slow and there was nothing for Deputy James Rice to do on the morning of August 12, but patiently wait until he was relieved from his duty station. He was tired from the fruitless loafing and the more his mind wandered aimlessly, the more sleepy he would become. Looking up toward the overhead fan that slowly turned at half speed, gently stirring the dank air, Rice followed the shadows disappearing from the blades, trying to invent a game to keep his mind occupied for fear of falling asleep.

The deputy's eyes followed a single strip of walnut molding that separated the painted ceiling from the soiled beige grass wallpaper. They came to rest upon the monstrous voice activated recorder that stood six feet high and seemed ludicrously out of place in the primitive office that consisted of a wooden counter supporting a telephone and two bar stools.

The deputy smiled as he remembered how the sheriff was criticized in the *Fort Lauderdale News* for spending so much money on an oversized recording unit. The editorial claimed there was no need for such a sophisticated device in such a small inactive office and demanded a public explanation. The sheriff, however, spoke only to his adoring constituents and left official statements and explanations to Major Kramer, the only articulate member on the entire staff.

"The recording unit would be activated by an incoming telephone call and receive all outside transmissions," explained the major. "A deputy on duty would field all the calls and catalog any citizen's complaints for attention."

What the major did not explain was that unless unusual exigencies existed to warrant otherwise, the tapes would be erased after a thirty day period and the recordings would thereupon be consigned to oblivion.

At exactly 6:18 A.M. Deputy Rice snapped awake from his reverie by the crackling of the telephone on the counter.

"Sheriff's Office," answered Rice as he picked up the phone and sat on the stool in one motion, "Can I help you?"

"I would like to report a murder." The voice was tense and agitated.

"Who is this?" asked the deputy.

"I just killed three people—please catch me before I kill more."

Deputy Rice leaped to attention and shouted, "You just killed three people?"

The distraught caller answered, "Please, please catch me . . . I ju—please!"

"Where are you?" thundered the agitated deputy, but the only response was a pathetic whimper, "I'm going to kill more tonight, too. Please, please, please!"

Rice looked up at the new oversized voice activated tape recording unit to make certain the weird telephone call was recorded. The caller's voice seemed to be too tense and fraught with emotion to be a crank call.

"This is Deputy Rice of the Sheriff's Department Complaint Desk. Are you serious about this?"

"I'm serious. Please catch me. Come and get me, please?"

"Where are you, son?" asked Rice.

"I ju—please!"

"Where are you?"

"I'm gonna kill more tonight, too. Please!"

"Where are you?"

The caller hung up and Rice stared at the dead phone in his hand as he asked himself if this was a crank call, or what? There were a few practical jokers now and then to test the new machine, but this particular call seemed the real thing to him. Maybe he ought to run it by his co-worker, Harold Lemore.

"Hey, Harold," shouted Rice, "Come here right away and listen to this call."

"What is it?" asked Lemore, strolling casually to the complaint desk.

"I just received a phone call from some weirdo that he just killed three people and wanted to be stopped before he killed any more."

"Do you have the call on tape?"

"Yes, the unit is working fine."

"You better alert the brass right away, unless you feel it's some kid playing games."

"This was no kid stuff," answered Rice. "Just play the tape back and judge for yourself."

Lemore, being the more experienced officer, replayed the taped message and whistled in amazement as he heard the agonizing words of the distressed caller.

"It seems to me," he remarked to his fellow deputy, "there was a possible disconnection in the transmission, and the chances are this guy will call again."

"Shouldn't we call the sheriff on this?" asked Deputy Rice, which brought a combination laugh and snort from Lemore.

"Never bother the sheriff on something like this," smiled the senior deputy, "and don't tie up this phone calling anyone else as I expect this dodo to call again. Just haul ass to Major Kramer and fill him in." At approximately 6:30 A.M. the phone rang again.

"Complaint Desk," responded Lemore.

"Ba . . . Brice, Brice—uh, Rice?"

"Rice? He's gone on an errand."

"I just killed three women. Hurry up and catch me."

"Who is this? Where are you?"

"If you want to find those women, go down to the airport."

"The airport?"

"Right."

"Fort Lauderdale Airport?"

"I don't know what it is, but it's an airport and I put one in the canal and one by the road."

"Now, wait, where are you calling from?"

"I'm at this, the race . . . the main highway here."

"Uh—Route 1?"

"She—Shell, the Shell gas station."

"Uh-huh."

"Hurry up, please, please!"

"Okay," replied the deputy, stalling for time and keeping the dialogue open for some clue or indication as to the caller's identity, "I must know who you are and where you can be found."

"You think I'm kidding?" was the retort tinged with a trace of disappointment, "Well I'm serious. You better come and get me before I kill again."

Once more the caller abruptly terminated the conversation and Deputy Lemore pulled a cigarette from a pack in the left upper pocket of his tunic and sat down on a stool reflecting on the unusual nature of the telephone calls. The cigarette was still unlit, dangling from his lips when Major Kramer burst into the room with James Rice in tow.

"Let me hear that tape, deputy."

"Yessir," replied Lemore as he sprang toward the recorder and rewound the tape to the 6:18 A.M. transmission so the major could hear for himself the self-confessed murderer's weird plea for help. The major's face was impassive as though etched in stone when the words captured on the tape spewed out its deadly message. The major was still stone-faced when the tape ended, and did not move from his seat.

"There is another transmission, sir," explained Lemore. "Came in at 6:30 A.M." The major still did not move a muscle, appearing to be deep in thought, whereupon Lemore took it upon himself to play back the 6:30 A.M. recording. There was complete silence in the room while the tape ran to its conclusion. Both deputies looked to the major for guidance and watched him slowly get up from the bar stool and, as the blood drained from his face, said with restrained excitement, "The 6:18 tape and the second transmission from that crazy caller must be preserved as critical evidence. Secure it immediately!"

"Right away, sir," and Lemore sprung into action, "and what does the major want me to do with them?"

"I want several copies made of the two calls for distribution to all police agencies in Dade, Broward and Palm Beach counties for voice recognition."

"Yes, sir," responded Lemore as he turned to leave with the tapes in his hand.

"Hold it!" ordered the major as the deputy froze in his tracks, "If this is not some psycho making waves, there's apt to be some dead bodies around. Alert all police units in the area."

"Yessir," answered Lemore, "I'll put the BOLO out immediately."

3

HE FROWNED AT the dusty Elgin clock adorning the green walls of his office and cursed. Seven-thirty. Half an hour more until his shift ended. The damn sun was already seeping through the plate glass window overlooking the tarmac of the Hollywood-Fort Lauderdale International Airport promising another scorcher. He rose from the rickety cane chair, loosening his cloying shorts with a practiced flick of his fingers and cursed again, "Dammit to hell." There ain't nothin' hotter than an August day in Florida and today's gonna be a bitch. Never should have left Georgia to become a security officer just 'cause an office went with the job. Hell, he fumed, he was just a night watchman and the office was nothing more than a broom closet. He looked around. An old desk with a dirt spattered ink blotter covered the frayed walnut top, sporting an outmoded dial telephone and a two burner electric plate for coffee to keep him awake through the long nocturnal vigils. In anticipation of the torrid day that would keep him from sleeping, he started to remove his shirt with the official insignia of the airport security guard and replace it with the short sleeved multicolored polyester when he spotted a small automobile at the end of the parking lot. "How in the hell did that get there," he mused. It wasn't there just a few minutes ago when he made his rounds. It was almost time for him to quit for the morning, so he wondered if he shouldn't leave the improperly parked car up to his relief.

Curiosity won, however, and stuffing his shirt back into his pants, he grabbed the peaked hat with the airport insignia and descended the single flight of stairs. A blast of heat hit him as he opened the door to the parking lot and cursed as he ploughed his way through the oppressive haze toward the little green car parked with both front doors wide open. Coming to an abrupt stop, he stiffened with horror and cursed, "What in the goddam hell is this?" A middle-aged woman lay sprawled on the passenger side of the car. He moved in for a better look at the sole occupant, recoiling at the sight of a woman's pudgy face and matted hair encrusted with dried blood. He knew she was not dead by her laborious breathing, and the gaping holes in her forehead and a perfectly round opening on the left side of her swollen nose were enough to galvanize him into running back to his office for help.

"Sheriff's Office?" he yelled into the telephone, "This is Lamar Hewitt, Airport Security in Fort Lauderdale. There is a lady in the parking area dying from gunshot wounds. Send a deputy and an ambulance right away." Hewitt's job done, he felt tired all over and could feel the sweat pouring from his armpits, head and chest. Now for sure, he swore, there would be no sleep for him today and began to curse more vehemently than ever and angrily spit on the floor as he waited for assistance of some kind.

Broward County on the southeast coast of Florida was affectionately known as the "Outlaw County" but the sheriff's office had very little police work to do. The only semblance of current crime was gambling which the inhabitants tolerated as they really didn't feel it was against the law. Law enforcement was actually left to the Federal officers in order to preserve tranquility and not disturb political and social equanimity. There were occasions when community problems or touchy situations would develop, but the wily sheriff would absent himself on a hunting trip in the Everglades, delegating the resolution of the controversies to the municipal police.

Traditionally all arrests for criminal violations were made by the local police, which accounted for the sheriff's continued and unchallenged tenure in office. Times were changing, however. The migration of Yankees from the north increased the county's population and the three story courthouse built in 1928 had increasingly inadequate room for any employees to conduct the county business. It may have been a geographical accident that pinpointed Broward County into prominence, nestling comfortably north of Miami and south of swanky Palm Beach, but it did have the Gulfstream Race Track, with thoroughbred racing during the day and the Hollywood Kennel Club where dog races were held at night. A Jai Alai Fronton with pari-mutuel wagering was being built and restaurants with gambling casinos flourished with official approbation. For a continuous stretch of fifteen years, Broward County led the entire nation in population growth and the area sprung alive in the post-years of World War II luring adventurers and starry-eyed tourists to its bosom. The county grew so rapidly, public services new residents required could not be provided, resulting in inadequate police and municipal supervision. In a cauldron of strangers, there was no leadership; anyone who requested employment in any governmental office was usually accepted, regardless of the position. A carpenter or plumber down from the north would declare himself to be a building contractor, and licensed accordingly. An itinerant with no trade skills would be accepted as a police officer. Incompetence was the norm. No questions asked. There was no need to. Broward was on a roller coaster and there was no stopping to assess what was happening; besides, who cared?

The grumpy security guard waited on the haze-dampened parking lot and was shaken from his lethargy by the screeching tires of a Broward Sheriff's official two-door DeSoto cruiser sliding sideways to a halt. All police cars in the area were souped up Fords or Plymouths, but the sheriff's brother Bob, his chief deputy, owned a DeSoto dealership in Fort Lauderdale and most employees in the courthouse drove around in the unusual and soon-to-be extinct vehicle.

"Hey Cap, whatcha got here?" grinned the youthful deputy as he sighted the green Falcon parked askew with its doors flung open. "Someone parked illegally?" He chuckled and smoothed his rich black hair, before carefully placing his newly blocked Stetson on his head not to disturb his duck-tail hairdo.

"Just looka here," fumed the security guard, ignoring the deputy's sarcastic remark. It made him angry every time he had to deal with one of the sheriff's relatives. This one was not dry behind the ears and should not have left his job at the Farmer's Market in Pompano where his biggest accomplishment was to sort snap beans and bell peppers in packing crates. Once he sported a deputy's uniform, badge and gun, there would be no return to the farm, and here he was at a major crime scene jauntily strolling toward the green car without the slightest idea of what he would find.

"Wow," exploded the deputy, "Someone had a turkey shoot here."

"More like a hurricane," chimed in the security guard, fluttering his fingers at the soiled food containers, torn paper bags and pieces of clothing strewn about. He looked with unconcealed distaste at the deputy who merely stood there mesmerized at the gruesome sight of the dying woman struggling for breath.

"Dammit man, wake up. Get on your radio phone and call an ambulance."

The deputy resented taking orders and demonstrated his displeasure by affecting a casual air of nonchalance while reaching for the transmitter, then turning his back from the agitated guard, spoke so his request for help was inaudible. In subtle retaliation the security guard took the initiative and opened the glove compartment of the little green automobile and extracted a frayed cloth woman's purse and the car's registration papers.

"Hold on," the deputy said, "this is police business and you're not suppose to touch the evidence. Lemme see what you have here." The purse yielded a few crumbled dollar bills, some coins, lipstick, keys, compact and a snapshot of a teenage girl. The two men glared at each other like two stray pit bulls. The tension was broken by the arrival of an ambulance from Fort Lauderdale's Broward General Hospital with the driver leaping out, running to the prostrate form in the car.

"This is a Code Blue if I ever saw one," he remarked, "give me a hand and I'm gone."

The deputy, deliberately ignoring the security guard, began making an inventory of the contents of the 1960 green Falcon and determined from the title and registration the automobile belonged to a Dorothy Clark of Clarkston, Georgia. He called in his findings to the Sheriff's Office and received orders to secure the scene as a back-up was on its way.

4

BADGE NO. 127 belonged to Hollywood's newest rookie cop. Blonde hair, ruggedly handsome and resplendent in his new police officer's uniform, Robert Erler cruised in a blue and white squad car in the early morning of August 12, reflecting upon his muddled life. He loved being an officer of the law. Maybe it was the wearing of the uniform or the regimentation that he acquired from his brief stint in the U.S. Army, but his dedication as a strict disciplinarian in the line of duty lifted his spirits, making his sordid existence more bearable. At the end of his shift he would reluctantly leave the muster room at the station, homeward bound to his lonely trailer in Dania to exchange his star spangled tunic for a white tee shirt. The glamorous mystique of the uniform seemed to vanish and the bureau mirror only disclosed a heavily muscled athletic figure with a tired, sad face. The glowing allure tarnished when he divested himself of his policeman's jacket, and the significance became obvious. He was only alive when clad in a police uniform.

"Is this all there is?" he asked himself. "There has to be more than this." He vowed to restructure his life in order to deal with the personal problems that were rapidly mushrooming out of control. The off duty hours he worked to earn the extra money he needed were interminably long and painful and the continuous blinding headaches denied him the surcease of sleep.

The warming sun did little to mollify Erler. His troubled thoughts were interrupted by the insistent blaring of an automobile horn coming from a blue sedan parked diagonally at the intersection ahead. As Erler pulled up, a middle-aged man on the driver's side rolled down his window and reported, "Officer, my wife and I just saw someone laying down in the dirt, right off the Industrial Park."

Bob Erler sprang into action. With one hand on the wheel

and the other clutching his radio phone Erler alerted head-quarters.

"This is Erler, Badge 127, on my way to Hollywood Industrial Park to investigate a report by a middle-aged couple about a human body lying in the field," was his terse message, and sped to the designated area where he frantically canvassed the city's new industrial park. His efforts were shortly rewarded by sighting the body of a girl or young woman clad in a polka dot and plaid combination bathing suit sprawled on the side of a new asphalt road. Upon approaching the body for a closer inspection he was appalled to note the girl's blonde hair thick with congealed blood and two dark brown rivulets dripping from wounds in her head.

Erler leaped to his police car and snatched the radio to contact headquarters.

"This is 127 reporting a possible homicide of a white female with several bullet wounds in her head. Send assistance and an ambulance immediately to the Industrial Park. Over."

"One twenty-seven, this is Lieutenant Cox at headquarters. Secure the area and preserve the scene. We're on our way. Acknowledge."

"Yessir, Lieutenant, ten-four." Erler procured a blanket from the trunk of his police car and covered the supine form of the young female and stood guard in the vacant, undeveloped area of the pre-planned Industrial Park.

It seemed like only a matter of seconds when the park became alive with an ambulance, police cars, photographers and detectives from the Hollywood Police Department. Lieutenant John Cox emerged from an unmarked car with another Hollywood police lieutenant, Irving Goetz, and sighting Erler standing forlornly over the covered body, walked over to view the object of an obvious homicide. Lieutenant Goetz took Erler aside and began an incisive interrogation.

"Bob, you were the first to report the incident, right?"

"Yes, sir."

"Did you get the names of the old couple that reported to you they had seen the body at the airport?"

"No, sir."

"Did you get the license number of their car?"

"No, sir . . . I guess I was too excited and too much in a rush to make the investigation."

"That's not good police work," soberly remarked the lieutenant. "Leave the scene immediately and write up a full report on this and have it on my desk as soon as possible." He abruptly turned away obviously irritated and dismissed the contrite Erler.

Erler wanted to say more. He should have apologized for his shoddy police work and explained he really didn't believe the report from the old couple and that was the reason for not taking their names or car license number. He panicked, realizing he failed in one of the most elemental basic procedures and dreaded the reaction of his fellow officers when they would learn of his incompetence. A blinding migraine headache hit him with severe intensity, rocking the sturdy rookie to his knees as he struggled toward his vehicle to escape homeward, away from the stress and strain of the murder scene.

Lieutenant John Cox, a craggy faced veteran with close-cropped iron-grey hair, stood by silently as Goetz humiliated the rookie for his poor performance. His steely gaze followed the hapless retreating figure and made a mental note to check out this Robert Erler. He heard him referred to in the locker room as "Super Cop" and was curious as to why his co-workers tagged him with that moniker. The lieutenant's ruminations were interrupted by Jack Mickley, the County Medical Examiner, an eccentric but brilliant pathologist who would be more at home in a Chair at Harvard, but would rather content himself with the warm tropical lifestyle Florida had to offer. Clad in a flowered sport shirt and pastel slacks, Mickley looked like a college student on Spring Break but his youthful appearance belied the forbidding intensity of his professional demeanor.

"What can you give us, Doc?" inquired Detective Cox.

"Just made a prelim," answered Mickley. "I fix the time of death at about 5:00 A.M. this morning."

"Was she sexually molested?" inquired Cox.

"Doesn't appear so offhand, but I will know more about it when I make a complete autopsy."

"Anything else you can tell us now before you take the body away, Doc?" Cox pressed on.

"Only that she died of multiple gunshot wounds," was Doctor Mickley's taciturn response. "She had been shot five times, four shots went into the left side of her skull at point-blank range, and a fifth missile went into her cheek."

5

MEDICAL EXAMINER JACK Mickley was bored. The autopsy of "Jane Doe" revealed nothing remarkable. It was just another run-of-the-mill homicide resulting from multiple wounds inflicted by a small caliber gun, most likely a .22. This disappointed Mickley as his fertile mind was always on the alert for a mystifying challenge to satisfy an enormous imagination. The only distinguishing feature of this routine murder was the five small bullet holes in the girl's head. So what?

Doctor Mickley arrived in Hollywood from Duke University at North Carolina with four bound volumes of case histories of his most noted investigations. He distinguished himself in a case where a husband and wife died in a raging fire while both were asleep at home. A huge inheritance was at stake, depending upon who expired first, the wife or the husband. Both bodies were burned to a crisp almost beyond recognition. After weeks of intensive study through innovative use of ultraviolet ray equipment, chemicals and microscopic examination of skin tissue and seared hair follicles, Mickley established to a medical certainty that the wife predeceased her husband. With that undeniable proof, all litigation and controversy came to rest and Mickley's laboratory technique was written up in current medical journals and lauded by his fellow pathologists. Mickley believed in his own instincts and followed his gut reactions religiously, but in this case his intuition remained dormant. This explained his irritation in presenting the autopsy report to John Neeley, the plump, balding State Attorney of Broward County who occupied a small office on the third floor

of the courthouse two days per week and unofficially practiced civil law in the Sweet Building in the heart of Fort
Lauderdale. Neeley's public duties were to impanel a grand
jury twice a year and prosecute first degree murders, but
saw to it that most of the homicides that occurred in the
county were declared to be lesser included offenses such
as second degree murders or manslaughter, in which case
he would pass the buck to the county solicitor below on
the second floor who would have jurisdiction for prosecution of such offenses. The county commissioners, in their
wisdom, did not allocate funds for the state attorney to
maintain a secretary because of the paucity of work. Neeley
was lucky to have an ancient Olivetti on which he did his
own typing of official documents, hunt and peck system.

"Hello, Doc," warily greeted the prosecutor, hoping
Mickley did not have any official business to burden him
with, "Whatcha got?"

"It's that little dead girl they found in Hollywood. Nothing spectacular," Mickley answered, "Here's the autopsy
report."

The state attorney read the report aloud very slowly
while Mickley stretched out on the faded green leather
couch under the stained circular window and tried to doze
off to avoid further boredom, when Neeley, in a dull tone
said, "You may have another autopsy to do real soon—
they found this old gal at the airport with five bullet holes
in her head and she is dying—"

"Did you say 'five bullet holes in her head?' " asked
Mickley shaking himself to attention, "Five bullet holes?"

Neeley looked up, surprised at Mickley's sudden interest.
"S-a-a-y, this little kid also had five bullet holes in her
head. What do you think?"

"Could be something," replied Mickley with an owlish
look on his handsome face, "Who's in charge of that one?"

"Luke Kramer of BSO told me, so he's the man to see,"
replied Neeley to the retreating backside of the Medical
Examiner who vaulted out of the office like a man in a
hurry.

Jack Mickley had a gut reaction. A medical man traditionally makes evaluations based upon scientific findings and

the Broward County Medical Examiner had no peer in the pathological field but he always yielded to his instincts and was firmly convinced that the young girl autopsied with five bullets in her head had a connection with the woman found dying at the airport coincidentally with five bullets in her head. Certain his hunch was right, Mickley sought out Major Kramer to compare clues, and to give him his opinion that the person who killed the little girl was also the assailant who shot the woman at the airport. As he was approaching the major's office he met Jerry Melrose of the Fort Lauderdale Police Department at the door.

"Glad I saw you, Doc," said Melrose. "I suppose you heard of this Georgia woman that was found almost dead at the airport?"

The doctor nodded his assent.

"Well," continued Melrose, "she was found in my jurisdiction and I'm in charge of the investigation."

Again the doctor nodded. "So?"

"In her personal effects found in the glove compartment of her car was this photo," and Melrose brandished a Polaroid snapshot of a smiling, pudgy faced girl with two front teeth missing, asking, "Could this be the girl you autopsied yesterday?"

The medical examiner took one look at the little girl's picture and knew his hunch was right. Whoever killed the little girl also tried to kill her mother.

Mickley's private world began and ended in his office just a few yards west of the Broward County Courthouse on Southeast Sixth Street in Fort Lauderdale. Marge Anderson was his assistant who wrote up all the reports and kept the office functional and had the distinction of being the only human being that was privy to the good doctor's deepest thoughts. There were no friends or associates in his life and he and Marge shared the frustrations and disappointments in their official duties, but also exulted in their victories and shared little humorous secrets like two giggling, zany conspirators. He took a liking to me, because we were both former naval officers and used to swap war stories when we'd meet at Mike Chrest's Bar and Grill on the corner of the Hollywood Bridge and Intracoastal Waterway. We were proud to have our names inscribed on

Mike's wall with the hundreds of other servicemen that frequented the bar. Mickley was so attached to Mike's place that when his wife, Esther, gave birth to their first and only son, he was christened "Michael." The medical examiner was as interested in my criminal trials as I was interested in his pathological experiences. We had a great rapport and worked well together on homicide cases even though we were adversaries in the courtroom. All I asked Jack to do when he made an autopsy was to measure and report the alcohol content in the body of the decedent. It was always helpful from a defense standpoint if the State's own medical examiner would report a .024 level of blood alcohol which would indicate the dead victim was highly intoxicated. Especially in self-defense cases.

When Mickley would take the stand and go through the litany of his medical findings I would ask him on cross-examination, "Doctor, what is the borderline level of prima facie intoxication restricted by our Florida Statutes?"

"The limit is .010," he would reply.

"What did you mean in your autopsy report," I would ask, holding up my copy of the report so the jury could see me read the official document, "when you wrote the decedent's blood alcohol content was .024?"

"That means the decedent was DRUNK," he would blurt out almost angrily, which invariably made the prosecutor wince.

Mickley would use me as a sounding board and try out some of his gags and jokes in the office with Marge Anderson as the appreciative audience of one. "Doctor Jack," as I affectionately called him, would set the stage for a joke, always looking at Marge to make certain she enjoyed the full measure of his efforts.

On the doctor's neatly arranged desk there were two skulls; one of a mature adult and the other was a small skull, presumably of a child.

"Do you want to know what these signify?" Mickley asked me, while Marge sat by with her hand over her mouth as if to suppress a laugh.

"Okay, Doc," was the invariable answer, "I'll bite."

"Well sir," replied the doctor with his impish smile, "the small skull is that of Pancho Villa, the Mexican bandit, at the age of fifteen, and the big one is that of Pancho Villa when he died at the age of forty-seven.''

Marge broke out in unrestrained laughter as though she never heard the joke before and I obligingly joined in to justify the amusement. I harbored a tremendous admiration for Mickley's brilliance, which the good doctor modestly surmised, and a bond of mutual respect developed between us. Other than the professional affinity between us, the medical examiner had a marked paucity of friends and associates. There were no pictures of public officials, diplomas or certificates adorning the office walls, only snapshots and illustrations of entry and egress of missiles through human flesh and bone as well as photographs of unusual or forensic pathological phenomena. In the extreme left corner a small foyer leading from the reception room to the doctor's private office sported an 8×10 photograph of a dark, stocky, well-built male immersed in an old-fashioned four footed bathtub with his head partially in the water. The man in the picture was obviously dead and in the throes of rigor mortis. His right hand clutched a vibrator whose electric cord was attached to a plug over the bathtub and his limp penis inclined toward his left side and an ejaculation of semen was evident by a large globule deposited on his upper thigh.

"What happened, Doc? How did the guy die?"

Mickley suppressed a grin and explained, "He was using the vibrator to masturbate and when the instrument touched the bath water, the electric shock did him in."

I glanced over to Marge, expecting some type of comical reaction, but her face was somber and reflected an untypical pensive mood. Pursing her lips she ventured in a dreamlike whisper, "The saline content of the semen was a good conductor of electricity which caused this man's electrocution."

In an attempt to recapture the jovial mood of the little group, I said what was intended to be a witticism and asked Marge, "How did you know about the salinity of semen?"

Marge's face reddened and blushed for the first time that I could recall. It was also the last time Marge ever spoke to me.

6

MAJOR KRAMER EXAMINED the wallet containing the Georgia driver's license. Its blurred photographic image stared out fixedly over the typed name of Dorothy Clark. Kramer settled his bulk in a comfortable leather executive chair behind a dark grey, war surplus steel desk and wondered why no one in the sheriff's office or Fort Lauderdale's police department contacted the Georgia authorities to confirm the identity of the driver. He took the snapshot of a smiling young girl with a pudgy oval face and wondered what connection there was between her and the wounded victim. It crossed his mind to have Plough Boy, the deputy who found the bleeding woman at the airport, check the license and auto identification, but then thought to himself, "That idiot will probably screw things up." Heaving a sigh, the major reached for the telephone on his desk and began to dial.

He barely had time to finish his second bottle of Coke when the mayor of Clarkston, Georgia returned the major's call.

"Sir, this here is Glen Hawley. I'm the mayor and chief of police of Clarkston. How may I serve you?"

"Much obliged to you, Mayor, for your kind offer to help. The Broward County Sheriff's Office in Fort Lauderdale is making a criminal investigation. Your motor vehicle commission office confirms one Dorothy Clark to be the owner of a 1960 Ford Falcon and she appears to be a resident of your town. The Clark woman is now in our local hospital trying to recover from five bullets in her head. We have no clues as to who tried to kill her and why, so whatever background information you can provide will be appreciated."

"How about her little daughter? Is she okay or was she also hurt like her mom?"

"Wait!" shouted Kramer excitedly, "There was a snapshot in the victim's wallet of a young girl, could be a teenager or not; black hair, round face. . . .''

"Dorothy Clark had a twelve-year-old daughter named Merilyn. Could be her. No other reason I can think of for Dorothy to carry around her picture. She had no kin of any kind around these parts."

"Maybe there is something in her background that might give us a clue. Also maybe the little girl is in the same kind of trouble if she was with her mom, and we will have to find her if she is down here, or maybe she is still up there in Georgia."

"No," explained Mayor Hawley, "little Merilyn went to Florida with her mother. Dorothy got divorced the second time around and when she lost her job as a typist at the courthouse, she decided to pull up stakes and try her luck in Florida."

"Any boyfriend trouble or some enemy that may have followed her down here?"

"Nothing like that, sir, but I suggest you look for Merilyn, pronto. The two were inseparable, and my guess is that little Merilyn is in danger."

"No one in this crummy town is interested in getting married to a two-time loser with a twelve-year-old kid," grumbled Dorothy Clark to herself as she shuffled application forms for city occupational licenses at the clerk's office in Clarkston, Georgia. She was bored with her job as a typist, besides the position was only temporary and had employment part time at the lumber mill where the only redeeming feature there was Bill Knowland, the cute foreman, but he was married and was only interested in her for a tryst in the packing shed which was getting dangerously close to fruition. Maybe she would do better in a big city like Atlanta where jobs would be more plentiful. At least the juke joints would be livelier and present more opportunities for amusement. Merilyn wouldn't mind, she just finished school and could start again this fall in a new town and maybe get a job after having her front teeth fixed with some sort of bridge. No one would know she was only twelve years old. She was large for her age and big busted like her mom.

Dorothy decided to discuss her idea of leaving this boring existence and make plans with Merilyn where to go and what to do.

The Sunshine State handled its publicity program well, heralding its many virtues: beautiful sunny weather on golden beaches, orchid jungles, fishing, boating and the languid life of a beachcomber on the fabulous Keys from Miami Beach to Key West. Florida—the "Tropical Wonderland" abounding with three horse tracks, numerous dog tracks and Jai Alai frontons with pari-mutuel wagering, where the major league baseball teams had their winter quarters—playground of the idle rich—utopia of leisure living. It was a young new territory, and land of opportunity calling out for adventure. Dorothy Clark and her daughter Merilyn answered the call. One early humid morning they packed their meager personal belongings in their 1960 green Falcon and headed south on U.S. 301 to the promised land of Florida. Not giving a thought to the finance payments on the car held by the First National Bank of Clarkston for almost the entire purchase price, or any of the other creditors left behind, mother and daughter cheerfully looked forward to a glorious adventure.

The two chugged along in the little green Falcon, chatting away like truant schoolgirls when a sign loomed on the horizon, "FLORIDA STATE LINE. WELCOME TO THE SUNSHINE STATE. FREE ORANGE JUICE AT OUR HOSPITALITY STATION." Dorothy parked diagonally in a lane across from the ladies' comfort station and took Merilyn by the hand to "freshen up" preparatory to plotting the course for their next adventure. Seated at a cool marble-like table, sipping iced orange juice from paper cups, the two wayfarers poured over the brochures they were given by the Florida hostess in charge of the hospitality house. The best idea they ever had was to go directly to Miami where all along the highway they would encounter attractions of caged birds, parrots and monkeys at gasoline stations and restaurants, as described in the pamphlets. They were happy with their choice. Miami it would be, and it was Merilyn who charted the route they would take. "We can take U.S. 41 all the way down the Tamiami Trail," while her mother proudly beamed at her daughter's cleverness.

The burning sun of tropical Florida yielded to lengthening shadows as mother and daughter looked eastward from Biscayne Boulevard at the breathless sight of Miami's coastline standing guard over the Venetian Causeway that split the tranquil waters of the bay.

"Where do you reckon that bridge leads to?" wondered Dorothy, as she retrieved some brochures and a map from her car that was parked on the boulevard. Merilyn took the map from her mother's hands, which was so well worn by this time that it almost automatically opened to the metropolitan section of Miami, and tracing a line with her pudgy index finger said, "It goes to a little island called Miami Beach, do you want to go there?"

"No," replied her mother, "we must remember this is not just a vacation. I have to find a job and hopefully we can live in Florida permanently." Ignoring her daughter's frown, Dorothy continued, "The first order of business is to locate a motel and rest up. Tomorrow morning I start looking for work."

They cruised past the Columbus Hotel on the boulevard and continued northward past the Everglades Hotel. Dorothy seriously contemplated making application to these two elegant hotels as a stenographer, although her shorthand was a bit rusty. She smiled at the thought of taking dictation from a rapid speaking executive, and her using a hybrid system which she improvised. Of all the motels along the highway, she was attracted to the Blue Star Motel whose neon sign flashed "VACANCY $8.00." Pulling into the parking lot she announced, "We're here, Merilyn, welcome to the promised land."

Dorothy's quest for employment was fruitless. August in Florida is a slow season and the only businesses that prospered were hotels and motels, supermarkets and restaurants that catered to family vacationers. The tourists walked in the bright sunshine wearing shorts and outlandish sport caps, visiting the various sundry stores where they shopped for souvenirs. Dorothy was amused at how the visitors were dressed, certainly not what they would wear in their own hometown, but these were the spenders who invaded the

tourist traps and bought baby alligators and crates of or-
anges to send back home.

On the second night, failure to locate a job dampened
her spirit and her hopes declined as well as her resources.
After dinner at a nearby Howard Johnson, Dorothy told her
daughter, ''You've seen about all the sights there are, so
party time is over. You stay home tonight and watch T.V.,
I'm going to a bar down the street, maybe get lucky, or
something.''

Merilyn really didn't mind being alone while her mother
went out. She was used to it in Georgia, and wished her
luck. Dorothy needed a lucky break as her finances were
running low, and there was no need to panic, but if she
didn't score one way or the other tonight, she would pick
up stakes and move north to Broward County where she
heard there were thriving communities away from the tinsel
and glitter of Miami. Dorothy checked herself in the full-
length mirror behind the door and was satisfied with what
she saw, a chic strawberry blonde with ample bosom, just
enough cleavage exposed in her powder blue sport suit to
make it interesting for some stud on the prowl. She blew a
kiss at her daughter, who was already glued to the television set, and stepped out into the parking lot and changing
her mind about taking her car, elected to walk two blocks
down to the Jewel Box Entertainment Lounge. As she approached the entrance a brightly lit ornamental sign proclaimed, ''STAR STUDDED SHOW FEATURING THE
INCOMPARABLE JACKIE MAY.'' Not having heard of
that particular performer, Dorothy did not know what kind
of entertainment to expect and ventured through the door.
The white baroque decor of the room impressed her as she
walked by the pastel shaded booths to the rear of the club
directly alongside a stage with an abbreviated runway. Se-
lecting a seat at the tastefully appointed bar she turned her
back from the bartender who moved forward to greet her
and surveyed the crowd. Most of the booths were occupied
with an unusual variety of couples. In one booth an elderly
matron of about seventy years of age held out her jeweled
hand to an effeminate young handsome man with a bored
expression on his face. Another booth harbored two
women, one slight of build with raven hair adorning a sweet

virginal face looking at her companion with a mixture of awe and trepidation, perhaps in fear of this large muscular woman's menacing scowl. The people were indeed strange looking to Dorothy, and when her eyes fell upon a middle-aged man, who was likely within the parameters of her search, she was discouraged by the intense attention he paid to his young companion who spoke with fluttering hands accentuated by raised eyebrows emphasizing every mincing word he uttered.

"When does the show start?" asked Dorothy turning around to the waiting bartender.

"Not until nine. What would you like to have?"

Dorothy was sorry she came to this club, it was too fancy and weird; besides, the drinks would be expensive and there were no jocks at the bar who would spring for a drink, let alone provide worthwhile companionship for the evening.

"Let me have a glass of white wine," said Dorothy hoping that her luck would change, and placed a precious five dollar bill on the bar. The bartender looked at the five spot with annoyance. This would not even cover a small tip, and decided to enlighten his uninformed patron.

"Do you know Jackie May?"

"No," answered Dorothy. "Who and what is he?"

"He?" asked the bartender in disbelief. "He is a she! Jackie May is the most famous female impersonator in the country. Hails from New York's Howdy Club. Don't you know what goes here?"

Dorothy did not wish to appear naïve, replying, "Oh sure, just came in for company, you know."

She took a dainty sip of wine and out of the corner of her eye perceived a half ton truck dressed in a woman's leisure suit waddle up to the adjoining stool and plop on the leather seat.

"Hi doll" said the female behemoth, "Looking for some company?"

"No thanks," said Dorothy as she slipped off the stool. "Just leaving, besides I don't go that route," and made a dash for the doors. She could hear the bartender and the dyke laughing as she made her exit.

Walking back to her motel, her mind was made up. The Miami area held no promise for her and her child. She would hit Broward County right after breakfast. Merilyn was surprised when her mother walked in the door so early.

"What happened Mom?"

"Nothing good," answered Dorothy. "First thing tomorrow we will head north for Hollywood. This place is infested with homosexuals and lesbians."

Merilyn silently nodded. The twelve-year-old child, wise beyond her years, understood why her mother's mission failed, and turned her attention back to the television program in progress.

Broward County. The third day. By late afternoon, Dorothy had exhausted all leads for employment and decided to lower her sights and seek work on a different level. There were many motels that could use a maid or cleaning woman. She and her daughter at least would have a place to sleep and eat until she landed a secretarial position with more money, which reminded her, their cash reserve was getting critically low. There was no reason why they couldn't park their Falcon in some safe place and sleep in the car for the night. They could always clean up in a public rest room. Then a great idea came to her. She would tell Merilyn all about it during dinner.

Hollywood-By-The-Sea* in Florida was the dream city of a visionary named Joseph W. Young who founded the tropical paradise in the Florida land boom in the early 1920s. Fashioned out of mangrove swamp and dense palmetto foliage, the area became alive in the post World War II years. Tourists flocked to the mecca which offered long stretches of golden sandy beaches and an amusement center with stores, entertainment, paddle ball courts, two golf courses, numerous hotels and the crowning jewel of them all, the famous Hollywood Beach Hotel that catered only to a select wealthy clientele. Dorothy and Merilyn were thrilled with Hollywood and enjoyed driving around the famed Hollywood Circle downtown and walking on Hollywood Boulevard, looking at all the stores lining the street. Dorothy just knew she would find work here and took Mer-

*Hollywood-By-The-Sea was the first name given to the community designated as Hollywood when incorporated.

ilyn into the Rainbow Grill for dinner and to unfold her plan for the following day.

They sat in a booth across from a large mahogany bar that spread lengthwise almost to the back of the restaurant. As Merilyn munched on her real southern style pork barbecue sandwich, her mother said, "I've got a good feeling about this town. It's got everything and I just know I'll get a job tomorrow, but we are really low on funds so we'll park our car on the beach and sleep there."

"Whatever you say, Mom," muttered Merilyn as she continued to chew the large bun dripping with barbecue sauce.

"There are comfort stations right on the beach so," she archly looked at Merilyn, "the beach will be our motel."

They both laughed and set about finishing their dinner. Merilyn licked her fingers while Dorothy daintily cleansed her hands after dipping her paper napkin in the water glass. On Hollywood Boulevard they drove around the Circle eastward to the ocean. It was dark and the beach was deserted. Dorothy drove to Johnson Street and headed to a secluded area where the bathers used the metal piped showers to wash off the sand. She parked her car.

7

TWO SWEATING, SCREAMING orderlies frantically wheeled the unconscious body of Dorothy Clark into the emergency ward of Broward General Hospital in Fort Lauderdale.

"This one's a goner, for sure" gasped the resident doctor, intercepting the new arrival. "Get a surgical team in the O.R. stat!" He rushed away to scrub for the hopeless task facing the entire staff.

The super-efficient nurse in charge of the operating room attired in surgical mask and gown, her white cap concealing an unruly shock of red hair, had the surgical team in a state of readiness. The anesthesiologist and surgical assistant prepped the unconscious body of Dorothy Clark while Doctor Donald Sheffel waited with controlled patience for preop examination and the expected ultimate surgery.

"Okay Scotty, which hole do we want to work on first? It looks like there are five of them that need attention."

The assistant stared at the various head wounds and replied, "One is as bad as the other, so take your pick." The surgical assistant pointed to the x-ray photos at the side of the operating table and noted some small leaden fragments lodged subdurally in the cranium dangerously close to the brain.

"These we must leave alone and take our chances," mused the surgeon. "It looks to me like all we can do is close up the wounds and leave the rest to her maker."

Doctor Sheffel was pleased to note the surgical team completed their operations in record time and Dorothy Clark was hurried to an intensive care unit for recovery if possible. When the news media and police converged upon Doctor Sheffel for a prognosis, he proclaimed, "She's alive at the present time but it's extremely doubtful if she will recover."

The politically oriented sheriff adroitly parried the inquiries of the *Fort Lauderdale News,* the only newspaper in town, by announcing he was designating his most experienced deputy, Major Luke Kramer, to supervise the homicide investigation and cooperate fully with the police departments of the county, FBI and all official agencies available to solve the murder of Merilyn Clark. The sheriff's brother, Chief Deputy Bob, was engaged in "monitoring" a carnival in Pompano, otherwise he would have spearheaded the task force. Detective Johnnie Melrose of the Fort Lauderdale Police Department had already assumed charge of the investigation and rushed to the hospital to see Mrs. Clark. Bursting into the recovery room, he sought out Dorothy for questioning and was confronted by an intern.

"Doctor Sheffel demands that this lady have complete rest, so you police officers please clear out."

"Can't do that, doctor," Melrose replied firmly. "This lady must be under full police protection at all times!"

"Why is that?"

"Because we expect the person who shot her to come

into the hospital room and finish the job. See—no witness—no identification.''

Melrose was angry at being rebuffed by the medical staff, from the doctors down to the orderlies. He needed clues! Some place to start the investigation. There were no shell casings or spent cartridges on the airport grounds or in Dorothy Clark's car; no significant footprints, and the green Falcon yielded no telltale fingerprints. There was no physical evidence of any kind and he had to start with talking to Dorothy Clark. If she died before giving a statement or giving any clue as to identification of her assailant, the incident would become another statistic—another unsolved crime.

Within forty hours of her arrival at the hospital, Dorothy Clark astounded the attending nurse by opening her eyes and attempting to speak. The nurse hurriedly procured the resident on the floor but Dorothy's eyes began to glaze and she lapsed into a deep coma.

Johnnie Melrose visited the hospital daily and was aware of Dorothy's brief recovery. He demanded an up-to-date report from Doctor Sheffel.

"I have administered some basic neurological tests," reported the doctor, "and I can tell you Mrs. Clark is wholly comatose. She has suffered a slight paralysis on the right side of her face and body. She'll undoubtedly experience some speech difficulty if and when she comes around because of the lead pellets lodged near her brain. Above all, she must not be bothered by police questioning." The doctor had sternly warned his staff, directing this last salvo to Melrose, who did not miss the point.

"Doc, when do you suppose she'll be able to talk to us?" inquired the anxious detective.

"Maybe never," retorted the annoyed doctor. "There may be complications—there is some evidence of brain damage—she may never remember any details of the incident." He strode defiantly out of the hospital room pointing a finger to his assistant indicating a silent directive.

Melrose glared at the nurses and doctors remaining in the room and immediately thought of a great idea. He would put his plan into effect, even if he had to get a court order. His plan was clever, even if he had to say so himself.

Nothing like this had ever been done, but he knew he could put his novel idea into motion. He was certain that the chairman of the Broward Hospital District would back him up. One hand washes the other and Chairman Watkins had a bad habit of driving while intoxicated and just loved to cooperate with the police. He once asked his friend Joe Hall, a Hollywood Realtor, how he could get rid of his red nose.

"Just keep on drinking," replied the jaunty broker, "and your nose will become purple."

At the Hollywood International Airport security office, the major was closeted with Lieutenant Goetz and Detective Cox. Melrose was annoyed at the presence of the City of Hollywood detectives because he had proclaimed himself to be the lead officer in charge of the entire investigation. The major sensed the jurisdictional dispute about to erupt but there was no room for prima donnas in the dilemma that appeared insoluble.

"Here's where we are, men," said the major, running his tobacco stained fingers over his haggard face. "We have found two victims so far; each victim with five shots in the head—presumably inflicted by .22 caliber type bullets—around the same time of the morning."

"It's safe to assume the perpetrator is one and the same person," broke in Goetz.

"Hold it, men," replied the tired major. "I'm gonna give you fellas all the info to date. I know Hollywood wants to take the lead because the dead girl's body was found in the Industrial Park, and Johnnie here feels he should be the case agent because the mother was found dying in the airport at Fort Lauderdale, but there is so damn much to investigate that you must join forces—not only with each other but we need help badly from the outside."

The detectives looked at each other like school kids about to shake hands and make up after an argument.

"Another reason," continued the major, "our office will give you folks complete support and cooperation, but we're withdrawing from this mess and leaving the entire investigation to you two."

Melrose tried to conceal his joy with a feeble protestation and thought to himself that he would ultimately emerge in

sole charge of the investigation because of the preponderance of man power in the Fort Lauderdale Police force,
whereas Hollywood was by far the smaller city and relatively inadequate. Lieutenant Goetz and Detective Cox
were genuinely sorry to lose the guidance of Major Kramer
and were content to capitalize on whatever intelligence the
major could impart to assist them in the homicide inquiry.

"There is no question that the two victims were mother
and daughter," recited the major, reading from his notes
on a steno pad. "The dead girl was wearing the bottom of
a polka dot sunsuit when found, and her mother was wearing the top part of the same polka dot suit when we located
her in the green Falcon three miles away at the airport."

Not to be outdone, Melrose pulled a leatherette notebook
from the inside pocket of his tight grey seersucker jacket
and began to read: "There was a picture of a young female
in the woman's handbag which the medical examiner confirmed to be the same girl he autopsied in the Hollywood
homicide."

"All in good time," sighed the major, in weary frustration as he mentally prepared to shock the detectives with
his next surprise.

"First out, the girl's name was Merilyn Clark, age
twelve. Secondly," Kramer placed two fingers in the
air, "her mother fighting for her life in Broward General is
Dorothy Clark of Clarkston, Georgia." At this point the
major looked around the room satisfying himself that the
officers were listening with rapt attention and loosed the
shocker he was reluctantly holding back and said, "Finally,
there is another dead body out there that must be found
right now!"

"What's this about another body?" the officers seemed
to ask in unison. Each of the three detectives plied the tired
major with a barrage of questions until the older man waved
his arms and restored quiet.

"The morning of the 12th, some crazy bastard called the
sheriff's recorder saying he killed three people and begged
to be arrested before he killed more tonight."

The police officers were transfixed as each stared at the
major with mingled emotions.

"You mean there is a crazy killer on the loose?" asked Goetz.

"And he promised to kill more?" exploded Melrose. Cox remained silent. He was afraid that a serial killer was loose and dreaded the impact on the women of the community when the news was released that an insane murderer was stalking his next victim.

"Excuse me, major, but are there any clues of who this person is who called, or any idea of where he could be found? Any idea at all of where to start?" asked Detective Cox.

"Only his voice," replied Kramer sadly. "Only his voice captured on tape. If you come to the sheriff's office by 0800 tomorrow morning there will be copies of the transmission made by the caller. I have ordered copies of the two calls made by the weirdo delivered to every radio and television studio in Dade, Broward and Palm Beach counties with instructions to play the tapes all through the day in the hope that someone may recognize this bastard's voice."

All the men absorbed the news in silence and only Detective Cox mused, "When the folks start hearing these recordings they will be imagining hearing a familiar voice and there will be hell to pay."

"That's not the big concern," replied the major. "You guys missed the point." And angrily snatching his Stetson from a nail on the wall repeated, "There is a third body of a murdered person somewhere in this area. It must be found!"

8

A SEARCH FOR the third body commenced early the next morning without any defined pattern or strategy. The Hollywood Police Department dispatched as many officers as they could possibly afford to the Industrial Park area, where the little girl's body was found. Lieutenant Goetz was able to recruit a few members of the local fire department into the searching party and the entire area was diligently explored without success. In Fort Lauderdale, Detective Melrose stripped the local police department to a bare bones skeleton crew and, with the remaining personnel, combed the airport area inch by inch but the frantic, prolonged search yielded no clues.

The fruitless morning wore on and it was only a matter of time when the newspaper reporters from both the *Hollywood Sun-Tattler* and the *Fort Lauderdale News* pieced together some of the fragments of the bizarre puzzle. Major Kramer distributed copies of the taped messages of the self-proclaimed killer for immediate publication to the local radio and television stations which blared out the news that two of the three victims were found, and a countywide search was on to find the third victim, alive or dead. Special newspaper editions were printed setting out the text of the taped transmissions, and the designation of the caller as the 'Catch Me Killer,' only added to the frenzy and fear of the community that a serial murderer was on the loose.

Doug McQuarrie of the *Fort Lauderdale News,* a handsome Scotch-Irishman with black hair and blue eyes and the tenacity of a bulldog, came down to Hollywood to scan the police reports seeking data he could use for his follow-up story, and found Patrolman Livingston's brief Incident Report about the confrontation on Hollywood beach with a mother and daughter being rousted northward to Dania beach. He knew something was there and excitedly sought out Officer Larry Livingston, who was in the searching party and not available for an interview, so he took it upon himself, in an extra edition of the *News,* to widen the scope of the 'Catch Me Killer's' activities to the City of Dania claiming the search for the third body should be extended northward, as it was highly possible that the killer was lurking in that district.

Telephone calls and complaints were made by frightened residents to the sheriff's office, police departments and city officials. The serial killer must be caught! Women and children were afraid to venture out of their houses unescorted and the Broward County Sheriff could no longer be an interested spectator and, as angry protests grew, he knew he had to become involved. As the chief law enforcement of-

ficer in the county, the sheriff used his power to enlist the
services of the R.O.T.C. on Federal Highway and Colonel
Richard Cobourn responded by procuring two army helicopters to patrol the entire section from above. Such a show
of force set well with the citizenry. The quest was twofold:
Find the third body and the killer.

The television and radio coverage of the sensational story
brought hundreds of curious onlookers flocking to the area,
most of whom willingly joined in the search in a concerted
effort, scouring the vicinity to find the third victim. Small
boat owners were pressed into service to probe the various
canals and dikes, human chains were formed and men and
women spread out in the barren wasteland and scattered
clumps of wild foliage in a frantic search. The relentless
efforts continued throughout the day and into the night. No
third body was found. The police feared another unsolved
crime was consigned to Broward's growing list of investigative frustrations.

During a lunch break at the Broward Woodworking Company on the Federal Highway at Fort Lauderdale, another
enterprise Chief Deputy Sheriff Bob Clark owned as a side-
line to his police activities, "Slick" Sullivan, the foreman,
sucked on a toothpick and pontificated to a few of his hired
help, "They ain't no third body in any of the canals around
here like the po-lice think. 'Sides, there's a ten foot gator
that hangs around Dania Canal that feeds on swimming
dogs and if there's a body or anything that can be eaten, it
will be long gone by this time."

"I feel sorry for those professional divers wading
through the slimy bottom of those canals. They could have
gotten their ass bit off by that alligator," ventured Earl
Shape, who also doubled as part-time deputy sheriff, "but
the worst of all is how the womenfolk are scared shitless
about that crazy killer on the loose."

"What's the sheriff's office doing about that?" asked
Sullivan.

Earl explained that the responsibility of the investigation
was now in the hands of the Fort Lauderdale and Hollywood Police Departments. He pointed out that copies of the
Catch Me Killer tapes were distributed to the various police

agencies in a one hundred mile radius as well as local radio stations. Directions were simple: play the tapes at every possible interval in the hope that some listener would recognize the voice of the killer.

All police and prosecution personnel were required to listen to the tapes for recognition determination. The reaction was mixed; several officers frankly believed the taped conversations of the alleged killer were the product of a practical joker engaging in some type of hoax. Others believed they had heard the voice somewhere before, but could not state with particularity whose voice it was. The power of suggestibility ran rampant and conjecture attained an extremely high level. All vagrants in the area were suspect and many suspicious-looking individuals were detained for questioning and thoroughly checked out. All the airports and railroad stations were monitored and investigators were dispatched to every Shell gas station in the area of Hollywood Industrial Park and Fort Lauderdale-Hollywood International Airport. The hunt was on. Copies of the snapshot of young Merilyn, as well as photographs of her mother, Dorothy, were circulated in the critical areas in order to determine whether these unfortunate victims were seen in the company of any persons who would qualify as suspects of the double crime. The manhunt continued and the weary police investigators combed the area, doggedly picking up bits and pieces of pertinent information. The news media and local radio stations kept abreast of every clue as it was uncovered and reports came filtering in sporadically from well-meaning individuals.

A gas station attendant advised that he believed he saw the woman and her daughter on Hollywood Beach the preceding day, which was Sunday, August 11; an owner of a Hollywood restaurant reported he met Mrs. Clark and she was to be interviewed for a position as a cashier that Monday morning. Another witness claimed he saw a woman and a teenaged girl in a saloon in North Miami, just over the Broward County line, Sunday evening in the company of a man wearing a blue polka dot sport shirt. Rumors abounded but no one was able to establish that mother and daughter were ever in the company of any person.

Detective Melrose had great respect for County Medical

Examiner Jack Mickley who suggested that a psychiatrist be retained to listen to the tapes and study the voice, perhaps draw some conclusion as to the emotional stability of the speaker. Melrose sought out Doctor Clifford McIntyre, a brilliant psychiatrist with offices on fashionable Las Olas Boulevard in Fort Lauderdale, and acquainted him with Mickley's suggestion, leaving copies of the 'Catch Me Killer's' double transmissions. Doctor McIntyre smiled as he accepted the assignment and wondered why the police delayed so long before seeking an evaluation of the taped messages.

Doctor McIntyre, a bachelor, was a frustrated criminal lawyer and was employed by defense attorneys because of his unique courtroom manner. On the witness stand, McIntyre would sit primly erect facing the jury panel and speak to them like a school teacher lecturing to a classroom of students. His quiet voice demanded attention as his light blue eyes would peer mildly through wire rimmed glasses. The doctor's sparse sandy hair was tufted and irregular, matching bushy, sun bleached eyebrows, all of which contributed to a professorial look of sincerity. Ordinary psychiatric practice bored Clifford McIntyre and he was only happy in the forensic arena in the criminal courtroom. He enrolled in the University of Miami Law School evening program which suited his lifestyle, having no domestic ties, and ultimately received an LLB degree, indeed making him an eminently qualified witness in medicolegal cases. His preference was the field of criminal law, and it was inevitable that we would become good friends and allies.

Clifford McIntyre was the perfect man to study the tapes of the 'Catch Me Killer' as he had a practiced ear. He was a proponent of the Sibilant "S" Syndrome which was successfully used in convicting an obscene caller whose speech had a distinct sibilant "S," which McIntyre, as a prosecution witness, explained to the jury was a form of hushed or muted lisping when pronouncing the letter "S," indicating the speaker to be bisexual or definitely homosexual. The handsome male defendant was obviously a gay person as the jury could observe by his effeminate movements and female characteristics, who dared not take the stand in his own defense lest his speech on direct and cross-examination confirm Doctor McIntyre's analysis of the sibilant "S."

The psychiatrist played the tapes repeatedly and isolated pertinent segments that were significantly susceptible to interpretation, making copies of the critical areas for evaluation. After intense study of the tonal inflections and phonetics, he drew charts of a pattern of hysteria that led him to the conclusion the 'Catch Me Killer' was real and not a hoax! McIntyre put his findings in a written report to Detective Melrose, which indicated the caller was motivated by Panic Hysteria Reaction, presumably after he committed the shootings of both women; was self-destructive and obsessed with a sublimated guilt creating a death wish, and above all, wanted to be caught and punished.

II

ROOKIE COP ACCUSED

9

THE ERLER FAMILY fell onto hard times. Robert, Sr. had a serious operation debilitating him so extensively, his wife, Winifred, had to take charge of the entire family. Leaving Adams, Massachusetts for the warm climate which her husband required, they came to rest in West Hollywood, an unincorporated area west of State Road 7, which was undeveloped and referred to as "Alabama City" because of the substandard living conditions and its underprivileged inhabitants. The rent was cheap and the stuccoed frame house only had one bedroom, but the entire Erler family crammed in, determined to cope with their unfortunate lot.

They only had one friend, Ellie Dooley, a registered nurse who attended to the father when he made an office visit to Doctor Ben Seltzer, but the acquaintance was of short duration. The Erler family had to move to another area where the weather was drier and more conducive to the father's health and hopefully where there were better employment conditions.

There were quarrels and unrest in the house they rented in Phoenix, Arizona, and it was difficult to adjust to the western lifestyle and the monotonous heat. It wasn't only the climate. Perhaps it was the mannerisms of the people, but young Bob Erler couldn't put his finger on the problem and he became restless and annoyed at the constant bickering between his brothers and sisters. There were too many fights and arguments at home so he made up his mind to leave. The only solution was to join the peacetime Army. He had observed a small recruiting station in the Phoenix Post Office building just off the west wall reserved for postal box rentals and it was a simple task for him to enter the open door and stand awkwardly before a smiling Master Sergeant seated at a desk.

Boot camp at Fort Benning, Georgia was not what young Erler expected. He could handle the grueling thirty mile hikes and the demeaning basic training. The drill instructors could be as tough as they wanted, the rigors of regimentation did not phase him one whit, but what dampened his enthusiasm was his permanent assignment to the mess hall as a company cook. What few friends he made in "D" barracks had plush assignments to communications school, gunnery school or construction battalion training centers, and all he had to look forward to was a pile of greasy forty gallon stainless steel tubs and endless piles of food trays that needed to be cleaned, sorted and put away for the next chow down only minutes away, it seemed.

Erler sought out the captain in charge of the Enlisted Men's Mess for an audience, but was held at bay by a staff sergeant in charge of the office.

"What do you want, soldier?" asked the staff sergeant who was seated behind a typewriter.

"Would like permission to speak to the captain," answered Private Erler, and as he saw the sergeant raise his eyebrows in a quizzical look, added, "concerning a transfer."

"All requests for transfers must be in writing," droned the staffer, with a bored expression. "Just write out your request and hand it to me and I'll see that the captain considers it."

A few days later Erler was serving hash brown potatoes in the enlisted men's chow line where Captain Bradley's clerk was noticed.

"Hello, Sarge," greeted Erler. "Remember me?"

"Oh, yeah," answered the sergeant with a smile of recognition. "You're the guy who wants to put in for a transfer. When are you coming in?"

"It's no use," replied Erler.

The staff sergeant, impressed by Erler's physical endowments, the huge muscles bulging out of the tee shirt covering his massive chest, felt he belonged in a combat area and not in a mess hall, and said, "Come to my office when you're free. Have an idea, if you really want a transfer."

That same afternoon Erler visited Captain Bradley's headquarters and greeted his new acquaintance, the staff sergeant. The captain's aide acknowledged Erler's salutation and motioned him to sit down.

"Do you want your transfer bad enough to get into rough duty?"

"The rougher, the better," grinned Erler.

"Okay, soldier, here's the scoop. There is a shortage of men in the Paratroopers, so any request for a transfer to that division will be favorably received. Get it?"

"Great," said Erler, eyes lighting up.

"Okay," replied the sergeant, "I'll prepare the request for transfer. In no time you'll be where you belong."

The transition from mess cook to Special Services School was facilitated by Erler's natural propensity for danger. His excellence in Gunnery School equalled his outstanding performance as a Paratrooper, which caught the attention of his superior officers, advancing him to membership in the prestigious corps of the Green Berets. This was the happiest period of his life. The only thing lacking was a war to be fought so he could distinguish himself in combat and had to content himself with idle dreams and fantasies. He missed his parents and his two sisters and brothers and regularly telephoned home to report his activities and inquire as to the health of his ailing father. On a regular Sunday phone call his mother told him, "Bob, the doctor warned us that Dad is terminally ill and will not be around much longer, so please come home right away."

"Sure, Ma," replied Erler. "I'll put in for a 72 hour furlough immediately, there should not . . ." and halted as he heard his mother crying loudly at the other end of the line.

"What's the matter, Mom? Please don't cry."

"You don't understand, Bob," sobbed Winifred. "We need you here. Your dad is dying, and you must take over as the man of the family."

Erler was stunned. His world with all his wonderful opportunities crashed all around him, reconciling himself to the fact that his glorious army career was to end abruptly. He always obeyed his mother and steeled himself to the inexorable fate that compelled him to return to Phoenix to assume his position as the head of the Erler family.

The cloak of maturity was just about settling on the strong shoulders of Robert Erler when he entered a Phoenix cocktail lounge that featured risque entertainment on the weekends, and saw a lovely go-go girl dancer that captured his fancy. Seating himself at the bar where he could make a close observation of the young beauty as she went through sensuous and suggestive gyrations, he remained mesmerized, looking at her longingly. At one point in her act, their eyes met, but Erler quickly broke the magnetic connection dropping his gaze in embarrassment, making an awkward exit. Erler became a steady patron of the bar on weekends when Pattie Gould, the go-go dancer, performed. It was inevitable that the two would establish a relationship, to the amusement of the regulars who encouraged the romance.

When Pattie announced that she had to quit the club because she was pregnant and could no longer perform her strenuous routine, Erler was confounded. The shocking news dissolved into reality, and believing he was responsible for the mishap, the guilt-ridden Erler decided to do the honorable thing and marry Pattie.

The four bedroom home the Erlers rented in a respectable neighborhood in Phoenix was spacious enough to harbor Bob and his wife, who gave birth to a lovely nine pound baby boy which made his father extremely happy as he had always wanted a son. He relished in the visions of his son growing up to be a great professional athlete under the tutelage and guidance of his Dad. He could hardly wait until the boy had grown enough to walk and run so the coaching and training could begin. Bob's reveries and hopes were all focused on the little boy and he was happier than he could ever recall. Erler confined himself exclusively to his home using every pretext so that he could attend to his son's care and upbringing. He shirked no chore, however menial or odious, and attended to his son's needs with exemplary and touching devotion. His wife, Pattie, was not quite able to adjust to being a young doting mother and was gradually becoming disenchanted with the new domesticity that was thrust upon her. Pattie found it difficult to become a part of the domestic tranquility that was the trademark of Mother Winifred's closely knit family.

Their wedded bliss diminished by degrees and Bob Erler, sensing Pattie's restlessness, tried to placate his wife's ennui by trying to show her a brighter side of their existence and optimistically promised a rosier future. Pattie refused to be so easily put off and became unhappily adamant. She realized that her lifestyle had to change and it could only be accomplished away from the matriarchal influences of Erler's mother. Bob Erler dwelled on his predicament and reasoned that perhaps his lovely wife was right. A new environment would indeed save their rocky marriage. Pattie envisioned new horizons for her youthful husband and infant son and continually pressed Bob to pull up stakes and move to glamorous Florida. Bob Erler was enamored with his young family and was easily persuaded to yield to his wife's mandate. Hasty plans were made for their departure and Pattie's excitement mounted as she realized she would soon be free from the influence and domination of her mother-in-law. Bob also caught the fever of adventure as he looked forward to facing a new challenge in a strange land.

On a bright clear morning the Arizona sun shown down from a cloudless sky where Mrs. Winifred Erler and her son and daughter watched Bob Erler cram the newlyweds' worldly possessions in his decrepit but serviceable little Mustang. Winifred turned to her daughter-in-law, Pattie, with outstretched arms and tearfully said, "Be careful on your trip to Florida. You know we all love you and you can always come back and make this your home if things don't pan out right."

Pattie avoided Winifred's conciliatory gesture and remained silent, holding the baby protectively in her arms. Bob, sensing the awkward stand-off, placed his arms around his mother and gave her a farewell kiss and told her, "Mom, I'll miss you and the family. When I find myself and settle down we will send for you."

Everyone laughed to mask the disappointment at losing the head of the household. Bob detected their sadness and rather than prolong the agony of sad goodbyes, made a hasty departure.

Florida was not the tropical paradise Pattie had in mind. The hot dusty ride cross country was uncomfortable, particularly with Bobby Jr. The baby was unable to sleep as the dilapidated Mustang piloted by Bob Erler jumped and bounced on the substandard roads he selected as "short cuts." The infant's continuous crying stretched Pattie's frayed nerves to the breaking point. Crossing the Georgia line lightened the spirits of the weary travellers. Moss-covered trees slowly disappeared yielding to the flattened terrain and thin scrub pines lining the two lane asphalt road with dried out foliage camouflaging endless potholes. Occasionally they would encounter a wood-framed general store advertising "Free Orange Juice," but chose to press forward to their destination where there were sure to be rivers of orange juice.

Many times during the tortuous trip Pattie asked, "Where are we going to finally make our home?"

"In Hollywood," answered Bob, trying to be cheerfully optimistic. "Lived there with Ellie Dooley many years ago. It's a great little town."

Pattie was fed up with "little towns." She wanted the glamorous life, and pictured herself in a black bikini basking in the sun on the beautiful sandy beaches that lined Florida's Gold Coast, visiting the bars and nightclubs on the strip at Miami Beach, betting on the horses at Hialeah Racetrack with the pink flamingos beautifying the regal atmosphere.

"Why can't we live in Miami Beach where all the fun is?" she ventured, trying to see how far she could push him.

"Have to try Hollywood first," he explained patiently. "There are a few friends there who may help out with a job. Once I find work, we can move anywhere you want, so please cool it."

Pattie sulked and her displeasure was studiously ignored by her husband, who compounded her disillusionment by failing to find suitable housing accommodations or employment in Hollywood. His old friend Ellie Dooley helped Erler get a job at the North American Boat Company in the neighboring city of Dania. American Boat was a boat manufacturing company on the Dania Cutoff Canal with a small improvised marina. Bob was elated at being gainfully employed, but Pattie hated Dania, and especially hated living in a secondhand two-room trailer in a "mobile park."

Dania was the oldest municipality in Broward County. It

was originally settled by a group of Danish immigrants in the early 1920s who wanted to establish a community with their own kind. They appropriately called it Dania, reminiscent of their origin, and their only claim to fame was a tomato canning plant which was used to process all the tomatoes grown by the local farmers. The sandy loam in the rich black mucklands, under a warm sun that shined almost every day, yielded bountiful tomato crops three times a year, and Dania's Chamber of Commerce modestly declared itself to be the "Tomato Center of the World."

The black population residing exclusively west of the Dania railroad tracks, which served as the city's east-west boundary, constituted the labor force for the small tomato industry. There were several bars and saloons in the area which forced the city to maintain a larger police force than usual for its population size. The entire police department was lodged in a corner of the city not more than forty square feet of space which included the complaint desk, the chief's office and a cubicle containing a bare wooden table used by police to write reports. There was no jail but on rare occasions when someone had to be locked up, the person arrested was transported six miles north to the county jail in Fort Lauderdale for safekeeping.

Robert Erler at the age of 23 reflected upon his future. He was tired of testing powerboats at the boat yard in Dania and longed to be back in uniform. He figured there was always room for promotion at the police department and Dania always seemed to be shorthanded since the members of the volunteer fire department often doubled as auxiliary police officers. Erler took the plunge one dull afternoon when he presented himself to Don Parton, Dania's Chief of Police. The chief solemnly regarded the earnest young man and liked what he saw, a strong, muscular fighting man who resembled Tony Zale in his prime when he won the middleweight boxing championship of the world.

"We're just a small town with a six-man police force, three of which are colored to take care of our troubles in colored town," said Chief Parton. Noticing Erler's look of disappointment, the chief hurriedly said, "But why don't you ride as an auxiliary officer in a squad car with one of the regulars? You can fill in a few hours at night, you know, learn the ropes and maybe the city council will spring for more money, or maybe one of the men may quit.''

"That's wonderful," replied a grateful Erler. "Do I get to team up with someone? When do I start?"

"You understand there is no pay as an auxiliary officer, just voluntary."

"Yessir, Chief," answered the enthusiastic candidate who checked himself before he could give the chief a smart military salute.

"Very well then," said Parton. "I'll arrange to have you ride with Dewey McCutcheon. His nickname is 'June Bug' and he's one of my best colored officers."

Erler did not like the idea of riding at night with a black man. For some inexplicable reason he did not like colored people. He could never understand why he felt that way but he simply did not like colored people. But that would not stand in the way of his riding in the squad car with June Bug since he made up his mind to get along as a team player.

Once when Bob was riding with June Bug they were dispatched to an area in colored town to quell a disturbance.

In attempting to disarm one of the fighters, June Bug was accidentally shot and he died en route to the hospital.

The very next day Robert Erler was sworn in as a full-fledged police officer of the City of Dania.

The canning factory was the nucleus of the tomato industry in Dania and was self-sustaining from a security standpoint, but the bars on Federal Highway and the saloons and nightclubs in the black section west of the railroad tracks required constant police supervision. Chief Parton was a good judge of human nature and knew that Erler was tough and made to order to cover the colored area that was formerly June Bug's beat. He assigned one of the city's three police vehicles to Erler, giving him a list of police signals with an explanation of their meaning and taught him how to work the radio and siren.

"I'm sorry, Bob, a town this size can't afford to send you to the Police Academy in Miami for training, but you just go out there and use your good judgment and don't be afraid to make arrests. The men here will help you along

and just ask questions if you have any problems whatsoever.''

That was the sum and substance of Erler's initiation into
police work!

"Thanks, Chief," beamed Erler. He was given a brown
police tunic with a shoulder patch with the words "City of
Dania" emblazoned on a background of palm trees, a .38
caliber revolver and a badge. He was informed that he
would have to purchase additional uniform and trousers at
his own expense. Erler proudly assumed his duties as a
patrolman and after a few days of indoctrination in the office and police yard, was permitted to drive the police
cruiser assigned to him.

Rookie Erler was a source of merriment and wonder to
his fellow officers. His bravado in raiding the bars in colored town was alarming. He exhibited no fear in responding
to a police call on a Saturday night where he would single-
handedly enter a trouble spot, without calling back-up units
for assistance, and pummel the drunken brawlers who were
disturbing the peace. He was regarded by the black community as a veritable scourge when his authority was challenged. They feared and hated him. Complaints drifted to
the mayor that their segregated area west of the tracks
should be policed by colored police officers who understood the people, their habits and ways of life and not by
the newcomer white yankee. June Bug was indeed sorely
missed and no one could take his place, certainly not this
racist upstart.

The mayor of Dania, Bob Houston, Sr., was affectionately known as "Mayor Bob" and loved by both the black
and white communities for his keen understanding of municipal problems and his personal sagacity. Plans for municipal improvements delighted the residents and they
enthusiastically supported him in all of his innovative ven-
tures. The mayor recognized his police force was in dire
need of renovation and advertised for experienced police
officers, encouraging them to apply for positions with Dania and spend their retirement in sunny Florida. There were
a few responses during the employment campaign and the
mayor hand-picked an applicant named Joseph Portelli who
claimed to be a sergeant with the New York Police De-

partment, which was probably the only mistake Mayor Bob made during his long and respected tenure in public office. Portelli, a suave, well-dressed, debonair individual, was immediately installed as a lieutenant in Dania's small police force and literally shoved Chief Parton to the background as he took charge of the department. But Portelli's aggressive conduct and whirlwind tactics conclusively indicated that he was out of his element in the rural atmosphere of the Tomato Capital of the World.

Erler did not win any popularity contest with any of the Dania residents or his fellow officers because he followed the rules rigidly and was unyielding in his treatment of offenders, which earned him the sobriquet of "Super Cop." His unorthodox methods of police enforcement amused his co-workers and no one on the force could get close enough to become friendly, which made him a "loner." He often quarreled with the two black officers as he felt they were incompetent and unable to write a police report properly. The task fell upon Erler to write it for them, which kept him at the station an extra forty-five minutes to an hour. He resented this intrusion on his free time as he didn't relish the idea of leaving Pattie and the baby alone more than necessary.

On one particular occasion Officer Robert Erler stopped a vehicle he perceived to be driving erratically on a side street in Dania. He walked over to the driver's side of the car and was engulfed by the strong odor of alcohol, and noting that the driver's pupils were dilated, told him, "You are under arrest."

The driver indignantly demanded, in a slurred speech, "Why the hell are you stopping me?"

Officer Erler replied, "Because you're drunk, that's why, and you shouldn't be driving. I'm arresting you for driving while under the influence."

"Bullshit," replied the driver, "you don't know who I am. Just call Lieutenant Portelli."

"I don't care who the hell you are. Just get out of the car, please!" retorted Erler.

"Well, I am a police officer just like yourself and we police do not arrest each other."

"You can tell that to the lieutenant when I bring you in.

Now please get out of the car or I'll drag you out."

When Erler brought the irascible driver into the station to be booked, Portelli immediately recognized the man to be a Hollywood police officer and said, "Bob, this is one of our neighboring police officers, so let's give him a pass."

"Not me," retorted Erler angrily. "This man committed an offense in my presence and I'm arresting him. Let Judge Black give him a pass if he wants to."

Portelli gave Erler a cold, hard look. This episode would cost Erler dearly in the future, but he stubbornly adhered to the law without fear or favor which did not enhance his popularity on the force.

He was addicted to police work and was happy in his newly chosen profession. His only disenchantment was with his home life and the constant feuding with his wife over financial affairs. She wanted a new trailer to live in as long as she was resigned to living in a mobile home in a one-horse town like Dania. She even offered to seek employment to help the family finances. Arrangements with a girlfriend were made to harbor little Bobby while Pattie worked as a check-out clerk at the Pic-and-Pay Supermarket on Dania's Federal Highway. That job terminated abruptly for some reason Pattie refused to discuss. Another attempt at employment as a waitress at the New England Oyster House on Dania Beach Boulevard ended in a disaster, and finally she abandoned the notion of working entirely.

Pattie was not a good household manager and, unable to cope with the sedentary life of a housewife, began to run up a stack of bills and charges. Their joint bank account was depleted. Pattie continued to write checks which would be returned because of insufficient funds and Erler was besieged by the resulting creditors. The only solution to his plight was to "moonlight" which he did. He took on as much extra work as he could possibly find, working at two jobs to keep pace with Pattie's extravagances.

Erler sat behind the wheel of his cruiser at a vantage point on Dania Beach Boulevard and Federal Highway, waiting patiently for a motor vehicle violation to occur. At the briefing session that morning, the lieutenant told the assembled police officers their quota of traffic citations had not been met and ordered them to concentrate their efforts in that direction. Erler liked this kind of duty because it gave him a chance to reflect and think about his problems. He didn't want to appear disloyal to Chief Parton, but the small Dania police force was the most ineffective agency in Broward County and Erler had serious thoughts of moving upward with a police department in a larger municipality, such as Hollywood. It paid double the salary he now received. Besides, he didn't like what was going on with his fellow officers, such as the Saturday night when he accompanied two officers to the Paradise Club in Liberia, west of the tracks. All three policemen entered the club presumably for a routine inspection, and were greeted by a hushed silence. The music and dancing came to an abrupt halt as the sergeant announced, "Everyone bring your guns and knives to the bar, immediately." The patrons, both male and female, slowly approached the bar and deposited an assortment of pistols and switchblades, quietly returning to their seats. No arrests were made, which seemed odd to a puzzled Erler, who asked the sergeant what was transpiring.

"We'll sell their weapons back to them. Don't worry, you'll get your split," the sergeant said.

Erler could certainly use the money, but respectfully declined as his displeasure mounted. He was fed up with the colored officers and their arrogance toward the white girls who were employed as barmaids in the nightclubs and entertainment bars in Liberty City, across the tracks. He often argued and exchanged curse words with the black officers when he felt they were making advances toward the white barmaids, growling, "Why don't you stay with your own kind?" This certainly didn't endear Erler with his black fellow officers and he was to pay later on for this indiscretion also.

The final episode in Erler's career as a Dania cop occurred when he came home one evening and confronted Lucius Wilson, a black officer, sitting in his living room occupying his pet La-Z-Boy recliner, and Pattie sitting in the next chair, all made up, wearing a tailored house coat.

Erler's face darkened with fury as he gave a withering, long look at Wilson.

"Just thought I'd drop in to see you, Bob," smiled Lucius. "Wanted to get your advice on a police matter."

"I'll give you advice, all right," said Erler, trying to restrain his anger. "My advice is never to let me catch you in my house again."

It was the last straw. Next morning Bob Erler quit the police force.

10

JIM WALSH, A patrolman for the Hollywood Police Department, was the only friend Robert Erler had in Florida and he knew how badly Erler wanted to join the Hollywood force. When Walsh learned of an opening in the department he immediately alerted Erler, who rushed to apply for the position. When Erler's application for employment was officially filed, Walsh interceded with some associates to facilitate his friend's acceptance. Assistant Chief of Police Carl King took an immediate fancy to the young and eager rookie applicant and accepted him on probation, making arrangements for Erler to receive a routine training course at the police academy in Miami to which Erler readily adapted. It was much easier than the rigorous training he had in Special Services at the United States Army Camp in Fort Benning, Georgia. When Lieutenant Delton Dollar, the Director of the Miami Police Academy, sent glowing reports to King about Erler's high ratings, the assistant chief knew he had made a good selection and decided to take him under his wing and personally mold his career.

The career advance, however, was dampened by gloomy, dark clouds continuing to hover over the Erler household in Dania's trailer park. The increased income from his new job and the proceeds of the sale of the old trailer to former boss, Dania Chief of Police Don Parton, encouraged the young couple to acquire the new trailer Pattie desired and a brand new Dodge Dart. Both were heavily financed and in order to make ends meet Erler still had to moonlight, taking on any employment available. His wife continued to write bad checks and Erler would scurry from one creditor to another asking for respite and arrange to make partial payments on his delinquent accounts in order to stave off threats of garnishment and harassing litigation. Erler worked at a frenzied rate day and night, even denying himself the luxury of eating lunch to save expenses. He doggedly maintained this frightening pace until it became apparent to Erler's superior officers that he was exhausted, physically and mentally. His work as a police officer, which he had heretofore approached with such enthusiasm, diminished to a point of lifeless inefficiency. It was inevitable that a confrontation with Carl King would occur and Erler was finally called on the carpet.

King sat at his worn oaken desk carefully going over the reports of his three shift commanders when Patrolman Robert John Erler meekly walked through the partially opened door. Observing the stately executive look up with a startled expression, Erler took a step backward and tried to knock on the half-opened door, fearful that he may have incurred the displeasure of his chief by not announcing his presence before making an unheralded intrusion.

"Come right in," sang out the chief with a ghost of a smile playing about his lips.

"Thank you, sir," responded the flustered rookie, and stood awkwardly at the chief's desk.

"Sit down, Bob," ordered King softly, his handsome face clouding to show concern for the distasteful subject he was about to discuss. "When you first came on the force, I was proud to be your coach and tutor because you were a true dedicated cop. I had high hopes for . . ."

"But sir," interrupted Erler, "I . . ."

"I know all about your troubles, Bob. You don't have to explain. That's why I gave you all those extra details. You're the only officer on the force that has permission to work seven days a week. I want you to get your finances straight so you can do your job. The ratings of your efficiency reports have dropped considerably. Why?"

"Chief, I have contacted all my creditors and worked out a plan to pay a little each month on the delinquent accounts, so that problem is under control . . .''

"Then what's bothering you enough to make you lose weight and wander around like a zombie?"

Erler felt he had to stand up, and with labored effort rose unsteadily to his feet. Here it is again, he thought, and flopped back into his chair before he blacked out. His mind started to drift as he felt himself become flushed and clammy. He was back in Dania in his high performance 360 horse-powered police car chasing a robbery suspect, cutting in and out of traffic at 100 miles an hour, racing through stop signs and traffic lights when he saw the Chevrolet loom within his sights. It was impossible to avoid the collision; he jammed on his brakes before hitting the car dead center. He remembered his head crashing through the patrol car windshield, then darkness. When he regained consciousness in the hospital, the doctor informed him that he had a severe brain concussion and prescribed rest and medication. All he remembered was the blinding painful headaches.

Erler snapped back to reality. The chief was waiting for him to continue with his explanation.

"It's those painful migraine headaches that are making me nauseous and dizzy—and they get so bad I sometimes forget where I am or what I'm doing. Didn't I report that I was in a bad car accident when I was on the Dania police force? Well, when I totaled that police vehicle I got a bad concussion that should have passed away, but the headaches remain, and I black out every so often.''

King suggested Erler visit the police surgeon for a complete medical examination, but Erler quickly protested, fearful that prolonged medical examinations were too time consuming and would keep him away from his moonlighting assignments, which were his first priority. Besides, he thought, the headaches and blackouts would soon go away. The assistant chief, reflecting upon Erler's unconvincing claims of fitness for duty and good health, made a decision.

"Bob, I'm taking you off active duty and assigning you to administrative work." Seeing his protegé was about to register an objection, he held up his hand to silence him and continued, "You'll be back with Lieutenant Goetz on the homicide investigation of Merilyn Clark. He needs an

officer to supervise the distribution and playing of the
Catch Me Killer tapes. It's easy work and will give you a
chance to recover your health and strength."

The assistant chief rose from behind his desk to indicate
the end of the interview. Erler rigidly stood at attention,
trying to conceal his chagrin at what he believed to be a
demotion, and promised to report to Lieutenant Goetz immediately. Erler left King's office with mixed emotions. He
realized that his job was safe for the time being, but certainly didn't relish the prospect of having to work under
Lieutenant Irving Goetz and his sidekick, John Cox. Goetz
was the officer who humiliated him in front of half the
police personnel in the city when he berated him for not
getting the names of the elderly couple who led him to find
the body of the dead girl at the Industrial Park. He remembered the look of disgust on Goetz's face when he mimicked Erler's high-pitched voice, "No sir, I didn't get the
number of their license plates on the car."

Erler also disliked the cold look in Detective John Cox's
eyes as he quietly stood by, just staring.

Erler's new assignment was to supervise the taped recognition program of the 'Catch Me Killer's' voice, aptly
named DO YOU RECOGNIZE THIS VOICE?

His duties were to play the two tapes to all civil service
personnel in the county and all shifts of the various municipal police officers and deputy sheriffs. Local radio and
television studios played the tapes periodically to mixed
reactions. Some listeners believed the taped conversations
of the alleged killer were the product of a practical joker;
others were apprehensive and fearful. Many believed they
had heard the voice somewhere before, but could not state
with particularity whose voice it was. The power of suggestion ran rampant and conjecture attained an extremely
high level.

"That guy is really whacked out," observed one police
officer who listened intently to the taped transmission.
"The more I hear it, the surer I feel the voice is familiar
to me."

"He's sick all right," chimed in another patrolman, who
had listened for the fourth time at the end of his shift.
"Didn't you guys hear what the shrink said about him?"

"What shrink?" questioned Erler. "What are you talking about?"

"Well," answered the patrolman, pleased that he was the center of attention and was about to impart a juicy morsel of gossip to the curious group of cops, "the big brass in the sheriff's office called in a phonetic expert and a shrink from the University of Miami to listen to the tapes and give an opinion . . ."

"So what's the scoop?" the officers excitedly asked in unison.

"The scoop is that he's nutty as a fruitcake and will probably wind up killing himself."

Erler remained silent amidst the amused sallies and raucous laughter of the departing officers and prepared the recorder for transmission for the next shift that would soon congregate for the voice identification experiment.

The part of the assignment Erler liked best was visiting the classrooms of the public and private schools in the area. The respect he received from the teachers and students as a uniformed police officer made him gregarious to the point where he found himself giving little talks to the assembled groups, until an incident occurred at Southeast High in Fort Lauderdale that deflated his spirits, discouraging further lectures.

Philo Levenson almost missed the privilege of attending public school in Broward's educational system. He was ten months old when his parents resigned themselves to the dire realization that their cuddly infant with bright owlish eyes was retarded. Five years and six pediatricians later, Philo's doting parents were informed their son was not retarded but slightly autistic and required special attention and training at a private learning facility. The Levensons continued to relentlessly pursue every medical avenue for assistance to their only son and a small ray of hope appeared when the last attending neurologist ventured his professional opinion that Philo was indeed a healthy normal child suffering from dyslexia, a reading disability, which could be corrected, and recommended the child enroll in a public school with children his own age.

The first grade teacher at Pinecrest Elementary School in Fort Lauderdale listened patiently as Philo's mother tearfully groped for words to explain away her son's slight problems with reading.

"Sometimes my Philo sees the printed words transposed, but he always works it out," she said while looking at the teacher's square-jawed expressionless face for some glimmer of empathy or understanding, but found none. Looking squarely into the eyes of the worried mother, the first grade teacher huffed, "He's just a slow learner. I'll take care of him."

Robert Erler was depressed on the morning he was scheduled to give a demonstration of the tapes to the entire student body at Southeast High. Driving slowly to his next assignment he thought about the fight with Pattie and her threats to take their son, Bobby, to her mother in Kansas City and not return. He didn't mind being saddled with all her debts and bad checks, but he couldn't bear the thought of losing his son whom he adored. Erler did his best thinking while driving his police car, but today he couldn't seem to shake the despair that engulfed him. He was afraid he would get one of his migraine headaches.

Philo Levenson was at the rear of the classroom when the stocky, well-built, good looking officer carrying a large black transmitting device entered and greeted his teacher. Philo was always at the rear of the classroom from the first grade at Pinecrest to the second year at Southeast, which prevented personal contact with his classmates and less chance to be ridiculed. The teacher rarely called upon him, but he was always ready with the correct answer on the current lesson. Philo never volunteered.

Erler gave the class a brief explanation of the purpose of the tapes and requested absolute silence while they were being played in order to ensure accurate voice recognition. The first transmission was being made and at the juncture where the tense voice pleaded, "I just killed three people—please catch me before I kill more!" Philo's arm shot up. The teacher bolted upright in her chair with a look of amazement on her face. This was the first time Philo ever raised his hand to volunteer anything or ask a question.

Officer Erler, observing the peculiar looking lad in the last row with his arm held straight up in the air, inquired, "Do you think you recognize the voice?"

"Yessir," gulped Philo. "That's your voice!"

Everyone laughed.

11

In a private room at Broward General Hospital, Dorothy
Clark reclined in a white metal bed with fresh, white sheets.
Her bandaged head was propped up on wedged pillows as
a uniformed police officer sat in an easy chair nearby and
read the *Fort Lauderdale News* to while away the time
during his guard duty. Melrose, who was in charge of her
security, took an active role as the chief investigator, and
constantly checked on Dorothy's progress. He would saun-
ter over to her side and surreptitiously ask the supine patient
questions as though he fully expected a reply. These intru-
sions began to bear fruit as he often detected Dorothy's lips
move in an attempt to speak. He threw caution to the wind
and defied the stringent directions of the doctors as he persisted with continuous interrogation. At one time Dorothy
moaned something incoherently and attempted to speak her
first words! Names of individuals and bits and pieces of
incoherent muttering came forth from her swollen lips and
Melrose exulted.

"Bingo!" he shouted to Detective Sweeny, who stood
at the door so he could warn Melrose if any doctor was
approaching the hospital room. "We've got her talking—
here are your orders—and if any doctor interferes I will go
to court on this!"

"What do you want done, Johnnie?"

"Get a voice activated tape recorder and put it right next
to Dorothy where it will pick up everything she says. I want
it operative twenty-four hours, around the clock!"

"I'll get on it right away, Johnnie. Anything else?"

"Those tapes are to be sealed and made available to no
one except me. I repeat, *no one*!"

August 19. When the news leaked out to the media that
Dorothy Clark recovered sufficiently from her comatose
condition to be taken off the critical list, police investigators, newspaper reporters, well-wishers and curiosity seekers all milled around the hospital room in quest of the

slightest ray of information to unmask the puzzle, but all were shunted away and denied personal contact by armed guards of the sheriff's office who were protecting Mrs. Clark constantly, in fear that her unknown assailant would make another attempt on her life. Officer Sweeny privately reported to Melrose that Dorothy would murmur a few non-sensical phrases and then fade out and suggested the county medical examiner, Jack Mickley, be consulted.

"Sure, I know that Mickley's jurisdiction is homicide and autopsies, but he's a friend of the police, where as here . . ."

"Yeah," agreed Melrose, "get Jack on the phone and he'll tell us where we stand. I'm tired of fighting with these doctors here." And raising his right fist in a menacing gesture said, "That damn resident doc and his flunkies will get their walking papers soon."

Doctor Mickley bounced in, white coat and crepe soled bone colored sneakers flashing in the pristine hospital room, and laughed at the serious faces of the two officers, "What's eating you guys?"

Melrose cooled down. Mickley always had a soothing effect on him, and asked the medical examiner to read Dorothy's hospital chart and medical records, and even examine her for "a reading."

Mickley went to the foot of Dorothy's bed and extracted the stainless steel clipboard encasing the patient's chart and flipped through the pages like a speed reader. He then made a cursory examination of Dorothy's wounds and, putting a small flashlight to her eye, remarked, "What is significant here is the proximity of a bullet lodged so close to this gal's brain that if she fully recovers her total recall would be markedly diminished."

"What are you trying to tell us?" asked a worried Melrose.

"I'm telling you this looks like a classic case of amnesia, and from what you have explained to me, you can expect this little lady to relate events up to the point of the traumatic occurrence, then there would be a mental block as to the details immediately preceding the attempted murder."

Melrose's shoulders drooped with disappointment and he thanked Mickley for his opinion but inwardly vowed to keep after Dorothy until she identified her would-be killer. She had good days and bad days. On the good days Dorothy would utter some disjointed statements and Melrose or the guard on duty followed through with pertinent questions, to no avail. For the next several days Dorothy's tiny room was crowded with police investigators and guards. Every little recorded utterance was analyzed and carefully considered for further investigation. Dorothy's memory was evanescent, but Detective Melrose remained optimistic and attempted to jog her memory by reading her the official police reports of the Hollywood Beach incident where the police officer refused to allow her to sleep on the beach and ordered her to leave and park her car at the beach in Dania. Melrose was scrupulously careful not to mention anything about Merilyn.

"What happened after the cop woke you up on Hollywood Beach? Tell us, Dorothy, when the cop woke you up on Hollywood Beach, you remember that—tell us, what happened after that?"

"Dorothy, do you remember that the cop woke you up on Hollywood Beach and you drove to Dania? Do you remember, Dorothy? Tell us what happened in Dania. Tell us, Dorothy, who did you see in Dania?"

This barrage of questions coupled with the detective recounting the events that had transpired: sleeping in the car, being accosted by a police officer telling her to get off the beach, evoked a vague response.

"Yes, I remember that," replied Dorothy.

"The police officer coming to you on the beach and telling you to move on?"

"Yes, I remember that, too."

"Now, Dorothy, remember you moved on and drove up to the beach in Dania?"

Dorothy replied in a monotone, "I know about that."

"Then who did you see on Dania Beach, Dorothy? You must remember. Who was it you saw on Dania Beach?"

In the same deadened, flat, expressionless voice Dorothy replied, "This fellow with a brown uniform. He had a round patch on his shoulder."

Melrose could hardly contain himself. He pressed for details. His extreme agitation overwhelmed Dorothy. A thin film of perspiration covered her upper lip as her eyes became slightly opaque and closed.

"Dorothy, Dorothy?" yelled Melrose, apprehensive that his charge would lapse into a state of unconsciousness and never again remember what she started to describe, but Dorothy had fainted away into a complete state of oblivion. The silence that fell over the hospital room was discouraging.

"She'll snap out of this," declared Melrose to a hushed, skeptical group. "And when she does," he looked around defiantly, "we will have our killer."

The determined lieutenant sat in the proffered chair, intently waiting for the patient to awaken, pleased that he was armed with the first clue of any magnitude. Dorothy's gentle snoring subsided to a complete stop after what seemed to Melrose an eternity, and she slowly opened her eyes and looked around the room, resting a vacant stare on the police investigator.

"Tell me about that fellow in the brown uniform. Do you remember what he looked like?"

"He was husky and had a blond crew cut; yes, I remember."

"What else can you tell us about him, Dorothy?" Melrose pressed eagerly.

"Ask Merilyn. She's a smart girl and has a wonderful memory. Merilyn will tell you much better than I can."

A hush fell over the room. No one had informed Mrs. Clark that the body of her daughter Merilyn was transported for burial to Clarkston, Georgia.

Melrose subdued his excitement. He decided to proceed slowly and handle Mrs. Clark with kid gloves, asking leading questions based on information that appeared on collective investigation reports including tips that trickled in from anonymous callers and well-meaning citizens. He realized there wasn't much to work with and the only degree of similarity in any of the clues was the description of the sandy haired man with a crew cut, young, stockily built, wearing a brown uniform-type shirt.

"Did he have sandy hair? Did he have a crew cut? Did he have a blue polka dot shirt?"

"No, he had a brown shirt with a shoulder patch," replied a troubled Dorothy. In straining to remember she volunteered, "He was husky and had a blond crew cut."

Melrose decided he would tell Mrs. Clark about her daughter later, when she was mentally and physically prepared for the traumatic news, but for now he would proceed carefully and milk the entire story from the only surviving eyewitness to the murder. He knew he was on the verge of a major breakthrough.

"Can you describe this fellow, Dorothy? Did he have a polka dot sport shirt? Was his hair cut short, like in a crew cut?" questioned the detective, groping for any plausible lead to an important clue.

"No, no polka dot shirt. None of that. It was brown, with a shoulder patch."

Melrose decided that when he was finished interrogating Dorothy Clark he would check the supply houses in Miami to see what kind of brown tunics were distributed to elevator operators, security guards, delivery services, repairmen and even police personnel.

12

IT WAS ALL over with the Erlers. The breakup started when little Bobby tousled his mother's perfectly groomed hair and received a slap in the face which sent him reeling. The father became so enraged he grabbed his wife's arm, spun her around and struck her flush on the right side of her face.

"Don't you ever hit my boy again," he thundered. "I'll kill anyone who lays a hand on him."

Robert's anger subsided and he apologized to his wife for his explosive outburst, but Pattie remained stone-faced. She had already made plans to leave her husband forever and take Bobby with her. That would be the cruelest blow of all, but it would serve him right.

All alone in his new trailer, Erler became depressed and lost all enthusiasm for the police work he loved. He sorely missed his son and cursed his wife who took him away.

He had to decide on a course of action. Should he fly to his mother-in-law's home in Kansas City to reclaim Bobby? That wasn't a good idea. It would mean a court fight for custody and he had no money for travel or attorney's fees. His health was deteriorating from missing too many meals and the extra jobs he took to cover expenses and pay delinquent bills were taking their toll on his vitality. Migraine headaches were becoming more frequent and he was afraid of the blackouts, and wondered whether he should continue with police work or chuck it all and go back home to his family. Florida had too many bad memories. He decided there was no reason to remain. The next morning bright and early he appeared at the office of his friend and mentor, Carl King, to announce his withdrawal from the Hollywood Police Department. He was embarrassed and didn't know how to break the news to the assistant chief. He felt like an ingrate and tried very hard to keep his tears from showing as he said, "Chief, I have decided to resign from the force."

"I can't believe that, Bob. You're a dedicated police officer and you love your work so very much. Besides, you're due for a hundred dollar a month raise."

"I'm sorry, Chief," croaked Erler, his face reddening, "but I must go back home to Phoenix to be with my family. Mother's health is not good, and she needs me."

Carl King was genuinely sorry to lose Erler, offering him a new assignment on the homicide investigating team. But the rookie was adamant, disappointing the assistant chief, who became business-like and snapped, "Please remember you were the one who received the original complaint that led us to find the body. You even secured the scene and helped conduct a hunt for the third body; and therefore you are a vital witness and will be called upon to testify when we arrest the murderer."

Erler noted the change in King's feelings toward him with a sickening sense of guilt, and assuring his superior that he would always be available to assist at the trial, backed out of the office just as a migraine headache was about to form.

The next few days were busy ones for Robert Erler. He peddled all his personal effects and made an effort to clear a few of his debts, but Pattie left him in such a financial hole, it would be futile to consider getting his affairs in order. There was no way out. He felt he had made the right choice. The sooner he left Florida, the better.

John Cox sat at his desk in the open area of the detective bureau intently pouring over the mushrooming reports that were coming in from well-meaning citizens and cranks. The police reports compiled from the various investigative agencies were in marked conflict and unproductive. Lieutenant Goetz entered the bureau and flopped down tiredly across the metal desk as Cox ceased assembling the sheaf of reports in his hands and looked up.

"John, does it bother you that Johnnie Melrose of Fort Lauderdale seems to be taking over this homicide case? After all, this is a Hollywood matter and he can stay in Fort Lauderdale and take care of Dorothy Clark's case."

"We have to work together," replied Cox solemnly, "and exchange clues freely, otherwise both prosecutions will be ruined. It took us three days to get the autopsy report from Melrose. There was no earthly reason for him to hold it from us. There was nothing there, no rape, no sexual molestation of any kind, nothing."

"I have to tell you, Melrose is angry with our department."

"Do you know why?" asked Cox.

"A number of reasons," replied Goetz, "but the big reason is that Dorothy Clark is in virtual isolation at the hospital with a recording machine set up right by her pillow monitored twenty-four hours a day to receive whatever utterances she may make while she's in a coma. Melrose gave strict orders that no one was to enter her room except hospital staff and armed guards, and lo and behold, one of our cops paid her a visit. Guess who?"

"Erler?"

"Right," answered Goetz. "He went to her hospital room and showed his credentials, explaining his interest as being on the department's investigating team and they let him in. Melrose blew his top when he learned of the visit."

A red warning sign flashed in Cox's head upon hearing of Erler's visit to Dorothy Clark. He had promised himself that he would check into Erler's background, but did not impart his concern to his associates. There were other problems that required attention. Too many people were being arrested "on suspicion" by both police departments at an alarming rate and were subject to the same frailty; worried residents would telephone the police department to report an odd looking stranger or some unkempt person moving in a suspicious manner, whereupon a police officer would be dispatched to "detain" the individual for questioning, and ultimately coming up empty.

"Another thing," said Irving Goetz, as though reading John Cox's mind. "We have to stop making these needless arrests. Have you any idea of the number of zero pinches we've built up? Do you realize what a smart defense lawyer could do with a record of irresponsible arrests? Our credibility would be destroyed," continued Goetz, answering his own questions, "and our prosecution diluted."

"I know we've picked up too many suspects for questioning but that's our job. How can we be faulted for that?" replied the detective.

"Yeah," retorted a worried Goetz. "What about the young kid we picked up on suspicion and held on an open charge of homicide just because he had a record? We even got a warrant for another suspect for suspicion of murder who had a criminal record just because he tried to book a flight to the Bahamas the day after the girl's body was found."

"I know all these things would make us vulnerable in court, but we have so many possible leads that it's our duty to follow them up and let the chips fall where they may. It'll be up to the prosecutor to do the explaining if we get our man and the case finally gets to trial."

"Vulnerable," echoed Goetz. "What about the fellow who called from Tampa claiming he killed three women in Fort Lauderdale. What a holiday a defense attorney would have with that."

"Old man Gore from the *News* had his usual sarcastic editorial on the ineptitude of the police," lamented Cox, "and he hit us rather hard on the nonsensical arrests we've been making."

"I'll tell you about a nonsensical arrest," parroted Goetz. "Wonder Boy Erler received a call from a barmaid at the

Hutchinson Hotel where a stranger with a briefcase was babbling about a dead girl and when Erler went to talk to him he seemed so shaky and nervous that Bob put him under arrest, handcuffed and searched him. He was even transported to headquarters where he was grilled, pushed around and finally released.''

"Why did you refer to Erler as 'Wonder Boy'?" asked Detective Cox, ignoring the lieutenant's narration of the arrest.

"Oh," replied Goetz. "That's one of the names his fellow officers call him. Another name they use is 'Super Cop.' Guess he brought that one from Dania.''

"How long was he on the force there?''

"Just about six months, and came here because of the money, but still lives in Dania somewhere.''

John Cox reflected on how little he knew of Patrolman Robert Erler and recalled an image of a stocky, muscular young man standing guard over Merilyn Clark's blanket covered body, with imperious defiance, until ordered away in humiliation by Irving Goetz's vitriolic criticism. They had to have a little talk.

The public was clamoring for action. More than two weeks had elapsed since the murder of the young girl virtually in their back yard and no clues or witnesses had surfaced. The news media maintained pressure on the various police agencies as the terrorized housewives maintained a strict vigil in their homes and kept their children off the streets. There was a crazed killer on the loose and they were justifiably in fear of their lives. It was imperative that the phantom murderer be found!

Cox and Goetz met early in the detective squad room every morning to sort out the available clues and leads for evidence. They lamented that there was no direct evidence to support the mounting circumstances that could possibly lead to a suspect. All anonymous calls were pursued to their conclusions with no hunch or rumor ignored, especially a strange telephone call received by John Cox which he discussed with Lieutenant Goetz at a pre-coffee briefing.

"An old buddy of mine who used to be on the force in Dania called to tell me of a hunch about the voice on the tapes. I told him to come on down and see what he's got."

Goetz signed, "Another hunch to 'dead endsville.' You carry the ball on this one. I'm just fed up." He strode from the office leaving Cox smiling at his partner's impatience. A few minutes later Detective Cox brightened as he recognized his friend walk into his office.

"Hello, Roger," he grinned, reaching out to shake the ex-Dania patrolman's hand. "You sure look funny out of uniform."

"Hello yourself, John," answered a smiling Roger Kelly. "Just because I gave up the police business doesn't mean I'm not interested in fighting crime. I still ride in a squad car now and then to get away from the old lady a night or two."

Laughing at this old squad room cliché, Cox answered, "You said you wanted to talk about a hunch you had—what gives?"

"Do you mind playing that tape for me of the Catch Me Killer? I have an idea who it sounds like."

Cox obligingly opened up his overstuffed briefcase that was lodged under his chair and extracted a copy of the original transmission. Inserting the tape into the recording unit, he casually asked, "What got you on this kick?"

Roger stretched out in his chair, folded his hands across his stomach and explained, "On one of my visits to the Dania squad room we were barbering about the case. We had all heard the tapes over and over. The more we heard them, the more familiar the voice became. Then I got my hunch but didn't want to tell the fellows because they would either laugh at me or all go along because the power of suggestion is so strong. That's not fair police work."

The detective agreed and as the tape began to unfold, placed his finger to his lips indicating silence. Both listened attentively to the tormented words pouring out:

"I just killed three people—please catch me!"

"Please, please catch me!"

"I'm going to kill more tonight . . ."

The recorder came to a whirring halt and the two men looked at each other. Roger broke the silence, "Do you know now who it may be?"

"Nope," answered Cox honestly, wondering what was in his friend's mind.

"It sure as hell sounds like our old 'Super Cop' we had in Dania."

"A cop?" asked the amazed Cox.

"Yes, a cop! He's one of your men," said Roger, jack-knifing out of his reclining position.

"I can't believe it," started the detective. "Tell me who you think it is?"

"Robert Erler—that's who."

An embarrassed quiet pervaded the bureau office as Cox slowly reached for the unit and rewound the tape. No words were exchanged between the men as the transmission was replayed. This time the flat nasal tones fraught with emotion and pathos acquired a new significance.

"It may be Erler," mused Cox to himself, and, turning to Roger, who was standing expectantly over the recorder, said, "Please do me a favor. The Dania P.D. has copies of this tape. Have some of the boys listen with you and see if they come up with the same impression. If there is some area of support, I'll get Erler's voice on tape and see if there's a match."

The two old acquaintances were saying their farewells when a young lady in a tailored police uniform announced that Lieutenant Johnnie Melrose of Fort Lauderdale would like to see Mr. Cox.

"Please tell Mr. Melrose I'll be with him in a minute and get ahold of Lieutenant Goetz and ask him to please come to the office for a meeting." Ushering Roger out of the front door and thanking him for his assistance, Cox greeted his visitor and led him to his desk.

"John," commenced Melrose, shunting aside all social amenities, and getting down to the business at hand, "I want to fill you in on some important new developments."

"Great!" acknowledged Cox. "I'm waiting for Goetz to get here, so please go ahead."

Melrose took a notebook from the left front pocket of his tweed sport coat and placed it gingerly on his crossed legs.

"Here it is for openers: Sergeant Portelli of Dania told

me he is certain the voice on the *Catch Me Killer* tapes is Bob Erler, one of your patrolmen.''

Detective Cox inwardly winced. He was just flattened by that same news a few moments ago, but remained impassive as he didn't know how much he could trust the Fort Lauderdale detective. He wondered what Melrose wanted. Why was he here in person? He never coordinated any investigative information with Hollywood before. Aware of the subdued reaction evoked by his big ''bomb,'' Melrose said, ''There's a helluva lot more.''

''It's possible the voice characteristics were similar to Erler's,'' replied Cox defensively. ''Besides, this Portelli has some kind of hard-on for Erler because of something that happened on the force in Dania, and Portelli gigs Erler every chance he gets.''

Lieutenant Goetz had quietly entered the detective bureau offices without making his presence known for fear of interrupting Melrose's interesting narrative. Cox looked up, acknowledging his partner's presence and pointed him out to Melrose, who curtly nodded and said, ''Mrs. Clark is starting to come around and remembers that the man who came to her car in Dania was wearing a brown, uniform type of shirt with a shoulder patch.'' He looked knowingly to his listeners for a response, but as none was forthcoming gushed, ''I checked with Chief Parton who tells me that last year the official uniform of the Dania Police Department was a brown tunic and a shoulder patch embroidered in silken gold thread with the words 'City of Dania Police Department'.''

''So . . . ,'' trailed off the interested Cox.

''So,'' continued the lieutenant, ''the Dania police officers were not required to turn in their old uniforms when the new designs and colors came out, and it's quite possible Dorothy Clark may have described a discarded Dania police tunic as the 'brown uniform-type shirt with a shoulder patch' her attacker wore that night she was shot.''

''Seems to me you're zeroing in on a suspect,'' said Cox, his closely cropped grey head lowered in thought, fixing an inquisitive stare on Melrose.

''Could be,'' he replied, ''and I'll tell you why. In my talks with Chief Parton he told me when he bought Erler's trailer in Dania, it was in filthy condition with dirty clothing, remnants of police uniforms, shorts, tee shirts, children's diapers piled in the kitchen and several spent .22 caliber casings all over the place. The same type of missiles were found in Merilyn's body and in Mrs. Clark's head!''

"Anything we can use as a standard of comparison on those shells?'' queried Goetz. "Perhaps something we can use on ballistics?''

"No such luck,'' answered Melrose. "The chief threw them away when he cleaned up the mess. The only thing I was able to salvage were Erler's personal pictures that I want to show to Mrs. Clark for possible identification.''

"Why are you harping on Erler?'' asked Goetz.

"All roads lead to Rome,'' Melrose sermonized in a patronizing manner, vaguely wondering if the two Hollywood officers knew what he meant, and deciding to elucidate said, "The strong fingers of suspicion all seem to point in your boy's direction. I want to see his log book for August 12.''

"Why?'' asked Goetz lamely.

"Here's a suggestion: When that girl's body was first found, it was off the highway and still dark. I sincerely doubt any motorist simply driving by could have seen it. Maybe—just maybe—there was no couple in a car to make such observation, and Erler could have faked it. That could explain why Erler claimed he 'forgot' to get the names of the elderly couple and didn't get the tag number,'' explained Melrose. "I want to talk to Patrolman Erler right now!''

"Impossible,'' stated Goetz sadly. "Erler resigned from the department and went back to Phoenix.''

"What!'' exploded Melrose. He was more furious than frustrated. His initial instinct was right and felt he was wasting his time with the Hollywood department. Melrose stood upright. He decided not to waste any more time with these Keystone Cops in Hollywood and to take matters into his own hands, making an abrupt departure, barely waving goodbye.

Goetz shook his head in resignation and told his partner, "We better fill Carl in on what's happening to his pratt boy.''

Cox slowly lumbered to his feet and said, "Let's go to the crucifixion.''

13

IT WAS CLEAR in Melrose's mind who the killer was, but there was no hard evidence, just an educated guess supported by innuendo, which was not enough to formalize any semblance of a prosecution. He was experienced enough to realize the paltry facts uncovered to date were mere inferences which did not rise to the level of reasonable circumstances. A case built solely on circumstantial evidence would not survive the rigors of a vigorously defended court trial. There must be more! He made his way to Dorothy's room and was pleased to note her sitting up and smiling pleasantly. The nurses apparently had just completed her morning toilette. Her shorn hair was making a comeback and a light blue shawl rested over her shoulders. Looking at her, a casual observer would never guess she was partially paralyzed by the bullets left in her skull. She had lost coordination of her right hand but her memory began to improve, much to the delight of the bevy of police officers that continued to frequent her guarded hospital quarters. During her waking periods, around-the-clock, she would be questioned at every interval but would only respond to Detective Melrose's prodding and insistent questioning, like a slave under a hypnotic trance.

She greeted her visitor, slowly articulating with slurred tones, "Hello there."

"Hi Dorothy," was the reply, with a forced smile that belied his anxiety. "I have some pictures to show you," and without ceremony or explanation, exhibited to the disinterested patient Erler's identification pictures when he was a police officer in Dania. Sweeney and the patrolman assigned to guard duty looked puzzled at the unusual turn of events.

"Wh-a-t that?" struggled Dorothy.

"This is a picture of a policeman in uniform. Does he look familiar?"

Upon receiving no response, the persistent detective

showed the reclining patient a snapshot of Erler and his wife taken during palmier days, and inquired, "Do you recognize this man?"

"Cl-oser. Let me see closer."

With eager hands, Melrose positioned the snapshot so Dorothy could have a better view and was rewarded with a nod. "Is this the man who took you and Merilyn to his trailer that night?"

Every person in the hospital room remained deathly silent, expectantly waiting for her reply. None came. Dorothy's head fell back to her pillow in resignation. Melrose waited patiently for her to regain her composure.

"She's coming back!" yelled Sweeney as Dorothy's eyes fluttered open and beckoned to Melrose with her good left hand.

"That looks like him—the sandy haired fellow."

Melrose was ecstatic and pounced on Dorothy like a terrier, "See the shoulder patch on the uniform? Doesn't that make you remember?" In his eagerness to produce an "eyeball" identification witness the detective disregarded the frailty of the human power of suggestion and how forceful it could be when imposed upon a weakened or subservient individual and relentlessly prodded her with the ultimate clue.

The positive identification was made! Melrose was on a hot roll and turning to an elated Sweeney ordered, "Let's play the *Catch Me Killer* tapes, maybe Dorothy will recognize the fellow's voice also." But Dorothy had retreated to the peaceful and gentle world of oblivion. She snored softly. Melrose, realizing he had pressed his good fortune to the utmost, picked up the telephone at the bedside and contacted John Cox at the Hollywood Police Department.

"Cox, this is Johnnie. Mrs. Clark just made a positive identification—Robert Erler is the 'Catch Me Killer'!"

At Hollywood headquarters, Carl King sat alone in his darkened office, partially lit by a small desk lamp covered with shaded green glass which cast an unearthly shadow on his handsome face. He was determined not to be stampeded into action merely upon Melrose's conclusion about Erler's involvement in the two crimes. He was aware of Melrose's technique in using questionable suggestibility by showing photographs to Dorothy Clark. It would not stand up in court. The only evidence that could be used were the tapes made by the "unknown" caller. If only Erler were around to put his voice on tape so a comparison could properly be made. Everyone missed the boat there, so the next best thing would be to play the tapes before Erler's closest friends and associates and hope for an honest answer. He telephoned Goetz at home. "Irv, I want Jim Walsh in my office at 0800 tomorrow and a few of the men who may have worked with Erler or were close friends with him, and tell Cox to be there with his recorder and tapes."

The next morning Carl King looked over the officers assembled in his office and abruptly reported, "Men, there have been some new startling developments on the Merilyn Clark murder case that call for immediate action. But," he looked slowly over the attentive group, "there is one area of conflict that must be resolved, and I want an honest and sincere evaluation." In an attempt to put the men at ease, King rose to his feet and walked over to Corporal Jim Walsh, who looked up in wonder.

"Jim, it's no secret that all the clues and tips seem to point to your old pal, Bob Erler, as the prime suspect."

Walsh remained noncommittal and looked at his chief for guidance, but King merely returned Walsh's mute plea of supplication with a blank stare. He wanted to be totally impartial and certainly didn't wish to influence the opinion of the young corporal. Addressing the entire group, King said, "You will soon hear the tapes of the Catch Me Killer and you must pay strict attention to the voice and see if any one of you recognize a familiar accent or tone that may ring a bell in your consciousness. The voice identification has to be made positively by a credible person who has a reasonable basis for venturing an opinion."

"That's true," interjected Goetz. "A bunch of officers hearing the tapes together would bolster each other with guesswork. The next thing you know, their imagination takes over and one guy's opinion influences the other, and they come up with an agreement of who they think the caller may be."

"Okay John, roll the tapes please," directed the chief as

the officers settled back in their chairs to hear the transmission. Cox obediently started the recorder and the emotional plea gushed forth: "I would like to report a murder."

"Who is this?"

"I just killed three people—please catch me before I kill more."

"You just killed three people?"

"Please, please catch me . . . I ju . . . please!"

"Where are you?"

"I'm going to kill 'em tonight, too. Please, please, please!"

The tape ended amid total silence. Cox withdrew the reel and inserted the second transmission and activated the recorder. The silence continued and as the second tape whirred to a halt the officers looked at each other; no one ventured an opinion.

"What about you?" asked the chief pointing to Walsh.

"I'm sorry to admit," the corporal commented sadly, "it's Bob's voice alright. I wonder what makes a cop go bad?"

Goetz and Cox looked at each other with knowing glances. Every person in that room had made up his mind as to who the killer was.

"That's it, gentlemen," pronounced King. "Erler is our man. Let's get him!"

Assistant Chief King was besieged by television and newspaper reporters intimating that certain reliable sources disclosed a suspect was about to be arrested for Merilyn's murder and clamored for details. Doug McQuarrie of the *Fort Lauderdale News* impishly suggested that a news leak hinted the prime suspect was someone close to the chief himself. This retort annoyed King, who fended off all the incisive questions by making a rather optimistic announcement: "Gentlemen, I am scheduled to attend a meeting shortly with certain police officers and investigators, and may be able to call a press conference this afternoon and report a most vital police action. Please leave and you'll be contacted officially."

"When will that be?" asked Al Topel of the *Hollywood Sun-Tattler,* with his perennial cynical expression.

"We'll call you," responded the beleaguered chief.

"I see," laughed McQuarrie. "Don't call us, we'll call you."

Topel flipped his cigarette out the office window in mock defeat and joined the group in their mass exodus, but looked back toward King saying, "We know who it is just as well as you." But the wary chief didn't rise to the bait.

14 _____

BOB ERLER BELIEVED in travelling light. He had divested himself of all his worldly goods, threw a duffel bag containing what was left of his personal effects in the rear seat of his small but serviceable car and headed toward Arizona to see his ailing mother and the rest of his family. He drove all day with a compelling obsession, stopping only to replenish his fuel supply and grab a light snack. He welcomed the darkness of nightfall as an escape from the humidity and oppressive September heat. When he felt weary, he would pull off the road for a brief nap, then doggedly resume his arduous journey. The further he got from Florida, the lighter his spirits became. Florida held no fond remembrances and he was looking forward to a new life, but first he had to make certain his mother was okay. She would ask about Bobby, and what was he to say? He hoped Pattie would at least contact Winifred. After all, she was Bobby's grandmother and entitled to some kind of respect; but knowing Pattie, he resigned himself to the fact that he lost Bobby for the time being. Someday things would be different and father and son would be reunited, and this time for good! These thoughts drifted through his mind and spurred him onward, driving relentlessly until he arrived in Phoenix thoroughly exhausted.

His reunion with the family was a happy one. Mother Winifred had survived the crisis that hospitalized her. Danny was only too glad to relinquish the role as the "man of the house" to brother Bob, who took up residence in his sister DeDe's apartment which she shared with her girlfriend Judy. Erler liked the idea of having two women minister to his new bachelor lifestyle, but he had to settle down and get a good paying job, maybe with the Phoenix Police Department. He remembered his boyhood friend, David Koelsch, who was a deputy with the Maricopa County Sheriff's Office and decided to call him and make inquiries.

Late on the evening of Friday the thirteenth, Carl King, in the company of Irving Goetz and John Cox, sat in the West Hollywood office of Assistant State Attorney Robert Fegers and recounted in minute detail all the evidence that existed to link Robert Erler to the homicide of Merilyn Clark and the attempted murder of Dorothy Clark. It was not King's intention to bypass Johnnie Melrose, because the Fort Lauderdale lieutenant had built up a close relationship with Dorothy Clark, who could turn out to be the only eyewitness in the case. But time was of the essence and an arrest warrant must be procured in order to extradite Erler from Phoenix. Fegers, a husky, balding person, sat behind his desk, his rolled-up sleeves revealing muscular arms folded across his chest. This posture of "body english" sent out negative signals to Cox that the prosecutor was disenchanted with the presentation thus far, but Fegers continued to sit impassively behind his desk absorbing the facts as they unfolded in chronological order and when the chief concluded his narration, asked, "What do you want me to do with this crap?"

"We want a warrant issued against Robert John Erler for Murder in the First Degree for the homicide of Merilyn Clark."

"No way," commented the experienced prosecutor. "First of all, you're going to need a lot more hard, direct, positive evidence before this can go to a Grand Jury. Secondly," Fegers went on, "the Grand Juries in Broward County only sit twice a year and I wouldn't consider calling a special session on this kind of flimsy evidence."

"Can't you, as chief prosecuting attorney of the county, issue a warrant? Maybe by the time we make the arrest we'll find some concrete evidence or a confession to justify a Grand Jury indictment," suggested Goetz.

"The system doesn't work that way," replied Fegers. "In a First Degree murder case, the Grand Jury issues the

arrest warrant *after* an indictment is returned, and no
Grand Jury would vote an indictment on this kind of
horseshit.''

''Where do we go from here?'' asked Cox. ''You know
our problem. Erler is gone from Florida. We think we know
where he is, but any more delay on our part—we can lose
him.''

Bob Fegers pursed his lips in a pensive expression and
declared to his visitors, ''Gentlemen, here is the format I
suggest: Go to a Court of Record judge and get your warrant for Second Degree Murder. As you know, a Court of
Record judge has authority to issue warrants for all crimes
that are not capital offenses. Then go after your man.''

''We think he's in Arizona now, but what if he's on the
lam and hides out?''

''Here's another device you can use if you feel your
defendant is running away: After you get your Court of
Record warrant, go to the office of the FBI on Broward
Boulevard. When you tell them a criminal defendant is on
the run and deliberately staying out of Florida's jurisdiction, they'll get a federal warrant charging the defendant
with 'unlawful flight to avoid prosecution.' Then the FBI
agents will hunt him down and, believe me,'' smiled Fegers
knowingly, ''no one can hide from the government for any
length of time.''

''Wonderful,'' exclaimed Goetz, fully understanding the
prosecutor's astute instructions. ''Then when the Feds get
Erler, they'll turn him over to Florida for formal arrest and
prosecution.''

''Exactly,'' nodded Fegers. ''Go get some Court of Record judge that will issue your warrant.''

As the three officers made ready to leave Feger's office,
John Cox remained seated, ''I'm a bit disappointed that you
feel our case against Erler is weak. Maybe we'll have trouble getting a judge to issue a warrant?''

''We'll need to find a tough, scrappy law and order
judge,'' said the assistant chief. ''The toughest and roughest
one on the Bench is O'Toole. Let's go to his house now.''

''It's almost midnight,'' laughed Fegers. ''That's no way
to endear yourselves to a person from whom you want help.

He's probably in bed and by the time you get to Fort Lauderdale it will be 1:00 A.M.''

"We'll have to take our chances," Cox replied quietly with genuine sadness. He was relieved to receive the concurrence of the other two members of his team.

In the squad car on the way to Fort Lauderdale, the trio talked over who could make the most diplomatic presentment and not offend the fiery jurist for invading the privacy of his home for police business. Their decision was for all three to approach the judge en masse and thus share his honor's inevitable wrath should it be forthcoming. They finally assembled at the front door leading to the foyer of the fashionable home in Fort Lauderdale's exclusive Coral Ridge neighborhood and with trepidation, Cox rang the doorbell. They could all hear the bell chime inside and waited. After what seemed an eternity, Cox pressed the button again. The lights came on and a visibly irked, handsome man with tousled jet black hair, wearing a blue bathrobe, opened the door.

"What's going on?" snapped the judge in a clipped Boston accent.

All three officers began apologizing profusely for the intrusion. "We have to talk to you about an emergency, Judge O'Toole," ventured King.

"Okay, come in and make it quick," said the judge, refusing to smile at the officers' apparent discomfort. The judge had been subjected to these episodes in the past and was acutely aware of this interruption of his privacy as an occupational hazard. Carl King assumed the role of spokesman, just as he did in Bob Feger's office, and recited almost word for word the chronology of facts he believed would justify the issuance of an arrest warrant against Robert Erler for the double crimes of Second Degree Murder and the murderous attempt to take the life of Dorothy Clark.

Over an hour had elapsed while the judge sat in his easy chair seeming to sort out the meager evidence in his mind. The incisive questions he asked made King's hopes wane. He knew this was the end of the line. If the judge, a rabid law and order man, could not find enough probable cause to issue an arrest warrant, then the whole investigation would be placed on the back burner and end up in the dead files—and Robert Erler would get off scot-free.

"Very well," announced the judge to the relieved triumvirate. "I'll sign the warrant for the arrest of Erler for the Second Degree Murder of Merilyn Clark and the attempted murder in the First Degree of Dorothy Clark, but this will only keep the defendant on ice. Your big job will be to get the county solicitor to file an Information in order to prosecute this cop. Good night . . . I mean good morning, so please get the hell out!"

It was past two o'clock in the morning when the three tired but happy cops dropped in at Lester's all-night diner, enroute to Hollywood, for coffee and breakfast to talk over the next procedural move.

"The issuance of O'Toole's arrest warrant will only hold Erler on ice as a suspect," said King, the ranking Hollywood officer in charge. "A formal complaint should be made by the county solicitor, before we can even begin to think about formalizing extradition proceedings against Erler to bring him back to stand trial."

"Mrs. Angeline Weir is the new county solicitor in Broward County," said Goetz. "Does anyone know her?"

"No," answered Cox, "but she used to practice domestic law in Hollywood before being appointed by the governor."

Goetz replied, "We have to join forces with Melrose and let him carry the ball in Fort Lauderdale with her if you want an Information filed on the homicide charges. He can probably sell a bill of goods to this new gal whereas we're Hollywood outsiders, and have no clout up here."

"Let's go with the Melrose deal," directed the assistant chief. "He probably has a bit more evidence up his sleeve that he refuses to share with us, so fill him in on what we've got and let's have a united front for once." Cox gave a meaningful look at Goetz who also noted the chief's displeasure toward Melrose, which made the feeling unanimous.

The job of formulating criminal charges against Erler was readily accepted by Detective Melrose. He went to the second floor of the Broward County Courthouse and visited Mrs. Angeline Weir, who was having "on-the-job" training in the area of criminal law. She leaned heavily for guidance on tall curly haired prosecutor Len Boone who was a carry-over from the previous county solicitor, and had the most experience in that office. Angie Weir didn't seek Boone's advice after her conference with Melrose, as she liked the idea of filing formal charges against the 'Catch Me Killer' and looked forward to the enormous publicity her official action would generate. Even though the decision was hers alone, in the back of her mind there was a gnawing feeling that guidance from a top echelon conference of prosecution officials would be more prudent before taking the big step. The lovely Angie tossed her head defiantly, and yelled to her top assistant, "Len, come in here, we're going to prepare my first murder Information."

Boone lumbered into Angie's office with an inquiring look of curiosity on his handsome, rugged face. When his comely "boss" explained what she had in mind, his reply was, "Hold your horses," emphasizing his surprise with outstretched hands and rolling eyes. "Let's slow down and get some reports and input from all the investigating officers on this case."

"Of course," answered Angie, who immediately realized her inexperience prompted her to jump the gun. "Let's set up a meeting with the Fort Lauderdale and Hollywood police investigators, and then we'll file the formal charge."

15

ERLER WAS GETTING cabin fever in his sister's small apartment, pacing up and down like a caged Bengal tiger. The annoying migraine headaches persisted and he became depressed. The fact that Pattie never got in touch with his mother did little to alleviate his frame of mind. At times, his headaches were so severe he was compelled to lie on the couch in a darkened corner of the room until relief ultimately came.*

"Why don't you go to a doctor?" suggested DeDe. "Can't you see what these headaches are doing to you?"

"I have some pain pills from my prescription," volunteered Judy, reaching into her purse to withdraw a small bottle from which she selected two pills, handing them to the bewildered Erler.

"Thanks, Judy," their boarder gloomily acknowledged, accepting the medication which he popped into his mouth and hastily swallowed.

Erler was unhappy. The constant headaches gave him a nauseous feeling and drained him of his energy. He realized sooner or later he must get a job but he didn't seem to have enough energy to venture forth into the marketplace. He certainly didn't like his present lifestyle of lounging around the apartment like an invalid watching television all day long.

One gloomy afternoon while he sat listlessly before the television, pondering his future plans, the programming was interrupted by a special news bulletin. "We interrupt this program to bring you this special news bulletin. Local police departments are involved with a nationwide manhunt under the supervision of the FBI . . ." The announcer went on to give a description of the person that was labeled a "mass murderer," mentioning the killer to be an ex-Green Beret. At the mention of the words "Green Beret" Erler bolted upright from his chair, calling out to his sister to turn up the sound. DeDe came running into the room.

"There's a special news bulletin about a manhunt for an ex-Green Beret!" shouted Erler. "See if you can catch the name because maybe I know the fellow."

---

*I later learned from Bob's brother, Danny, the probable reason behind Erler's severe headaches: In 1963, as an amateur boxer, Erler went up against a well-known fighter named Florentino Fernandez. During that bout, Erler suffered a severe concussion. Later that night he went berserk in Hollywood's Diplomat Hotel. When he started smashing furniture, security was called and it finally took eleven policemen to restrain him. Shortly after that episode he would awaken some mornings, pillow soaked with blood that gushed from his ear during the night.

They both listened attentively and heard the announcer continue, "There is a nationwide search to apprehend a dangerous killer who is believed to be a Phoenix resident, for the brutal slaying of a twelve year old girl in Florida."

"Hey, that's got to be the case I worked on. I found the body. Listen to this."

"Is that the murder you told us about . . . finding the little girl in the field?"

"Shh," said Erler. "Let's hear what the announcer has to say."

"Be on the lookout for Robert John Erler, age twenty-five, five feet ten inches, weighing approximately one hundred seventy-five pounds, blond hair, crew cut. He is armed and dangerous. Call in any leads or information to this station on your local FBI or police office."

Erler jumped up rubbing his eyes fiercely with the palms of his hands. It had to be a mistake! He went before the television and sat transfixed, staring into the screen, waiting to hear his name mentioned again. He couldn't believe what he heard, and ran to the sofa to stretch out. The headaches were about to start. He could always tell. First there was the nausea, then excruciating pain. He hoped there would be no blackout as he had to collect himself and think. He knew he should do something, but what? The television in the small apartment was going full blast and the newscaster was warning the local townspeople about Erler, the fiendish 'Catch Me Killer,' painting him more violent and hideous with every report. The announcer warned his viewers about the veritable arsenal Erler commanded—hand grenades, automatic weapons and tear gas. The broadcaster cautioned extreme care because the murderer was a former Green Beret, trained to kill with his bare hands—and a Karate champion capable of pulverizing a human skull.

DeDe was horrified to see the pathetic figure of her brother Bob as he writhed and fumed in his chair. She had never before seen him in such condition. She called out to Judy, "Come here quick and help me with Bob."

Judy responded and was surprised at the sight that awaited her. Erler's eyes were rolling wildly and spittle formed on his lips. The only help Judy could offer was contained in her ever present bottle of barbiturates which she always carried on her person.

"Here Bob, a couple of these will calm you down."

Erler snatched the bottle from her outstretched hand, frantically tearing the lid off and greedily gulped down several pills. After a few moments he still continued to shake and tremble, and swallowed another handful. Tension rose among the occupants in the small apartment. The girls were helpless and in fear; the now irrational and frightened ex-cop, unsure of what to do, ordered, "Get Mom on the wire, quick!"

DeDe hastily went to the telephone and with trembling hands dialed her mother's number. "Mother, did you—yes, Bob's here. Please stop crying, dear, and Bob will speak with you."

"Mom . . . ?"

"Oh Bob," Mrs. Winifred Erler asked tearfully, "what have you done? There are police all around the house looking for you—waiting to arrest you."

"Mom, please . . ."

"I'm afraid they'll hurt you. They have guns and are hiding behind all the cars piled up out here and, oh, I don't know what to do!"

"It's all a big mistake, Mom. I'll call the police in Hollywood and work it all out," pleaded the tormented Erler. "Just give me a little time."

"Please Bob," begged his near hysterical mother, "don't come to the house. I'm afraid you'll be shot and killed!"

"Don't worry Mom, I'm going to check with the television station and my old chief in Hollywood. Get them to clear the police from around your house."

"All right, son," replied the partially reassured mother. "Danny wants to come over and talk to you."

"No, no, no!" thundered Erler. "Danny will only lead the police to this apartment. Another thing, Mom, we have to cut this conversation short because the police may have placed a tap on your phone, knowing I'd call you sooner or later."

He abruptly slammed the receiver down and cut off his mother's entreaties. What to do next? He felt unsafe, unsure and unable to make a rational judgment. His confusion blended into panic. His sister and Judy could offer no advice or help, and just kept milling about, crying and trying to comfort each other, while Erler paced the floor and wrapped his arms around himself, rocking back and forth in mute agony.

"Please call Ellie Dooley in Doctor Seltzer's office in Hollywood," he whimpered.

"Right away, Bob," obeyed DeDe, and picked up the phone, asking the long distance operator for Doctor Seltzer's office number. She remained on the phone until the connection was made.

"Hello, Doctor Seltzer's office? Let me talk to Ellie Dooley."

"Just one moment," replied the receptionist, "she'll be with you shortly."

"Hello, Mrs. Dooley speaking."

Erler grabbed the phone. "Ellie, this is Bob Erler, please help me. I'm in a terrible mess and need help."

"Bob, where are you?"

"I'm in Phoenix."

"Okay Bob, I heard what's going on and what they're saying about you. We don't believe it and we'll do everything in our power to help you. Come back here where you belong with your friends."

"No, Ellie, it won't do any good. They won't give me a chance. I'll kill myself before I let them take me alive."

Mrs. Dooley, a pretty blond, blue-eyed and trim of figure, was a registered nurse and a highly trained medical technician. She quickly assessed the situation and tried to placate the wild unmanageable Erler at the other end of the phone and pleaded, "Don't say foolish things like that. What you need is an attorney to advise and represent you down here."

"What do I need a lawyer for? I'll just end it all—I can't take this kind of pressure."

"A good lawyer can make judgments for you and guide you because I can see you're not capable of thinking clearly."

"I'm broke, Ellie. I have no money for a lawyer."

"Frank and I will help out. There's a criminal lawyer here in Hollywood that happens to be Doctor Seltzer's friend and patient. I'm certain we can get him to help. His name is Joe Varon."

"I've heard of him and how expensive he is."

"That's our problem. You just take it easy and we'll call you later. What's your telephone number?"

"No, Ellie, no one must know where I am or they'll come and kill me. I'll call you later."

The connection was broken. He looked at the receiver in his hand and sorrowfully concluded the telephone was the only means by which he could reach out for help, but phone calls were treacherous and could be traced. He wanted to call the television station to tell them everything they said was a big mistake, but that would only be a wasted call. No use calling the local cops. They were out to kill him on sight. He decided to chance a telephone call to Mrs. Claire Kaufman of Hollywood, a former part-time employer with whom he established a close friendship during his moon-lighting days.

"Hello, Claire, this is Bob Erler. I'm calling you from Phoenix. What's happening back there in Hollywood?"

"They're saying you killed a little girl but we know it's not true."

"Oh Claire, I have never been so scared in my entire life. The police here are all out to get me. They want to kill me, but I'll kill myself first."

"Don't talk like that, Bob," she shot back. "You have to fight to clear yourself. There's all kinds of silly rumors. Is any of this stuff true?"

"I tell you it's a mistake! I can't understand it. I think I'd better call my old chief, Carl King. He'll tell me the truth of what's going on down there. He's always been on my side and he can be trusted."

"If you want," answered Claire, "I'll call Mr. King and tell him that I just spoke with you, and need his help, and he can tell you what to do."

"Please, Claire, just leave it alone—I must think—have to figure out what to do by myself."

"Bob, you sound so awfully strange . . ."

The phone went dead. Erler flung himself prone on the couch and sobbed in utter frustration. He was trapped in an apartment with two helpless women and an infant. On the end table rested the telephone silently beckoning him like a sinister force to use it as a key to the bizarre, overpowering puzzle that was destroying him. There was no rhyme or reason in initiating the calls to the television station, the Maricopa Sheriff's Office, or the Hollywood police, only to hang up once the call went through. The closest he ever came to making contact with the Hollywood police as he promised Claire Kaufman was to ask for Assistant Chief Carl King. When Chief King's cheery voice responded, Erler choked and said, "Chief, this is Bob Erler."

"Oh yes, Bob," replied King, "glad to hear from you, but first I must advise you of your rights. You have the right to remain silent, you . . ." Erler slammed the receiver. It was final! He *was* a suspect in a murder case, otherwise there would be no purpose for the chief to read the constitutional Miranda warnings to him. He decided to call his former chief again and tell him to forget about the Miranda crap. He knew what his rights were. Didn't he graduate at the top of his class? Didn't he administer the Miranda rights to many arrestees while he was a cop? All he wanted was help and guidance right now!

In his office, Carl King was dwelling pensively on Robert Erler and his dilemma. He surmised all the hang-up calls were from Erler who wanted desperately to talk, and perhaps he made a tactical mistake in reading Erler his constitutional rights, but proper police procedure mandated that it be done. If Erler confessed to the slaying without first having been warned of his right to remain silent, the confession could be successfully nullified in court. He reported to Goetz that Erler angrily hung up on him in the middle of reading his Miranda rights, but he knew Erler. He knew Erler would call him again, and waited patiently, looking back upon their past relationship.

The assistant chief had been impressed by Erler's polite demeanor and his ability to handle assignments with efficiency and dispatch. It was perhaps that avuncular feeling that caused him to forgive Patrolman Erler's oversight in not getting the names or identification of the couple in the blue car that reported a possible homicide. Carl King could live with that, he rationalized the incident, chalking it up to Erler's inexperience. The real irony of the situation made him uneasy with every recollection. It was with considerable chagrin that he recalled how he ordered Patrolman Erler to stand guard over the twisted body of Merilyn Clark and secure the scene. He could still remember Erler standing over the blanketed body of the young girl in a windswept vacant area, keeping the curious onlookers away. Now, Erler was accused of killing that very same child he so fervently guarded that memorable day. The assistant chief was snapped out of his reverie by another phone call from Erler.

"Chief, those Phoenix cops are looking for me. I can't let them take me alive. I'm going to shoot myself right now!"

"That's not right, Bob. Take hold of yourself," King advised in a calm, soothing voice. "You will only hurt your family and loved ones. Just turn yourself in quietly and come back to answer the charges."

"I know what everyone is saying about me. What do you think about it, Chief? Tell me, what does Jim Walsh say about this? How are the other men on the force taking this? What are they saying about me?"

It was apparent to King that Erler was losing touch with reality as he babbled continuously, and the conversation focused entirely on what his former buddies on the police force thought of him. King thought it unusual that Erler was more interested in the portrayal of his image rather than the immediate peril of his predicament. At a convenient pause, King broke in, "Where are you, Bob?"

Erler hung up. The assistant chief sighed in disappointment. He felt he had sufficient rapport with Erler to effectuate the arrest without presenting danger to anyone. He discounted the rumors of Erler being armed with guns and high explosives and was genuinely alarmed that Erler believed the police were out to kill him. He sat pensively behind his desk groping for some solution to Erler's misconception, and shared the latest developments with Cox and Goetz in the office of the detective bureau down the hall.

"Guys," said the assistant chief, "got another call from Erler. He's still hung up on the idea that the cops in Phoenix are out to kill him. He really got pissed off and hung up the phone when I suggested he turn himself in.''

"Did he say where he was?"

"No, just in Phoenix, that's all.''

"Between the FBI and the Maricopa County Sheriff's Office they'll soon pinpoint his location and nab him.''

A worried King observed sadly, "That's not the real problem, fellows.''

They both looked at King's handsome face with curiosity and noted his ordinarily merry blue eyes were clouded with genuine concern, and looked as though he was carrying the world on his shoulders.

"What's bothering you, Carl?" Goetz inquired softly.

"It's the way things are going. We may be responsible for a needless murder or suicide. We have to retrench and handle Erler's capture another way. The news media blew this whole case out of proportion. The reports of Bob Erler being armed with hand grenades and high explosives may trigger off some gun-happy cop to take desperate measures if Erler is ever found.''

"I see what you mean," agreed Cox. "They also reported that Erler swore he wouldn't be taken alive. Some gung-ho cop in a searching party could jump the gun and that's all she wrote.''

"On top of that," added King, "Erler told me he was so afraid of being killed by the police in Arizona he would blow his brains out first. And there's more.''

King leaned back in his chair and looked up at the ceiling, saying, "You fellows know Bob Erler is a fighting machine. If the Phoenix police surround him like a cornered rat, he'll go down fighting, but he'll also take a lot of good cops with him!''

"That means . . ." started Goetz.

"That means," King stated firmly, "we cannot go that route. There must be another way. We must find it soon or there'll be a blood bath, and the blame will be ours.''

On Sunday, September 15, Erler called King. "Chief, do you know what the newspapers and TV stations are saying about me?"

"What are they saying, Bob?" answered King thinking of some ruse whereby he could resume a friendly conversation with Erler.

"Sergeant Hamilton of the Phoenix police is calling me the 'Desert Fox' and I'm suppose to be holed up in a fortress in the desert with an arsenal of gas grenades and automatic rifles."

"Of course it's bullshit, Bob. Do you want to talk to me about this whole affair? I really and truly want to help."

"Well, I would like to talk to you about . . ."

"Wait," interrupted King, "You were a police officer—and a good one at that—so I'm sure you'll understand your rights under the law."

"What?"

"You have the right to an attorney present while you tell me about the case. You don't have to speak to me at all if you don't want to, but whatever you say may be used against you in court and I'll have to testify . . ."

"Again," came the anguished cry from Erler. "You're doing it to me again!" He slammed the receiver down with a shattering noise, ending the conversation.

Carl King shook his head sadly. He was so close to solving the problem that was eating away at his heart, and now he was certain he lost Erler forever.

That same afternoon, a tall, heavyset man in his early fifties, dressed in a flowery sport shirt and tight blue slacks, draped his bulky form in King's doorway and drawled, "May I come in?"

"Certainly, Chief," said King jumping to his feet and pulling out a chair for his boss, Woody Malphurs, who was the duly appointed Chief of Police of Hollywood. Woody remained at the doorway until he fully completed his acknowledgement of the greetings of each person on the floor. He was a genial, warm and friendly native cracker who worked his way to the top spot in the police department and was dearly loved by the entire community. Still smiling, the chief extended a piece of paper with a name and telephone number with semi-legible scribbling and said to King, "Take a look at this!"

"What is it?" inquired the assistant chief.

"This little lady called me to say she spoke to this Erler fella—you're handling that case, aren't you?"

Carl King leaned forward in his chair with excitement. "She spoke to Erler? When? Who is she?"

Malphurs gave King an amused lopsided grin. "I figured you might want to check this out."

"Maybe she's a crank," ventured King, not knowing what to say.

"Nope, she's not," replied the chief, tossing the strip of paper on King's desk. "She and her husband run the Jiffy Clamp Company here in town, name's Kaufman. Better give her a call."

King reached for the desk phone and as he dialed the telephone number written on the note, observed from the corner of his eye the retreating form of his boss, waving and bellowing greetings to everyone out in the hall.

The phone rang four or five times before a feminine voice meekly responded, "Yes?"

"Hello," began King, trying to contain his mounting excitement, "would I be speaking to Mrs. Kaufman?"

"Who is this?"

"This is Carl King of the Hollywood Police Department. Chief Malphurs requested that I call Mrs. Kaufman."

"I'm Claire Kaufman, and I spoke to Mr. Malphurs about some calls that I received from Robert Erler."

"Do you know Robert Erler?"

"Very well indeed," she answered.

"Mrs. Kaufman," King replied with forced restraint, "it's urgent that I speak with you. May I come over?"

"Certainly," was her reply and gave her address in Hollywood. "I'm anxious to see you as it's equally important for me also."

In a matter of minutes, King and Detective Cox appeared at the beautifully appointed pink stucco home with contrasting darkened Bermuda tile that was the Kaufman residence. King reached for the brass knocker on the door and perceived a fluttering of the lace curtains at the vestibule window, reasoning that Mrs. Kaufman was anxiously waiting for his arrival. A pretty lissome brunette not more than twenty-five years old opened the door and cheerily announced, "Hi, I'm Claire Kaufman."

"I'm Carl King," smiled the assistant chief, bringing forth a black leather wallet containing his police badge and identification picture, "and this is my partner, Lieutenant John Cox." Cox acknowledged the introduction with a huge grin, obviously pleased with the prospect of interviewing and hopefully working with such a lovely young lady.

They were invited to the living room.

The two officers made themselves comfortable in the tastefully decorated room and were poised expectantly to learn what Mrs. Kaufman knew about the case.

"Why did you call Chief Malphurs?" asked Cox.

"Robert Erler has been calling me constantly but he wasn't coherent and in the middle of our conversation he would hang up the phone and then call again saying the same thing over and over."

"Can you give us an example?"

"Yes. He first told me that he called to say goodbye because the police were hounding him and he was going to kill himself before they shot him down like a dog. I told him not to do anything foolish like that and I would call the Hollywood Police Department and get those police away from there. That's why I called Chief Malphurs who turned me over to you."

"Anything further?"

"Only that Bob said he didn't know if he had time or not and then he hung up."

"Do you remember any other conversations with Bob Erler during this period?"

"He kept repeating the same things. He kept saying everyone was laughing at him and he felt like a parakeet in a cage. All I did was keep telling him to turn himself in and he was willing to do that except he was afraid if he let the police know where he was hiding out they would kill him."

John Cox was thoughtfully listening to the conversation between King and Mrs. Kaufman and a plan of action began to germinate in his fertile mind. He could use the good graces of Claire Kaufman to get Erler's voice on tape for additional positive evidence. A voice-print comparison could be made with the initial transmission of the 'Catch Me Killer' and if they matched, the circumstances pointing to Erler's guilt would be more credible. Another good use that could be made of Claire Kaufman would be to induce Erler to make some incriminatory statements that would facilitate the prosecution. "That's it!" he said to himself. "Claire Kaufman would be the perfect lure!"

"Mrs. Kaufman," broke in Cox. "I have an idea. We'll furnish you with the telephone number of Erler's mother in Phoenix and you can talk to her. Tell her you have contacted the police in Hollywood and they want to be of assistance in calling off the dogs in Phoenix so Bob can turn himself in peaceably."

"I'll do anything to help."

Cox exchanged knowing glances with Chief King and opened his notebook, flipping the pages until he located the phone number of Mrs. Winifred Erler's home. Claire obediently made the call. An unknown male voice responded and Mrs. Kaufman proceeded, "This is Claire Kaufman of Hollywood, Florida. I'm a very good friend of Bob's. He has been calling me to help him out and I would like to speak with his mother, Mrs. Winifred Erler."

"My mother is too sick to come to the phone. This is Bob's brother, Danny. You can talk to me."

"Your brother used to work for me and my husband at the Jiffy Clamp Company here in Hollywood and we became good friends. Bob has been calling for help. He keeps telling me dreadful things and is deathly afraid the police in Phoenix will shoot him down like a dog."

Danny remained silent and after a few seconds inquired, "What did you want to say to my mother?"

"You can check with Bob to prove he's been calling me for help."

"That's not necessary," responded Danny. "Just how do you think you can help him?"

"First, I tried to advise Bob to turn himself in peaceably and not try to fight with anyone, but he's convinced he'll be killed on sight and is threatening to harm himself."

"He can't think properly," replied Danny. "I can hardly blame him. It's a no-way-out situation."

"I have a solution," Mrs. Kaufman announced. "There are some good friends of mine on the Hollywood force and I took it upon myself to ask them to intervene and keep the Phoenix police away from Bob to give him a chance to surrender."

"That's a great idea!"

"All I want to do is get this message to Bob," Claire continued.

"Thanks," replied Danny. "I'll go see him and tell him what you're trying to do."

Danny Erler, a handsome younger edition of his brother Bob, and almost a head taller, was the man of the house and seriously assumed the responsibility of making critical decisions. He agreed that Bob should turn himself in and fight the charges. The only way to convince him was to go along with Mrs. Kaufman's efforts and let the Hollywood police run interference to call off the armed police that were surrounding their house. "This way," thought Danny, "there would be no violence, no one would be harmed and Bob could forget his threats of suicide." Assuring himself that this was the only solution, he hastily repaired to DeDe's apartment to give his brother the good news.

A tearful DeDe cautiously opened the apartment door and admitted the edgy Danny, who eagerly burst in to talk to his big brother. "Danny," blurted Erler. "What are you doing here?"

"Listen Bob, I just spoke to your friend, Claire Kaufman of Hollywood, who is working with the police down there on a plan . . ."

"No, dammit!" shouted Erler. "You just blew my cover!"

"What did I do wrong to make you so mad at me?"

"You led the cops to this apartment by coming here. I'm positive you were followed. Now they'll be here with their bazookas and tear gas to bomb us out."

"I'm sorry, Bob . . . just wanted to help . . ."

"Just get out of here quick before all hell breaks loose," retorted Erler, as he hurriedly ushered his brother out of the apartment.

Erler realized it would only be a matter of time before the dreaded Phoenix police converged upon him and dragged him out of the apartment. He panicked at the thought of being shot. From the bottom of his duffel bag he produced his .38 caliber police service revolver and thrust it in his belt, giving him some small degree of comfort. He put his head in his hands and desperately struggled for a solution. In a flash it came to him! He remembered his friend from his early Phoenix days named David Koelsch who went into police work and became a deputy sheriff in the Maricopa County Sheriff's Office. "Maybe," he thought, "my old friend Dave would be a connection to the Phoenix police who are hot on my tail?" He rushed to the telephone and called information for the number of the sheriff's office and frantically dialed.

"Let me speak to Deputy David Koelsch."

"Who's calling, please?"

"This is Robert John Erler, the man you all are looking for. I want to speak with Dave."

"He's not here. He's on a juvenile call. Give us your number and we'll contact Deputy Koelsch by radio."

Erler was trapped. He was cunning enough to realize his telephone number would be traced to the apartment and knew he'd be captured. "Nothing doing," retorted Erler. "Just tell Dave I'll call back," and terminated the conversation abruptly.

"Hey fellows!" shouted the deputy at the receiving desk. "That was Robert Erler on the phone, the guy we're looking for!"

"You're kidding?" replied the astounded desk sergeant.

"No, I'm not. He wanted to speak with Koelsch and said he'd call later."

"Where's Koelsch now?"

"He's on a juvenile call."

"Contact Koelsch immediately and have him report to headquarters. I want him in a state of readiness."

"Why do you suppose Erler asked for Koelsch?"

"I don't know but I sure as hell will find out when Dave gets here. Something must be going on."

Erler went from room to room methodically closing all the venetian blinds and drapes, carefully peering from each window to survey the street and area around the apartment complex. He strode around the darkened rooms nervously fingering his gun, cocked and ready in his belt. The two confused and frightened women with the baby secluded themselves in the kitchen while Erler stood ominously quiet in the center of the living room pondering his next course of action.

16

Deputy Edward David Koelsch, known as "Dave" to his friends and acquaintances, was a tall wiry young man with a dark complexion and short black hair. His small piercing black eyes had the intensity of a religious zealot, and were it not for the starched tan sheriff's uniform, one would unequivocally mistake him for the minister of a local Baptist church. The juveniles in the detention center hated him and hoped another supervisor would take his place, but there was no one on the entire staff low enough in stature or seniority to merit the post of "Supervisor of Delinquent Juvenile Detainees." Koelsch was doomed to the lowest echelon of police work. He longed to move up to the investigative branch of the sheriff's office, but his monthly efficiency reports filed by his senior officers precluded that possibility. Koelsch continued to nurture his ambition and all his waking hours were clouded with fantasies. He believed some day, somehow, his luck would change for the better. He was on the force for two years now and would give it one more year, and if the brass didn't take him out of juvenile, then they could "shove it" and he'd take that job his brother-in-law offered at the supermarket.

Deputy Koelsch drove his police vehicle into the parking lot behind the one story courthouse and hurried into headquarters in response to the radio summons directing him to report immediately. His duty sergeant sat patiently waiting for his arrival and ordered, "Dave, come to my office right away."

A puzzled Koelsch took off his hat and sprawled his wiry frame over the sergeant's desk, mopping his dark brow, glad to be out from the searing Arizona sun.

"Dave, what do you know about this fellow Erler we're looking for?"

"Well Sarge, I knew him when we were kids years ago, before he and his family moved to Florida. We were good friends then, but I haven't heard from him since, especially now that he's a killer on the loose."

"Well, he's not on the loose any longer," replied the sergeant. "He put in a call for you a little while back and said something about trying to reach you again."

"Gee, I wonder why? What the hell can I do for him?"

"Plenty," remarked the sergeant. "You may be the lead to making him surrender."

"I'll do anything Sarge . . . just tell me what you want from me."

"All your duties and assignments are hereby suspended. You will remain at the receiving desk just in case Erler calls for you again, and don't leave that duty station without my permission because I want to know the minute he contacts you."

"Yes sir, Sarge," answered the excited Koelsch, feeling that he was about to play an important role in one of Arizona's biggest and most publicized manhunts. "What is the plan when we make contact?"

"The plan?" exploded the sergeant. "The plan? God dammit man, this is the biggest collar we will ever make! The 'plan,' as you call it, is to get Erler's ass behind bars immediately, if not sooner. This guy has to be arrested, and it looks like you're the one to do it."

The receiving desk in the Maricopa Sheriff's Office was an eight foot length of imitation parquet with a thick black plywood top that served as the complaint desk. It was purposely made four feet high so the complaint officer sitting on a bar stool could look down upon the visitors. When Dave Koelsch took charge of the incoming calls, as directed by his superior, the two officers regularly assigned to the "desk" moved away with an awed reverence. They felt Koelsch was selected for a highly sensitive undertaking. So did Dave Koelsch.

There were a few incoming calls that Koelsch fielded with a slight sense of importance, although his heart jumped each time the telephone rang. He comforted himself with the knowledge that in a celebrated case that held the attention of the entire country, the 'Catch Me Killer,' the most wanted man by the FBI, singled out ole Dave for help. Well, ole Dave will help all right, but ole Dave will not be handling juvenile assignments anymore. No sir, after ole Dave snatches the brass ring, the sheriff will have to promote him to homicides and big time stuff befitting an officer of his caliber. He had a good feeling that he would be the star performer in this case and he glowed inwardly, ready to take center stage.

The phone rang.

"Deputy Koelsch speaking," he announced in a very professional tone.

"Dave! This is Butch Erler . . . I gotta talk to you . . . I need your help!"

"Sure, Butch," replied Koelsch trying hard to conceal his excitement. "Tell me where you're holing up and I'll come see you."

"It's not that simple, Dave. All those things the papers and television are saying about me are not true. The police have my mother's house surrounded. They've got machine guns and are looking to kill me—I'll kill myself first— they've got to let me alone—"

"Hold on Butch," cautioned the deputy. "You're talking like a crazy man. Are you on something that's making you talk goofy?"

"Only a few pills to calm me down."

"Lay off that stuff and tell me, Butch, where are you now?"

"Dave, I trust you for old time's sake. I don't want to be shot like a dog in the street . . . it's not fair. I'm a cop, a good cop, and don't deserve this kind of treatment from my fellow cops."

"Okay Butch, you'll be safe with me. Just tell me where you're staying and I'll protect you and guarantee your safety."

"All right, Dave, I'm putting my trust in you. Please come to DeDe's apartment, you remember my sister, she's living in the Sheridan Arms. Please come quickly, I'll wait for you."

Barricaded in his self-imposed stockade, Erler sought solace from the mounting pressure in the bottles of tranquilizers Judy freely supplied. During lucid intervals, he would feel relieved that the solution to his dilemma was soon to be resolved. He would be able to surrender to the authorities with dignity and return to Florida to defend the charges against him. His friends, the Dooleys, Jim Walsh, and the Kaufmans, would assist him in his fight for exoneration. When the dark moods would appear he must chase them away. His friend Dave was clearing things up, so he must be patient and wait. That's it. Just be calm and wait for Dave Koelsch.

A tense Erler sat in his sister's living room awaiting the arrival of Dave Koelsch. It should only be a matter of minutes when his buddy would appear. He turned on the television to while away the time, and as he vacantly stared at the screen, his short period of relief dissolved into shocked disbelief. He sat upright with agonizing slowness. There, right before him on the screen, was depicted the very same apartment building he was living in, with a cordon of uniformed police officers milling around the complex, a few armed with riot guns had stationed themselves at vantage points on all sides of the building. Erler herded the two women and the baby in a bedroom and ordered them to keep the door closed and lie on the floor, fearful that at any moment a fusillade of gunfire would shatter the windows and rake the apartment with bullets and tear gas bombs. The women were terrorized when they became aware of what was happening. Amid their cries, an electric megaphone blared out an ultimatum:

"Erler, come out with your hands above your head and surrender. You have one minute before we start shooting the windows out with tear gas."

"I'm not coming out!"

"Who else is in the apartment with you?" asked the police officer manning the speaker, in an abundance of caution before opening fire, and possibly hurting innocent bystanders.

"Two women and a little child," was Erler's reply.

"You don't want them to get hurt, so just walk out with your hands on your head and surrender to us," thundered the officer on the bullhorn.

"Where's Dave Koelsch? I want to see Dave!" he shouted to no one in particular. Erler felt betrayed. He depended on his old friend, and reasoned that Dave gave the police the location of his hideout, and now death was staring him in the face. He reached into his pocket for some of Judy's pills but they were all gone. He took his service revolver from his belt, flicking the trigger device, toying with the gun, trying to decide what to do. In his dull state of indecision, he heard a knock on the front door and growled, "Get away—no one's gonna take me alive!"

"It's Danny," came the muffled voice from outside. "Please let me in Bob?"

Erler let Danny into the apartment, and asked angrily, "How did you get through that mob of blood-thirsty cops?" Danny looked at his brother and wanted to cry at what he saw.

"I asked you how you got through!" repeated the fugitive.

Danny noticed his brother's speech was slurred and his eyes were darting wildly about. His service revolver was dangling loosely from nerveless fingers.

"Answer me!" ordered Erler thickly.

"The police let me through. They want me to calm you down and take you in."

"Nothing doing," snarled Erler, brandishing his gun. "This is the only way out. I'm going to kill myself!"

"That wouldn't help any of us, Butch," reasoned Danny, praying and hoping Bob would calm down until Deputy Dave Koelsch arrived. The phone rang. Danny answered and handed it to Erler saying simply, "Here's Dave. He wants to speak to you."

"Hi Butch, this is Dave."

"Dave, you're just in time to see me kill myself."

"Butch, just let me come in and talk to you."

"It's no use," cried Erler. "I don't want to hurt anyone. You can come in, but I'm going to die one way or the other."

"Don't do anything crazy. Everything is all taken care of. Put Danny back on the phone."

Erler moved slowly as if he were sleepwalking and handed the phone to Danny who apparently was receiving instructions from the deputy at the other end.

"Yes Dave, okay Dave. I'll try Dave—please hurry," he murmured.

Erler was now swaying drunkenly behind his brother and

grasping his shoulder. Roughly turning him around, he demanded, "What did he say?"

"He wanted me to get your gun so you wouldn't shoot him when he came in. Dave is afraid you might do something foolish . . . maybe hurt someone or even yourself."

Erler gazed woodenly at his little brother who was on the verge of tears and waved his gun in the direction of the Lazy Boy chair in the corner, indicating that Danny sit down. They both waited in silence. The women peeked out from their bedroom to see what was going on. Finally, a knock on the front door was heard and Koelsch called out, "Let me in Butch. It's Dave!"

Danny ran to unbolt the door and Dave Koelsch was let into the apartment. He nervously approached his old friend Butch, who was brandishing a large service revolver.

"Please give me your gun, Butch," was the calm demand, but Erler only clutched the revolver more firmly and spat. "I'm not surrendering. They're all out to get me— I'll kill myself first."

Danny burst into tears. "Bob, if you do anything like that the whole family will be stranded." Wiping the tears from his eyes with the back of his hand, he added, "How can we get along without you? We need you!"

Koelsch noticed how the young man's pleas about the family made Erler pause and think, which gave him an idea. Cautiously keeping his distance from the erratic Erler, the deputy said, "Butch, your mother has been asking for you and is so worried about the way you're behaving it's making her sicker than ever."

"Keep my mother out of this!"

"I can't Butch. Winifred wants you to come with us and when you are safe in our protective custody she can visit with you, the rest of the family can visit." He broke off, eyeing his prize catch for a sympathetic reaction, or how his new pitch was working. Then in a smooth comforting tone, "Your friends will be visiting you and work out plans for a safe return to Florida to stand trial."

"What good will that do? I'll never get a fair trial in Florida, with all this phony publicity about me. What chance does a cop have when the public is already convinced he has gone bad?"

Koelsch, still keeping a respectable distance from Erler, reached for the telephone and dialed a number, huddling over the receiver, and spoke quietly out of Bob's hearing. Erler sensed something unusual was in the making. He didn't appreciate his friend Dave talking privately to some unknown person in his presence, as though he didn't exist, and not knowing what was said, or to whom. It had to be about him and Koelsch didn't let him in on what was taking place. He started to have second thoughts about Koelsch and wondered if he should really trust him. While trying to decide if his new intuition may be right, he pulled his revolver from his waist, holding it low with both hands, trying to make a decision.

Koelsch maintained his vigil, eyes darting toward the door, while he nervously drummed his fingers on his bony knees. He jumped when he heard a knock on the door and rushed to open it. Framed in the doorway was Robert Erler's mother, Winifred, a middle-aged ash blonde, withered and distraught. In happier days she must have been a beautiful woman; it was apparent that the ravages of her dreaded illness had taken their toll on this lovely person. With faltering steps she made her way across the room and stretched out her arms to her oldest son. The moment Erler saw his mother, he began to sob and embraced her with one arm, tightly gripping the revolver with his other hand. He recoiled and regained his composure rapidly, upon realizing how thin and bony his mother felt under the light summer dress, and flushed with shame because of the stress and pain he caused her. Look at what his sister and brother went through, just because of him. He resolved then and there not to allow his family to be tortured any longer. This ordeal had to end right now.

"Oh Bobby," cried his mother. "Please turn yourself over to Dave and no one will be hurt. We have all suffered so much in too many ways. I'm so sick with worry and can't take much more."

"Mom, I love you! I can never forgive myself for causing you even one moment of pain. Please leave with Danny. Dave and I will work out the terms of a surrender."

"Whatever you do, Bobby, we all know you're innocent. The whole family is behind you."

"As long as you believe in me, Mom, that's all I care about," and placing his left arm around his mother's brittle shoulders and awkwardly maneuvering his right hand, still tightly holding the service revolver, around Danny's waist, he walked them to the door amid tearful heart-rending farewells.

Koelsch was pleased at the scenario he just witnessed. The prize was within his grasp and he was about to distinguish himself in the annals of Arizona police history.

"Let's go, Butch. Give me your gun and I'll notify the back-up squads that we're coming out peaceful and quiet like."

"Not so fast, Dave," Erler said to the startled deputy. "I want to lay down some ground rules."

Dave didn't like this turn of events. He, Edward David Koelsch, was the conqueror. He was the one to make the rules, not the vanquished. His mind raced quickly. He had come too far on this caper and was within a hair's breadth of success. He didn't want to blow the deal by being hard-nosed, and deciding to be prudent inquired, "What kind of ground rules?"

"Number one, you alone drive me to the police station to be booked."

"What else?" asked Koelsch apprehensively.

"Number two, I'm not giving up my gun until I arrive safely at the police station."

Koelsch was getting nervous again. "Anything else, Butch?"

"That's all."

"I'll have to get approval from the captain. Let me get to the telephone." Koelsch picked up the phone to call his supervisor keeping a wary eye on his quarry as he couldn't figure out what idiotic thing that drug-crazed Erler would do next. The telephone conversation with the captain consumed very little time and Koelsch happily announced, "Butch, it's okay, you got yourself a deal! There's only one thing: you must promise not to use your gun on me or anyone else."

"I promise, Dave. I don't want to hurt anyone but they better leave me alone and not try to kill me," threatened Erler.

Koelsch opened the front door of the apartment and stood aside so Erler could precede him. His crowning moment of glory was at hand. He eagerly anticipated the envious police officers parting the crowds to allow the heroic Deputy Edward David Koelsch to escort the 'Catch Me Killer' to jail single-handed.

"Just a minute, Dave," broke in Erler. "I want to say goodbye to DeDe and Judy. They were locked up in the bedroom with the kid when your guys threatened to bomb the apartment."

"They're not here, Butch. They left some time ago." He wanted to add, "They took off when Danny was here but you were bombed out of your skull you pill-popping freak," but bit his tongue. He didn't want to rock the boat, and what a sweet little boat it was for him.

A highly agitated Erler entered the squad car of Deputy Koelsch who very cautiously took his position at the driver's side and commenced to make the long journey to the Maricopa County Sheriff's station. As soon as the car containing Erler was under way, a fleet of police cars converged upon the departing vehicle. This maneuver excited Deputy Koelsch who was shouting to his fellow police officers, "Stay away, keep out of this. I'll take care of this delivery."

Although the police vehicles yielded in reluctance to Koelsch's directions, the reporters and television cameramen followed constantly, flashing lights, taking pictures of the crowds of onlookers filling the streets to witness the historic surrender to police authorities.

The 'Catch Me Killer' was finally in police custody and the long fight for vindication was about to start.

17

ANGELINE WEIR, A pleasant, saucily attractive young lady in her early thirties, started her career as a legal secretary to a politically influential lawyer in Hollywood who encouraged her to study law. He not only encouraged her, but restructured her working periods so she was able to study. One of the few women lawyers in the area, Mrs. Weir became an extremely vocal activist in feminist politics, long before the movement became fashionable. When Bob Adams, the county solicitor, resigned his public office in a fit of anger, rebelling against the arrogant demands of an overly aggressive police investigator, Angie was appointed by the governor to fill the remainder of his term. Her appointment as the chief prosecutor was met with approval by all the police agencies in the county. She was a novice, never tried a criminal case, and her political motivation and inexperience in the field of criminal law made her a cooperative ally to prosecution officials to whom she would have to turn for guidance and indoctrination.

Fortunately, she inherited an entire staff, seasoned and schooled by her predecessor, who subscribed to his rigid policy of fairness and was headed by Chief Investigator Robert McElroy, a spectacled, blondish grey-haired man of middle age with a slightly bent frame. Another asset Angie acquired was Len Boone, the department's chief trial counsel. Boone, a former Florida Highway Patrol trooper from the center of Florida's redneck district, became an attorney and brought his law certificate and southern drawl to the Gold Coast. As a law and order man from the Bible Belt, the tall, good looking cracker, whose curly brown hair was always trying to escape from under the three gallon trooper-style Stetson which became his trademark, was greeted in the county solicitor's office with open arms as a natural prosecutor. Len was a ''good ole boy,'' charming and soft-spoken but deadly as a cobra.

Detective Melrose had a good rapport with prosecutor

Len Boone. They worked many cases together, becoming good social friends, although Boone would socialize with almost anyone who would bend an elbow with him, even defense attorneys, after a dry spell of abstinence. Melrose had a motive in singling out ole Len. He wanted to bypass the standard operating procedure of the chief prosecutor in formalizing a murder charge against Erler. He knew Len preferred to follow protocol, requiring the arresting officers to present a detailed report of a crime, together with names, addresses and statements of witnesses, and a written recommendation of the charges that should be filed. Melrose did not like the procedure at all, especially not in this case. He was aware of the duties of the assistant county solicitor designated as the "filing officer" who, after reviewing the police report, would prepare an Information for the county solicitor's signature. There have been occasions when the "filing officer" would review the police reports and evidentiary material presented and decline to file charges because of the paucity of evidence and the resulting improbability of procuring a conviction. Robert Erler's case merited different treatment. The wily Melrose, spearheading the prosecution, would certainly not chance submitting the huge accumulation of police reports and supporting evidence to a mere assistant who may decline prosecution because of the frailty of the case built solely upon circumstantial evidence and conjecture. There had to be a selling job done on the chief prosecutor and his newly appointed boss, Angie Weir. Melrose had little cause for concern. Len Boone would prosecute his own brother, and as for Angie Weir, she was impatiently waiting in the wings ready to make her grand entrance into the blinding spotlight of national publicity.

Melrose had a plan. With Boone's help, the county solicitor would call a top-level conference where Angie Weir could hear from the Hollywood investigative team, and Sergeant Portelli of Dania on the matter of voice identification; Chief Parton regarding the spent .22 caliber shells in Erler's old trailer as well as the highly circumspect inference of Erler's "finding" the body of Merilyn Clark. The suspect's total disregard of police investigative procedures in getting the names of the informants who told him where to find the girl's body, or even the license number of their car, was the icing on the cake.

Boone laughed to himself. It didn't take him long to figure out his boss's mental process. He expected her to react with feminine coyness to Melrose's proposal, pretending to studiously consider, and ultimately accede. Len Boone knew women and was content to sit on the sidelines and let the scenario unfold. The plan to overwhelm the inexperienced and naive county solicitor by sheer numbers at the conference was unnecessary as Weir was eager and willing, subtly concealing her delight at the prospect of her first prosecution of a major homicide case.

At the prearranged office conference, Weir presided like a reigning queen over the veteran police officers assembled to discuss the feasibility of filing charges against Robert Erler for murder. She invited Chief Investigator Bob McElroy and Chief Trial Attorney Len Boone to sit in conference with her during the decision-making process. Only Boone smiled; he knew what Angie was going to say and do. The others were grim and hopeful. Angie knew her first big case had to be a resounding, successful prosecution, and asked to no one in particular, "Do we have any real hard evidence to go on?"

"Not really," admitted Carl King. "In fact, there is no hard evidence whatsoever, and unless we can come up with some direct or solid proof, we may as well scrub the whole deal."

"And another thing," chimed in Lieutenant Goetz, "it may not be Erler at all. Maybe we're jumping too fast on this. Let's slow down."

"I think we have enough," growled Melrose. "There are enough witnesses that recognize Erler's voice on the tapes. We have Dorothy Clark's identification and some good evidentiary material to back up Mrs. Clark's story . . ."

The new prosecution chief, attempting a weak bluff, broke in with a half-hearted laugh, "It looks like you fellows are not quite ready. If you need more, let's get more. I'm going to run with the ball, so back me up."

Lieutenant Cox rubbed the top of his closely cropped grey hair and sighed, "Maybe I can come up with some-

thing to get Erler to admit his part in this." All heads turned
expectantly toward the speaker.

"I've got an idea," grinned Cox. "Just give me a few
days to put things in order and we'll soon be in business."

"I'll work on the Information and hold matters in abey-
ance until John comes up with his clincher," said Weir,
tapping her pencil on a yellow legal pad, and contemplated
the tremendous publicity she would receive from the Erler
prosecution. The entire nation would know her name and
she would be acclaimed for her meteoric rise from lowly
legal secretary to the intrepid chief prosecuting officer who
convicted the 'Catch Me Killer.'

Melrose knew better than to ask the departing Hollywood
officers what John Cox's secret weapon was. The rivalry
between the two police departments was still smoldering,
but they had one common interest: "Get Erler!"

Seated in the passenger side of the squad car, King
looked at Cox as he positioned himself behind the wheel
and asked, "The key is the Kaufman woman, isn't it,
John?"

"Yes," replied Cox, "she'll be at headquarters tomorrow and wants me to arrange it so she can speak with Erler
in the county jail in Phoenix. She can't get through, and
thought, you know—" shrugging his shoulders. "Police to
police, they'd put the call through if a police agency
called."

"Erler's got himself a lawyer, so be careful you don't
speak to him and ask any questions."

"I know, I know . . . only Claire Kaufman will speak
with him . . ." and grinning at his partner, continued with,
"It's no crime if I listen in."

Tuesday, September 17. Mrs. Claire Kaufman sat primly at
Detective Cox's desk and earnestly repeated her desire to
"be of assistance."

The detective wondered who she wanted to help, Erler
or the police and decided to put her to a test.

"Just how do you suppose you can help?"

"Well," his attractive volunteer suggested demurely, "if
I could only speak with him, he will listen to me and agree
to come to Florida to answer these horrible charges. I sim-

ply cannot believe what the papers are saying about him. It just isn't fair.''

"Let me try the sheriff's office in Phoenix, and they may extend their courtesy to another police agency.''

"I tried to call the jail so many times, but they refused to let me talk to Bob.'' Looking hopefully at the detective, she went on, "It would really be important if you could help me with that.''

"All I can do is try," ventured Cox. "But there is one thing I would like to do.''

"What is that?'' inquired the eager young lady.

"You wouldn't object if I recorded the conversation, would you?'' Cox asked casually.

"I don't suppose so,'' replied the puzzled Claire. "The main thing is to speak with Bob.''

John Cox fought hard to conceal his excitement and maintain a casual façade while reaching into the large drawer in his desk, pulling out a recorder and induction coils.

"What's that?'' asked Claire.

"This is a recording machine. When I put this suction cup on the telephone receiver and hook it up to the recorder, we will be all set.''

Cox deftly assembled the recording device and after affixing the induction coil to the telephone handset explained, "We're now ready to call Bob at the Phoenix jail.''

"What do I do about all this?'' asked the confused Claire.

"We will now put in the call for Bob Erler at the jail in Phoenix, and you can speak with him. Of course, you don't have to tell him the conversation is being recorded,'' he added, maintaining the same casual attitude.

"What do you want me to say to him in particular?'' asked Claire, sensing the conversation she was about to have was highly critical.

"Oh, just speak naturally as you have in the past,'' counselled Cox. "And play it by ear.'' He sat behind his desk and carefully dialed the sheriff's office in Phoenix. After two rings a voice responded, "Sheriff's office.''

"This is Detective John Cox of the Hollywood, Florida

Police Department. I'd like to speak with your Captain Edmondson, please.''

"The captain may be hard to locate," was the reply. "Is there something I can do for you?''

"Certainly,'' answered Cox. "I want the captain's permission to have Robert Erler, who is in custody, speak with Mrs. Claire Kaufman, a cooperating witness, who is here with me at the station. I was wondering if it would be possible to get him on the line?''

"Who, Erler?''

"Yeah,'' replied Cox a trifle apprehensively.

"Well, if he'll talk. He's got a lawyer, you know.''

"Yeah, well, she just wants to talk to him.''

"What's her name?''

"Mrs. Kaufman, tell him.''

"Kaufman?''

"Yeah, he used to work for this lady and her husband and they're very close friends. In fact, she was on the phone with him the other night when he surrendered. She was instrumental in it, and extremely helpful,'' ventured Cox, trying to give the deputy on the other end of the line a hint that Claire Kaufman was a valuable ally, and worried that if he made it any plainer, Mrs. Kaufman might balk at initiating the vital conversation for fear it might result in harm to Erler. The detective had no cause for alarm. Claire Kaufman was not the naive dupe Cox intended to manipulate, as she had sized up the situation quickly and effectively before she decided to become a team player. She was beautiful, but also smart.

"Tell you what,'' answered the deputy, "I'll reach out for the captain for his okay and then have the prisoner call you at the police station. Give me your telephone number and extension. At least I'll know you're who you say you are.''

"That would be fine,'' agreed Cox. "He can call and ask for Mrs. Kaufman at our number. Do you have our number? It's area code 305, 922 . . .'' and after he gave the last four digits, said, "The captain will recognize our number, I'm sure.''

"All right. If he doesn't call in the next thirty minutes, you'll know he won't call.''

"Well, I sure appreciate it," acknowledged the detective. "Thanks very much."

John Cox cradled the phone and shut off the recorder. Directing his attention to the impatient Claire, he told her, "We have to wait at least thirty minutes until Captain Edmondson gives his approval for Erler to speak with you. Can I get you some coffee or something to pass the time."

"No, thank you," was her reply. "I'll just wait."

In the dismal, small solitary cubicle that isolated Robert Erler from the jail population, he peered through sleep encrusted eyes to see the bulky frame of a uniformed jail guard looming menacingly over his cot. "Get up, Copper!"

Erler was rudely shaken awake and told, "The captain wants to see you."

The prisoner was yanked to his feet as another guard entered the cell with leg irons and handcuffs. Erler was puzzled and backed into a corner. He didn't like the idea of being manacled like an animal again and fear replaced his bewilderment, debating whether to be submissive or put up a fight. His head started to throb and a wave of nausea came over him as he touched the left side of his head, following the path of the migraine headache which made him stumble to his knees. It only took a single jailer to handcuff the debilitated prisoner and affix leg irons to his ankles. The senior jailer shoved Erler through the small steel door of the cell and laboriously propelled him toward the open recreational area where a guard standing by the telephone waved for his attention.

"Over here, Erler," the guard beckoned. "I have orders to make a phone call for you."

"I don't want to talk to anyone," replied Erler. ". . . er, hold it . . . who is it?"

"I'm to call a Mrs. Kaufman in Hollywood," answered the guard. "Do you want to talk to her or not?"

Erler's eyes lit up hopefully, "Yes, I do."

With deliberate reticence the guard directed his prisoner to wait by the wooden partition booth while fumbling in his upper left pocket for the telephone number of the Hollywood police station where Erler's friend and confidante Claire Kaufman eagerly awaited his call. An optimistic Detective John Cox also awaited, with the recording device and necessary apparatus to tape the telephone conversation. Whether such interception tactics were admissible was not the detective's immediate concern. Everything was riding on this call. Erler's voice would be used as a standard for comparison with the voice on the *Catch Me Killer* tapes. Another possibility that excited Cox was that he knew Mrs. Kaufman would ask Erler pertinent questions about Erler's involvement in the girl's murder and maybe, just maybe, Erler would incriminate himself. What a deal! What a master stroke! It was all there, a perfect Machiavellian plot, so let the game begin.

The call was made. "Bob, this is Claire. What are they doing to you? What's happening to you?"

"Thank God you called, Claire. There's nothing you can do for me. Don't waste your time or your money, Claire. I'm not worth it."

"Sure you're worth it. We want to help. Tell me about your trouble."

"What's Jimmy doing? A fine friend he turned out to be."

"What do you mean? What does Jimmy have to do with this thing? Is he in on this trouble you're in?"

"Nothing. Just forget about it, Claire, please."

"Let's get this over with. They're going to bring you back anyway . . ."

"I told my brother Danny to tell his lawyer friend not to fight extradition and send me back to Florida."

"Well, tell that lawyer to go to hell. You don't need him. You're quite capable of signing a paper. Just tell him you want to waive extradition and you're coming home. The Dooleys and Al and I will stick by you all we can, you know that."

"Thank you, Claire, I know that," was the response. "Everyone is laughing at me and making fun of me."

"Well, as far as them making fun of you, I think that's a shame."

"What's Jim think?"

"What does Jim think? Jim doesn't say much of anything. Why do you keep asking about Jim? Are you both in this trouble together? Tell me what he's got to do with this business?"

"Nothing at all," answered Erler hastily. "I'm just wondering if he's on my side."

"Get serious. Why don't you think Jim's your friend anymore?"

"I don't know," replied Erler, changing the subject. "My hand's all numb. I can't feel any feeling in it."

"I know. You put your hand through the window. Don't do anything dumb like that again, please. My nerves are already shot."

"I feel just like an animal now. They talked to me . . ."

"Why do you feel like an animal?"

"I don't feel like I'm a police officer anymore, you know?"

"Bob, did you do it?" persisted his interrogator.

"I don't know, Claire, really,"

"You don't know if you did it or not?"

"No," answered Erler flatly.

Detective Cox, who was monitoring the recorded conversation, was ecstatic. He wanted to jump for joy! He restrained the urge to run into Carl King's office and tell him Robert Erler practically confessed to the murder, but there was more to come. Maybe Erler was becoming unglued and would incriminate himself deeper. Cox congratulated himself on his strategy. It worked! All it needed was a woman's touch, a sympathetic ear, and bingo! There we have the 'Catch Me Killer!'

Claire Kaufman continued the dialogue with Bob Erler, as Cox watched her eyes narrow and lips compress with distaste. At that point, the lieutenant knew he had acquired a valuable ally who needed no encouragement as she turned a friendly conversation into a prosecutorial interrogation.

"Did you do it?"

"I don't know, Claire, really."

"You don't know if you did it or not?"

"No."

"Do you remember these people at all?"

"I don't know, aahhh."

"Don't be afraid of me, Bob. Do you remember anything about this little girl?"

"I don't want to talk about that on the phone, Claire."

"Do you want me to come out and talk to you? Do you want to talk to me?"

"Yes, Claire."

"All right, then. I'll come and talk to you, okay. Now what else do you need, honey? Do you need a priest?"

"I don't know, Claire."

"Do you want to talk to a priest? I'll bring one with me."

"No, thank you," replied Erler. "But I'd like to talk to Ellie Dooley."

"You mean you want to talk privately with me and Ellie?" quickly retorted Claire Kaufman, being very careful not to lose her position as sole confidante of the befuddled prisoner. She didn't want the Dooley woman sharing center stage with her in the most spectacular performance about to unfold.

Adroitly shifting to another subject, she asked, "You keep talking about Jim Walsh. Is he in on this with you?"

Cox couldn't help but marvel at Mrs. Kaufman's native instinct that impelled her to tie Jim Walsh, a City of Hollywood police officer, into the homicide. This idea was exactly what the lieutenant had in mind. Another cop gone bad; two cops, two victims. Claire Kaufman was doing just fine with the inquisition of her friend. Cox felt a bit sorry for Erler's predicament at the hands of this strange woman, which gave rise to an old expression heard many times, "With a friend like her, who needs enemies." The interrogation persisted until Erler became silent, not answering any of the woman's questions. Mrs. Kaufman, recognizing a stalemate, also remained silent.

"Claire, I'm sorry."

"Sorry for what?"

"Everything."

"What's everything mean?"

"They all sit out there and gawk at me like I'm an animal you know. I just . . . I don't know what's going on right now, Claire."

"You don't?"

Lieutenant Cox, the "silent observer" whose sole part in the devastating telephone conversation between Claire Kaufman and Robert Erler was merely to "listen in," was now beside himself with apoplectic frustration. His normally passive face was flushed as he brandished a yellow legal pad in the face of his female cat's paw, wordlessly mouthing directions to ask the questions he scrawled on the pad, but she shook her head with an imperious air and continued the questioning at her own pace and in her own way.

"Bob," she asked, "is there anything else you can remember that I can tell your new lawyer that may be of some help?"

"I don't know. I'd rather . . . I'd rather run and have them shoot me, or something," replied Erler, unable to follow the trend of her inquiries and moving to another subject.

"Don't do anything foolish," she cautioned. "What I'd like to do is come out there with Ellie after making arrangements here. Mr. King has been very nice to me."

"He's a pretty nice guy."

"He is . . . and I will make arrangements with him and see if we can bring . . . a deputy with us and we can all come back together. Would you like to do that?"

"I told them yesterday I'd come back," answered Erler in a plaintive voice. "I don't care. I wasn't trying to run away. I just came out here to see my family. Would you believe I was just sitting watching television, and all of a sudden they said I was wanted for murder. It scared the shit out of me. I started cracking up."

"That's just terrible," soothed Mrs. Kaufman, looking at Cox to see if he also noted Erler's change of attitude, only to receive a blank look as if to indicate a neutral nonparticipating role in the charade of obvious entrapment. "Please stay where you are until we get there, will you?"

"I don't know. I can't go far, that's for sure."

"Yeah, but don't try to make any breaks for it or something, because they'll shoot you down, so don't be ridiculous."

"I'm not being ri . . . I don't want to hurt you. I don't . . ." he answered brokenly.

"Will you wait for us to get there?"

"Okay, I'll keep praying."

When Claire Kaufman put down the phone, Detective Cox came over and exchanged knowing glances. He re-

moved the taped cassette from the recorder, marked it with
his initials, date of transmission and carefully, almost lovingly, placed it in a plastic envelope marked "EVI-
DENCE" in large red block letters.

"Was everything all right?" queried Claire.

"Just perfect," smiled the detective. "I have to tell you
that you may be required to appear in court as a witness,
and I assume you will be available when necessary."

"Oh yes," readily agreed Mrs. Kaufman. "My husband
already anticipated this and said we should leave town so
I won't be bothered by the press or lawyers, or anyone."

"That's fine with us," Cox assured her, "as long as we
know where you are and you're available for the trial."

"No problem," replied Claire. "My husband or I will
keep in touch with you as soon as we get situated at our
new address."

The elated Cox walked rapidly to the office of Assistant
Chief Carl King and burst into his office, "Excuse me,
Carl, for crashing in on you like this," and holding the
plastic evidence bag containing the tape cassette triumphantly over his head exclaimed, "but this should do it!"

"Do what?" asked the puzzled King.

Cox sat down in a chair at King's desk and explained in
full detail the results of his visit with Mrs. Kaufman and
delightedly recounted how Erler's conversation with her
was captured on tape and said, "Let me play it for you,
Carl, and you'll see where we've got Erler cold. As far as
I'm concerned, this is as good as a confession."

The assistant chief received this startling news with characteristic equanimity. He moved slowly but effectively and
subdued the excited lieutenant with a rewarding smile.

"Sounds good," remarked King. "What are you waiting
for? Let's go ahead and roll it."

Cox rushed back to the detective bureau, procured the
recorder and returned to King's office, setting up the equipment for a replay of the intercepted conversation between
Erler and Mrs. Kaufman. Both men remained silent as the
pointed queries of Claire Kaufman and the agonized responses of Erler unfolded. After the transmission was replayed a second time, King heaved a sigh and said, "Let's

get hold of Irv Goetz and Johnnie Melrose for a little input. This thing is shaping up where our evidentiary position seems a bit stronger—not really enough,'' he cautioned, primarily to dampen Cox's exuberance.

The lieutenant chuckled and said,''Did you get that part when Claire asked him 'Did you do it?' and Erler said 'I don't know'?''

''Forget about that for now,'' advised King. ''Set up a conference in the county solicitor's office and we'll play the tape and go from there.''

Cox nodded, stone-faced beneath his closely cropped iron grey hair. He knew this would be reviewed by Angie Weir, who Melrose said was on the edge and just needed a little push. ''Well,'' mused Cox to himself, ''when she hears Erler on the tape, a team of wild horses couldn't hold her back.''

18

AT 8:00 P.M., daylight savings time, the hot August sun started to descend, casting long shadows over a one-story office building on Hollywood Boulevard whose reception room lights illuminated the black and gold lettering on the door, announcing ''Law Offices of Joseph A. Varon.''

As a product of Chicago's 55th Street, on the wrong end of fashionable Hyde Park's south side, there were a few rough edges left and a relentless nature that my adolescent years failed to eradicate. The only American-born son of a large, uneducated immigrant Portuguese family, the basic instinct for survival impelled fighting and clawing my way from the age of thirteen, working by day and attending school at night to achieve a consuming ambition. From my earliest recollection as a child I was obsessed with the desire to become a lawyer, but never understood the motivation for such intense ambition. There were no role models in my family, nor any near relatives that were attorneys or affiliated with a kindred profession to justify such aspiration, but working all day and going to school at night, my most fervent desire became a reality. Learning shorthand and typing helped me land a good paying job as secretary to the president of a local cereal mill which I sacrificed to gain a much more coveted job—a law clerk to a mediocre ambulance chaser who paid seven dollars for a six day week, 8:00 A.M. to 6:00 P.M., half days on Saturday. Working as a law clerk and legal secretary made me feel I was in heaven. Going from courtroom to courtroom, I watched Chicago's outstanding lawyers select juries and try cases. Having a chance to study their varying techniques proved invaluable years later. Before long, the courtroom personnel and several judges began to notice the friendly, nice-mannered kid with the ready smile and black curly hair. There was no happy childhood, nor was it missed, and when admitted to the Illinois Bar at the age of twenty-one, I was mature beyond my years, facing the world with confidence and burning intensity of purpose. To become a criminal defense attorney was my goal and through a series of fortuitous investments and occurrences, I answered Florida's magical call to the young and adventurous.

"Yankee" lawyers were not readily accepted in the legal circles of Florida, but with the passage of time I gradually assimilated to the milieu of the south and married a beautiful titian-haired southern belle. Broward County began to grow and so did my reputation as a criminal trial lawyer, but unfortunately success and prosperity had a dark side. Unremitting dedication to the legal profession made our marriage flounder, as my lovely wife so aptly put it as she walked out of my life, "You are married to the law, which will always be your only love. Goodbye!" She was right! The law was a jealous mistress, and I was passionately devoted to it. I was a hopeless, incurable visionary. Now, middle-aged, balding, with a respectable crown of silver hair, I was riding the crest of popularity engendered by complimentary media accounts of some highly publicized criminal trials. This intoxicating crescendo of plaudits from the media fulfilled every waking moment of my isolated existence. I was happy when I was immersed in my profession, insulated from the social pressures of the outside world.

*   *   *

Enough woolgathering, I promised myself, sitting at the twelve foot mahogany table in my law library, toying with a few citations while waiting for Ellie and Frank Dooley to keep their 8:30 P.M. appointment.

The headlights of the Dooley car flooded the front of the office building and I blinked away my reveries to open the gold anodized heavy glass doors and greet my visitors. I knew they wanted to speak about the 'Catch Me Killer' case, which was highly publicized and the subject of everyone's conversation. It was certainly interesting enough for me to pass up a dinner at Joe Sonken's Gold Coast Restaurant. I remember meeting Ellie Dooley in Doctor Seltzer's office where she worked as a head nurse and wondered what her interest in the murder case was. The couple was ushered into the large, brightly lit library which also served as a conference room and when all were comfortably seated, noting the strained look on Ellie's face, I tried to put my visitors at ease by telling an amusing anecdote about Doctor Seltzer, and how his cronies called him "Bromo Seltzer" because he always fizzles out on the golf course. Ellie tried a polite smile, but her anxiety made her come to the point, and began to tell of her sincere concern about Bob Erler. Frank Dooley, a tall, slim, dark-complected man in his forties, sat quietly in his chair and comforted his agitated wife as she related her long friendship with the Erler family.

"When the Erlers came to Florida several years ago, they settled in the West Hollywood section and the senior Erler had trouble making a living. There were too many mouths to feed and they were all crowded together in a rental unit that was just too small. They had to break up the family and young Bob came to live with us."

"Okay. Now what's the last information that you've heard from your friend," I asked.

"Only that he's hiding out somewhere in Phoenix. He keeps calling us to say how scared he is and afraid that if the police find him they'll kill him. Oh, please, Mr. Varon . . ." An avalanche of tears burst forth, "He threatened to end his life before that happens."

"Don't worry about that," was my reply, trying to console the weeping woman. "People who threaten suicide never go through with it. Please calm down because I want to give you some instructions and you're not helping the cause if you continue to carry on this way.''

''Then you'll take the case?'' asked Ellie, brightening up.

''Glad to be of service,'' I answered, pleased at the opportunity to tackle the perplexing challenge evident in the 'Catch Me Killer' enigma. ''Just a small detail: the accused must select his counsel. It is a personal right that he alone can exercise. When Mr. Erler calls you, which I'm certain he will, tell him of our meeting and have him call my office 'collect' from wherever he is, and by all means, tell him to speak to no one until I see him in person. Just remember, he must not speak to anyone, not to police, not to any of his friends, no one!''

The Dooleys left the office somewhat mollified but uneasy over the new developments reported. They apparently missed the radio reports about the Hollywood police calling a press conference to announce they were investigating some critical evidence on the 'Catch Me Killer' case and would formally charge a prime suspect with the murder of Merilyn Clark within twenty-four hours. Once they reached home, Frank Dooley later told me, Ellie went inside her darkened bedroom and sank to her knees, offering a prayer of thanks that I had promised to fight for her Bobby. Her strong belief gave me the boost I needed.

The next morning, I opened the back door of my office building at 7:30 A.M. and turned on the ten-ton air conditioning system because the weatherman promised another bright, sunny, beastly hot and humid day. It was my favorite time in the office. With no one around to encroach upon my thoughts, the office schedule could be restructured depending on what matters required my priority treatment. Certainly, first and foremost was the Erler case. He would be charged with murder for sure and it was important to get him back to Florida immediately. It was just a matter of time when Erler would be nabbed and the longer he remained in hostile territory, the greater the probability of his being coerced into some zany incriminatory statements which would later be used against him. I didn't like that morning's news flash from the Hollywood Police Department heard on the radio. The report indicated that "a prime suspect would be charged" with the murder of the little girl within twenty-four hours. It could only be Robert Erler, but he would have to be arrested first before he would be returned to Florida. He would have to be found before he could be arrested. Even the Dooleys, who were in telephonic contact with Erler, didn't know where he was, only that he was in Phoenix, Arizona. Until I spoke to Erler personally, or at least on the telephone, I was technically not officially retained, and didn't represent anyone in the case.

My intuition told me to stretch the technicality and call Assistant Chief Carl King. Carl would understand and level with me.

The twelve mile journey to the central compound in the Maricopa County Courthouse seemed an eternity to both occupants in the sheriff's squad car. To a casual observer, it would seem that the uniformed deputy was being held hostage by the passenger who toyed with a service revolver on his lap. True to his word, once the squad car squealed to a halt, Erler turned over his gun to Koelsch. On cue, as though a signal was given, four armed deputies stormed the squad car, two positioned at each side, and dragged Erler, forcefully hurling him to the pavement. His arms were pinioned behind his back and another group of police officers who were following in unmarked cars jumped out, pointing shotguns at the captive's head as he was dragged and hustled to the booking desk. Eager reporters jammed the corridors yelling questions, clawing and shoving for a closer look. Flash bulbs were popping in Erler's face as he cringed and begged, "Leave me alone—I don't feel good."

Erler could never remember the booking process, being fingerprinted and photographed. The large quantity of drugs he ingested was responsible for his disorientation and ultimate blackout. He vaguely recalled being stripped naked and flung into an ice cold shower amid insulting taunts and vile remarks from his jailers, but he thought it was one of his bad dreams. The stupefied Erler was unceremoniously led to a small solitary cell where he flopped on a tiny cot and slept.

Next morning, Erler was deeply immersed in a turbulent drug-induced sleep when he was roughly shaken awake by a jail guard.

"Get up, *officer*!" shrilled the custodian with sarcastic delight, hoping to impress his partner with his cleverness. "We're going across the street to the magistrate." Smirking with sadistic glee, he grabbed Erler's loose denim jacket with both hands and roughly shook him out of his stupor.

Erler rose from the cot with unsteady legs, his face broken by many hours of drugged sleep; tousled hair and wrinkled clothes made him look unsightly and unkempt, presenting a pathetic picture. He was helpless and bewildered but managed to inquire, "What are you going to do with me?"

"You were a cop once," teased the jailer. "Where the hell do you think you're going?"

"I dunno . . ."

"You're going before the judge, asshole, to the committing magistrate for openers."

The handcuffs were snapped on Erler's wrists in front of his body and he was shoved from his cell toward the waiting open elevator. When the descent was made to the downstairs hallway, a host of reporters blocked the elevator door to confront the stunned captive. They packed the room armed with cameras and floodlights in order to photograph the famous 'Catch Me Killer,' and surged forward taking pictures and snapping flash bulbs in his face, shouting questions, making him scream, "Get them away from me!" The two custodians valiantly pushed their way to the street, but the short walk across from the jail to the courtroom of the committing magistrate was a nightmare. The word was out. The 'Catch Me Killer' was caught and it seemed as though the entire population of Phoenix lined the streets to view the killer on parade. The persistent newspaper reporters, television cameramen and photographers converged upon the hapless prisoner, taunting him and hurling insults and invective. "Hey, copper, let's have some action for the press," an eager TV cameraman sneered. "Come on, Erler, show us how tough you are—give us something for your adoring fans."

Erler lowered his head like a wounded bull in an arena and begged his captors to "Keep these people away from me. I want to be left alone." His pleas and entreaties fell on deaf ears; the insults and catcalls continued unmercifully until the beleaguered captive could contain himself no longer, and lashed out at his nearest tormentor, kicking him and repeatedly kicking and spitting at the gleeful photographers until he was subdued by his police guards.

"Listen, asshole," snarled one of his jailers, "any more trouble from you and we'll go right back and put you in body chains and leg irons."

"I'll behave," promised Erler. "But they're treating me like an animal. Where's Dave? He promised to protect me from this stuff."

As the trio reached the middle of the street the reporters and curious onlookers formed a barricade around the jailers and their prisoner, impeding any further progress toward the magistrate's courtroom. Traffic was stopped, impatient motorists honked horns, but the crowd refused to disperse. They were at an impasse. One reporter advanced upon Erler, cruelly thrusting a camera directly in his face for a close-up shot. Erler retaliated with a vicious kick in the groin and the photographer doubled over in pain, his camera clattering to the ground. Still on the offensive, Erler smashed the camera with his foot.

"That's it, buddy," growled the angry jailer. "Back you go. We're gonna put irons on you so tight you won't be able to fart."

They fought their way back to the sheriff's office while deputies rushed to bar the riotous horde of newsmen and curiosity seekers pushing to enter the building. Erler was fitted with a waist chain and leg irons that restricted his mobility so severely he could only move forward ten inches with each stride. Checking to be certain Erler was incapable of making any more trouble, the guard announced, "You've got a date with the judge. Let's get started. The going will be slow, but you brought it on yourself."

The trio retraced their steps toward the magistrate's courtroom across the street, but nothing had changed. The

press rushed at Erler, asking pointed questions, grabbing
him for attention, while television photographers were busy
cranking away at their minicams; flash bulbs exploded in
Erler's face and the bolder members of the burgeoning
crowd were having a Roman holiday, shouting inane questions and hurling insults at the tormented prisoner. The
manacled Erler laboriously made his tormented way across
the busy street, tears of suppressed fury and frustration
welling in his eyes. Silently he prayed, "Dear God, please
let this nightmare end." At the end of the hall near the
judge's courtroom was the court's chambers, where Erler's
guards had planned to check in rather than buck the growing crowds congregating at the double doors of the courtroom. As one of the guards started to remove the leg irons,
the other jailer yelled, "What in the hell are you doing?"

"Taking off the hardware, that's what."

"Don't you know this crazy bastard will flip at any time
. . . he's got to be trussed up."

"Sorry, Mac," replied the senior guard. "You know the
rules, no prisoner goes into court in irons, even a bad bastard like this one."

The Superior Court Judge of Maricopa County also acted
as a committing magistrate, conducting his own preliminary
hearings. He instructed his bailiff to spirit the defendant
into his chambers for the initial judicial confrontation as
required by law. The bailiff led Erler and his guards to the
judge's chambers where the sign on the upper glass portion
of the pine door read,

CHARLES F. COPPOCK
SUPERIOR COURT JUDGE

The bailiff tried the chamber's door but it was locked.
Reaching into his pocket for the keys, he tried the door
again but still couldn't get it open. Cursing to himself, he
tried another key just as the crowd of people standing in
front of the courtroom door began to drift toward the
judge's chambers. The unruly mob jammed the small hallway and surged forward in undulating waves, accelerating
its vocal display of ridicule and invective toward Erler. He
began to panic. Fearing for his life, he lurched forward,

raising his manacled hands and, handcuffs and all, smashed through the frosted window of the chamber's door, severing an artery in his left wrist. The blood spurted like a fire hose; people began screaming and pandemonium set in. Only the newspaper photographers and television cameramen remained to memorialize the gruesome sight.

"Get an ambulance," shouted the alarmed bailiff. "This guy is liable to bleed to death!"

The unruly crowd began to back away, not so much in a spirit of cooperation, as to avoid being spattered with Erler's blood that was now cascading on the wall and all over the wooden floor outside the magistrate's chambers. A deputy sheriff lowered the dazed Erler to the floor and, removing his own black uniform tie, applied a tourniquet above the prisoner's left elbow in an attempt to temporarily staunch the pulsating jets of Erler's life blood.

No ambulance appeared and the jail guards could wait no longer. They dragged and half carried the helpless Erler to a waiting squad car, rushing wildly to the emergency room of the Maricopa County Hospital.

"Doc," said the senior jail custodian, addressing a young intern who was examining Erler, "stitch this guy up, pronto, 'cause we got to bring him back to court."

The intern held a pencil flashlight to his patient's eyes and directed a small beam to check his reflexes and dilate his pupils. He stood away from Erler and mused to the white-garbed nurse in attendance, "Just a tetanus shot and nothing else. He's so loaded right now, he'll feel no pain when I suture the wounds."

In record time the efficient emergency room team repaired the severed artery and closed the jagged gash with innumerable stitches. Erler looked at his bandaged wrist and through an uncomprehensive fugue, as though the object he was observing belonged to someone else, muttered, "What's up?"

"Back you go for your date with the judge. This is our third try and it better be the last. I'm getting fed up with you!"

The two guards handcuffed Erler's good right hand to the waist chain around his body. The senior jailer, recognizing the improvised restraints might be inadequate, hissed through clenched teeth, "Listen, you rotten bastard, one more false move out of you and I'll blow your goddam head off. Now, let's haul ass. The judge is waiting for us."

Erler's appearance before Superior Court Judge Coppock was a mere formality in obedience to the constitutional mandate that a person arrested for a crime be brought before a magistrate without delay. The kindly judge peered down from his elevated bench and went through the required litany. "Are you Robert John Erler?"

The groggy defendant standing between the two jail custodians replied in the affirmative. The court went on, "Have you been apprised of your constitutional rights . . . ?" and was interrupted by the defendant.

"I know my rights. I'm a police officer."

"Very well," said the judge with a smile. "It is my duty to tell you what the charges are against you. I will read them to you from this arrest warrant in my hand . . ."

"That's not necessary," broke in Erler once again.

"Since you are a fugitive from Florida, I must inform you that you can either waive extradition and return to the demanding state of Florida or you may wish to contest the extradition in this court."

"I haven't spoken to anyone since my arrest, Your Honor, and don't know what to do."

"Perfectly understandable," replied the affable jurist. "I am now instructing the jailers to allow you the use of the telephone, and suggest you get a lawyer to advise you what to do. Oh yes, Mr. Erler, if you want a lawyer and cannot afford one, please let me know and an attorney will be furnished at the expense of the State of Arizona."

"Thank you, Judge," replied Erler, pleasantly surprised to hear kind words from anyone since his surrender.

"I will set this matter for hearing on . . ." He thumbed a well-worn diary and, stopping at a sparsely filled page said, "October 1 at 9:30 A.M. If your lawyer advises you to waive extradition and go back, there will be no need for a hearing."

"Any bond to be set, Judge?" reminded his secretary, who also acted as court clerk.

"Oh yes, thank you," acknowledged Judge Coppock. "I

will set bail at $85,000.00. Court is adjourned."

The bailiff directed Erler to the two guards stationed in front of the witness stand, motioning them to take the prisoner away. There was no use telling Erler what was in store for him. His latest episode unequivocally established that he was violent, emotionally unstable and dangerous to himself and others. He was placed in solitary confinement in the county jail to await the pleasure of the prosecution officials of the State of Florida. He was not aware of the passage of time. He slept fitfully on a tiny cot, gradually recovering from the doses of barbiturates he ingested, and was awakened only by his guards at feeding time. He refused to eat and begged to be left alone, turning away so he could sink into his world of dreams: He was back as a police officer in Dania cleaning up on a saloon full of drunken, brawling rednecks, fighting his way to the top in the Golden Gloves National Tournament, parachute jumping behind enemy lines with his buddies in Special Services, and the best dream of all—being cited by the Chief of Police of Hollywood for meritorious service. He longed for the affection, respect and warm adulation of his fellow police officers. He would suddenly jackknife out of his drug-induced reveries, alarmed, bewildered and bathed in sweat, only to flop on his stomach gripping the iron sides of his cot and force himself back into the comfort of his world of dreams where again he was the super cop, the scourge of the criminals and law breakers. He was Erler the Avenger, the terror of the police department, and refused to recognize or think about his predicament. As he would drift back into consciousness and look at his surroundings through the slits of his sleep-swollen eyes, he viewed the sight of his small solitary cubicle with disbelief. There was no place in his thoughts for reality. Sleep was his sanctuary; the dark concrete wall, his security.

Ellie Dooley got an emergency appointment and came bursting into my office waving a newspaper. "You came in at the right time, Ellie," I began. "Heard that Erler is in the county jail on an arrest warrant and was about to call him. He doesn't know me, so you can introduce us on the phone."

"Please look what the newspaper is saying about Bob," said Ellie, angrier than I could imagine, holding the newspaper with both hands so the emblazoned headlines were easier to see. "KILLER COP TRIES SUICIDE!"

Taking the journal from Mrs. Dooley's shaking hands, I reclined in the leather chair behind my desk and slowly read the accounts of Erler's erratic behavior outside the court's chambers, kicking and fighting with newspaper reporters and spectators. The paper carried a picture of Erler slamming his hands through the "plate glass door" of the judges chambers in "an emotional outburst." Another photo showed Erler breaking the frosted upper panel of the magistrate's door and being wrestled to the ground with the inscription, "He rams his cuffed hands through glass door and fights off the guards . . ."

I slowly put the newspaper down and nodded to Ellie Dooley in sympathetic understanding. My real reaction was that this type of journalism was a precursor of things to come, and the trial by news media was just beginning. I yelled to my secretary in the adjoining office, "Call the Maricopa County Jail in Phoenix, and tell them to please get Robert Erler on the phone, his attorney must speak with him."

While listening to my secretary order a person-to-person call, I turned my attention to Ellie, who had a dull lifeless look on her face. "Something troubling you?" I asked.

"The newspapers are referring to Bob as a 'dangerous maniac' and that he is 'emotionally unstable,' and . . ." She started to cry, "He tried to commit suicide by slashing his wrists."

"Please calm down. That's part of the game. Don't ever believe what you read in the papers, half of what they print isn't true and the other half is fabricated."

The secretary buzzed on the intercom to report that permission must first be procured from the sheriff before Erler could be released from solitary confinement and arrangements made for the prisoner to take the call. "I asked them to please return our call collect and that you would wait by the phone until Mr. Erler called."

"It will be a few minutes before we get clearance from the authorities," I explained to Ellie. "So while we're wait-

ing, there's another very important call to make." Dialing
the telephone number of the Hollywood Police Department,
I asked to speak with Carl King. The assistant chief of
police immediately answered: "Hello, Carl," I greeted my
old friend warmly. "This is Joe Varon. I've just been retained by the Erler family and will be filing a formal appearance on behalf of Robert John Erler."

"I was afraid you'd be called in on this. In a way I'm
glad because I've always liked Bob and he certainly has
been through an awful lot," said King with genuine sincerity.

"Thanks, Carl. I just wanted to report that Erler is being
contacted and I'll advise him to waive extradition. Oh, Carl,
by the way, when he gets back here, please see to it that
no one tries to interview him or get a statement. You know
the rules."

"Don't worry, Joe, I'll pass the word," promised the
assistant chief. I contentedly terminated the call knowing
Carl King to be a man of his word, a perfect gentleman
and an honorable police officer. We both knew the law:
when an attorney notifies the police or prosecution officials
that he represents an imprisoned client, no questions relating to the charges must be asked of the accused and no
attempts made to procure any incriminating statements. I
was comfortable in the belief King would personally honor
this simple request and follow the mandates of the law.

The telephone call from Robert Erler finally came
through. Handing the receiver to Ellie, she was asked to
make the introduction.

"Hello, Bob! This is Ellie. Yes, yes, I know Bob. I'm
here in Mr. Varon's office. He's the criminal attorney we
talked about and has agreed to be your lawyer. Wait, Bob
. . . please do everything he says."

Taking the telephone from Ellie, I came to the point immediately, "I know how tough things are with you in Phoenix and the first thing we want to accomplish is to get you
down here as soon as possible. That means you will waive
extradition."

"But sir, my brother got hold of a lawyer friend of his
who wants to fight extradition."

"Listen Bob," I replied firmly, "and listen well. You

are to waive extradition immediately and tell that to your brother's friend. He will know how to accomplish that.''

"Yes sir," was the meek response.

"The idea is to get you down here in familiar territory as soon as possible among your friends and the Dooleys. We can then have a long talk and prepare for your defense.

"I understand sir, and thank you sir," was his polite response.

"Good. You get going on the waiver of extradition and I'll see about expediting your transportation back to Florida. Another thing, Bob, and this is most important. I do not want you to talk to anyone about this case, understand? No one!''

"Yes sir," confirmed Erler, "no one!''

19

A TOP-LEVEL meeting in the county solicitor's room on the second floor of the courthouse was more like a birthday celebration at the Riptide Bar on Federal Highway—a well-known open-air bar in Ft. Lauderdale. Johnnie Melrose was in such high spirits he unwittingly placed his arm around Irving Goetz, not noticing Goetz cringe imperceptibly from his arch rival's embrace. John Cox was light-headed from the praise heaped upon him for his master stroke in orchestrating Mrs. Kaufman's telephone call to Erler in jail which unleashed a wealth of incriminating admissions. As always, King remained quiet. Erler's pathetic responses to Claire Kaufman's barbed questions could conceivably be construed by a biased listener as a tacit confession, but his many years of police experience told him this was a far cry from a confession. As to the others in the room, they felt the investigation was over. Cox dreamily said to no one in particular, "Did you get that part when Claire asked him if he did it and Erler said, 'I don't know'?''

Detective Melrose chimed in with, "How about the part when Erler said he was sorry for everything, that was dynamite.'' Angie Weir viewed the new evidence with great relish.

.''This is an absolute confession in the true meaning of the word.'' Looking at the officers sitting around her desk she announced, ''A Second Degree Murder Information will be filed in the clerk's office before you fellows even leave the building.''

In the small unpretentious home of Mrs. Winifred Erler in Phoenix, Danny Erler and sisters Lynn and Betty were trying to sort out with some degree of sanity the crisis that befell brother Bob. Family friend Lieutenant David Koelsch had advised them that extradition warrants were en route from Broward County, Florida, and Bob's attorney had directed him to waive extradition so all future activity would take place in Florida.

"My job is over, Mrs. Erler," said Koelsch. "Might be best if you folks scoot to Fort Lauderdale where Bob will be sent shortly."

"Oh David, thank you for all your help," replied a grateful Winifred. "Bob always said you were a good friend."

"Glad to help you and your family, ma'am," answered Koelsch, his lanky angular frame twitching with eagerness to run away from the mother's trusting gaze. Danny started to have inner doubts about Koelsch. When the deputy left, the younger brother reached for the telephone and called Ellie Dooley in Florida.

As Bob Erler's legal representative, I was more disappointed than angry. The first inkling received about Robert Erler being charged with murder was my secretary opening a special edition of the *Fort Lauderdale News* in front of my face so I could see the oversized headline, "EX-HOLLYWOOD COP CHARGED WITH MURDER."

I grabbed the newspaper from my secretary's outstretched hands and devoured the news in bitter silence. The opening salvo of the media is expected to be brutal but this special issue abused the traditional privilege and it dawned on me this was one of those cases that would be tried in the newspapers. As I read on, I was mentally countering the critical assertions made in bold print. The media had been flailing away at Erler when he was a prime suspect and now that he was charged with murder, it characterized their favorite villain as an emotionally, unstable, dangerous person who was a deadly Karate black belt champion with a lust to kill with bare hands, and exercised poetic license to the utmost as to Erler's vicious propensities. His maniacal antics at the preliminary hearing outside Judge Coppock's chambers, and the ultimate episode of smashing his manacled wrists through the judge's glass door were artfully catalogued.

Lucy, my private secretary, had been through many of these traumatic incidents before. She sat in a comfortable tan leather chair across from my desk waiting for the instructions that would follow when my emotions subsided to normalcy.

The newspaper was allowed to fall from my numbed fingers as I spoke to the patient blonde, dutifully waiting with pen poised over her ever-present steno pad. "The only valuable information in this bunch of trash," pointing to the newspaper strewn over the floor, "is the news that Erler signed the extradition waiver last Friday, September 20. Do you know what that means?"

"For openers," replied the astute secretary who also doubled as a paralegal assistant, "the . . ."

I didn't let her say anything further and really did not expect her to as I hurried on, "It means, first of all, I must deal at arm's length with Carl King and everyone else on the prosecution side. The honeymoon is over. Carl should have told me about the formal murder charge and that Erler had waived extradition . . ."

There was really no justification for my outburst. The battle lines were drawn. I realized that and shouldn't be short-tempered with my old friend King. This was by far the most publicized homicide case Broward County ever had, even surpassing the sexually bizarre case of that high society doctor Fielding-Reid from Baltimore. I represented the doctor after he was charged with murder during a drunken Christmas party on his yacht. Snapping out of my invective mood, I ordered Lucy to call the Sheriff's Office in Maricopa County, as I decided to talk to Erler before he made the long trip from Phoenix to Fort Lauderdale. Many things could happen on a protracted journey with a prisoner in tow. The attending police officers would have ample time to establish a rapport with Erler and an innocent conversation could be disastrous, particularly in the jaundiced view of the deputies. Grave concern arose in my mind: Erler must be intercepted before he made his trip back and warned not to speak about the case. I also worried that a two or three day automobile ride from Phoenix would encompass too long a period of time for a seemingly unstable Erler to remain passive and noncommittal. An idea came to me. Without waiting for the result of the secretary's call to Erler, I grabbed the phone at the corner of my desk and called the new sheriff of Broward County, Alan Michel. Erler's return to Broward County was imminent and it was important that the manner and method of his transportation be resolved. Fortunately, the Broward Sheriff could see me immediately and the trip from Hollywood only took twenty minutes.

Michel was waiting for me in his office on the sixth floor of the county courthouse building. He rose from his desk, perpetual cigar in his hand, greeting me cordially, and ushered me to the comfortable worn leather chair in his large office adorned with pictures of himself with political notables and a large array of plaques and certificates of merit and acknowledgments of his community service. The sheriff was a veteran police officer, having been a chief of police in Philadelphia before coming down to Florida for his retirement. Michel was respected by lawyers and police alike because of his warmth and compassion.

"Sheriff," I began, "Erler waived extradition in Phoenix and I'd like to have him flown down here as soon as possible and would appreciate your expediting his transportation."

"What's the hurry?" he asked smiling with a twinkle in his soft brown eyes.

"Since formal charges have been filed against him," I answered, "there will be a concerted effort by you police fellows to get some kind of confession or incriminating statement, and the longer the delay, the more opportunity for you guys to work on him."

My grim accusation was said in a lighthearted manner

hoping to dilute the harshness of the complaint, but it was not necessary. The sheriff grinned, showing his tobacco-stained teeth. "I know where you're coming from, Counselor," he now guffawed openly. "I've been there, believe me. I'd really like to help you," he responded sincerely, "but it's impossible."

"Why can't you do this?" I asked, trying to conceal my frustration.

The sheriff ran his fingers through the sparse light brown hair that almost matched his sallow complexion, giving him a sorrowful demeanor that belied his good nature and said, "I heard Erler is a dangerous character and the airlines won't accept armed guards on the airplane. It's against regulations, but I'll send a couple of men by car and you can rest assured there will be no 'automobile confessions' attempted."

"I know that, Sheriff," was my relieved reply, knowing I could rely on Alan Michel's word, and thanked him for seeing me on such short notice, making haste to rush back to the office to see what other surprises were awaiting me.

Early Tuesday morning, September 24, 1968, Detective Andy Murcia, Sheriff Michel's trusted chief deputy, brought his unmarked police car to a halt directly behind the Broward County Sheriff's booking office, without fanfare or notice to anyone. This low-key, matter-of-fact approach was characteristic of Murcia, a retired New York police detective who knew more about police work than all the rest of Alan Michel's staff put together. He was entrusted with the pickup and delivery of Robert John Erler, fulfilling that commitment with his usual efficiency and dispatch. He opened the door on the driver's side of the vehicle and grunted audibly as he moved his bulky frame, pulling down the seat to allow his prisoner to free himself from the cramped quarters he shared in the rear seat with Murcia's companion, another deputy.

"All right, son," he gruffly addressed the prisoner, "just walk through that door for processing." And seeming to have another thought added wryly, "Guess you know about being fingerprinted and mugged?"

"Yes, sir," was the somewhat rueful response. "Many's

the time I did that to others—now it's me . . .'' He broke
off abruptly just as George Duncan, the head of the booking
division, came forward to relieve the burly detective bellowing, ''Andy, how could you let this Erler fellow roam
around here without handcuffs and restraints?''

''Just relax, George, I had no trouble at all from Phoenix
to Fort Lauderdale.''

''I'll still have to double the guards and put the restraints
on him . . . haven't you heard? Don't you read the papers?
My God, Andy, this fellow is a one-man disaster!''

''So long, Bob,'' said Murcia as he threw a two-fingered
salute in Erler's direction giving him a fleeting smile of
understanding, and left the booking area.

Erler stood woodenly at attention as his fingers were
blackened on an inked slab and didn't move a muscle as
George Duncan took each finger from each hand to make
an imprint on a light cardboard form designating the identity of each digit. The thumb and palm print received the
same treatment and Erler was ordered to sit down while his
picture was taken, front and side views. When the news
leaked out that the 'Catch Me Killer' was being processed,
officers and detectives began to filter into the booking division to size up their celebrated prisoner. Erler kept his
eyes glued to the floor, fearful that an eyeball confrontation
with any of the police officers present would trigger off an
unpleasant incident. The kindly George Duncan, realizing
the awkwardness of the situation, hurried his routine processing procedures and personally whisked his famous prisoner into the private inner elevator up to the head jailer.

Lieutenant Sullivan, a curly haired, slightly built man in
his late thirties, could have easily been taken for an Irish
priest were it not for the sheriff's uniform he wore. He took
immediate charge of Erler and wordlessly ushered the prisoner into an overcrowded, steamy jail that reeked of perspiration, urine, and strong penetrating antiseptic solution.
The overhead lights threw an eerie glare on the huge iron
door that led to the cells lining the narrow corridors with
cream-colored bars painted over and over to hide the accumulated rust and grime. The lieutenant opened the
ponderous door and motioned Erler to precede him, and

upon entering, the huge door closed with a deafening clang that made Erler flinch.

"Here, take this," said the lieutenant as he handed Erler a prison jumpsuit similar to denim coveralls. "Hope they fit." The lieutenant then inserted a key in the door of a little cubicle and pushed the prisoner into the solitary cell saying, "This is maximum security, and you're going to remain in solitary confinement until you can prove to us that you'll behave like a human being."

"Wait!" shouted Erler to the retreating lieutenant. "I've been on my best behavior since I came here . . . why are you putting me in maximum and solitary too?"

"For several reasons," sighed the lieutenant. "You're a cop! The inmates hate cops. The police personnel hate an ex-cop that goes bad. If I were to let you in the general area, the prisoners would try to kill you . . . there would be fights and stabbings, all because of you, so who needs that kind of trouble? Erler, you spell trouble . . . just watch and see what happens and we'll talk again."

The barred door to Erler's cell clanged shut, and a flash of pain behind his eyes gave him a sick headache. When the massive main door of the general area banged with a deafening noise, Erler held his hands over his ears in fright and glared wildly around the small cell with disbelief. The floor was wet and littered with pieces of napkins and toilet paper apparently used by the previous occupant to clean the contents of the toilet bowl that overflowed. He sat on a filthy cot amid the acrid stench of stale urine that pervaded the dismal atmosphere, and bemoaned the strange fates that led him to such degradation. The pervasive smells of unwashed bodies and human waste sickened him, adding to his misery. He felt there was no way out, and forced his mind to reject the urge to escape from his inhuman surroundings. Any such attempt would not only be futile, but would subject him to greater disciplinary measures. Exploring all his options, including the possibility of a hunger strike, he finally decided to block the outside world out of his consciousness and ultimately drifted into a troubled sleep.

*   *   *

It was a tense morning for me. I knew the celebrated Bob Erler was due at the Broward County Jail at any moment and I was anxious to meet him and reiterate the most important instructions every criminal lawyer gives his client: "Do not talk about your case to anyone!" It always worried me that a slip of the tongue by an accused in custody could be interpreted by his jailers to his detriment. The hiatus period from the time an accused is arrested to the instant he meets with his attorney is the most sensitive. In this case, there was no cause for alarm because of my unbounding confidence in the integrity of Deputy Andy Murcia, but years of bitter experience dictated caution and I always worried about everything. The motion and trial calendars were suspended this day because all the judges in the courthouse were called to attend an important judge's conference. My presence was not required at the courthouse so I was content to wait, albeit nervously, for Erler's arrival. It was impossible to concentrate on depositions, briefs and investigation reports on other cases, including many lucrative ones, because the Erler case was proving to be a real puzzle. There was never a voice identification case in Florida, although a "voice print" technique was attempted in New Jersey, where a Rube Goldberg apparatus was constructed to measure the decibels of comparative sound. Certainly the prosecution staff of fledgling Broward County was not knowledgeable or sophisticated enough to engineer any technical device to evaluate or compare the 'Catch Me Killer's' voice with any "known" standard, assuming one was available. I couldn't help dwelling on the circumstantial evidence aspect of the case when my secretary put through a call directly to my desk. Our office had an inflexible rule: Never ask "Who is calling?" Put the call through at once! Perhaps the caller wishes to remain incognito or maybe it was a fugitive on the run and this confidence must not be violated. Often a person is calling from jail and this could be his one and only call.

"Hello, Joe," a deep voice boomed. "This is Murcia. We've got your man here, if you want to see him" and rung off before I could adequately express my thanks.

It took twenty minutes to drive from the Hollywood office to Fort Lauderdale for the initial confrontation with the former Hollywood policeman. The newly constructed six-story addition to the Broward County Courthouse had barely been completed, but was already too small to service the needs of its citizens due to the burgeoning population explosion. The building exterior was cosmetically appealing, but the detention area where the prisoners were jailed was in a deplorable state of disrepair and not conducive to amiable visitation. With a tremor of excited anticipation, I approached the heavy plate glass window and asked to see Bob Erler. The deputy in charge knew me and never asked for identification. He flashed a knowing smile.

"Just go right in to the private conference room. It will take quite a while to get him out."

Instinctively, I sensed something unusual and asked, "What's the problem?"

"This guy requires special attention. Orders are cuffs and leg irons before we move him out of solitary."

"Solitary?" I exploded. "What's he done?"

"Nothing here, but you know . . ."

"No, I don't know," was my cold reply. "But I sure as hell will find out!"

The conference room where lawyers consulted with their imprisoned clients was private and small with green tinted windows on all sides permitting the jail guards to monitor the actions of the occupants. A weather-beaten walnut table and two once-varnished chairs constituted the sum total of the furnishings, except for an eight-ounce rusted tomato can that served as an ashtray. Jail trusties walked back and forth, glancing in curiously. They were prison elite who either had a few more days of servitude before release or were serving a minimal sentence for a misdemeanor, and had full freedom of the cell block as "assistants" to the harried jail guards. They were trusted not to escape and were model prisoners, hence the nickname, "Trusty." As I waited patiently, a dour-faced guard approached Erler's cell, rattled keys along the thickly painted plastic-like bars and said, "Your lawyer's here to see you. Do you promise to behave yourself or do I call for backup?"

"I don't know why you think I won't behave," replied Erler. "What's the matter with you people? I'm gonna tell my lawyer to get me out of solitary. I'm entitled to be out with the others waiting for trial."

"I'm still putting you in cuffs and irons. Those are my orders and you can tell that to your lawyer!" With the help of another guard, Erler was put in restraints and escorted to the conference room where I viewed my new client for the first time, and liked what I saw. The prisoner appeared to be a somber, sincere young man about twenty-five with a square jaw and frank demeanor; but seeing him in handcuffs and leg irons upset me. "Hold up there, men," I yelled to the departing custodians. "Is Lieutenant Sullivan on this floor?"

"The lieutenant is on coffee break and he'll be back soon."

"Thanks. I'd appreciate it very much if I could have a word with him when he gets back."

"Okay Counselor," replied one of the guards. "We'll pass on your request."

"Thanks again, fellows." I waved in salutation and turned to my client who politely stood by during the brief exchange. With a firm grasp to one of his manacled hands I guided him gently toward a chair.

"Hello, Bob."

"How are you, sir? Thanks for coming."

While pulling the other chair close to Erler, I started the conversation. "The first order of business is to get rid of those restraints. Have you done anything since you arrived from Phoenix to warrant this type of security?"

"No sir. There were some catcalls and insulting remarks I heard all the way into solitary, but I ignored them."

"Of course," I cut in, "you can expect all kinds of flak from the other inmates because you were a cop. I know you don't belong in solitary, and especially in maximum security, so let me work on that."

Erler gave a nod of understanding and smiled. "That's why I want to speak with Lieutenant Sullivan," I explained. "He's in charge of this jail and I have to go through the chain of command. If we receive no satisfaction then I can go over his head to the sheriff, but I'm certain the lieutenant will be reasonable."

Erler seemed well-oriented and comfortable. I intuitively

felt he would not hesitate in reposing his entire confidence in me and welcomed dispensing with small talk to concentrate on the business at hand.

"I know you want to make bail, but all the possibilities have been explored and it looks like they want to make a special case out of you. The standard bond for second degree murder is $15,000.00, and the prosecutor won't come down from the $100,000.00 set by the court. We'd be wasting our time with a motion to reduce bail. Once we see what the State's evidence is, I'll move for a speedy trial so you won't be held in jail longer than necessary."

"Sir," Erler interjected meekly, "I didn't do this."

"I'll get your entire story later." Noting the disappointment on Erler's face, I hurriedly explained, "There are certain procedures that we must follow so we will know what's happening. I'll be at your side when you go before the judge for arraignment. We'll enter a plea of 'not guilty' to the murder charge and . . ."

"But really, I am not guilty of anything!"

"Okay. That's fine," not wanting to encourage the protestations of innocence. In all my experience as a criminal trial lawyer I never asked a client if he committed the crime charged. Frankly, I didn't want to know. I was dedicated to the principle that an accused was innocent until proven guilty beyond a reasonable doubt, and my mind was conditioned to give the defendant the best defense the law allowed, no more, no less. If the prosecution should prevail despite all the constitutional protection and trial experience at my command, so be it; but I certainly would always know in my heart and conscience that every possible avenue of defense was fully explored and exhausted. No stone was left unturned, to borrow a phrase.

"By the way, my investigator will meet with me tomorrow and there will be some things to talk about. Until then, and I can't stress this enough, Bob, you are to speak to no one about this case."

"I think I did too much talking already."

"That may be true," I replied, wondering just what he meant with that remark, but was reluctant to inquire at the time. "I want to leave you with one more warning. You will be a target because the other prisoners will try to test you. They love to go after cops in jail. Please control your-self and don't get into any fights.''

"I promise to behave, and sir,'' Erler pleaded in a child-ish manner, "can you get me out of solitary? I'd like to join the others. They have television and radio and they play cards and read books.''

"Of course,'' I answered. "This problem will be re-solved within twenty-four hours. Just continue behaving yourself and you'll be transferred for certain. That's my guarantee.''

Erler was happy, his eyes lit with trust and confidence. He whispered, "Thank you, Mr. Varon,'' in grateful re-sponse.

Maurice Sullivan, the head jailer, walked by the window of the conference room. Making a mental note to explain the abrupt termination of my first interview to Erler later, I bid a hasty farewell and ran to intercept Sullivan.

"Hey, Maury, can I have just one moment with you?''

"One of my men said you wanted to see me, and I know why.''

"That's fine, lieutenant,'' I grinned. "My client, as you know, is entitled to the presumption of innocence and should be treated the same as any other prisoner in your cell block.''

"Gee, don't you think I know that,'' he grimaced. "Your man came here with a rep as a mean, tough guy. You must know how he tore up the jail in Phoenix and if he goes on a rampage here, it's my ass.''

"I understand, Maury, but let me get you off the hook. Maybe a little talk with Sheriff Michel would ease your responsibility.''

"No, no,'' he whispered. "Don't go to the sheriff.'' Running his hands through his curly hair then rubbing his face as though he could erase the worried look from his countenance, concluded, "I'll have your man transferred out of max, but so help me—one false move and back he goes into solitary and irons.''

"Thanks, lieutenant,'' was my sincere reply, "I'll see Erler tomorrow and read him the riot act.''

The chief jailer was somewhat mollified but not entirely

satisfied and a trifle apprehensive at the monumental decision he made, but he had to follow the law; besides, he
knew damn well Sheriff Michel wouldn't stand for discrim-
ination among his prisoners.

20 _____

BROWARD COUNTY'S JAIL never housed a more unique defendant than Robert John Erler. The news media unmercifully hammered at his macho image as a former Green
Beret commando, Black Belt Karate expert and trained
killer, subtly suggesting his explosive conduct and homi-
cidal propensities. The jail guards and inmates regarded
him with mixed feelings and warily studied his variable
moods. It took Erler a few days in the cell block before he
attempted any communication with his fellow prisoners, but
the conversations were reserved and laconic. They learned
via the grapevine how Erler fought like a demon when attacked by some hardened inmates. A few young Turks appraised their chances to challenge the highly touted bruiser
but prudently declined any overtures when Erler returned
their stares with an even more belligerent glare. From the
safety of their cells, they nevertheless hurled insults, their
favorite expression being "pig," a pointed jibe to remind
Erler he was a hated cop. It took all his self-control to keep
his temper in check and he was almost at the breaking point
when the jail guard called him for his court appearance at
arraignment.

Erler was escorted from his cell clad, in a wrinkled but
clean tee shirt he had washed himself with his meager water
supply. Wrists handcuffed behind his back, feet shackled
and an iron restraining bar around his waist, he was taken
to a courtroom on the third floor, where Judge Robert
O'Toole was the duty judge that week. Newspaper reporters
and photographers jammed the courtroom door, thrusting
microphones in his face, attempting to goad him into some
personality trait providing fuel for the media fires, but the

hapless prisoner was tightly bound and could only move a few inches at a time.

Seated in the jury box with a few lawyers while waiting for Erler, I heard a disturbance erupting outside the courtroom door, and instinctively knew what it was. Hurtling out of the jury box, I ran from the courtroom to the side of my client and was horrified at the sight.

"Cut it out, fellows," I yelled to the reporters and was angered at seeing my client trussed in irons. The abashed guards stood by as I gently led Erler into the courtroom, step by step, just as Judge O'Toole ascended the bench to commence the arraignment. I respectfully addressed the court: "Your Honor, I am counsel of record for the accused, Robert John Erler, and must register my objection to the carnival atmosphere being enacted by the jailers for the benefit of the press and media. There is no reason why my client should be brought before this court in this disgraceful fashion, shackled in irons."

O'Toole, an experienced and seasoned veteran, quickly viewed the situation and inquired of the custodian, "Is there any reason why the defendant is restrained in this manner?"

"No, Your Honor, but our regulations require that any prisoner in transport be handcuffed."

"I understand that," the judge replied impatiently, "but I'm asking you again if there is any valid reason why Mr. Erler should be in leg irons and handcuffed to an iron waist bar?"

"None that I know of, sir."

"Remove all the restraints immediately!" the judge commanded sternly. "Please see that this nonsense doesn't happen again—or do you want me to enter an order to that effect?"

"No sir," the jailer replied hastily. "That won't be necessary. I'll relay Your Honor's directions."

The courtroom filled up quickly with spectators and courthouse employees. The newspaper reporters and photographers crowded in the seats just beyond the rail and waited expectantly for the routine arraignment to begin. Judge O'Toole glanced around the room, satisfying himself that order had been restored, and said, "I must caution the

members of the press and their photographers there will be
no pictures taken inside this courtroom. Moreover, you are
directed not to interfere with the mobility of the defendant
after these proceedings have terminated, and in no way im-
pede his return to custody. Is that clear?''

The clerk of the court dutifully called the case of "State
of Florida vs. Robert John Erler, Defendant," and Erler,
head lowered, with the "Green Beret Paratrooper" tattoo
visibly prominent on his muscled arms, stepped forward,
grateful for the first consideration received since his arrival
in Broward County.

"Counsel," inquired Judge O'Toole, "does the defendant request a reading of the charges before entry of a
plea?''

"Your Honor, the defendant desires to waive the reading
of the charges, as we already have a copy of the formal
accusation, and now enter a plea of 'not guilty' to each and
every allegation.''

"The not guilty plea is accepted and the defendant will
be granted twenty days to file defensive motions. Anything
else to come before the court?''

"Yes, if Your Honor pleases. I would request permission
to confer with my client privately in the anteroom before
he is taken back to his cell.''

"Permission granted," ordered the judge. "Just let my
bailiff know when your conference is concluded.''

"Thank you, Judge," was my response, taking Erler by
the arm. I escorted him through the door of the room that
was used by the jurors for their deliberations during a trial.
The guards grudgingly tendered their high-risk prisoner and
took their positions outside the court's anteroom while we
conferred in private.

Making ourselves comfortable at the highly burnished
mahogany conference table, I pointed to the water cooler
and asked Erler if he cared for a drink. He shook his head
imperceptibly. "How about some coffee?" I pursued, moving toward the table with a decanter resting on an electric
warmer. Once again Erler shook his head, leading me to
believe he was still in a state of exasperation.

"Now, Bob, I want you to know exactly what's going
on. At this point, the case is at issue. That means the battle

lines are drawn. Before I tell you what lies ahead, it's important that you don't do anything while in custody to create any prejudicial publicity.''

"Well, sir, I've been having one hell of a time trying to get along with everyone, like you said. I was warned that an ex-cop is a sitting duck in jail, but every day is a nightmare. I wake up in the morning terrified at what will happen next.''

"Tell me what's been happening to you.''

Erler heaved a sigh. "Let me give you these for openers—when I was taken out of solitary and put into the general cell block, there's a telephone for use by the prisoners and I decided to call my family. As soon as my back was turned and I started dialing the number, someone hit me on the back of the head. I started to black out but fought back until the guards separated us and I was sent down to the nurse for emergency treatment and they gave me something to ease the pain. The next day,'' Erler continued, "a new prisoner, a total stranger, for no reason at all came up behind me and struck me on the head with some sort of billy club. I chased him and started to punch him out until the guards pulled me off. I was dizzy and drenched with blood and they rushed me to Broward General Hospital emergency room. The intern told me I had a concussion.''

"My God!'' I exclaimed, shocked that no one ever informed me of what was developing. Neither my client nor any of the jailers. "Why didn't you contact me about this?''

"I can take care of myself,'' was the reply. "Right now I've got my eye on a tall dude who told me he didn't like me because I was an ex-cop. He showed me one of those homemade shivs and threatened to knife me, but don't worry, I know how to discourage him.''

"Bob, I can see this case will have to be expedited. The longer you remain in custody the more vulnerable you become to outside influences, and I intend to file a request for a speedy trial which will guarantee us a final hearing within ninety days.''

"The sooner the better,'' said Erler.

"Not too quickly,'' I mused. "There is still some discovery that has to be made and new evidence is cropping up that must be explored. My investigator, Harry Long, has been meeting with me regularly and we are getting an insight on the prosecution's case against you. The prosecutor, Len Boone, promised to show us all the evidence the state intends to use at the trial.''

"What *do* they have against me?''

"So far, nothing concrete. No fingerprints, no identification witnesses, only circumstantial evidence, but . . .'' and wondered if this was the appropriate time to tell him of the most recent annoying development.

Noting my hesitation, Erler pointedly asked, "But what?''

"The police found a girl's hair band crammed in the front seat on the passenger side of your old car which they believe belonged to the dead girl. The rumor is that Dorothy Clark will identify that hair band as belonging to her daughter, Merilyn Clark.''

"Impossible!'' Erler blurted. "Wait, I remember, my wife Pattie left her hair band between the seats of my Mustang. Yes, that hair band belongs to Pattie.''

"I sincerely hope so because in a day or two the newspapers and television stations will blast the story and all hell will break loose.''

"I'm telling you, it's Pattie's hair band, don't you believe me?''

"Sure I do, Bob,'' I replied soothingly, trying to suppress his mounting agitation. "There will be numerous tests made . . .''

"What tests? For what?'' he broke in forlornly. I sensed that this piece of news would trigger off a negative reaction and made a mental note to have him evaluated by a psychiatrist.

"Let me explain about the tests, Bob,'' I said, smiling in an effort to calm him down and restore his composure. "There were a few strands of hair on the hair band. The police intend to exhume the body of Merilyn Clark and snip a sample of her hair as a standard of comparison. The two hair specimens will be analyzed by a laboratory technician, or sent to the FBI lab in Washington. The results will tell us a great deal.''

"What if they phony up the tests? You once told me you

wouldn't be surprised if the cops tried to plant some evidence just to nail me.''

"That's true, I did caution you about that. Some police have resorted to that type of tactic in my experience, but the Hollywood group isn't like that. Besides, if we aren't satisfied with the results of the lab tests we can have our own independent test taken by a laboratory of our own choice.''

"You do believe me when I tell you that hair band belonged to Pattie?'' he demanded, staring levelly into my eyes as though he dared the slightest suggestion of disbelief.

"Of course I believe you, Bob, and I hope you aren't too upset, but many of these surprises pop up and we have to meet each challenge as they appear.'' Erler seemed to settle down, but disturbing notions of his emotional instability entered my mind and I decided to venture another sensitive subject. "By the way, Bob, I'm seriously considering having a psychiatrist visit you for a cursory examination and evaluation.''

"Why?'' he asked. "I'm not a psycho. Do you think I'm nuts?''

"The reason a psychiatrist's examination is necessary,'' I answered, summoning all the patience at my command, "is because for a while you had been taking a lot of pills which made you say and do a lot of foolish things. I know a great psychiatrist who might be able to ferret out some logical explanation for your irrational behavior and may even help establish a defense of diminished capacity. The exam can't possibly hurt and since it's a private evaluation, whatever is disclosed is confidential and considered a work product of the defense attorney.''

I knew this idea of having Erler examined by a psychiatrist would not sit well with him, but in the short period of the relationship with my client, it appeared that the ex-police officer possessed a dual personality which may be indicative of latent schizophrenic tendencies. Several people have attested to Erler's gentle and considerate demeanor, but I was also painfully aware of Robert Erler's vicious propensities and his belligerent conduct when irritated by outside influences. It was important that a possible insanity defense be considered, or ruled out completely.

Robert Erler received this explanation in thoughtful silence and lowered his head as if he were studying his hands. He was obviously annoyed at the prospects of being examined by a psychiatrist, so I brightly broke into his thoughts.

"Bob, such an examination can't possibly hurt us and since it's a private evaluation, whatever the doctor reports is strictly confidential. If it weren't important, I wouldn't ask for the examination."

"Okay, let's go with it," he agreed. "What else is cooking?"

There were some other urgent matters that required discussion but Erler was obviously in no mood for any further discourse and I decided to terminate the conference. I knocked on the door and the guards came in.

"Are you through, Counselor?"

"Yes, thank you very much," I replied, lingering to make certain Judge O'Toole's orders of minimal restraints were observed, and upon being satisfied said, "So long," as a smiling Erler made his way back to the cell block.

The criminal justice system of the early sixties left a lot to be desired. Prosecution officials were not yet required to make available to the defense any relevant evidence, nor did the Rules of Criminal Procedure then in existence enable the defense to anticipate surprises they might encounter at the trial. For that reason, Harry Long was the most sought after and efficient private investigator in the area. A plump six footer, Harry had been a police officer for the City of Fort Lauderdale for many years and was liked and respected by lawyers, judges and prosecutors. When Harry was assigned to an investigation, he would simply stride into the police station and rifle through the Incident reports as though he was still the shift commander. His old comrades loved the way Harry filled up a chair with his huge bulk, his unruly forelock drooping down his forehead, discussing the pros and cons of the criminal case under investigation. All the trial lawyers in Broward County gravitated to Harry Long, and I was no exception.

Alone in the semi-darkness of my office, I apprehensively waited for Long, who called for an urgent appointment at 9:00 P.M., recalling the terse statement: "Counselor, I have some ball busting stuff for you." I stretched to ease the tension and looked at my reflection in the glass partition separating the library and the reception room, for lack of anything else to do, and staring back at me was a mid-sized, placid looking man in his middle fifties with short cropped, sparse silvering hair, but the mirror-like glass pane did not reflect the seething stress and agitation I was experiencing. My instincts told me some bad news was on the way. Harry Long sounded like the voice of doom over the phone and I waited for him to arrive shortly and deliver his report. Looking through the glass, I perceived a large image darken the door to the reception room and moved to greet the investigator with a bright beaming smile to cover the sinking feeling at the pit of my stomach.

"Are you the man with all the goodies?" I teased in an attempt to set the tone of the conference in a light vein. Harry was quick in returning my feeble sally with a cheery laugh which eased my tension somewhat. "After all, things couldn't be that bad if Harry seems to be lighthearted." I also reminded myself reluctantly that Harry Long was always lighthearted and cheerfully asked, "So what have you got?"

"Whoa," answered the investigator. "Let me sit down and catch my breath . . ."

"Forgive me," was my chastened apology. "I forgot my manners. Have a seat. Can I get you something to drink?"

"No thanks," replied the investigator, sinking his ample frame into the largest of the library chairs. Harry Long grinned as he pulled out a Baby Ruth and slowly removed the wrapping just enough to take a huge bite. In the midst of devouring his choice morsel Harry said, with an owlish expression exposing his chocolate-covered teeth, "Pretty cozy." Pointing to the glass partition, he continued "You have a one-way mirror so you can see what's happening out there?"

"Not at all," I responded quickly. "Check it out if you want to. The trouble with you, Harry, is you're still a cop, but I'm glad you have a police mentality. That way, you can play devil's advocate and between the two of us we can figure out what the hell is happening.''

The investigator didn't seem convinced about the non-existence of a one-way mirror, but was more intent upon finishing his chocolate bar than accepting the invitation to examine the glass pane. When the one-story office building on Hollywood Boulevard was built, I deliberately designed the reception room alongside the library, where clients would hopefully congregate and could look right into an imposing array of law books lining the three walls, cradled in neat mahogany bookshelves, and be subtly impressed. I was inordinately proud of my library, which contained all the latest reports from the Florida Appellate Courts, as well as Federal Courts of Appeal throughout the nation, and every conceivable textbook on the forensic technical aspects of criminal law. There were many times when I would return to my office late at night, after a stormy session in the middle of a trial that presented a knotty legal problem and go into the library, looking around at the multicolored tomes that seemed to look mockingly back at me with a challenge. I would touch the bindings lovingly with my fingertips and say to myself, ''Somewhere in this room full of decisions, in some remote state, at some distant time, this same problem came up and the answer is in one of these books. I'm staying right here until that decision is found.''

Harry Long spread his notes out before him covering the head of the oversized burnished conference table, and wiped his mouth with the back of his hand, indicating he was ready to proceed.

''For openers,'' Harry began, fingering the sheaf of crumpled papers, ''your man Erler didn't win any popularity contests at either the Dania or Hollywood Police Departments, so you can look on both forces to testify against him.''

''That's too bad,'' I muttered to myself. I never relished having police officers take the stand as prosecution witnesses during a trial, as I always seemed to feel jurors traditionally accepted a police officer's testimony as gospel truth. Even though they are sworn to treat the testimony of a police officer with the same dignity accorded to a lay witness, jurors never did. There was something about an officer on the witness stand, replete with badge and official regalia, that intimidated the average juror, tending to influence his or her judgment.

Noting the look of dismay, Harry's cherubic face broke out in a grin. "They have a nice long taped conversation between Erler and" he resorted to his notes, "a woman by the name of Claire Kaufman where your client practically confessed to the crime . . ."

"Wait!" I shouted. "How did that come about?"

"It seems Erler used to be real close to that woman and she 'cooperated' with the Hollywood police. They set up a monitored call to Erler while he was in custody in the Phoenix county jail and she got him to make some incriminating admissions."

Shocked beyond belief, I began furiously making notes on a legal pad as the investigator spoke. I realized Harry was just skimming over the salient features of his investigation, but they were important leads that would be thoroughly explored to the nth degree.

"I'll get those tapes on my motion for discovery, but from what you tell me, it looks like entrapment."

"Right," Long agreed, "but you'll have to establish that the Kaufman woman either didn't know her conversation was being recorded or that she didn't knowingly give her consent."

"I'll address that problem on the pretrial level," I replied. "What about the Clark woman? Anything on that?"

"Hold on," Harry smiled with his impish leer. "Here's the worst part . . ."

"Lay it on me, Harry." The sinking feeling returned.

"They intend to use the tapes for a voice identification and several police officers that worked with Erler in Dania will swear they recognize it's Erler's voice. There are some Hollywood cops who will also identify the 'Catch Me Killer' voice to be that of Robert Erler."

"Do you know which Dania officers will testify to the voice ID, and why?"

"I know one in particular," replied Long. "It's Portelli, that fancy New York cop that was Erler's sergeant. As to the 'why,' I'll tell you why: your eager beaver client arrested one of Portelli's buddies for driving under the influence, and when Portelli asked Erler to tear up the citation and give his friend a pass, Erler refused, so Portelli is hot to trot." The investigator paused as though he wanted the information to sink in, but I kept making copious notes, head bowed, intensely concentrating on everything Long had to say.

"Okay, there's so much to tell you. Are you up to it?" asked the investigator, almost gleefully.

"Go ahead," was my quiet reply.

"There are a couple colored cops from Dania that will testify, if necessary, as to the voice ID. Erler apparently didn't like black cops and resented one in particular that would hang around Erler's trailer and visit his wife when Bob was on duty." Harry looked at me with an impish leer to see if I was following his drift and continued, "The word on the street is that Erler came home unexpectedly and there was a big three-way fight."

"Did you have a chance to interview Pattie Erler?"

"No," replied Long. "She took her kid and went to stay with her mother in Kansas City. She's not coming back, so you may as well forget about her."

"Getting back to the voice identification," I snapped, referring to the notes just made. "Is there any standard of comparison the police have to match the voice of the *Catch Me Killer* tape?"

"Only Erler's voice on the tapes with Claire Kaufman." Long's eyes gleamed as a new thought struck him. "Let's get the Kaufman tapes and match them ourselves with the killer's voice. That's how you'll be able to determine firsthand if your client is innocent or guilty."

I remained silent for what seemed an unusually long time. Decision time, again. My own investigator was forcing me to violate a cardinal rule of my practice—never to pre-judge the guilt or innocence of an accused. I desperately strove to change the subject and asked, "What do you have on Dorothy Clark?"

"The Incident reports filed in Hollywood and Lauderdale are very brief. Even Johnnie Melrose didn't have much on Dorothy's background. Let's see what we have here," and going through his crumpled papers for accuracy intoned,

"Dorothy Clark, a native of Clarkston, Georgia, married and divorced several times; worked as a secretary typist at the county courthouse there for a while, jumping from job to job. Mrs. Clark came to South Florida a few weeks before the shootings taking her twelve-year-old daughter, Merilyn, with her and spent plenty of time in the bars and saloons along the strip."

"Do you mean 'strip' on Fort Lauderdale beach?"

"No, the strip in Miami Beach. That's 'motel row,' better known as the amusement district on A1A right off the ocean road. According to John Cox's report, Dorothy worked in the shipping department of Howard Johnson's for only three days, then had to check out of her motel in Miami Beach because she was destitute. For the following week or so, Mrs. Clark and her daughter slept in the 1960 Falcon every night."

"Is that all you have on Dorothy Clark?"

"That's it so far. Don't forget, she's been in a coma and the five slugs in her head gave her partial facial paralysis. Melrose says she's just getting around to talking."

"The burning question is eyeball identification. Does any department have a report or knowledge that Dorothy Clark was able to identify her attacker?"

"If you want a gut reaction, I'll have to tell you Melrose is working on some plan to have a line-up arranged and hopefully have Dorothy identify the defendant on the spot."

III
ENTRAPMENT

21 _____

THE GRAND JURY room on the third floor of the courthouse was only used for a single short session every six months and was tacitly appropriated by the employees of the clerk's office next door primarily for coffee breaks and brown baggers during the luncheon period. It was past five and the employees congregated for a birthday celebration for Pinkie Harrison, the chief courtroom clerk, including a few favorite "outsiders" invited to participate in the festivities. They could always rely on me to underwrite the cost of the sandwiches and beer, including the traditional decorated birthday cake. The party was in full swing and I was making the rounds preparatory to leaving when Robert McElroy, the chief investigator for the county solicitor's office, sidled up, looked around nervously to see if he was being observed, and with a quick bird-like wave of his hand murmured, "Speak to you in private?" looking away as if to escape detection.

"Certainly," I replied, pretending to look over the shoulder of the agitated chief investigator, then slowly turned and whispered, "where?"

"How about in Hollywood?"

"Okay," I answered. I was heading homeward anyway, and ventured casually, "Howard Johnson's on Hollywood Boulevard?" McElroy nodded, turning away to reach for a glass of beer that teetered precariously on a covered typewriter, hoping no one noticed his action as he never indulged in alcoholic beverages and, if observed by anyone who knew him, it would appear to be suspicious. McElroy was afraid. He was already sorry he made the appointment but his conscience was bothering him and he had to do something about it.

I drove to a secluded spot in the rear parking lot of Howard Johnson's, just a few blocks west of my office and waited for McElroy, wondering what the county's chief investigator wanted. Why was he behaving so strangely, with his furtive demeanor at the party, and now this clandestine meeting? A few minutes later, an unmarked police car eased into the lot and I almost laughed out loud. Anyone can spot an official unmarked car, with its telltale antennas protruding from the trunk and top; the traditional pristine two-door green Ford coupe.

"Might as well have police markings with red and blue flashers," I muttered, noting McElroy's slim figure exit his car, slowly scanning the area. Spotting my car, he walked over, opened the door and sat in the passenger's seat of the Lincoln Continental.

"How are you doing, Robert?" I asked, reaching for his trembling hands.

Before making a response, McElroy looked around apprehensively, adjusting the spectacles on his thin nose, and said, "This is graveyard talk, do you understand?"

"Anything you say, Robert. Go ahead."

"I've been working on this Erler case day and night and I don't like what I see." Turning his troubled face to stare intently at me he continued, "I'm not convinced Erler did this. I feel it was someone else."

"My God, Robert, do you have another suspect in mind?"

He shook his head. After all these years in the arena, I became a good judge of human nature and knew McElroy was worried about something. I could sense the man's inner struggle with his conscience. McElroy was a fair-minded, humane person and I decided to appeal to his equitable nature, hoping to strike a nerve of religious consciousness.

"If you feel Erler is not guilty of this charge, you owe it to him, and to yourself, to make sure he doesn't stand trial for something he never did."

McElroy nervously adjusted his wire-rimmed glasses with a trembling hand and said sternly, "I can't interfere with an ongoing investigation. My loyalty is to the County of Broward and the prosecution."

"How can you, in good conscience, let the police send an innocent man to jail? Can you live with the thought that Erler will face a murder rap when you, in your own heart, believe the 'wrong man' is being prosecuted?"

His silence heartened me and I detected thoughtful reflection in McElroy's eyes and went after him; pleading, cajoling and imploring.

"Robert, it's your Christian duty to prevent a miscarriage of justice. How will you be able to sleep at night if you conceal evidence and a human being spends a lifetime in jail because of misguided loyalty?"

McElroy seemed to weaken. I continued talking rapidly in the same vein when the investigator's hand signalled me to halt. "Okay, I'll give you some clues, though I don't know what you'll do with them."

"Thanks very, very much," I answered with genuine gratitude. Turning to the rear seat of my car, I clutched my briefcase and pulled out the perennial yellow legal pad and a pen.

Seeing that I was in a state of readiness to take notes, McElroy pursed his lips and warned, "If you breathe a word where this tip came from, I'll deny it and call you a liar."

I became so excited and so eager to grasp at any hint of beneficial evidence to help my client that the devil himself could have extracted a Mephistophelian promise of silence and divine loyalty.

"I solemnly promise," I vowed, knowing I was on the verge of a huge revelation, "I'll keep the faith. Now please, what can you tell me to help this poor bastard?"

Torn between loyalty to the prosecution staff and his own religious scruples, McElroy, with a pained expression on his face, began to speak.

"When Dorothy Clark was in a coma at Broward General Hospital, Melrose had a tape recorder at her bedside around-the-clock. She did a lot of talking while she was unconscious and mentioned the names of several fellows that presumably assaulted her." Paranoid with fear, his eyes scoped the dark parking lot for possible eavesdroppers. Grabbing one of my jacket lapels, McElroy entreated, "Get those tapes!"

"You've got to tell me, Robert, what's on those tapes?" I pleaded. "I know this is bothering you, but you must give me some idea of what I am suppose to be looking for."

"All right," sighed the harried investigator. "But you

must swear to me on your honor that you will never reveal the information I give you.''

''I give you my word that I will keep your name out of the entire case.''

Robert McElroy, being somewhat mollified, shook his head sadly as he brought out a clipboard of reports from his well-worn attaché case.

With pen poised, I waited for McElroy to say something, anything. The investigator seemed subdued, as though he was at peace with the world at last, and read aloud in a firm tone:

''Tapes of Dorothy Clark during illness:

August 14, 1968	Mentioned the names of Renee Dusentona and Dave. Said Renee had shot her.
August 15, 1968	Said Robbie put her here. Tall, dark and handsome, twenty-eight years of age, black hair. Lives at Cocoa Beach and works with tools. Robbie Lane lives in a small house in Cocoa and drives a blue car. She once found Merilyn in his car.
August 16, 1968	Fellow had new yellow car. She shot Merilyn and then shot herself.
August 23, 1968	(In answer to question by police 'Who did this to you?') Reply was 'Jerris, he is the one.' California Pete shot her. Came to the airport. Works at Methodist Hospital. (When nurse on duty asked Mrs. Clark 'Who shot you?' her reply was, 'Carl Winkle').

August 24, 1968   Made three different statements
                     to detectives Cox and Basor, in
                     essence that 'There was no way
                     in the world to tie Erler into
                     this.' ''

The chief investigator sorted his notes, methodically placing the clipboard in a larger brown fiber folder marked ''County Solicitor's Office'' and peered through the windshield as if nothing unusual had occurred. He opened the car door and slipped away without saying a single word. I felt sorry to see that McElroy was emotionally drained and felt a twinge of guilt for putting him through such an agonizing experience, but I had a client to defend and now that I was told by the county's chief criminal investigator that Erler might be innocent of the murder charge, my burden and responsibility became heavier.

The early evening gloom of the darkened parking lot at the rear of the restaurant matched my mood which had suddenly become more somber. The invaluable data just received from McElroy was more a curse than a blessing for many reasons, and I heaved a big sigh while mentally kicking off every obstacle cast in my path by the now conscience-relieved public servant. The cardinal, inflexible modus operandi of a criminal defense was disrupted. I never pre-judged the guilt or innocence of a client, keeping an open mind, challenging the prosecution officials to prove guilt beyond a reasonable doubt in the face of every constitutional protection I could build around an accused. Now, almost officially informed of Erler's innocence, my self-imposed charade of neutrality was not applicable and the comfort of utilizing constitutional safeguards wasn't enough to ameliorate the dreadful burden of defending an innocent man of a heinous crime. It was difficult to tear myself away from the parking lot, although the office was only a few blocks away. The office was my haven, my sanctuary, where I could wrestle with these new problems in comparative comfort, but I was transfixed with a growing dejection.

Dorothy Clark's utterances captured on tape during her comatose period certainly would exclude Erler as the only suspect, particularly when the case being made against him rested only on slight and untrustworthy circumstantial evidence. It would also serve to create a reasonable doubt as to Erler's involvement. The problem now was how to flush out the tapes. I couldn't subpoena the tapes because I wasn't supposed to know they existed. Even if that hurdle could be overcome, it would be almost impossible to specify what tapes were sought or when they were made and by whom, because such disclosure would betray the confidence reposed by McElroy. The only solution would be a pretrial motion before the trial judge requiring the State of Florida, and all of its prosecution officials, to make available to the defense all evidence in their possession which might be beneficial to the accused. I started to feel better. That was it! But I knew in my heart that neither Melrose nor the county solicitor would relinquish the tapes because disclosure of their existence would erode the prosecution, even though any such beneficial evidence deliberately suppressed or withheld is violative of a defendant's constitutional rights. "At least that is what the United States Supreme Court said," I remarked caustically to myself.

As I started the car to go home, I recalled Mr. Boone was to present me with a list of witnesses he intended to use at the forthcoming trial together with a schedule of evidentiary material to be introduced in evidence. That would be a good time to ask him if there was any evidence the state may have in its possession which may be beneficial to the defense. I chuckled and thought I would just casually mention the new United States Supreme Court decision on that subject to the prosecutor, just to see what reaction I could perceive. I could almost guess.

It was too early for my appearance before Judge B. L. David, who was assigned to the Erler case, so I made the usual pilgrimage to Tom's snack bar in the courthouse lobby and exchanged greetings with the clerks piled two deep around the counter who were sipping coffee and munching doughnuts. I called out to the proprietor for my usual fare of toasted English muffin and black coffee when Tom acknowledge the order by squinting conspiratorially, beckoning me to come over to the end of the counter. His covert glance meant that Tom was about to impart some important news and I asked, "What's cooking?"

Tom narrowed his eyes and looked over toward his customers, making certain his conversation could not be overheard and said, "Just learned that B. L. David is going to have Republican opposition for his judgeship."

"Who is it?"

"Stokely just qualified for the job."

"Who's Stokely?" I asked.

"A bad bastard, that's who," spat out Tom as he left me to give his attention to the needs of his hungry customers.

I made a mental note to meet with the all-knowing, knowledgeable Harry Long to find out about Judge David's political opponent. The election was scheduled for November 5, and if there should be another Republican landslide like the last one, Stokely would be the new trial judge designated to hear the Erler case. "It would be a shame," I thought, "because there are many legal questions to be resolved and an experienced jurist like Judge David would follow the law, whereas a new, inexperienced fledgling would be inclined to yield to the public clamor, ignited by a relentless press."

Shrugging off these gloomy thoughts, I walked up the rear marble steps to Judge David's courtroom and opened the door to find Assistant County Solicitor Len Boone at the counsel table, his fingers tapping a large fiber folder. He gave me a knowing smile which was more like a leer and said, "All the stuff you're looking for is in here, Joe. You didn't have to make a motion for discovery."

"Thanks, Len," I replied, willing to bet my life the tapes made of Dorothy Clark while she was in a coma at Broward General Hospital would not be disclosed. "Maybe Boone didn't know of the existence of the tapes that would exclude Erler as the sole suspect," I thought. But that was hard to believe because Boone and Melrose were good friends and the odds were that the prosecutor had to know.

"Court's in session," shouted the bailiff. "All rise, the Honorable B. L. David presiding." The smiling, black-robed jurist motioned to the rising spectators and court personnel to remain seated and boomed a resounding "Good morning, folks," to the partially filled room. The judge was a kindly, compassionate individual, a native Floridian, loved and respected by all members of the bar. His large, ruddy face lined with countless wrinkles was testimony to years of farming and exploring wildlife in the Everglades.

I joined in the chorus of "good mornings" in response to the judge's hearty greeting, looking sorrowfully at the pleasant face that would soon vanish if the Republican juggernaut continued to displace all Democratic officeholders this coming November, just weeks away.

"What do we have here this morning?" asked the court, smiling broadly to all the attorneys and court personnel within the enclosure of the bar.

"May it please Your Honor," I began, "the defense has two routine motions for discovery."

"I suppose there aren't any objections the state can make. Did you read the motions, Mr. Boone?"

"I have received copies, Your Honor," replied Boone in his pleasant North Florida drawl, "and they appear to follow the rules."

"Very well" announced the judge, relieved there was no controversy requiring him to make a ruling. "The defendant's motions for discovery are hereby granted. Anything else, gentlemen?"

"One more thing by way of explanation," I broke in. "The first motion for discovery is routine and the clerk's minutes will suffice, but there is a second and special motion for discovery in accordance with the latest pronouncement by the United States Supreme Court."

"What specifically do you want, Counsel?" asked the judge.

"I would appreciate it very much if I may present a written order on my special motion to require the state to produce exculpatory evidence, or any evidence beneficial to the accused that may be in the possession of the prosecutor or prosecution officials."

"Don't see any purpose in that," volunteered Boone.

"It is very important that the state follow the law on this particular point," was my answer. "A written order would serve as a constant reminder to the state of its obligation to provide evidence favorable to the defense."

"I'll sign your special discovery order," said the judge,

reaching over the bench to receive the coveted document from my outstretched hand, and beaming like a proud father at Boone. "I'm sure Len will give you the discovery you want and certainly not hold anything from you," the judge said.

"Yes sir," affirmed Boone with a short vigorous nod, "I'll do that."

"He'll do what?" I wondered as I left the courtroom. It was expected there would be some evidence forthcoming, but would the state produce the Dorothy Clark tapes, or would they play games again? I already made the first move, and their official response would let me know soon enough if Erler would get a fair trial. Many times I cursed the fates that led me to sell my soul to the devil. If only I could reveal that Robert McElroy, the county's chief investigator, knew about the tapes made of Dorothy Clark during her stay at the hospital, naming names of her attackers, establishing the existence of genuinely valid suspects. There was no way of subpoenaing the tapes without divulging the source of the information. The solemn pact I made with McElroy had to be honored at all costs. Unless the state voluntarily disclosed the existence of the tapes under the obligation of the court order and the mandate of the U.S. Supreme Court, the defense team would never know if any of the named suspects mentioned by Dorothy Clark while in a coma were ever contacted or investigated by the prosecution officials.

There was small comfort to be found in creating a two-pronged trap to confound Boone and protect Erler from prosecutorial misconduct. The first facet was the "routine" motion for reciprocal discovery where both sides were obliged to exchange the names and addresses of witnesses who may be privy to the criminal charges made against the accused. McElroy had a list of the named suspects taken from the Dorothy Clark tapes. Melrose knew everything about the tapes. It was his brain child. Certainly there were other police officers in the hospital room when Dorothy Clark uttered the names of her attackers into the recording device that was by her side twenty-four hours per day. I could only make an educated guess that Len Boone also knew, and reasoned, "These named suspects were 'witnesses' within the spirit of the 'reciprocal discovery' rule, and a failure to give these named witnesses to defense counsel constitutes 'violation number one'.''

I abstractedly held up two fingers, saying to myself, ''Violation number two is colder than a whore's heart.'' I knew a deliberate refusal or failure to produce evidence favorable to the accused that may be in the possession of police officials was a transgression of such magnitude it would prove fatal to the prosecution, if uncovered. I sighed, ''It would be so much easier for everyone if only the Dorothy Clark tapes would be disclosed,'' but my heart and mind told me they would remain a deep, dark secret, forever.

By previous arrangement, pursuant to the court's discovery order, I met with Assistant County Solicitor Len Boone in his office on the third floor of the courthouse to examine the evidentiary material the state had in its possession, for use in Erler's murder trial. On the credenza, behind the prosecutor's desk, reposed a three-gallon Stetson hat that was part of Boone's uniform when he was a State Highway Trooper. He wore that on occasion with highly polished, medium-sized motorcycle boots, heralding to all and sundry that he was a law-and-order man. Len was a likeable person, but a cop all the way. Our meeting was very cordial and Boone, taking a large brown bag from the corner of his office, said brightly, ''Here's all there is.'' It was too much for me to hope the large brown bag of evidence also contained the precious Dorothy Clark tapes, but decided to be patient.

''That's just fine, Len,'' I exclaimed eagerly. ''Suppose we make a list of what photos, reports or tapes,'' emphasizing the word ''tapes,'' almost choking as I got that word out. ''I may want to see a copy.''

''Good idea,'' agreed Boone and called in his secretary, directing her to catalogue the pertinent bits of evidence the state had in its possession. ''Here is a photograph of Robert Erler and his wife and child.''

''I don't need a copy of that picture Len, but can you tell me if that singular photograph was ever shown to Dorothy Clark?''

Boone looked at me with a frank, open face and answered, ''Yes, she was shown that picture about five days ago." Then feeling that he had gone too far, Len continued, "That's all I'm going to say about it."

"You showed Mrs. Clark the picture of Erler and his family?" I demanded.

"Sorry, Joe, no more on that subject. Let's go on."

I let my thoughts stray to the courtroom when I would be cross-examining Dorothy Clark and ask, "Mrs. Clark, did anyone ever show you a photograph of the defendant Robert Erler prior to this trial?" "Oh, no sir," she would reply, and I envisioned glancing over to see if Boone would correct his star witness's erroneous statement. "Fat chance," I grumbled to myself. Shaking off my habitual woolgathering fantasies, I returned to reality and saw Boone systematically taking items from the brown bag, one-by-one, which were of problematical importance such as Merilyn's bloodstained clothing, and gory pictures of her body on a slab in the county morgue, depicting five bullet wounds prominently displayed in a partially shaven head. I became angry. I knew the morgue photographs would be placed in evidence. Prosecutors loved to do that in order to shock the jurors and create a subconscious prejudice against the accused. I stopped fuming and sighed, sitting back in my chair with forced resignation. That's the way the game is played.

After depleting the contents of the bag, Boone opened a thick case file on his desk and selected a few sheets of paper.

"Are those lab reports?"

"Yes," answered Boone, "but there's nothing there," and shoved the papers across the desk for examination. I gave them a peremptory glance because my investigator had already advised me that all lab reports were negative.

"I see you fellows even tested the tire prints at the scene. I was never informed about that," I complained.

"We came up lame on that one," said Boone sadly. "No blood samples, no fingerprints, nothing tangible." He acted as though he was about to conclude the meeting. I began to lose my poise because the real purpose of the meeting, the Dorothy Clark tapes, was not even mentioned.

"What about the tapes of any type of conversations?" I asked almost too casually.

"Oh yes," replied Boone, "There are some tapes of a telephone conversation between a Mrs. Kaufman and Erler made at the Hollywood police station, with her permission," he added coyly. "Here's a copy of the transcript of that conversation you may have."

I took the proffered transcript, and didn't let on that I had received a copy long ago, then took the final plunge: "Aren't there any other tapes that the police took in this case?"

"Don't have anything like that here," answered Boone blandly. Then asked, "Are you looking for something specifically?"

I couldn't divulge that I knew what the police had. For the time being, I had to rely on the integrity and honor of the prosecution officials and play a waiting game.

"Just thought," I ventured weakly, "there were some other tapes made by now, you know." I hesitated and faltered, "Maybe by some of the state's witnesses."

Len Boone gave me a crafty look. Maybe he knew what I was driving at, or maybe he didn't. Maybe that was his cute cracker way of enjoying my discomfort. "Tell you what I'm gonna do," said the prosecutor, "I'm just gonna scribble at the bottom of this list that 'any other evidence coming into my possession or knowledge will be immediately turned over to Mr. Varon.' How's that?"

I groaned as Boone raised himself to his full six feet behind his desk and flung out his arms like a Baptist preacher experiencing a catharsis, and happily exclaimed, "Now you have it all, don't you?"

"Not really *all*, Len," I replied, and turning to leave the prosecutor's office, received the classic cracker gig, "Come see us any time, hear?" The parting was just as cordial as the conference, except that a cat and mouse game seemed to be unfolding. After recapping what transpired at the discovery conference, I concluded that Eagle Scout Boone lost a couple of merit badges.

22

BROWARD COUNTY, ON the eastern coast of the Florida peninsula, was a sleeping giant drawing to her shoreline adventurers, real estate speculators, entrepreneurs, pioneers and a variety of misfits. Its population grew so rapidly the United States Chamber of Commerce officially rated the area as the number one growth city in the entire nation, a distinction that prevailed for seventeen consecutive years. New residents were absorbed into the mainstream of the community for a myriad of compelling reasons and an ill premonitory wind impelled Harris Stokely, a thirty-five-year-old Kentucky lawyer, to pull up stakes leaving his domestic woes and other sordid personal affairs in limbo. He desperately needed a new locale where he could forge a new image and make a fresh start among strangers. Florida beckoned, and Stokely responded.

Easter Lily Gates, a beautifully groomed southern belle with a merry face and twinkling eyes, was the Supervisor of Voter Registration for Broward County from time immemorial. No one could remember her predecessor but recalled with sorrow when, after thirty years of public service, Easter Lily retired. The Democratic party had lost their ace recruiter. When a new, aspiring resident came into her office to register, Easter Lily would personally take the application and demurely ask, "Political preference? Democratic of course?"

One morning a man by the name of Stokely came in to register and to file a change of domicile.

Mrs. Gates said, "I see you are an attorney, single, age thirty-five; and now if you please, political preference? I presume Democrat . . ."

"Hold it," snarled Stokely, showing strong, large, yellowing teeth. "Nobody tells me what I am! Put down Republican!"

The blood drained from Easter Lily's face as she gave Mr. Stokely a cold hard stare. Insulted by the crass attitude

of the new resident, practically accusing her of using her
official position for political purposes, which was a violation of the election laws. She made a mental note to have
a talk with Malcolm Porter, the Mayor of Fort Lauderdale,
about this strange, hot-tempered new resident.

The clerk's desk in the municipal courtroom of Fort Lauderdale was directly to the left of the judge's bench and
was occupied by Maria Jordan. The stack of file folders on
her desk bore the case numbers, defendants' names and
municipal offenses charged, corresponding to the docket
sheet from which she would call each case in sequence
when the judge opened court and commenced proceedings.
At the center of the stage she knew the attorneys and court
attachés were looking at her. But her eyes grew cold with
hate when new Assistant City Prosecutor Harris Stokely
strode into view. Maria knew from the very beginning she
had made a mistake in agreeing to go out with him, but
after all, he was a fellow employee and single. She was
divorced with two teenaged children and there weren't too
many unattached men around for companionship. Maria
made a note on her legal pad to seek out Blackie Graham,
the Fort Lauderdale detective, as to the status of her criminal complaint against Stokely, just as Judge Goodman
burst from his chambers and sat down in his large executive
chair behind the judicial bench. The entire courtroom rose
en masse at the judge's explosive entrance, but were hurriedly waved down by the jurist's impatient gesture. The
bailiff halted immediately prior to calling the court to order,
and just as well, as he hated the boring litany of "Hear ye,
hear ye . . . ," but he knew the judge was in his usual hurry
and would make short shrift of the docket so he could return to his law office on Southeast Sixth Street. Arnold
Goodman, a "street smart" Brooklyn boy, accepted the
judicial appointment not for the salary but the prestige, as
well as a good source of business for his law practice. Business was good and the judge was anxious to finish the
docket and get back to the lucrative real estate deal he was
working on, but was annoyed by the slow-moving hayseed
deputy prosecutor impeding rapid progress in his court. Another thing that rankled him about Harris Stokely was the

arrest warrant he signed charging Stokely with the municipal offense of "Discharging a Firearm within the City
Limits." Judge Goodman was well versed in criminal law
and, if the facts as stated on the affidavit for the arrest
warrant were accurate and Stokely had indeed fired a gun
into the home of Maria Jordan, he wondered why Harris
Stokely wasn't charged with a felony as provided by the
Florida Statutes. There was a cover-up somewhere by
someone who wanted to protect Stokely; but who and why?

That afternoon, Maria Jordan sat at a desk in the Fort Lauderdale detective bureau facing Blackie Graham, trying
hard not to cry in disappointment and frustration. Graham,
a suave and worldly fourteen year veteran police investigator, was attempting to let Maria down gently while trying
to convince her that the complaint against Stokely should
be dropped. Placing his beefy hand over Maria's, which
held a piece of Kleenex poised for a cascade of tears, Graham soothed in his most avuncular fashion.

"Honestly, Maria, it's a no-win situation. First, Stokely
is a prosecutor here and a fellow deputy prosecutor in the
next courtroom won't like the idea of going after a col-
league; and there's no way a special prosecutor would be
appointed to handle the case. Second," Graham continued,
"this guy Stokely is about to announce his candidacy for
judge of the Court of Record of Broward County, and none
of us here at city hall want to spoil his chances."

"What?" sputtered Maria. "You guys are giving this
moron a pass at my expense? Have you any idea what a
creep he is? That pot-smoking bastard . . . and you're in the
deal with the rest of them," she sobbed, tearing herself
away from Blackie's attempt at an embrace.

Maria reflected on her options. There had to be some
recourse. She knew where there was a wrong, there had to
be a remedy. Maybe the new county solicitor, being a
woman, would be a kinder spirit and understand how she
was victimized by this uncouth bastard. She continued to
relive all the events leading up to her making the criminal
charges against Stokely.

It took only one date for Maria to decide she wanted no
part of Harris Stokely. She couldn't abide his peculiar man-

nerisms, inane manner of speech, slurred and disjointed, as though he were under the influence of some kind of drugs, and thought it prudent to discourage further association with him. Besides, there was Jack Hansen, a handsome eligible bachelor who evinced a romantic interest in her and she directed her full attention to him. Hansen was a successful, exceedingly well-dressed Fort Lauderdale stockbroker who was highly regarded in the community. Maria was content with him for the first time in the years following her divorce as the two became a familiar sight in the bistros and dining parlors around the city. One evening, as the couple sat in Maria's living room, Stokely crept stealthily up to the open window, and under the cover of darkness peered in to see the visitor of the young lady who was the object of his affections. Unable to identify the man, Stokely yelled into the house, "Who's in there with you?"

The couple stared at each other in disbelief but remained silent. When no response came, the nocturnal intruder shouted, "Whoever is in that room better come out of there immediately!"

Maria put her fingers to her lips warning Hansen to remain quiet. "Sounds like he's drunk or something," whispered Maria. And trying to dispel her fright added, "Just be still and he'll go away."

"Do you know who he is?" asked Hansen.

"It's that Harris Stokely again," was her reply. "Just hush."

Stokely would not be put off and screamed, "If whoever is in that house doesn't come out, I'll start counting backwards and shoot! Here goes: ten, nine, eight, seven, six, five, four, three, two, one," and a gun shot rang out.

Maria and Hansen flung themselves to the floor fearing the gunman would unleash a fusillade of bullets and mortally wound them. Hansen crawled to the window where the shot was fired and peered out. In the darkness he could make out a man standing in the yard holding a gun in his hand. He sank back to the floor and motioned Maria to make a telephone call. Maria, nodding, crawled to the end table where the phone was nestled and dialed the police emergency number. Next she managed to reach the light switch, plunging the room into utter darkness, crawled back towards Hansen and, both frightened, awaited the police. It seemed like an eternity before two Fort Lauderdale police officers arrived at the darkened house and entered throwing their powerful flashlight beams on the cowering couple then piercing the darkness at random through the foyer and living room.

"Why are you sitting here in the dark?" asked the corporal who was the ranking officer.

"Because," responded Maria with a mixture of excitement and fear, "there's a man out there who shot a gun into my home and I'm deathly afraid he isn't through with his shooting."

The corporal looked at Mr. Hansen who he recognized, and asked, "Is that about right, Jack?" and upon receiving a nod of confirmation said, "Let's put the lights on."

"You better look outside in the front to make sure the gunman is gone," suggested Hansen to the corporal who smiled agreeably as though he had the same thought in mind and went to the open window accompanied by his assistant. Both officers sprayed the penetrating beams of their flashlights over the front lawn. Satisfied that the intruder was gone, the living room lights were turned on and they began searching the room for evidence that a shooting had occurred, as reported, before sitting down for the background information, statements and possible identification.

"Look here, Ed!" exclaimed one of the investigating officers, pointing to a leaden slug imbedded at the top of the window sill.

"Was this bullet here before, Mrs. Jordan?"

"No sir, that just happened, and it was Mr. Harris Stokely who shot that bullet just a few minutes ago!"

The officer called "Ed" whistled with disbelief. "Are you saying Lawyer Stokely who works at the hall was the one that did the shooting?"

"You know who that is, don't you?" broke in the junior officer.

"I suppose I do," sighed Ed. "Yessir," he added, heavily. "I'm afraid I do."

"Well, I don't care who he is," Maria snapped. "He almost killed us and it's my intention to prosecute him to the fullest extent of the law."

The corporal now in command of a serious investigation, took out a pocket knife and rooted the leaden missile from the soft wood of the window frame. Tossing it up and down in his hand several times he surmised, "Looks like a .32 caliber to me," and closed his fist over the slug.

"I suggest, ma'am, you stay clear of Attorney Stokely until we contact him. The city attorney will ask you to sign an affidavit for an arrest warrant, maybe make a formal statement," and looking over to Mr. Hansen standing nearby said, "You, too, Jack. As I see it, you were also an intended victim."

"What charge will be made against Stokely?" asked Hansen.

"Oh, probably some kind of felony, but that's up to the city attorney who'll take it up with the county solicitor for prosecution."

Maria went to Len Boone for help and went to great length to acquaint him with the events that led to her almost being killed by Stokely's erratic behavior of shooting a gun into her house. She explained that when she made a formal complaint to the Fort Lauderdale Police, they chose to treat the incident as a violation of a municipal ordinance, rather than a felony charge which should be prosecuted in the criminal court.

"To make matters worse," she went on, "the local police are trying to cover up the affair because of politics."

Boone explained, "I know all about the case . . ."

"You do?" exclaimed Maria in surprise.

"You see, Jack Hansen and I both belong to the Fort Lauderdale Country Club. We discussed the entire matter during lunch, and what happened afterward made Jack so angry he wanted to file a criminal complaint against Stokely."

"Jack never told me," replied the astonished lady. "What else happened?"

"Well," chuckled Boone settling himself comfortably behind his desk preparatory to a long dissertation, "it seems Jack was in his office at the brokerage house when he received a call from Stokely. Jack asked what the hell he wanted and Stokely told him there was a rumor that he had fired a pistol into Maria Jordan's house and that there was no truth to it. Jack told him, 'That's no rumor. I saw you out the window with a gun in your hand and even identified you to the police.' What do you think the crazy fool said to Jack?''

"Can't imagine," Maria replied dutifully.

Boone laughed, "Stokely told him he used to be a marine and was a crack shot. If he wanted to shoot Jack or you, he would have no trouble doing it."

"I'm afraid of this man," said Maria. "He's not only a liar, but on some kind of drug. His strange behavior scares the heck out of me and I can't understand who is trying to protect him, or why?"

"Just an estimated guess, honey," ventured the prosecutor. "No factual basis, no proof. Do you want my feeling on this?"

"Sure," replied the distressed Maria, eagerly at attention.

"We . . . ll," drawled gentle Len in his folksy manner, "your boy Harris Stokely has agreed to be a candidate for the criminal court bench this November on the Republican ticket . . ."

"Republican?" Maria laughed. "It just shows how crazy he is. There are no Republicans around here."

"Hold on, sweetheart," cautioned Boone, placing both palms outward in the direction of his guest. "There's some serious politics developing which are too complicated to talk about now, but with the Vietnam War going on and President Lyndon Johnson's popularity at the lowest point of his career, Republicans have a good chance to be victorious."

"That must be why Blackie Graham has been trying to get me to drop the charges against Stokely," said Maria. Looking up defiantly to the prosecutor across the desk, she asked, "Is that why you didn't file charges on behalf of Jack Hansen?"

"Not at all, dear," reassured the slightly annoyed prosecutor. "It was a matter of protocol. The local police must bring their reports, evidence, list of witnesses and recommendation of charges to this office for evaluation. They didn't do that. Instead they opted to prosecute in city court.

It was their choice, their decision and apparently the city chose not to prosecute.''

"But you have the power to file a direct criminal charge, don't you?" she asked firmly.

"Yes," answered the prosecutor. "But the Speedy Trial Rule prevents me from taking any action at this time. I'm genuinely sorry."

Boone was sorry about more than Maria's unpunished perpetrator. His entire career was now at stake because of the coming Republican landslide. Angie Weir was a Democrat and an interim candidate. The new Republican county solicitor would clean house of all Democratic employees and Boone would be thrust out with them unless a drastic change in his political ideology occurred. He agonized over the decision he was inexorably compelled to make. Boone was a native son of Chipley in the northern part of Florida, a dyed-in-the-wool Democrat like his forefathers before him who grew up believing the word "Republican" to be synonymous with "Damn Yankee Carpet-bagger." But he was relatively new in Broward County and had a family to support. The handwriting was on the wall: approach Easter Lily Gates with a request to change his voting registration. And he did.

23

IT WAS FRIDAY and I completed the mandatory calendar call requirement in Broward's Criminal Court of Record, as well as disposing of pretrial motions in pending cases. I enjoyed Fridays at the courthouse. The employees and court attachés were happily looking forward to the long weekend. Their jovial spirits usually caused a holiday atmosphere to permeate through the marble-floored halls. I was caught in the upbeat aura that prevailed and decided to touch base with my famous client before heading homeward for a pleasant weekend of golf.

The security guard at the county jail always let me through the gate without the usual identification prelimi-

Robert Erler (far left) with fellow Hollywood Police Department Officers and a news reporter looking at the covered body of the murdered girl, Merilyn Clark, at the Hollywood Industrial Park. She was found with five bullet shots in her head. Photo taken shortly after Officer Erler reported discovering the fatal shooting.

This photo of the victim, 12-year-old Merilyn Clark, was found in her mother's wallet after the mother was found nearby with five bullet shots in her head.

Dorothy Clark's 1960 Falcon discovered at the Fort Lauderdale Airport where she was found in a critically wounded condition.

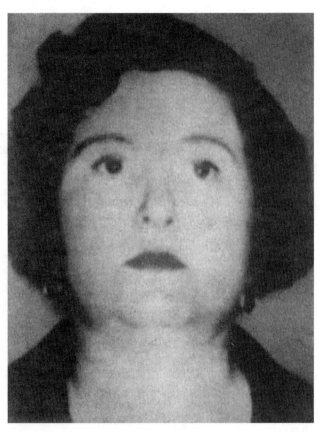

Mrs. Dorothy Clark

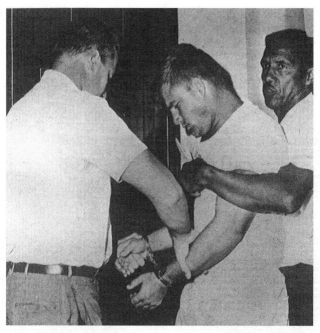

Handcuffed and under heavy guard, Erler is shown here being taken to the Magistrate in Phoenix, Arizona for arraignment.

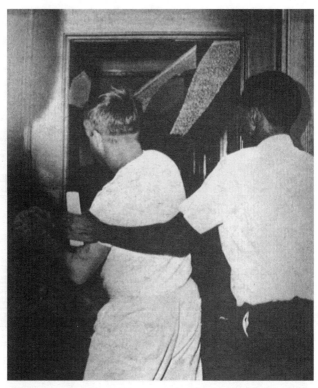

Under the influence of countless pain pills and after being subjected to taunts from police and reporters, Erler smashes the glass of the Magistrate's door.

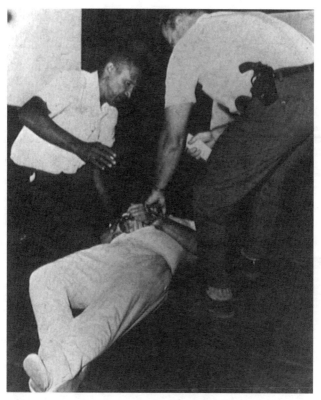

The accused is shown here unconscious and on the floor of the courthouse after his outburst. He had to be rushed to a nearby hospital to have his wrist stitched up before proceeding with the hearing.

A montage of the headlines on this infamous case.

naries because he was always "remembered" at Christmas, birthdays, holidays and even made up special occasions that required "remembering." I was directed to a smaller type conference room as the main consulting room was occupied by an assistant public defender who was working on a new case.

"Let me get you into the big room," suggested the guard. "I'll kick those guys outta there."

"No, please," I begged. "I'm only going to be there a minute, just to say 'hello' and I'm gone. Thanks anyway," I smiled, rewarding the jailer with an unobtrusive handshake enclosing a neatly folded ten dollar bill. The grateful guard left and I was thinking about what to say to Erler to justify the visitation, and thought I would report that the motion for a speedy trial was filed and the state would have to bring Erler to trial within ninety days or be forever barred from future prosecution. There would be no continuances and the trial would go forth no later than the middle of January 1969. I only hoped that Judge B. L. David, to whom the case was assigned, would be re-elected in November. Judge David was a Democrat, but would be unable to survive if he was opposed by any Republican. My thoughts were interrupted by a sober, grim-looking Erler who stood stonily erect in front of me.

"How goes it, Bob?" I asked more out of habit than anything else, as it was apparent he was obviously perturbed about something. Erler clenched both his fists causing his heavily muscled biceps to ripple menacingly.

"Those bastards called me out of my cell because 'someone important' was going to talk to me, and took me to the conference room where this asshole cop was pretending to be the psychiatrist you were to send over!"

"Wait a minute, Bob," I cautioned. "Please take it easy. Did you find out the name of the police officer who came to see you?"

"His name is Melrose," came the angry retort.

I was slowly becoming furious. It was against the law for a police officer to interview an accused who is represented by an attorney of record and, although the courts have universally declared that any statement or evidence procured from a defendant under those circumstances is inadmissible, Robert John Erler was a 'special target' who I feared would be given a special interpretation of the prevailing law, to his detriment.

"Please relax," I urged. "Let me put this in its proper perspective," trying to assuage the agitated Erler. "You have to admit you were anxiously awaiting a visit from my psychiatrist, Dr. McIntyre, and when you saw this stranger you probably asked, 'Hello, are you the psychiatrist?' and a clever police officer like Melrose would probably have said, 'There are certain areas I want to examine,' or perhaps, 'I'm here to make an observation'—or maybe even used the word 'evaluation.'" Frankly, I was angry that Melrose visited Erler at all, deliberately violating the law, and wondered how this episode would affect Erler's frame of mind.

"It was just by luck that I found out that prick was a lieutenant on the Fort Lauderdale police force."

"How was that?" I questioned, relieved to note Erler had calmed down.

The security guard at the door poked his head into the conference room and said, "Lieutenant Melrose, one of the trusties back here would like a word with you when you're through with Erler." I made a mental note to "remember" the jailer at my earliest opportunity, and laughed, "So that's how you were tipped off?" Erler nodded, obviously pleased that he had uncovered Melrose's ruse. Relieved to note that Erler's rage had subsided and rather than further discuss the detective's motives, which would only serve to arouse my client, I suggested, "So far there were no blood stains found on any of the old clothes taken from your old trailer—no fingerprints—nothing—so they are grabbing at straws. Maybe that's why Melrose came to see you. Did you say anything at all to him?"

"No, sir. I remembered you told me not to speak to anyone, so I just told this guy to bug off."

I smiled and said, "That's excellent," and since Erler seemed in a receptive mood, I thought this would be a good time to discuss the telephone conversation with Mrs. Claire Kaufman. "Bob, do you recall anything about your telephone calls with a lady by the name of Claire Kaufman?"

"She's my friend," was the quick reply. "I called her a

couple of times before I was arrested in Phoenix.''

"Do you remember Mrs. Kaufman calling you while you were in custody in Phoenix—remember you were in county jail after you surrendered?''

"Oh, yes, I have a vague recollection," and frowned as he tried to recall the conversation.

"Did you know," I pressed on, "that she was calling you from the Hollywood Police Department?''

"Of course not," he answered in surprise. "Why would she call from the police department?''

"And did you know, or did she tell you, that your telephone conversation was being taped and monitored by the Hollywood police?''

"No, no one ever told me that—what does that mean? What's this all about?''

I took a calculated risk. There was no way of knowing if my client, after all he'd been through, was mentally equipped to cope with the news about to be imparted. "Bob, your friend Mrs. Kaufman went to the Hollywood Police Department to see Detective John Cox. A call was put through to the Sheriff's Office in Phoenix and Cox was at the other end, taping the call. That tape is the biggest piece of evidence the state has against you.''

Erler ran his fingers through his hair. "I can't believe this. Claire is my friend—she would never do anything to hurt me. Frankly, I don't remember anything I said—too many pills and stuff—I was half out of my mind." He looked around the room in despair and asked, "Did I say anything wrong?''

"Not really," I equivocated, "but I'll try to have a talk with Mrs. Kaufman and get to the bottom of things.''

"Absolutely, Claire will cooperate. In fact, I'm going to call her this evening and tell her you'll be contacting her. She's my best friend.''

"Thanks, Bob." I rose to my feet and moved toward the door, "You did very well by not talking to Melrose. Just keep Rule Number One in mind—no talking to anyone!''

"I guess I did too much talking already," was his wry response.

I tried to comfort him by saying, "We'll see, we'll see,"

but was inclined to agree with his sad remark that he already did too much talking.

Good, competent legal secretaries are made in heaven, and Lucy, my personal secretary should have been elevated to sainthood for putting up with my inexplicable idiosyncrasies. In countless criminal trials, Lucy, having graduated from legal secretary to "legal assistant," would sit in the front row behind the defense counsel table, notebook in hand, pencil poised to render a myriad of services to assist me. Rarely would there be any communication or sign discernible to an outsider, but a raised eyebrow or a knowing look would set wheels in motion, particularly during jury selection at the preliminary stages of a trial. When a prospective juror was being qualified and asked about previous jury service on another criminal case and the juror answered in the affirmative, I would ask, "When did you serve and in whose courtroom? Do you remember the name of the judge?" When the juror answered and the pertinent data was provided, Lucy needed no signal. She would slip unobtrusively from her seat, running to the judge's chamber on whose case the juror had previously sat, and find out from the secretary what the verdict had been. I would stall the jury selection process, going on to the next juror, until I saw Lucy back in her seat. If she gave me a "thumbs up" signal indicating the prospective juror was one of the panel who voted for acquittal the juror would be accepted. On the other hand, if Lucy gave a "thumbs down" signal it meant the juror voted to convict, and was casually dismissed peremptorily.

Claire Kaufman was among the missing. Phone calls were not answered. Letters from my office were returned by the postal service marked "acceptance refused." Her obvious lack of cooperation was of great concern to me since she was a vital witness in the murder trial. The burning question was, "Whose side was she on?" Bob Erler advised me most assuredly that "Claire was his best friend and would do anything to help him." I was inclined to doubt this and resigned myself to consider Mrs. Kaufman a hostile witness until one morning, when no court work required my presence in Fort Lauderdale, Lucy was reviewing my schedule for the day and calmly stated, "At 2:00 you have an appointment here with Mrs. Claire Kaufman."

I absorbed this bombshell with the same equanimity with which it was delivered, and like all vain employers who unnecessarily withhold due credit, assumed a casual air and replied, "Thanks, I'll be here." Lucy concealed her disappointment and walked briskly away. I looked at her retreating figure in awe. "How did she manage to pull this off?" and shook my head in amazement. Perhaps accolades were in order; at least an expression of gratitude or congratulations for an impossible job well done. I didn't, but in hindsight I should have at least said, "Thanks, Lucy."

At 2:00 P.M. on the button the receptionist announced that Mrs. Kaufman had arrived for her appointment. I all but flew down the corridor to the reception room and saw a lovely brunette, tastefully attired in a black and white cotton suit, rise from the leather couch as soon as I entered the room and announce, "Hi, I'm Claire Kaufman."

"And I'm Joe Varon, Bob's lawyer. Thanks for coming." Taking her arm, I gently ushered her towards my office in the rear of the building all the while making a quick appraisal of the woman's attitude, but gleaning nothing from her vapid patrician features. "This one's an enigma," I decided. "She's a flake that could go either way: defense or prosecution." What she had done to date made me feel there was little to gain from her unless Mrs. Kaufman would admit being lured into making the recorded telephone conversation with Erler or that the tapes were made without her knowledge or consent.

In such eventuality I could make a motion in court to exclude the tapes from evidence because of illegal or impermissive telephonic interception. The whole legal concept rested on her. The crux of the whole case boiled down to a single, solitary issue: "Did she, or did she not, authorize the police to tape her conversation with Erler?" Yes or no, just as simple as that!

My educated guess was that Mrs. Claire Kaufman became a willing dupe of the police who took advantage of her cupidity and used her to entrap her friend into making a dubious, left-handed admission that he committed the girl's murder. I could just hear the prosecutor arguing to the jury, "When Erler was asked, 'Bob, did you do this thing?' his answer was, 'Gee, Claire, I don't know!' " It was abundantly clear to me why Mrs. Kaufman was making herself scarce. Another element that flashed across my mind was Claire's husband, Al, may have been slightly suspicious of his wife's friendship with the handsome ex-cop, and it was possible that he exerted an appreciable amount of influence on Claire's actions, well intended or not.

"It was very nice of you to come and help Bob Erler," I began sincerely. "Just want a little background first; how you met, what kind of work he did for you and your husband, and in general your relationship . . ." I stopped in the middle of my question, noting Mrs. Kaufman was about to say something.

"I know, I know," repeated Claire. "The first time we met was when Bob was a police officer in Dania and he stopped me for speeding, and after we became more acquainted, he did some work for us—we own Jiffy Clamp Company in Hollywood," she added proudly, "and it was because of our friendship that I prevailed upon him to waive extradition and surrender to the Florida authorities. In fact," she went on, "Detective Cox of the Hollywood Police gives me credit for Bob's safe return."

"That was very nice of you," I agreed wondering if that wasn't part of John Cox's con game to enlist Mrs. Kaufman as a member of the prosecution team. I also had to wonder when a cop gives a person a ticket for speeding, such an act does not exactly endear the motorist to the police officer, unless some special dispensation is given to forgive the annoying and costly traffic infraction. "I'm glad you mentioned Detective Cox," I said, getting down to business. "The principal reason for this meeting is to see if you recall the details of a telephone call you made to Bob Erler last September."

"Certainly. I spoke with Bob many times in September. He called me from Phoenix right after the news broke that he was wanted for murder."

"The telephone call I'm interested in," I suggested warily, "is the one you made on September 17, 1968, to Robert when he was in the Maricopa County Jail, just after he surrendered."

"At my request . . ." she pridefully interjected as a reminder to me of the power she wielded over Bob Erler. "Yes," she continued. "I vividly recall the circumstances of contacting Robert when he was in the county jail there."

"How did it come about that you made the call from the Hollywood Police Department?" I asked in a most casual manner, attempting not to betray how crucial this particular line of inquiry was. I had a feeling that Mrs. Kaufman was enjoying her role in this murder drama. She displayed a modicum of modesty in order to minimize the importance of her participation. She looked at me with a blank, childlike, innocent stare. I waited for her answer to this question, and kept my eyes focused on her lovely face, beginning to understand why Erler had an affinity for her. She adjusted her beautifully groomed raven hair in preparation for a long discourse and finally began.

"I had been trying to reach Bob in the jail in Phoenix and no one there gave me any consideration and finally I contacted Woody Malphurs—you know—the Hollywood Police Chief. He turned me over to his assistant, Carl King, who came over to my house with Detective John Cox."

"I'm beginning to understand the chronology, Mrs. Kaufman. May I ask what you said to the police and what they said to you?"

"Well"—she paused to examine her meticulously manicured nails—"I told them Bob was threatening to commit suicide because the Phoenix cops were going to kill him and if I could reach him and speak with him, he would listen to me and do anything I asked."

"That's probably true," I encouraged. "Then what?"

"Detective Cox was very understanding and considerate, and suggested that perhaps he could help get the call through for me from the Hollywood police station, you know—one police department to another."

"Good ole Cox," I mused to myself. It was plain to me how the detective maneuvered her with his wily avuncular tactics. I could even write the script. Here was this timorous, well-intentioned young lady in an emotional quandary and this kindly, grey-haired, sympathetic police officer would solve her problem. The telephone call would be made from the Hollywood Police Department, at no cost to her, and for cutting through the red tape she would be grateful. The rest would be easy.

"Claire, I'd like to ask you some very important questions and I know you'll be truthful. Your answers will mean a lot to Bob's defense so please consider carefully before you reply."

"I'll answer to the best of my recollection."

"Thank you, Claire. First question. Did you know your conversation with Bob Erler was being taped?"

"Not really," was the reply. My heart leaped.

"I don't understand what you mean by 'not really.' Either you knew your talk with Erler on September 17 was taped, or you didn't know. Which is it?"

"Sorry, but I didn't know what was going on. I was so wrapped up in speaking to Bob, everything was in a state of confusion."

"Second question, Claire. Did Robert Erler know the conversation was being taped?"

"Oh, no," she hastily replied. "He never knew. I certainly didn't discuss that with him."

"Now for the third and most important question. Did Lieutenant Cox or anyone else in that room where the call was being made ask you for permission to tape your telephone conversation with Erler?"

"Not exactly," was the equivocal response.

My head started to ache fiercely and I could feel my blood pressure rising. "This woman was either being cute," I fumed, "or had committed herself to the side of the prosecution." I hated being toyed with by this poker-faced woman, but she was deadly and exercised a great restraint in the next series of questions which only infuriated me more. All of her responses were masterpieces of evasion, leading me to conclude Bob Erler lost what he thought to be a valuable ally. She was definitely on the side of the prosecution. Forcing what I hoped was an understanding smile, masking my disappointment, I asked, "Claire, don't you remember if Lieutenant Cox or Carl King or Lieutenant Goetz, or any other police officer asked for permission to record your conversation with Bob Erler?"

"I really don't recall any such thing," she admitted.

"Would the answer then be," I hopefully asked, " 'No one in that room asked me for permission to tape my private talk with Robert Erler.' "

"The answer is," she firmly stated, "I don't recall anyone asking me for specific permission to tape my telephone conversation with Bob."

"I'll settle for that answer, Claire, and thank you very much for your assistance. Your testimony will be important at the trial." I briefly sighed with relief, but the gnawing doubt of inadequacy prevailed.

"If Claire Kaufman truly wanted to help Erler," I theorized, "she would hold fast to her statement that 'no one asked her for permission to tape her private talk with Robert Erler,' and at an evidentiary hearing in court, on a defense motion to suppress the tapes, the judge hearing the motion would refuse to allow the prosecution to use them at the trial."

"Is there anything further you want from me?" Claire asked coyly.

"Yes, Mrs. Kaufman," I answered. "I would like to call in one of the stenographers and take your sworn statement so there will be no misunderstanding . . ."

"Sworn statement about what?" asked Mrs. Kaufman, drawing herself up in her chair as though she were personally insulted.

"A sworn statement by you," I replied speaking slowly as a chill enveloped my entire body, "to the effect that no one asked your permission to tape your private conversation with Bob Erler when he was in Arizona last September 17."

"Sorry," she answered. "No statement."

"But why?"

"My husband doesn't want me to get involved, and that's why we are leaving town."

"I need you as a witness in court at a pretrial hearing," I pleaded, trying to hold on to the last vestige of hope.

"Sorry, Mr. Varon, we are leaving this afternoon, so don't bother to look for me," and clutching her black patent leather bag, turned and unceremoniously marched out of the office, leaving me both dejected and agitated.

24 _____

THE RUMOR MILL kept grinding away and well-meaning courthouse employees who were sympathetic toward me would come up with juicy morsels and tidbits in the stairwells and corridors, then dart away in conspiratorial secrecy. Only Harry Long's rumor of a line-up had any basis of reasonableness, which reminded me there was another chore for the investigator. No valid information was forthcoming about Dorothy Clark from Broward General Hospital. Was she recovering? What about her mental faculties? Could she make an eyeball identification? Detective Melrose and the hospital staff kept an iron lid on security, but I knew my investigator could penetrate the secrecy that surrounded the mother of the dead girl. On the telephone, I directed that Long make discreet inquiries about Mrs. Clark's mental and physical condition but was interrupted by Long's cheery laugh.

"Way ahead of you, pal. Maybe you should meet me in the conference room at the courthouse library, there are so many things to discuss."

"Like what?" was my curious response.

"Like everything! You pick it," chortled the investigator, enjoying my frustration. "Which do you want first, the good news or the bad news?" This type of trite banter infuriated me. But I knew from experience that Harry Long just loved to tease me. Harry was the best investigator around so I had to abide his little quirks in order to accomplish good results. Suppressing my annoyance, I promised, "See you there in twenty minutes," and made a mad rush out of the office to meet my tormentor, curious to learn what new aggravation he had in store for me.

I approached the sundry counter on the first floor of the courthouse run by old reliable Tom, who used to be a semi-professional baseball player until he lost most of his eyesight. I never knew Tom's last name, but we became friends over the years and Tom greeted me warmly.

"Hi there, Tom. Can you rustle me up a few of those Baby Ruth bars?"

"They're no good for your waistline, Counselor," answered the ex-ball player.

"Not for me, Tom." I smiled. "It's for Harry Long. I'm meeting him in a few minutes and want to sweeten him up."

Tom ran his fingers over several cartons on the back shelf, coming to rest on the box containing the proper candy bars and handed me three, accepting a five-dollar bill in payment for which no change was expected. "C'mere," whispered Tom. I moved closer.

"Hear there is a line-up due for your boy and a lot of special preparations being made to shaft you."

"Thanks, Tom," I replied sincerely. "I'm to get some low-down from Harry who is waiting upstairs."

"Keep the faith," and gave me a thumbs-up sign, as I waved my hand in return, not knowing whether the vendor could see my abrupt departure.

Harry was sprawled in a large chair with the usual unruly clutter of papers scattered before him on the otherwise barren conference table. He casually accepted my offer of candy and thrust two into the right-hand pocket of his pastel green sport jacket; then, with maddening slowness, began to unwrap the bar hidden in his meat-like hand.

"Okay, you had your jollies," I started. "Now tell me what you've got in that twisted mind of yours."

The investigator laughed with genuine gusto. "I have so much to tell you I just don't know where to start."

This was the price that must be paid for having the best investigator in the state. I resigned myself to my fate and simply sat quietly in the chair until Harry decided to begin his report. Fanning through the pieces and bits of crumpled notes, although the investigator knew the contents of each by heart, he said, "Dorothy Clark is on the road to recovery."

"What about her physical and mental condition?" I broke in impatiently.

"She still has the five leaden pellets imbedded in her head. The surgeon in attendance can remove at least three bullets, and may have already by this time, but two have to remain in her head because of their proximity to the brain. There's a partial paralysis in her face but she can speak well enough.''

"What about the possibility of an eyeball identification? Can she do it?"

Harry reached into his jacket, retrieving a second Baby Ruth, and looking at me with amusement before he unleashed some disquieting information said, "They are doing a real job on that girl. They have been showing her pictures and orienting her to events that may have happened."

"Who is doing it?" I asked, as if I didn't know.

"Who else?"

I remained thoughtfully quiet in the chair. My worst fears were now being realized. The showing of photographs of the defendant prior to viewing him in a line-up is morally and legally improper. This type of impermissive suggestibility is designed to aid a victim make an identification of an attacker or assailant.

A police line-up is an old tried-and-true investigative procedure where a suspect is lined up with five or six other individuals presumably of the same height, weight and coloration and wearing similar clothing, and required to stand under glaring lights on a stage or raised dais. The victim or potential witness is placed in another room at a vantage point, or behind a one-way mirror, undetected by the individuals being viewed in the line-up and make an identification if possible.

The officers conducting the line-up must not give any hint or indication in what position the suspect is standing. To make certain the viewers do not speculate or make a random guess, the positions of the line-up are changed. Sometimes the individuals in the line-up are changed. Sometimes the individuals in the line-up are given placards with numbers on them, and asked to utter a few words, usually catchphrases used in the commission of the criminal offense under investigation. Of course, the criminal investigators arranging the line-up are legally and morally prohibited from showing the viewers any photographs of the principal suspect immediately prior to the viewing. The courts have universally condemned such impermissive suggestibility and zealously guard a suspect's rights when a line-up is conducted, even to the right to have a lawyer present to supervise the procedure.

"Got a couple of unfounded rumors," continued the investigator. "Can check them out if you wish. One is that Dorothy Clark was spirited out of the hospital by Johnnie Melrose and spent a cozy afternoon in the East Side Saloon in Fort Lauderdale." Long looked in my direction for an outburst which never erupted and recited another rumor he heard about Dorothy Clark attending a grand old southern cookout where a beer party was in full swing. Booze, Brunswick Stew and barbecue at Len Boone's home.

"That means," I reflected, "Mrs. Clark is in pretty fair shape physically and will participate quite effectively in a line-up, should there be one."

"Oh, there surely will be a line-up. That's gospel," said the investigator. "You didn't tell me if you wanted any of these rumors checked out."

"Not necessary," I answered. "It looks like the prosecution is grooming its star witness, but let me tell you, Harry, if they do have a line-up, it will be fully supervised by me and conducted according to the law."

The investigator wiped the last vestige of chocolate from his face and lips and asked, "Anything you want done for the line-up?"

"Not now, Harry. I'll have a list of things to be done, but we'll cross that bridge when we get formal notice."

"They don't usually give formal notice," warned the investigator. "We never did when I was on the force."

"Things are different now," I replied, "but maybe you have a point. As long as I'm in the building, I'll pay a visit to Erler and direct him not to participate in any kind of line-up without my being present."

I was getting a jittery feeling in my stomach. It had been a long afternoon and it was obvious the investigator was by no means finished with his report, but I had heard enough disconcerting news to occupy me for the present. Moreover, the matter of the forthcoming line-up was of major importance.

I waited impatiently in the main conference room of Broward's jail for the arrival of Erler, to orient him on strategic procedure for the police line-up inexorably due to be held. It shocked me to see an enraged Robert Erler burst into the room, his handsome face distorted, eyes rolling wildly and so distraught he couldn't speak coherently. I thought to myself, "My God, now what?"

"What on earth is happening?" I asked in amazement. I had been under the impression Erler was in good spirits and calmly looking forward to his trial.

"It's the head jailer, Sullivan. He came into my cell locked the door and tried to grill me . . ."

"What was he grilling you about? What did you do?"

"He wanted me to tell him what I did with the gun. Said I hid it and insisted on my telling him where."

The anger in Erler's voice was alarming. I believed he was approaching the emotional level of violence and was greatly concerned. There was no reason for Lieutenant Sullivan to get into the act on his own volition, unless he was requested to do so by someone on the prosecution staff or investigating officers, which was improper!

"Just take it easy," I ordered, reminding myself that Erler needed a psychiatric evaluation, and it became even more evident by his current emotional display of ungovernable temper. It was imperative, despite Erler's unstable condition, to make an effort to explain Maurice Sullivan's conduct, hoping my explanation would calm him down.

"Listen Bob, finding the gun is very important to the prosecution's case. Unless the murder weapon is found, there can be no ballistics test to establish that the bullets found in the dead girl's head came from a particular gun."

"You should have seen how that bastard Sullivan kept ragging me about the gun. He insisted I had stashed it somewhere and said I better tell him or I'd be back chained up in solitary."

"He'd be some great hero if he came up with the gun," I said. "The missing weapon could be traced to its owner, or witnesses might be found who could testify to its ownership." Erler was nodding his head, absorbing the logic of my argument, and I added, "Sullivan's job must be boring and he wanted to get into the action."

"I won't take this shit much longer. First Melrose posing

as a psychiatrist and now this jerk Sullivan pulling rank.
I'll take care of that guy," said Erler.

"Don't do anything you'll be sorry for," I pleaded, trying to placate him. "I'll talk to the sheriff about this and
it will never happen again." Nothing Erler's convulsed facial features receding to normalcy, I tried to reinstate a
serene atmosphere by saying, "The reason I came to see
you today was to alert you. It's possible the state will try
to run a line-up on you. Are you familiar with the concept
of a line-up?"

"Yes, sir," replied Erler, straightening in his chair, fully
attentive and clear of eye. "We had all that at the academy."

"You will probably be called upon for a line-up any time
now. Regardless of whether it's a line-up for another inmate
or even yours, you are not, I repeat—you are not to be in
any line-up unless I am present. Do you understand?"

"Yes, sir," answered Erler, now fully alert. "Unless you
are there, no line-up of any kind."

"Good," I smiled, and just as I shook hands with Erler
prior to departing from the conference room, Maurice Sullivan approached the doorway and beckoned to me.

"Have some news for you, Counsellor," greeted the
jailer. "I was ordered by the prosecutor to arrange a line-
up for your client."

"And I have news for you, too," I quickly replied. "You
better make all the arrangements with me, because there
will be no line-up unless I am personally present to supervise the procedure." I didn't like the idea of Maurice Sullivan, whose sole duty was to control the general population
of the county jail, having such close ties with the prosecutor's office. I debated with myself. Should I talk to Sullivan about playing detective with Erler? Finally, I decided
to make a private complaint to the sheriff, who would handle the problem in a diplomatic manner.

Bob Erler heard the discussion between us and signified
his understanding by making a "zero" with the thumb and
index finger of his right hand. It was gratifying that Erler
was able to smile again, but two chores remained. I had to
see Sheriff Michel; and second, but more important, Erler
had to be examined by a psychiatrist. It was apparent that

my client seemed to yield to the most trivial extrinsic pressures and I wondered how Erler could cope with the line-up, let alone the trial. What would happen if a witness testifying for the state gave damaging evidence that Erler knew was untrue? Would he demonstrate his displeasure by a violent outburst in the courtroom?

Such an occurrence would certainly prejudice the jury against Erler. Another sickening thought: how on earth could Erler, in his volatile state, withstand the grueling cross-examination the prosecutor would administer when he took the stand? That possibility presented another dilemma. The only way to prevent Erler from being crucified on cross-examination was to keep him off the witness stand. An accused, in a criminal case, is not required to take the witness stand in his own defense, nor can he be compelled to testify at his trail, but I knew from experience that the jury wants to hear the defendant's story from his own lips. The court always instructs the jury that an accused need not take the stand in his own behalf, as the "Not Guilty" plea he entered at his initial arraignment constitutes a denial of the charges, and no presumption or inference should be made when the defendant exercises his privilege not to testify; but those words fall on deaf ears. The jurors want to hear the defendant's version of the case, and if he doesn't take the stand on his own behalf, they usually accept the prosecution's testimony and evidence as being true. With this strategy, the defense almost invites the jury to find the client guilty of the offense charged.

The decision as to whether Erler would take the stand in his own defense was a strategic one that would be made at time of trial depending upon how matters were developing. I shrugged off these troubling thoughts and walked across the hall to use the telephone available to all lawyers, as well as engage in small talk with the judge's secretary. I always made it a point to cultivate friendship with the secretaries and court aides to the trial judges for the purpose of exchanging juicy morsels of gossip along with helpful hints: the judge's moods, inclinations and sometimes, his proposed rulings.

"Hello, Mr. Varon," greeted the judge's secretary with a bright smile. "Did you want to see my boss?"

I said, "No thanks. Just want to use the phone to call the sheriff."

"Oh, did you hear that the sheriff just married his secretary?"

"Gosh no," was my surprised answer. "I must see him. Hope he's not on his honeymoon."

"Probably not," replied Jennie, folding her arms. "From what I hear, they've been having their 'honeymoon' for the past four months, so as soon as her divorce became final, they tied the knot."

"Shame on you, Jennie. I do believe you're jealous. Maybe the same thing will happen to you," I replied.

"Not a chance," smiled Jennie, and her softly molded features took on a serious demeanor. "I'll be lucky to have a job after this November. The old man told me he expects a Republican landslide and we will both be kicked out of here."

"Does the judge have Republican opposition?"

"Not yet, but we hear the assistant prosecutor in Fort Lauderdale municipal court, Harris Stokely, will run against him."

"Stokely?" I answered. "The name sounds familiar."

"Some weird nut," replied Jennie, bravely brightening. "So we'll see," and turned her attention to the file of papers on the desk to keep from dwelling on her problematical future.

I was fortunate to get through to the sheriff's beautiful blonde secretary, and after congratulating her on the sudden marriage to Alan Michel told her of my urgent need for a personal talk with her boss. "Hold on a minute," she ordered, checking the sheriff's availability. She returned to the phone with a cheerful "Come right over." I thanked her profusely, "I'm on my way."

Alan Michel was seated in his large, cheerful office behind a massive desk puffing contentedly on a long cigar. "What can I do for you, Joe?" he asked in his usual pleasant manner.

"Sheriff, I have to make a serious complaint against the head jailer, Maurice Sullivan," and went into detail about how Sullivan grilled my client about the gun he was supposed to have used in the murder of Merilyn Clark and demanded being told where the gun was hidden.

"I can't understand that," answered the sheriff, knitting his brows, which further darkened his sallow features. "If Maury did anything like that, you can believe it was without my knowledge or consent."

"I know that," was my quick response. "Just had an idea that some of the police investigators may have pressed him into doing a favor or pressure must have come from the prosecutor's office."

"Or maybe," mused the sheriff, "Maury was bored and wanted a little action. You know," he smiled, "duty in the cell block can become monotonous and he wanted to be a big man."

"Sheriff, you of all people should know that nobody has the right to interrogate a prisoner who is represented by an attorney, and even though Lieutenant Sullivan is the head custodian of the cell block, he still wears a badge and is still a cop with a deputy sheriff's insignia."

"You're absolutely right. He should be fired or transferred to the road."

"Please don't do that, Alan. Just tell him to leave Erler alone and not bother him anymore. My client got very upset at the lieutenant's action—"

"I know," smiled Michel relieved that he wouldn't have to take disciplinary action. "I heard about how Erler gets upset. There have already been a number of incidents and a few inmates got their heads bashed in. Frankly, I'll be glad when he gets the hell out of here; that guy is a walking time bomb."

"Just wanted to clear this problem up with you before going for a court order," I said, slightly ashamed of myself for making an unnecessary veiled threat.

"Leave everything to me," assured the sheriff. "I'll call Maury in and give him specific orders to stay away from your client and not to ask him any questions bearing on the case."

"Thanks, Sheriff." I rose from my seat, reaching over to shake hands.

The sheriff reiterated in a stern voice, "If he ever does anything like that again, I guarantee he'll be canned!"

25

A CRUCIAL DECISION had to be made almost immediately. Pangs of guilt assailed me as I realized Erler simply must be examined by a psychiatrist without further delay. There were too many areas of stress emerging and I worried how my client would address each incident as it arose. "How would Erler react when he was told of his 'friend' Claire Kaufman's lack of cooperation?" The line-up was due in a few days and I had to prepare Erler, instructing him about the format, what questions he would be asked, the manner of his responses, and above all, I worried about what the piercing lights on the stage would do to his mental stability. Erler had said he knew about line-ups from his training at the police academy, but Erler never stood under the blinding lights like an insect being examined under a microscope. There was no time to lose. I felt derelict in delaying this vital duty and looked to my old friend, Doctor Clifford McIntyre, a prominent Fort Lauderdale psychiatrist-neurologist for assistance. I had been greatly impressed by Doctor McIntyre when he first testified in a criminal case as an expert witness. In addition to his brilliant courtroom testimony, he had the unique faculty of capturing the jury's undivided attention and general acceptance of his expertise. The good doctor, dressed neatly in a plaid sport jacket, probably with the design of his family's Scottish clan, light brown slacks matching his sparse, reddish brown hair, would cross his long legs, adjust his glasses and face the jury, beginning a lecture-type testimony in simplistic terms as if he were a professor in a classroom explaining to his students the complex machinations of human behavior. Doctor McIntyre had such a consuming affinity for criminal law that he enrolled in the University of Miami Law School, eventually procuring his coveted law degree, a rare combination of doctor and lawyer.

I was impelled to impose on my friendship with Mc-

Intyre and telephoned, "Doctor Mac, I need some help with a client—"

"Hold it," replied the doctor. "What about the cordial amenities? No 'Hello, how are you?' You sound like you need some help yourself."

"Sorry, Mac," I apologized sheepishly, chagrined for my lack of manners, "but I have to ask for a big favor."

"Fire away," said the doctor expectantly.

"I realize this is short notice, but I'm really pressed for time. I have a client in jail that requires a psychiatric evaluation. His name is Robert John Erler and he's in the Broward County Jail on a homicide charge. I must have an immediate report."

"Any emphasis on a particular area?" asked the doctor.

"I'm concerned about his erratic behavior and wonder if there is some underlying psychosis present."

"Are you considering an insanity defense?" the doctor asked, the sublimated trial lawyer in him coming out.

"Just want to rule out that possibility in an abundance of caution," was the answer.

"I'll take a look at him and see what's there. Please inform your client to expect me."

"Thank you, Doc. I'll see Erler this afternoon and give him your name and description. Don't be surprised if he seems a bit wary, or asks for identification. One of the clowns in the Fort Lauderdale Police Department pulled the 'doctor' act on him, after I alerted Erler a psychiatrist of my choice would be visiting him soon."

"Then you goofed and sat on your hands," chided the understanding doctor. "That explains the rush."

"I know, I know," was my contrite response. "Thanks for helping me out of this mess."

The daily eight-mile trek from my office to the Fort Lauderdale courthouse gave me time for thoughtful reflection in the privacy of my automobile. By the time my destination was reached, a format of meetings and court commitments were solidified. The first order of business this morning was Mr. Robert John Erler, and I skipped the usual stop at the snack bar, taking the elevator directly to the cell block that housed my notorious client. Approaching the heavy plate glass window to request permission to see Erler, the deputy at the receiving station saw me and rolled his eyes upwards, which was his way of telling me that Erler was involved in another jailhouse fracas.

Waiting for Bob to appear in the conference room, I conjectured about what mood he'd be in as there was much to discuss. I decided to play it by ear. After a few moments of speculation, in strode Erler, smiling broadly, once again holding his hands high above his head proudly demonstrating his new-found freedom from restraints. I decided there and then to give him the full treatment.

"You look wonderful Bob," I began, pretending not to notice the almost raw abrasion over his left eye. "How's everything?"

"Under control. Just a few rhubarbs with some of the new inmates, but nothing I couldn't handle."

"We've got a lot to talk about. First and foremost, my good friend Doctor Clifford McIntyre will come to see you for a cursory examination."

"Is he the shrink you wanted me to see?"

"He is a well-qualified psychiatrist," I corrected pointedly, "and you will like him. I'd appreciate your full cooperation. Please be as candid and open with him as you are with me."

"Tell me what he looks like so I can be sure who I'm talking to. I don't want to be suckered like that Fort Lauderdale cop tried to do to me."

"Doctor McIntyre will show you one of his business cards. If he doesn't start off that way, just ask him for identification; he'll understand. He is about forty-five, six feet tall, around 185 to 190 pounds, wears glasses and has reddish brown thinning hair and is light complected."

Erler thoughtfully absorbed the description and discerning his continued reluctance to be examined, I ventured on to another subject. "By the way, I told Sheriff Michel all about Lieutenant Sullivan and how he ragged you about the gun. Michel was so angry he wanted to fire the lieutenant. I begged him not to do that, just order him to get off your back."

"That's a help. I have to watch out from all ends. Everyone seems to be gunning for me. There are no friends in this place, only enemies.''

Now was the time for a rude awakening. Noting Erler was comparatively at ease, I addressed another troublesome problem. "Speaking of friends," I began cautiously, "I met your friend Claire Kaufman and asked for a sworn statement concerning the telephone call she made to you in Phoenix from the Hollywood police station. She refused and demonstrated a marked lack of cooperation."

"What?" he slowly exhaled with a genuine puzzled demeanor. "Claire is my friend. She's the only person who called to help me when I was in jail in Phoenix. I can't believe she would turn her back to me now."

"She gave the lame excuse that her husband 'didn't want her to become involved,' reporting that she was leaving town and told me it's no use looking for her." It was painful to see the sorrowful expression in Erler's eyes and I tried to explain there seemed a groundswell of ominous conspiracy in the air and he should not be too optimistic about getting any help from his old friends. Erler had to be made to understand that it was that very same phone call Claire Kaufman made to him in jail, supposedly to help him, that the prosecution was relying on as a type of implied confession.

"But I never confessed to anything, especially when I didn't do anything," pleaded Erler.

"Let me give it to you straight, Bob," I said bluntly, making myself as comfortable as possible on the hard wooden chair, preparing for a long explanation which Erler would have to understand. "You may not remember, but when she called you from the Hollywood police station she specifically asked, 'Bob, did you do this?' and in your drugged stupor you answered, 'Gee, Claire, I don't know.' That constitutes a damaging acknowledgement that you committed the murder, but didn't know why you did it." I let this sink in and waited for Erler's reaction.

"Oh God, I can't believe she did that to me," he answered, visibly agitated.

"Really?" I continued, trying to veil my sarcasm. "Let me read you another excerpt of the conversation," and opening my briefcase pulled out the transcript of the telephone conversation, leafing through the pages to find the pertinent part and read,

Mrs. Kaufman: 'You don't know if you did it?'

Erler: 'No.'

Mrs. Kaufman: ' . . . Do you remember this little girl?'

Erler: 'I don't want to talk about that on the phone, Claire.' "

It was too dangerous to dwell on this unforeseen turn of events for fear my client would plunge into an abyss of depression that could create additional problems, which I certainly didn't need right now. Gathering up my notes, preparing to leave, I perceived Erler to be in reasonable control of his emotions and asked, "Are you all right, Bob?"

Erler shook his head like a prizefighter in a boxing arena, abruptly snapping out of his trance he asked, "Why is Claire so important?"

I returned to my seat, satisfied that my client had returned to the real world, and tried to answer the question. "You must know it's against the law to intercept or record a person's private telephone conversation unless the party at the other end is aware the call is being taped."

"Understood," was the laconic response. "I never knew the call from Claire was being taped. She never told me."

"However," I went on, "an exception to this rule would be if the caller, who in this case is Claire Kaufman, authorized the police department to tape her conversation as a part of a criminal investigation. In that event the tapes would be admissible in evidence against you and the jury would be allowed to speculate on the nonsensical statements you made and the sinister connotations the prosecutor will attach to them, claiming they are tacit confessions."

"I'm sure Claire didn't give the police permission to tape our private conversations," Erler said hopefully. "What if she says in court that she didn't authorize the Hollywood police to tape the call, then what?''

"In that case," I smiled, "there can be no voice comparisons and the jury will not have the opportunity to hear the foolish answers you gave when you were asked if you murdered the little girl.''

I was not as optimistic as Erler about which way Claire Kaufman would testify. Erler sat silently in the conference room engrossed in his own thoughts. I also had my private thoughts about the case, but kept my own counsel. As my worried client began to wring his hands, he looked up and asked, "So they need those tapes to bury me in court. Is that the whole issue?''

"If that tape gets into evidence at the trial, the prosecutor will also use it as a standard of comparison and have witnesses testify that your voice on the tape sounds like the voice of the 'Catch Me Killer' who called the sheriff's office last August to report the murders of three people.''

"It looks bad for me, doesn't it.''

"My job," I continued, not answering my client's question, "is to move to suppress the taped conversation because it was illegally procured. If we are successful in keeping the tape from being admitted into evidence, there can be no voice identification, nor will your so-called 'confession' be read to the jury.''

"Claire really nailed the coffin, didn't she?'' Erler asked. "It can't be, it just can't be," he said pounding his clenched fist on the table in disbelief.

I was sorely tempted to tell Erler that he should write off Mrs. Claire Kaufman from his diminishing roster of friends but somehow felt he already was resigned to that conclusion, and would receive no comfort in relying upon her as a cooperative defense witness.

"Okay," I cheerfully burst into the gloom in an effort to brighten the atmosphere, "now I have some good news.''

"Like what?'' Erler asked with renewed interest, willing to accept any kind of respite from the depression that was permeating the close quarters of the conference room.

"My investigator reported that the FBI laboratory in Washington gave the county solicitor a report on the strands

of hair from the headband found crammed between the
seats of your old Mustang and three tresses clipped from
Merilyn Clark's head. You recall I told you about the ex-
humation? The follicles on each hair specimen didn't match
any of the hair samples from the headband, and there being
no other pertinent points of similarity, the official report
was negative.''

"I told you that headband belonged to my wife Pattie,"
sulked Erler like a spoiled child who was wrongly accused
of a misprision.

"And I believed you," was my placating reply, "but
don't forget, all this was strictly hush-hush. If it weren't
for Harry Long, we wouldn't have known about the headband, or their sending it to the FBI in Washington for a lab
comparison with the dead girl's hair samples.''

Erler slowly shook his head in disbelief. "Any more
deep, dark secrets I should know about? The line-up, for
example?"

Realizing Erler's attention span was being stretched to
the limit, I cut off further discussion with an airy laugh,
"Have to rush off," and extended my outstretched hand in
a parting gesture that either Erler was unable to perceive
through his glazed, staring eyes or didn't care anymore.

On the eight-mile ride back to Hollywood, the late afternoon traffic on Federal Highway gave me time to dwell
on the type of preparations and progress the prosecution
officials must have made in order to declare they were
ready for a line-up. It had to be assumed the murder victim's mother, Dorothy Clark, was on the road to recovery
despite the five leaden pellets imbedded in her head, which
had to remain in her cranial area because of their perilous
proximity to the brain cavity. Undoubtedly she had recovered well enough to be indoctrinated on how she would
identify Erler in the line-up. My educated guess was that
Dorothy Clark was shown Erler's picture over and over
again so she would have little or no trouble picking him
out in a six man line-up.

One more logical assumption to be considered was the
possibility of the existence of an eyewitness to either the
shooting of Merilyn or her mother, but I shrugged that off
as being too remote. Besides, if there were truly an eyeball

witness, Harry Long would have known about it. As I parked the car in the rear parking lot of my office building, I fully realized that the first and foremost order of business would be to prepare for the line-up which would play a critical part in the proceedings.

As soon as I walked through the conference room into my office and saw a huge stack of unfinished correspondence on the desk, a sudden weariness came over me. It was a reminder that things were getting too intense and that I needed a little R & R. I had just shrugged off all thoughts of a long weekend vacation and was starting to read some letters when Lucy announced that Meyer Lansky, a long-time client, was in the reception room and just wanted to "touch base."

I was caught a little off guard because Meyer usually called ahead of time before a meeting. When Lucy escorted Meyer in, he seemed to be in unusually good spirits, although I couldn't figure out why. He lost his fabulous Florida gambling empire in 1952. He was kicked out of Cuba in 1956. It was now an open "secret" that he was running the Lucayan Beach Casino in the Bahamas. After some amiable small talk, I asked about accommodations for the following weekend. On the one hand, Meyer denied even to me, that he had anything to do with the Bahamas operation. On the other hand, however, he suggested that I call "Dusty" Peters who would "comp" me and attend to all my needs. That was my tip-off that Meyer was indeed involved in the Bahamas but wanted to keep it under wraps because I knew Dusty had been his personal bag man for years.

After Meyer left the office, I called Dusty, made arrangements, and kept my fingers crossed that the Erler line-up next week would not dampen my well-needed getaway to the islands.

IV
THE LINE-UP

26

THE SOOTHING, CARIBBEAN weekend passed too quickly and early Monday morning I was back in my office going over the chores listed on a yellow pad in their respective order of priority. I was certain Doctor McIntyre had visited Erler but there was no time to wait for the written evaluation, so I called him at home using the unlisted number reserved only for emergencies.

"Doctor Mac," I began apologetically, "please excuse my impatience, but every time I've seen Erler he alarms me by exhibiting different types of personalities. There are some very sensitive pretrial procedures he has to go through and I'm wondering if he has the mental stamina to withstand some rough spots."

"What kind of sensitive procedures is your client facing?" McIntyre asked in his quiet hypnotic voice, making me speculate if it was the doctor who was so inquisitive or "Counsellor McIntyre" wanting to know what was going on with the case.

"Bob Erler is due to face a line-up and being a former cop, he knows how these things are rigged. I'm worried about whether he is mentally tough enough to take the heat."

"I was just formalizing my report," countered the psychiatrist, "and since you want the bottom line, your client is sane. He certainly can distinguish the difference between right and wrong. Although there appears to be a slight clouding of his sensorium, no evidence appears of a psychotic disorder. As for his ability to withstand the rigors of a line-up, the answer is a definite yes! Your man is a survivor, so go ahead with the line-up."

"What about the rest of the report?"

"You'll have the entire report in a couple of days. Let me read the summarized conclusion:

The psychiatric examination showed Mr. Erler to be moderately depressed with intermittent fearfulness.

This seemed to be directly related to feelings of anguish and loss of his wife and son. His personality characteristics suggest he is an overly determined person who could act repulsively and angrily when those controls were broken down by strong emotional feelings. In other words, Mr. Erler seems to be a sociopathic personality; an angry and hostile person under a controlled façade.

Frankly, I was disappointed at the doctor's evaluation, which was not even borderline psychosis. The psychiatric report was of no value from a defense standpoint and only served to rule out an insanity plea. There could be an area, I considered, where the psychiatrist could use his courtroom magic interposing a defense of "diminished capacity," but on reflection, it would not be feasible to go that route as the criminal act would have to be conceded before trying to avoid criminal responsibility because of mental aberrations or emotional instability. The maneuver was a classic example of what defense attorneys call "Confession and Avoidance." This strategy was immediately dismissed from my mind since Erler steadfastly maintained his innocence. "So, here I am" I lamented, "with a mentally crippled client, but not incapacitated enough emotionally to explain his irrational behavior."

The latest addition to my office staff was a young lawyer from the University of Florida who had never practiced law, but immediately upon graduation from law school taught a class at the university on appellate brief writing. Eddie Kay was a slightly built, handsome young man with an aquiline nose and blue eyes under a bountiful head of curly black hair. I invited him into my office one afternoon and explained to the eager neophyte the posture of the forthcoming Erler trial and the role he would play in the line-up procedure.

"I want you to contact Leon Gagliardi who lives here in Hollywood, and tell him he is needed to photograph the entire line-up procedure." Nothing the law clerk's puzzled glance, I continued, "Gagliardi must faithfully record everything that goes on in that viewing room." For emphasis, I repeated, "Everything, and be certain to tell Leon he may be required to testify about what he saw or heard. The pictures he takes will lend validity to his testimony, which I'm certain will be required."

"Excuse me, but isn't Gagliardi affiliated with the Hollywood Police Department?" Eddie asked.

"Not exactly. Leon is an ex-officio police officer who does freelance work as an independent. The Hollywood police use him extensively because he usually gets to the scene whenever there's been an accident, shooting or murder before any of the police arrive, so they buy his pictures."

"Gotcha," Eddie responded. "I'll get on it right away. What's my job at the viewing?"

"You'll be stationed in the anteroom with Dorothy Clark, and whoever else will be there behind the one-way mirror, to make certain no police officer exerts any influence on her or any other viewer. Take notes of what anyone says to Dorothy Clark, because you also may be called to testify about what went on in the viewing area. Who knows? Many peculiar things occur and we want to be ready for any eventuality."

"You mean, in case someone throws a hint to Mrs. Clark to help her make an identification?"

Pleased that the young clerk quickly understood the defense strategy, I stressed the importance of memorializing the coming events. "Just keep taking notes. Take notes of everything. No matter what anyone says, just take notes. If anybody there winks, raises an eyebrow, coughs, belches or farts, take notes."

September 24, 1968. The much heralded line-up was scheduled in a specially constructed facility in the courthouse abutting the county jail. Newspaper reporters and media photographers were barred from the line-up viewing, but had collected outside the room, eagerly awaiting the results expected by the confident prosecution staff. Eddie Kay, impeccably attired in a three-piece striped blue suit with a leather envelope under his arm containing an ample supply of note paper and a Norelco recorder, was in an impatient state of readiness, waiting for the festivities to commence.

Leon Gagliardi completed setting up the cameras and lighting equipment and sat on the corner of a desk mopping his
brow and muttering inaudibly to himself, anxious to get to
work. It was considerably past the appointed hour but no
police officers or representatives of the prosecution team
made an appearance. This unusual delay puzzled me. There
were ground rules to be agreed upon and a format of conduct established.

Lowering his head like a bull about to make a charge,
Gagliardi growled, "Something funny is going on." His
menacing glare was directed to the sound of a door being
opened from the adjoining jail portion of the newly built
viewing room, as Wayne Madole, a Broward County Deputy Sheriff, made his entry.

"Hello, Wayne," was my greeting. "What's the delay?"

Madole was noncommittal, which was one of the reasons
I didn't like his attitude, along with his insolence and air
of superiority. Gagliardi didn't like the deputy's arrogance
either and looked in my direction for tacit permission to
confront the annoying deputy sheriff. It was tempting to
turn Gagliardi loose on Madole, but the result would be
counter-productive. I inwardly laughed, imagining the
burly, heavily muscled police photographer tearing into the
swaggering, sneering deputy, and shook my head imperceptibly to Gagliardi, who returned to his seat on the desk
corner, clenching his fists in frustration.

"We've been waiting for over an hour," I complained
to Deputy Madole. "No one has discussed the ground rules
with me. I'm entitled to see my client and the other five
subjects that are to be viewed. I want to check their clothing
as to similarity. Also, where the hell is Dorothy Clark?"

Wayne Madole merely looked at me as though he was
seeing me for the first time. The deputy's serpentine
bronze-like face was devoid of expression. He slowly
turned away indicating there would be no response to my
question. I could feel the animosity Madole had for me so
I told him heatedly, "If this line-up doesn't start in five
minutes, we're leaving and there will be no line-up."

Madole walked briskly out of the room while Gagliardi
prominently displayed his chronometer-type watch to mark
time, his perpetual menacing stare promising that there

would not be a second's delay beyond the allotted period. The dilatory tactics were puzzling and I began to harbor a number of suspicious thoughts. "Perhaps," I wondered, "Dorothy Clark was being prompted, or pictures of Erler were being exhibited to her hinting toward an identification. Also, it was possible that Mrs. Clark was still debilitated from her traumatic assault and unable to participate in the line-up procedure."

A burst of floodlights cascaded over an elevated dais positioned directly across the viewing room which was protected by a one-way mirror. I realized activities would commence momentarily and immediately dispatched Eddie Kay to his command post in the viewing room. Leon Gagliardi, camera in hand, snapped to attention, alert and ready. Deputy Madole opened the door leading from the jail and escorted five inmates and Erler to the highly illuminated stage, all dressed in white tee shirts and nondescript trousers. As Deputy Madole was positioning the subjects under the large black numerals painted on the rear wall, I hazarded a guess that the wily deputy would place Erler under the numeral "5" since that was the first digit that traditionally comes to mind in the event a viewer has uncertainties. I cursed myself for being right. Madole placed Erler under the huge numeral "5" and stepped back as if to admire his handiwork.

My mind was racing. Things were happening a bit too fast for comfort. Gagliardi was taking pictures of the inmates standing at ease under their respective numbers, which gave me an opportunity to scrutinize the physical appearances of the subjects on the stage. "Wayne," I complained, "none of these inmates are as clean shaven as my client, which makes my man a 'standout'."

"Why do you say that?" asked the deputy with mock innocence. "They're about the same height and they're all wearing white tee shirts."

"Yes, but the hair styles on the other five are all different, their weights are radically different, one guy has elongated sideburns and another has a small moustache and goatee."

"So what?" replied the deputy.

"So, I want new men in the line-up who are clean shaven

with uniform hair styles and approximately the same weight.''

"Sorry,'' said Madole, turning away as I shouted to Gagliardi in a loud voice so Eddie Kay, in his viewing room, could hear and know what was happening center stage, "Leon, take accurate pictures of this phony line-up with particular emphasis on the hair styles and moustaches of the men.''

All six prisoners stood at attention under the glaring lights on the dais, awaiting the viewing and identification by the state's star witness.

It was no surprise to see Lieutenant Johnnie Melrose in the crowded viewing room. The real shock was that Johnnie was present without his prodigy, Mrs. Dorothy Clark. Before the question could form on my lips, it was answered when I observed Mrs. Clark gently ushered into the viewing room resting on the proffered arm of Prosecutor Len Boone. Her closely cropped hair and dark sunglasses created a melodramatic atmosphere, and she was obviously savoring all the deferential attention bestowed upon her. Walking with mincing steps to disguise her awkward corpulence, Dorothy disengaged her arm from Boone's protective embrace and stumbled heavily into the chair held out by Deputy Madole. I sidled over to Eddie Kay, and our eyes met with mutual confirmation of what must be closely monitored. Both men watched Dorothy Clark and her bevy of police escorts to make certain she would not be prompted or coached into making an identification.

The six inmates to be viewed obediently waited on the dais under their respective numerals. Erler was the number five man in the group. I felt comfortable with Eddie in close proximity, openly taking copious notes, discouraging the likelihood that any of the prosecution officials in the viewing room would dare venture a sign or hint to the witness as to which one of the six men on the stage was the person who shot her and killed her daughter Merilyn.

"Now, Dorothy,'' Len Boone drawled pleasantly, pointing to the dais in the next room, "tell us please, ma'am, if you have ever seen any one of these men before?''

Mrs. Clark looked intently at the six individuals on the

stage and haltingly, almost apologetically, said in a low, subdued voice, "No, I'm sorry."

A hush fell over the room as Prosecutor Boone and the officers present conducting the line-up looked at each other in agonized silence. Lieutenant Melrose and Lieutenant Cox were shocked by Dorothy Clark's inability to make any kind of identification. I drew a great sigh of relief and said with an air of finality, "I guess that does it! Let's clear out of here—the ball game's over."

"Hold on!" commanded the prosecutor. "Let's shift the positions around. Maybe different areas have different lighting features and will give Dorothy a chance for a better look."

Despite my vigorous protests, the officers took Boone's cue and in a matter of seconds, congregated on the stage with Wayne Madole, rearranging the positions of the inmates for a second viewing by Mrs. Clark. A fleeting thought flashed through my mind: "Perhaps this would be a propitious time to make an irate display of vexation and angrily walk out of the room, calling a halt to the aborted line-up." On the other hand, I reasoned, "If, upon a second line-up, Dorothy Clark was still unable to make an identification, the murder charges in all probability would be dropped." I mentally rolled the dice and took a calculated risk, reluctantly agreeing to the second attempt at identification. Naturally, Dorothy Clark had to be aware of the dialogue and discussions that ensued as a result of her failure to point out a suspect. The victim also had to be worried because she knew an identification of a suspect was required of her. I was bordering on the edge of paranoia. My troubled mind orchestrated the drama about to unfold: The police officials were relying heavily upon Dorothy Clark to make a positive identification. She had to repay them for all the medical attention and favors she received during her miraculous recovery. It was payback time.

The state's star witness slowly rose from her armchair, waving away the outstretched hands of Boone and Madole. Nervously adjusting her sunglasses, she stared into the next room with a fierce determination to reward the prosecution officials who were relying so heavily upon her for a satisfactory performance. She looked at the stage a long time, focusing on one person, then another, then repeating the procedure and finally turned to Lieutenant Melrose, "I don't see the man who shot me and my Merilyn," and began to weep softly, knowing she failed to be of service to the people who were of such great help to her.

"That's it!" I shouted triumphantly, and yelled over to the puzzled inmates standing on the stage. "Show's over. No more line-ups!"

I deliberately made my remarks to the group, generally, as I didn't want to pinpoint Erler in case Dorothy Clark was still in the viewing room with Madole and the rest of the police officers.

Quickly dismantling his lighting equipment, Gagliardi muttered, just loud enough for me to hear, "Let's get the hell out of here before the cracker gets any more bright ideas."

I ran out the door with my two assistants into a swarm of newspaper reporters and television photographers. "What happened in there?" demanded the anxious reporters almost in unison. Angie Weir emerged from nowhere with a visibly pained look on her face, Len Boone by her side looking more angry than disappointed. I shamefully exhibited a latent mean streak I never realized I possessed, standing smugly by to force the county solicitor into making the announcement that the state's star witness failed on two occasions to identify a suspect.

"Angie," pleaded Doug McQuarrie, the ace reporter and hatchet man for the *Fort Lauderdale News*. "Did Mrs. Clark identify Erler as her attacker?"

"She was unable to make an identification," was her quiet reply.

"Does that mean the murder charges against Erler will be dropped?" questioned the reporter.

"Erler will go to trial on January 27," Boone broke in, as he steered the crestfallen county solicitor away from the milling throng.

My happy smile began to fade as I worried, "How does the prosecution intend to overcome two failures of Dorothy Clark to identify Erler?"

27

DURING THE CIVIL War, or the "War Between the States," as the deep down, dyed-in-the-wool Southerners preferred to call it, Florida had aligned herself with her sister southern states in the Confederate cause. In 1865, with the abolition of slavery and the ending of the war, Florida was penniless and reeling from the exploitation of northern investors scornfully referred to as "Carpetbaggers" by the resentful local gentry.

Historians record the peacetime economic and political reorganization of Florida as the "Reconstruction Era" rampant with land theft, corruption at every level of political office, flagrant fraud at the polls so the power structure of the new Republican Party reigned supreme. It was not until the election of 1876 that the Democratic Party burst forth in unprecedented aggressiveness to overthrow the radical Republican Party.

When the last Republican left the state capital at the end of the Reconstruction period, Florida started the slow process of restoration of her pride and economic distress, in that order. For almost a century there was no such word as "Republican" in Florida. Every resident was a registered Democrat, and many a transplanted emigrant sought refuge in the Democratic closet of intimidation. There was no need for a Republican primary election. Every aspirant for political office ran on the Democratic ticket and whatever candidate won the Democratic primary was considered the duly elected official, since there was no Republican opponent to render opposition. This lopsided condition prevailed until 1966 when President Lyndon Johnson's popularity sunk to ominous depths due to his generalship of the Vietnam conflict. His "Great Society" had quickly gone away. The citizenry became angry and rebellious as a dormant Republican party was reborn with a vengeance. At the voting booths, the mutinous voters utterly destroyed the Democratic slate of candidates for public office.

Professional and career politicians along with appointed bureaucrats learned a lesson from this voter upheaval and changed their registration from Democrat to Republican. They wagered the landslide would be repeated, thus allowing them to retain their positions in local and state offices. A two-party system was crystallized in Florida. The Democrats were doomed, and there was every reason to think the 1968 general election of Richard Nixon would result in a Republican sweep at the polls on almost every level.

In Claude Anderson's Bonding Company on Southeast Sixth Street just west of the courthouse, the only bail and surety office in the entire county, Harry Long was permitted to use gratis a converted storage room for his investigation office. Harry didn't have his name on the plate glass window in front. It was not necessary, because everyone in the courthouse knew where the burly investigator could be found, except when on the road in quest of cover-ups or hidden secrets which he relished and savored like an antique dealer zealously coveting an invaluable artifact, just discovered.

Harry summoned me to his office for a "hot" report on Stokely and I obediently sat stiffly in the single steel framed chair in his office, careful not to let my dark blue silk suit jacket scrape against the torn, leatherette backing. On a small wooden desk rested an ancient black Royal typewriter whose flaking paint was randomly sprinkled on the desk's surface. "Of course," I noted to myself, looking around at the dismal surroundings, "Harry would make certain he would have a spanking, brand new executive leather chair for his big, fat ass." It irked me to look at the grinning investigator sprawled in his overstuffed judge's chair, gobbling a chocolate bar, taking his blessed time, knowing all the while I was chafing at the bit, just dying to know what he learned about Harris Stokely, the attorney who may be the new judge on the Erler case.

Harry Long finished eating his candy bar. He licked his fingers; licked his lips. He folded the candy bar wrapper and consigned it to a wastebasket at the side of his desk.

I was fuming and ready to explode, but maintained a cold, steady gaze on the twinkling dark eyes of the playful investigator. Harry delighted in teasing and knew exactly how to cause me distress. I was aware of this masochism but the investigator was a genius in ferreting out inaccessible data. "So," I reasoned, "what if I do get an ulcer from this cat and mouse game? It's the results that count."

"Okay, Tubby," I began, "you had your fun, now what can you tell me about this fellow Stokely?"

"Why do you want to zero in on this guy?" countered the investigator.

"Because I've been hearing so many negative things about him and he is a cinch to replace Judge David come next election. I want some input to decide if a change of venue is prudent or maybe petition for a different judge to hear the Erler case."

"What you may have heard is nothing compared to what I have to report. For openers, this guy Stokely is as crazy as a loon. Sit back and relax while I tell you the bad news." The investigator just loved it when he saw the unhappy look on my face. He scored a bull's-eye, and having accomplished his mischievous purpose, reverted to his role as investigator and divulged the information he was being paid for.

"Harris Stokely is a loner. He came from farm country in Virginia and after a nasty divorce, left a lot of creditors holding the bag. Stokely's drinking problems landed him in a sanitarium and his old law partner could not say if he was institutionalized because of the booze or a mental breakdown. The joker has done a lot of crazy things that you wouldn't believe."

"Like what?" I grumbled.

"There is a barbershop in Fort Lauderdale that has women barbers. It is rumored he would go in for a shave, and stretch out prone in the barber's chair. When the female operator placed the sheet over him preparatory to shaving, he would take out his dick and try to guide the lady barber's hand under the sheet to fondle him."

"That was a dangerous thing to do," I replied, "with a razor in the lady barber's other hand? He's lucky she didn't circumcise him."

"Oh, the gals knew what the score was," laughed the investigator. "He's pulled that act many times before."

"Sounds like a nut, all right. What else?"

"After getting a job as an assistant prosecutor in the Municipal Court in Fort Lauderdale, he started dating a gal who worked as a clerk in the courtroom, and when she gave him the freeze, he shadowed her night and day like a hunter stalks his prey. He spied on her one night when she was entertaining a new boyfriend and this crazy bastard shoots a gun right into the living room. He could have killed somebody."

"Are the felony charges still pending against him?"

"Felony charges, hell," sputtered the investigator, "he was only cited for a simple violation of the city ordinance of discharging a firearm within municipal limits."

"Who engineered that abomination?" I asked in surprise, obviously disappointed because a felony conviction would automatically disqualify Stokely from judicial office.

"Detective Melrose was the Fort Lauderdale police officer who executed the affidavit accusing Stokely with the watered down charge," answered Long.

Melrose was becoming too prominent in the Erler prosecution and loose ends of the puzzle were sprouting in all directions, like the snakes of Medusa's head. I began to pinpoint mentally who the principal adversary would be, when the sadistic investigator snickered, and broke into my thoughts, "Now are you ready for the really big news?"

"What now?" I asked uneasily, always becoming gravely concerned when the ace investigator gave his diabolical snicker.

"Harris Stokely has a big hard-on for you," and he roared until he was breathless, choking with paroxysms of laughter.

"Me?" I exploded. "A hard-on for me? I never met him. Don't know him. Never spoke to him and if he walked through that door, I would never recognize him!"

"Sorry, Counselor," said the investigator, becoming serious in a genuine effort to allay my consternation, "but that's the story in the Stokely camp."

"This whole thing is crazy," was my subdued response. "When this guy becomes a judge," I looked stonily at my investigator, "remember I didn't say 'if he becomes a judge,' I said 'when he becomes a judge' it will be my turn to make a decision."

"You mean to petition the court for his removal because of personal prejudice?" asked the experienced investigator. There was no reply to be made. My thoughts were intent upon the bottle of Rolaids reposing in the glove compartment of my car parked outside the bail bond office, which was the only panacea to quell the raging torment in my stomach. Another ameliorative remedy was to get away from that grinning Buddha-like, fat ass ex-cop of an investigator.

November 5. Election day in Broward County. The Republican juggernaut that made political history by electing a Republican governor of Florida for the first time in a hundred years rolled over the entire Democratic slate in Broward. Mrs. Angeline Weir, the incumbent county solicitor running for re-election on the Democratic ticket, lost to a virtually unknown lawyer, James Geiger, whose only attribute was that he belonged to the Fort Lauderdale Republican Club. A serious, tragic casualty to the community at large was the loss of the judicial post of Democratic incumbent B. L. David to an unknown Republican, Harris J. Stokely, who would be the designated trial judge in the Erler murder case next January.

28

THE MORNING PAPERS had headlines screaming, "MRS. CLARK FAILS TO IDENTIFY ERLER," and went into detail about the two line-ups that were unfruitful. If and when the case went to trial, it was hoped the prospective jurors would remember how Dorothy Clark failed to pick Erler out of the line-up after two attempts. But the trial would not take place until January 27, almost three months away. This critical episode would be forgotten by then, but it was my intention to make an issue of the line-up incident at the trial and envisioned Dorothy Clark admitting she could not identify Robert Erler as her assailant, even though he stood directly in front of her. Eddie Kay and Leon Gagliardi would make good, credible witnesses. Although the utter failure of Dorothy Clark to identify Erler undoubtedly dealt a crippling blow to the prosecution's chances for success, there remained one gnawing question that lurked in the back of my mind: "How would the prosecutor overcome it?" I began to feel uneasy. Erler's chances of acquittal were too good. There was a total lack of evidence which the prosecution must use in order to procure a murder conviction. There were no eyewitnesses; no murder weapon; no ballistic tests or paraffin tests for gunpowder stains on Erler's hands; no spectrographic or scientific tests to compare Erler's recorded voice as a standard of comparison for voice identification with the original recorded on the *Catch Me Killer* tape. I worried, "Things look too good for comfort."

There were many other criminal cases that occupied my time and attention while awaiting the Erler case to come to trial. Balancing the paradoxical equities of the case, it was prudent to reluctantly abandon the idea of moving to have Stokely recused as the trial judge, because any further delay of the trial would create insurmountable problems. There was Erler's propensity toward violence in the event an inmate or jail guard tormented him, which could result in generating prejudicial publicity. Another probability was the state would have more time to come up with some new or surprising evidence to solidify their position. Of course, there was the ever-present news media lurking dangerously on the sidelines, keeping the bizarre story of the 'Catch Me Killer' painfully alive with suggestive inferences, none of which were favorable to Erler.

Within two weeks after Judge Stokely ascended the bench as the duly qualified Associate Judge of the Broward Court of Record, the entire courthouse was buzzing with his strange behavior in the courtroom. There was one incident that positively horrified me. It seems that Judge Stokely was presiding in a civil trial for compensatory damages where a celebrated orthopedic surgeon, Doctor John Richard Mahoney of Fort Lauderdale, was testifying on behalf of the plaintiff. Judge Stokely suddenly interrupted the testimony and spontaneously asked Doctor Mahoney if, in his experience, he had ever "had an opportunity to observe persons under the influence of alcoholic beverages and formulate an opinion as to their sobriety."

The doctor answered, stating that very often he was called upon to make a judgment and give an opinion as to whether or not someone had been drinking or was intoxicated. Judge Stokely pursued the subject, and asked Doctor Mahoney, "What is your opinion relative to this court?"

"As to you, the judge?" the surprised doctor asked.

"Yes, as to me," Stokely replied.

Doctor Mahoney carefully considered his reply before responding, fearful that he would insult the judge in the presence of the bemused spectators in the courtroom, and the confused jurors sitting in the jury box. He was a witness under oath and required to answer the judge's question.

"I am of the opinion, from my brief observation that Your Honor is under the influence of some drug or alcohol."

"You mean on a previous occasion or on this date, sir?"

"On this date, Your Honor," replied the doctor.

"I hereby declare a mistrial" announced the befuddled judge.

Francis D. O'Connor, the attorney for the plaintiff, seeking to placate the court and also extricate his medical witness from impending peril before the erratic judge, addressed the court: "Your Honor, the court asked the doctor a question after his testimony had been concluded, with respect to his opinion of the court's condition of sobriety."

"That is exactly correct," replied the judge.

"And the doctor indicated the court might be drinking or drugged," explained attorney O'Connor.

"That is the reason I asked the question," the judge explained. "Because earlier I heard the same similar reports. Now I do not recall who from, or from whom, but I am not going to continue this trial if you gentlemen of counsel think I am not in a condition to preside over this case."

The two opposing attorneys agreed to go ahead with the

trial, whereupon O'Connor asked the court, referring to Doctor Mahoney, "May the witness be excused?"

"He may be excused," ruled the judge, "but I'm tempted to hold him in contempt of court."

Doctor Mahoney quietly left the witness stand shaking his head with disbelief as he exited through the small swinging doors of the enclosure.

Early one morning, a telephone call came in from Len Boone, who was retained in his job by James Geiger, the newly elected successor to former County Solicitor Angie Weir.

"Hey, Joe," greeted Boone. "How y'all this morning?"

"Fine, thanks," was my puzzled response. "What prompts this call so early in the morning?"

"Oh," said the prosecutor nonchalantly. "Spoke to Judge Stokely last night. He wants us in his courtroom at 2:00 this afternoon on the Erler case."

I didn't like what I heard, nor particularly care for the manner in which I was summarily ordered to some sort of undisclosed hearing before the eccentric Stokely. "Moreover," I burned to myself, "how come Boone met with the judge last night? If there was to be a hearing of any sort, the proper method would be by official notice to appear, and not the 'buddy, buddy' system where the prosecutor and judge play 'footsie' behind the defense attorney's back." Seething inwardly, I maintained an artificially cool façade.

"What do you suppose the judge wants us there for?" I asked, knowing full well the prosecutor and the judge had a lively ex parte discussion about the case last night.

"Well," drawled Boone with deliberate slowness, "the judge wanted to do a little general housekeeping just in case you had a few motions that needed disposition."

"Thanks, Len," was my reply. "I'll be there." I slammed the phone, muttering to myself, "Yeah, thanks for nothing, you redneck. There goes a couple more merit badges."

My secretary Lucy brought in two steaming cups of black coffee on a tray that contained her steno pad and pencil. After placing a cup on my side of the desk, she opened the fly leaf on the opposite side where she primly sat, ready to commence the early morning ritual of programming and dictation. I was not ready to do either. I was still angered by Boone's telephone call.

"Cancel everything this afternoon," I barked. "I have to be in Judge Stokely's courtroom at 2:00 on the Erler case."

"But it's not on the diary," ventured Lucy, fearing that perhaps the hearing date was inadvertently omitted when the diary was prepared at the close of business last evening.

"No," I replied bitterly. "Boone and Stokely had a nice cozy meeting and decided to call me up for an impromptu housecleaning." The secretary made no reply and waited for the next salvo that was certain to erupt.

"I've got to figure out now who my real antagonist is on this case, the prosecutor, or the judge." I looked at my docile secretary, the perfect sounding board, and continued, "It's both! I'll have to guard my backside from both of them!"

Promptly at 2:00 P.M., the judge quickly strode to the bench, his black robe billowing behind him, glaring at me like I was the only person in the courtroom. He ignored Boone, who he already knew, but focused his venomous look on me. This was my first glimpse of the large, raw-boned jurist with strong, gnarled hands who would have looked more at home behind a plow than in a courtroom. I greeted him with a smile that was not returned.

"What do we have here this afternoon?" he inquired, without indulging in any cordiality. His face was flushed and he seemed to be perspiring.

"Your Honor," I began, introducing myself as attorney of record for the defendant Robert Erler, to which the judge muttered some grudging acknowledgment, "there are a few items of unfinished business . . ."

"Why didn't you attend to this unfinished business before Judge David?" he broke in, visibly annoyed.

"Because," I explained, "an important motion to suppress the taped conversation between my client and a state witness by the name of Claire Kaufman requires an evidentiary hearing. My motion to suppress the tapes because they were illegally procured was timely filed. When Judge

David lost the election in November, it was futile to have him make a ruling because the new trial judge who succeeded to Judge David's calendar may not wish to be bound by the decision, and would prefer to conduct the hearing anew.''

''Why do you say the taped conversation was illegally procured?'' asked the judge.

''When my client was arrested in Phoenix, Arizona, he was lodged in the Maricopa County Jail. Claire Kaufman, an old friend, went to the chief of police of Hollywood to enlist his assistance in contacting Robert Erler in jail for the purpose of persuading him to waive extradition and return to Broward County.'' I paused to look at Stokely to see if he was absorbing the explanation. The judge maintained a blank, stony stare but I continued anyhow. ''The Hollywood police managed to put a telephone call through to the jail and Mrs. Kaufman was able to speak with Erler, but the telephone conversation was monitored and taped by the police.''

''Where's the illegality?'' Stokely asked again.

''It is my belief that Mrs. Kaufman did not give the police permission to tape her telephone conversation and Erler certainly did not. Under Florida law this renders the telephone conversation inadmissible in evidence and this tape is what the state intends to use at the trial.''

The judge sat back in his leather chair and began opening and closing his eyelids as though he were in pain. He haltingly addressed Len Boone to give his version of the taped telephone calls.

''It's very simple, Your Honor,'' the prosecutor responded quickly, ''Mrs. Claire Kaufman did, in fact, know her conversation with Bob Erler was being taped and the recording was done with her consent and approbation.''

Talking through clenched teeth the judge ruled, ''I will accept Mr. Boone's version. Motion to suppress denied! What else?''

''But, Your Honor,'' I pleaded, ''most respectfully, there cannot be a ruling on the motion to suppress because an evidentiary hearing is required, and it would be Mrs. Kaufman who would tell the court, under oath, whether or not she gave consent, and not Mr. Boone.''

"You will get another chance to bring this out at the trial as to whether Mrs. Kaufman consented to the taping. What else do you have?" he snapped.

I felt a chill wind starting to blow, and sensed the "housecleaning" meeting was well orchestrated and rehearsed. I could no longer afford to be over-respectful and unnecessarily pliant in these proceedings. The kid gloves were coming off.

"Your Honor," I said, looking sideways to the prosecutor standing at his side with a smug look of innocence, "my most important motion is a continuing one that remains viable and operative throughout the entire trial . . ."

"What is it?" asked the judge with marked impatience.

"It deals with the disclosure of any evidence in the possession of the prosecution officials that would be beneficial to the defendant. I am suggesting that there may be some other taped conversations or other tapes that may be in the hands of the police or the prosecution, and, if so, I am entitled to have them."

"What about it, Len?" the court asked. "Is there anything like that?" I flinched when the judge called the prosecutor by his first name in such a cordial manner, especially when he evinced a most hostile attitude towards me throughout the entire initial confrontation. Boone replied, "Nothing that I know of, Your Honor."

"Anything else?" the judge asked, looking at me with a baleful eye.

"Your Honor," I reminded the court, "I had a specific order entered by Judge David which is in the file directing the prosecution to furnish me with any exculpative or beneficial evidence it may have in its possession. I am addressing this question to the prosecutor once again in open court: Do you have any other tapes of any witness, or anyone else that I could use to benefit my client in his defense?"

"Counselor, Mr. Boone has already told you that he didn't have anything, so stop right there!"

I felt like someone gave me a swift kick in the stomach. Those tapes made of Dorothy Clark in the hospital were in existence! No doubt about it! Johnnie Melrose had them in his possession, but my lips were sealed and dared not reveal my source of information. The burning questions was:

"Did Len Boone know of their existence?" Perhaps Johnnie Melrose didn't tell him about Dorothy's mentioning the names of persons who assaulted her and shot her daughter. I desperately needed those tapes to formulate Erler's defense, and raise a reasonable doubt in the minds of the jury. The introduction of other suspects in the slaying would definitely demolish the circumstantial case against the defendant. "There must be a way," I agonized, "how these tapes could be flushed out," and made an impetuous attempt, almost to the point of breaking faith with my informant, Bob McElroy.

"Judge," I ventured boldly, "I heard a rumor that while Dorothy Clark, the state's main witness, was in the hospital convalescing, there was a tape recording device at her bedside in order to get some clues as to any utterances or names that she may have mentioned while in a comatose state. It is just possible that in her delirium Mrs. Clark could have mentioned names, events or something of benefit to aid the defendant in his defense. If so, it is important that we be permitted to examine and hear these tapes as they may constitute beneficial evidence."

"That's enough on that point," the judge thundered angrily, abruptly dismissing my argument. "Now I have some ground rules for the trial."

We both listened attentively. We had to because the judge continually spoke through clenched teeth. "The first six rows to my left are to be used exclusively for the press. The family and friends of the defendant are to sit on the opposite side of the courtroom and not fraternize with any members of the press. The lawyers are admonished not to make any statements to the newspaper reporters, or radio or television reporters, while the trial is in progress." Then, with a pointed look toward me, said "And any violation of my orders will be dealt with severely."

"Yes sir, Your Honor," agreed Boone with typical slavish style, looking over to me for agreement and saw instead, my regarding the judge with a cold, brooding look. I gathered my papers and slowly walked out of the courtroom, leaving the two antagonists to their own devices. The die was cast. Erler would soon go to trial against a stacked deck.

V

TRIAL

29 _____

JANUARY 27. THE sun-kissed beaches of South Florida beckoned invitingly to the influx of tourists who inaugurated the winter "season," providing a welcome respite to the local natives who patiently endured a hot, uneventful summer. On the third floor of the courthouse in Fort Lauderdale, the 'Catch Me Killer' murder case, the solitary exception to their boredom was about to commence.

Boone, the prosecutor, met me outside the courtroom door by sheer coincidence and we smiled to each other as we witnessed the milling throng of spectators scramble, push and maul each other for seats in the small courtroom. Space was limited because of the judge's ruling that most of the seating area was reserved for the local press, and additional facilities put aside for the arrival of newspaper reporters and photographers from other areas. We could not get near the door to make an entrance, but Len Boone towered over the squirming mob and shouted in his special police voice, "Hold it, everybody! Just hold it! There'll be no show if you don't back off and let us in!"

The mob dispersed for a brief moment. Boone plowed through with me in tow, forcing our way to the counsel tables within the enclosure at the bar. Patiently awaiting me was Robert Erler seated at the defense table, calm and unruffled, resplendent in a conservative blue suit, narrow tie and white shirt. His hair was neatly combed and long enough to reveal a wavy forelock over an unperturbed brow. He was engaged in looking back at his mother, sisters and brother seated directly behind in the first aisle, who returned his smiles and cross-fingered gestures of good luck. He snapped to attention when he saw me approach the table.

"How do you feel, Bob?" I asked.

"Okay, now, I guess."

"Tell me, Bob, were there any incidents or something that happened?"

"Only that I caught a lot of flak from the guys in the cell block. You know, the usual . . . trying to grab me and calling me names; doing their best to rile me up, but I remembered your orders to keep cool . . ."

"Good boy, Bob. You can lean over the aisle for a visit with your family for a little chat, but remember—no bodily contact! Explain that to them—no hugging or embracing."

"I understand, thanks," he said cheerfully as he scurried over to his delighted family.

The brief reunion was interrupted by the bailiff heralding the arrival of the judge who lumbered toward the bench gathering his unruly black robe about him, and fixed a stony stare over the crowded courtroom. Satisfied that a reasonable degree of order and quiet prevailed, he addressed the court clerk, "Mr. Clerk, please call the case on the docket."

"Yes, Your Honor," obliged the spectacled Pinkie Harrison, who intoned, "State of Florida vs. Robert John Erler. Second Degree Murder."

"Is the state ready for trial?" asked the judge, looking toward the counsel table where Boone sat.

"Yes, Judge," replied the prosecutor.

"And what about the defense?" asked the judge, not looking in the direction of the defense table but lowering his head to avoid eye contact.

"The defendant is ready for trial, Your Honor."

"Since this is a second degree murder case, only six jurors will be required to qualify," the judge announced for the benefit of the news media and general public. "Mr. Clerk, how many prospective jurors do you propose to bring in here?" asked the court.

"There are twenty-four waiting in the corridor, Your Honor."

"Clear the courtroom," ordered the judge. "We must make room for the jurors. Only the press and court personnel may remain."

This maneuver started another melee. Those spectators who were comfortably ensconced in their seats volubly expressed their disapproval as their vacated positions were rapidly filled by prospective jurors. The courtroom filled quickly and Judge Stokely looked over the panel of would-be talesmen, addressing the entire body with a toothy grin,

"Ladies and gentlemen, you have been selected at random from the voting lists to serve as jurors, if accepted, in the case of 'State of Florida vs. Robert John Erler.' You have all previously been sworn on oath and the court must ask you collectively a few questions:

"Do any of you know the defendant Robert Erler?" There was no response.

"Have any of the prospective jurors here heard of Robert Erler, or anything about the case we are about to try?" Still no response.

I groaned inwardly. This was the part I always hated, where the majority of jurors professed not to have heard about Bob Erler or the 'Catch Me Killer' case, although the newspapers were having a field day almost daily about Merilyn Clark's murder. "Lying bastards," I grumbled to myself, knowing in my heart there was no malice implicit in the jurors' equivocation, merely an innocuous eagerness to serve on the jury panel of a highly publicized homicide. If they were to show prejudice one way or the other, they would be excused from jury duty and prudently withheld any comment that might make them unacceptable as impartial jurors.

The court continued its interrogation: "Do any of you know the prosecutor, Len Boone, or anyone in the office of James Geiger, the county solicitor of Broward County?"

Again no response.

"Do any of you know the attorney representing the defendant, Mr. Joe Varon?"

Still no response.

"Mr. Clerk," ordered the court, "fill the box with the first six men on your list and Mr. Boone can commence the *voir dire*."

Pinkie Harrison, the deputy courtroom clerk, dutifully called six prospective jurors to be seated, preparatory to their being questioned as to their qualifications to serve. The novice jurist, seeking to impress the jury panel almost choked in his attempt to utter the phrase "voir dire" without explaining to the prospective jurors what the phrase meant. The term is an old French expression that means "to speak the truth" but I knew from vast trial experience not to expect a prospective juror to give honest responses to questions as to his prejudices or predisposition as to the guilt or innocence of the defendant, merely because he stands accused of a murder charge. The jury selection process ideologically is an attempt to procure a panel of impartial jurors who harbor no views that would influence a fair evaluation of the evidence, but it could be expected that most of the jurors would conceal their opinions under questioning by the respective attorneys.

Len Boone stood up before the jurors seated on the panel, with clipboard in his left hand, and pencil poised in his right, looking every bit like a drill sergeant, surveying the panel before questioning the prospective jurors. In his soft, northern Florida drawl said, "Now folks, jes a few questions so we all can git to know each other." He smiled to put the wary jurors at ease. Boone dutifully went through the litany of interrogation, touching on the experience and views of the impaneled group as to circumstantial evidence and whether or not they had discussed the case with friends, family or neighbors. The prosecutor tried to assure the prospective jurors that the state was only interested in a fair, unbiased evaluation of the evidence and hoped that the jurors, if accepted, would seek the same goal. All of the jurors in the box nodded in agreement, causing Boone to reward them with a munificent smile like a Sunday school teacher in church.

As a battle-scarred veteran of many criminal trials, it was ludicrous to hear the members of the prospective jury panel answer the questions Boone propounded in the manner they knew the prosecutor wanted to hear. I never ceased to be amazed at the inflexible pattern of the pristine jurors convincing the prosecutor they never heard about the case, never discussed it with anyone, and certainly had no opinions or preconceived notions about the defendant's guilt or innocence. If they were telling the truth, they had to be the most ignorant and illiterate people in all of Broward County. It was a juror's white lie that was always told for fear of not being accepted on the panel. I could see that good ole Len pretended to be satisfied and tendered the jurors to me, as defense counsel, for further examination; but I was already disenchanted with the integrity of the panel and went along with the charade of jury selection.

I had my own method of picking jurors.

"Your Honor," announced the prosecutor, "The State of Florida tenders the jury panel to the defense."

The judge hesitated and barked at me, "Defense may inquire."

I rose to my feet, introduced myself to the jury panel and smiled to put them at ease. Perhaps if they were comfortable, they would be inclined to make some truthful answers. I decided to utilize some hard and fixed rules that I had crystallized over the years, since it was obvious the prospective jurors were responding to questions as to their qualifications only in the manner in which they anticipated their interrogator wanted to hear. I was a believer in simple, visual inspection, which was more revealing to me than the spoken word. I shied away from jurors with cold blue or steely grey eyes and Nordic types whose roots were indigenous to European countries such as Germany, Sweden or Poland. It was always my belief that persons whose antecedents stemmed from France, Italy or Spain or the Latin American countries exhibited more empathy and were influenced by their basic emotions. They were capable of understanding human frailties and prone to forgive transgressions. This type of juror would be compassionate, sympathetic and would usually give an accused in a criminal case the benefit of reasonable doubt, "Just as the law required."

Leaning over the jury box, presumably making routine inquiries of the prospective jurors as to their acceptability, all the while making an imperceptible eye contact, I placed my concepts into practical application. If the proposed juror had icy blue eyes or steely grey eyes in a Nordic or Germanic face, the juror would immediately be excused without explanation. Dark brown eyes indicated a Latin or warm ethnic background and if the prospective juror had an olive skin or swarthy complexion, his acceptance as a juror would almost become a certainty. A few prospective jurors on the panel were summarily dismissed by me without a single question being asked. When the panel was yielded to Boone for additional questioning, Eddie Kay, who was sitting at the defense table, leaned across Erler to whisper, "Why did you discharge juror number three without even asking a single question?"

"Tell you later," I whispered.

Judge Stokely announced, "We will have a fifteen minute break," and as the crowd began to stir, he looked toward the press section and asked, "Are you gentlemen comfortable?"

One of the wags facetiously remarked, "Those benches are hard—just like church pews."

Stokely turned to his bailiff and directed, "Please provide that man with a pillow. Anything else?" he inquired looking in the direction of the press section and receiving only puzzled looks, he got up from his chair and left the bench.

During the short recess, my secretary provided the defense team with hot, steaming black coffee in paper cups. It was too much of a chore to venture out in the corridor and fight the mob of spectators and news photographers so we chose to remain within the enclosure of the bar. "Was there anyone on the jury panel you particularly liked?" Erler was asked.

"I'll leave everything up to you, sir. Whoever you select will be fine by me," was his response.

"I know that, Bob," I replied, "but sometimes there are people on the jury you particularly don't care for. When you look at a man and you dislike him for no apparent reason whatsoever, the chances are that he doesn't like you either. So why waste time asking questions regarding his views. It's more comfortable to just get rid of him at an early stage rather than have the uncertainty gnaw at you throughout the trial."

"So that's why you excused some of the jurors without asking any questions," exclaimed Eddie Kay, raising his eyebrows as though he uncovered a mysterious secret.

"That's part of it, Eddie," was the response in a preoccupied tone as I studied the master jury list to determine how many more jurors remained to be examined. The tedious process of jury selection continued throughout the long afternoon as I systematically weeded out the undesirable prospects in accordance with my unorthodox, but unalterable rules. At every juncture when the prosecutor would tender the jury panel to me as defense counsel, Boone would make a theatrical display of accepting the jury on behalf of the State of Florida, inferentially indicating the jury was okay by him, but the defense attorney did not approve of the prospective jurors sitting in the box.

It was 5:00 P. M. I sensed an aura of tedium permeating the courtroom atmosphere. Prospective jurors on the hard oaken benches and those in the jury box squirmed, crossing and uncrossing their legs, showing weary discomfort. I looked up at the judge's flushed face, thinking, "It's probably past time for his booze," noting with satisfaction the jurist licking his lips, glaring down at me, smoldering, biding his time for an excuse to spew his venom. It was time to act.

"Your Honor, the defense will accept the jury."

The prosecutor made another dramatic display of unrestrained boredom and stated to the court, "The State of Florida *again* accepts the jury."

"Very well." Judge Stokely looked toward the jurors in the box and clenched his jaw as he addressed them, "Please rise and be sworn."

The jurors in the box all rose as one and remained standing at the direction of the courtroom clerk who recited the juror's oath. I called Eddie Kay's attention to the demeanor of the jurors as they were sworn in and how their composite visage changed abruptly from the jocular manner they evinced during the selection process to their present serious vein. "As soon as they took the oath, their entire attitude changed. This will be a tough jury," I remarked. "Not too bright, but strictly law and order."

Judge Stokely stumbled to his feet and turned his florid face to the expectant panel, and said in his usual pattern of speaking through clenched teeth, barely parting his lips, "We will adjourn until 9:00 A.M. tomorrow morning at which time you will hear the opening statements of the respective attorneys. I'll explain in the morning about the opening statements—we are all too tired now." He turned and fled toward his chambers, his black robe puffed out like a kite ready to soar.

"A real Batman," I thought to myself.

30

THE SECOND DAY. It was early when I approached the brown leatherette-tufted double doors of Judge Stokley's courtroom and greeted the bailiff. He was trying his best to discourage the throng of spectators waiting to get inside. Recognizing me, he cleared the crowd back long enough so I could enter. Once inside, I tried to speak with the courtroom clerk, Pinkie Harrison, just to get his views on the jury panel, but the prosecutor was already seated at the counsel table, poring over his notes preparatory to his opening statement to the jury. After an exchange of greetings all around, Robert Erler was escorted to the defense side of the table. No words were passed between lawyer and client while the handcuffs were removed from the defendant, who had a troubled look on his boyish face.

"Anything wrong?" was my question as we both sat down at the defense counsel table. Erler hunched over and whispered, "Would you believe this? Judge Stokely's secretary visited me last night up in the jail conference room."

"What?" I exploded. Then lowering my voice to a forced hissing tone, "What was that all about?"

"Her name is Marsha Fitzgerald and she feels sorry for me because I'm being set up as a patsy on this rap."

"Where did she get that idea?" I asked.

"There have been some meetings with the judge about how the case should be prosecuted."

I gave no indication to my upset client what my reaction was to this startling news, and tried to minimize its importance by smiling knowingly as though such harmony between the court and prosecution officials was commonplace. I had my own personal views.

The conversation ended as abruptly as it started when the bailiff asked everyone to clear the courtroom to allow the duly impaneled jurors access to their private jury room. In the process of vacating the courtroom, I slowly walked backwards in order to look at the jurors for some sign or expression, but none of the jurors looked at me. I didn't like it when jurors refused to return my gaze. It worried me.

At the opening of the court session, the trial judge lumbered toward the bench as if he were awakening from a deep sleep, and nodded to the prosecutor, ignoring the defense counsel. Boone greeted the court, "Good morning, Judge." I remained silent, awaiting the next move. There would be no more courtesies from me.

"Mr. Clerk, please bring in the jury."

The bailiff, knowing the care and attention of the jury was his own personal responsibility, jumped in front of the clerk and opened the door of the jury room, directing the jurors to take their respective places in the jury box.

The judge looked over to the expectant panel and advised them, "The next order of business is the opening statements of the prosecutor and defense counsel" and reading from a prepared text in his notebook continued, "The court hereby admonishes you that the opening statements of the prosecutor and defendant's attorney are merely a blueprint of what the prosecution and defense would be. You are not to take into consideration any of the statements made by the lawyers as it does not constitute evidence, but merely their respective theories of the case, and what evidence, if any, they may elect to present."

The judge signalled the prosecutor to rise, saying, "Mr. Boone will be the first to give his opening statement."

Len Boone approached the jury box and drew himself up to his imposing six foot height, his brown curly hair falling over his forehead, and surveyed the jurors as he commenced to outline the state's case against Erler. A long list of witnesses was read to the jury to impress them with the overwhelming preponderance of evidence that would be forthcoming. The longer Boone spoke, the more emotional he became, and glancing contemptuously at the defendant told the jurors, "You will see a parade of the defendant's former fellow police officers, his comrades in arms who he has betrayed and sullied, testify against him. Each bit of testimony will be like a piece in a jigsaw puzzle. When all the pieces of the puzzle are put together, we will have proved that Robert John Erler is the man who shot five bullets into the body of that sweet little girl and cast her broken and twisted body in a prairie in a remote airfield to linger and die.'' The prosecutor sat down with a great display of sorrowful heaviness.

Judge Stokely woodenly waved his hand in my direction, which was an indication to start the opening statement to the jury. I tried to gently remind them that whatever statements the attorneys make at the opening of a criminal case did not constitute evidence but merely represented what the lawyers expect to establish by way of proof during the course of the trial. I also gave my standard pitch in a circumstantial evidence case, telling the jury, "In weighing the evidence in a criminal case sometimes the lack of evidence cries out more loudly than any direct or positive evidence. In this case there were no eyewitnesses to the offense, nor any fingerprints. The prosecution will have to rely upon speculation and conjecture from the mouths of individuals who have no basis for formulating any suppositions. Witnesses cannot be called to the stand to give opinions. They are only allowed to testify as to what they saw or heard. They are certainly not allowed to testify as to what they guess or what they think."

I made certain the jury was advised that Dorothy Clark, the star prosecution witness, had two opportunities to pick Erler out of a six man line-up and failed both times, and seeing the prosecutor stir uneasily at the table, crossing and uncrossing his legs as though he were running the high hurdles at a track meet, said, "I suspect that Dorothy Clark will walk into this courtroom and point the accusing finger today at my client, Bob Erler. So you will have to ask yourselves why was it that she could not identify him last September, but four months later can make a positive identification?"

From the corner of my eye, I detected the prosecutor slowly rising to his feet, inciting Judge Stokely to promptly shout, "Sustained!" This was shocking and unprecedented and I angrily asked the court, "Judge, how can you sustain an objection that was never made?" The members of the press, witnessing a most usual episode unusual episode, laughed at the judge's ludicrous antic, nearly sending him into an apoplectic fit.

"He was going to make an objection," the judge yelled. The entire courtroom snickered.

The snickering continued as the judge glared at me, the sole cause of his chagrin. Obviously aware of the court's mounting displeasure, I brought the opening statement to a hasty conclusion, making way for the trial to commence in earnest.

Judge Stokely looked at the jurors dutifully seated in the box and spoke with ill-concealed rancor, "We had enough for today," then consulting the ever-present manual on his desk, read, "I must caution you not to discuss this case with your friends or anyone in your family, and you are not to read anything about this case in the newspapers. If you are watching television and something is said by the commentator, you must turn the set off, or leave the room. Do you all understand my instructions?"

The entire jury panel nodded its assent. "Mr. Bailiff," ordered the judge, "no one is to leave the courtroom until the jurors have left the building."

The court's required admonition to insulate the jurors from communication with the outside world and not discuss the case with anyone, was a futile gesture. Jurors who are not sequestered can hardly wait to get home and see what the newspapers reported about the case they were working on. It is unrealistic to visualize a juror's wife or husband, or girlfriend or boyfriend, asking about his or her experience in court and the intrepid juror refusing to discuss the matter. Idealism always yields to realism, and jurors are only mortal beings.

I accompanied the jail guard who took Erler through the back door, up the elevator to the general cell area where the events that transpired in the courtroom were recounted.

"That judge acts like he's against us," suggested Erler.

"The understatement of the year," I affirmed. "Now comes a parade of witnesses, so if anything is said on the stand that you may want to challenge, just lean over and tell me."

"Who do you expect to be the first witness on the stand?" he asked.

"Ordinarily, prosecutors follow the same format in a homicide case. The first witness will be the person who found the body of the little girl, and then the medical examiner will testify as to the cause and time of her death . . .''

"But I'm the one who found her body," interrupted Erler.

"The state will produce someone else to testify where the body was found, and from that point on there will be an imposing array of uniformed cops to impress the jury, even though they may have little to talk about. There will be a great deal of guesswork, but that's to be anticipated in a circumstantial evidence case."

As we reached the communal area of the jail, one of the inmates shouted, "Hey, Erler, get your ass in here. We've got a hot poker game going."

"Be right there," called back the grinning Erler, who bade me a hurried goodbye, as he happily took his place at a large table surrounded by shouting and laughing inmates.

For some endless period of time, I watched the poker game in progress and witnessed Robert Erler shuffling and dealing the cards with glee, appearing not to have a care in the world, although his murder trial would resume first thing in the morning. I thought to myself, "I wish I could learn Bob Erler's secret for serenity. Here I am, worried to the point of not even being able to eat or sleep properly but the one who really has everything to lose is playing cards and having a ball."

31

SPECULATION RAN HIGH as to who would be the prosecution's first witness at the trial. Boone refused to comment but promised a surprise. The convening of the court was a repetition of the previous day's fiasco, except that the spectators were even more vigorous in their quest for seats in the courtroom. The jury was assembled in the box, and everyone rose as his honor stiffly walked to his plush leather seat behind the bench.

"Is the jury panel all present?" the judge inquired formally, and upon receiving the equally formal response in the affirmative by the bailiff, further asked, "Counsel for both sides ready to proceed?" We both indicated our readiness, whereupon the judge looked over to the jurors and said, "I'm sure none of you jurors discussed this case with anyone or read about it in the newspapers, right?" All of the jurors, without exception, nodded. I looked upwards at the ceiling in silent supplication. I really didn't blame the jurors for fibbing, but it was discouraging to try a serious criminal case before a patently mendacious jury.

"Very well," beamed the court, "Mr. Boone, please call your first witness."

"The state will call Mrs. Dorothy Clark to the stand," announced the prosecutor, to everyone's surprise.

"Why would Boone call the state's cleanup witness first?" I wondered. "Perhaps Dorothy Clark's orientation would be diluted if she were required to wait until the end of the state's case to testify." The entire courtroom noisily whirred with eager speculation causing the judge to vigorously rap his gavel for silence. On cue, Mrs. Dorothy Clark, with her close-cropped hair and darkened sunglasses, was led to the witness stand, weakly tottering on the elbow of a very attentive deputy sheriff. She haltingly made her way to the witness chair and the very first question after establishing her identity was, "Mrs. Clark, do you know Robert John Erler?"

Upon receiving an affirmative reply she was asked, "Would you point him out for the gentlemen of the jury, please?"

Without hesitation, Mrs. Clark pointed directly to the defendant at the defense table. The graveyard silence in the courtroom was ominous. I was glad that in my opening statement the jury was reminded that Dorothy Clark had two different opportunities to pick Erler out of a line-up, and failed, and hoped they would remember my prediction that Mrs. Clark would walk into the courtroom and identify Erler as the man who shot her.

"Please tell us, Mrs. Clark," began the prosecutor, "what you were doing here in Florida and how you met the man you just pointed out as Mr. Robert Erler."

"Came down to Miami with my daughter Merilyn to

Olston's Employment Agency; they have a branch in Atlanta. They got me a job at Howard Johnson's commissary, but only worked for three days and moved on.''

''Where were you staying?'' asked Boone.

''We stayed in two different motels, but we checked out and went north toward Dania. It was dark by then so we stopped on the beach to rest . . .''

''By the way,'' broke in the prosecutor, ''how old was your daughter Merilyn.''

''She was twelve years old,'' was the tearful response.

''I'm sorry, Mrs. Clark,'' said Boone to the abject witness, trying to evoke as much pathos and sympathy as possible. ''Can you tell us what happened next?''

''We were resting in the car when a police officer told us we couldn't sleep on the beach and ordered us to move northward toward Dania. We followed his advice and went to this other place. Merilyn was sleeping in the back seat. The night was real hot and the mosquitoes were terrific. I took a sanitary napkin from the glove compartment and burned it. It didn't burn; it just smoldered and made a lot of smoke.''

''Then did you see Robert Erler?'' hinted Boone.

I jumped quickly to my feet, ''Objection, Your Honor, the prosecutor is leading the witness.''

''Please continue, Mrs. Clark,'' said Stokely, not deigning to rule on the defense objection. By ignoring the objection Dorothy Clark assumed the court overruled the defense complaint, and the narrative continued.

''The purpose in burning the sanitary napkin was to make enough smoke to drive the mosquitoes away. Mr. Erler came over to the car and naturally he thought the car was on fire, and we managed to put the damn thing out . . . because he had a policeman's uniform shirt on, I just assumed he was a guard.''

''Mrs. Clark, will you describe what you just said, 'A policeman's uniform shirt'?''

''It was a khaki shirt with a police patch on the shoulder,'' she obliged. ''I told Mr. Erler about the officer in Hollywood telling us we could come up here, but he said 'No.' He said he knew of a place we could stay the night.

I assumed he meant parking, so we followed him to the trailer camp.''

''What happened when you got to the trailer park?''

''I expected to see a wife and a young infant son.''

''Why?'' broke in Boone.

''Because he told me he had a twenty-two-month-old son—and his wife should have been home, but there was nobody in the trailer . . . We went into the trailer and Merilyn went over to the couch; there were two couches facing each other, and they had comforters and pillows on them.''

''What happened then?'' urged Boone with a pained expression on his face, forewarning some devastating evidence about to erupt.

''He pulled out a pistol with white handles and pointed it at me and then did something that made me know there was something he had on his mind.''

''Tell us what he did,'' asked the prosecutor.

''Well, he started masturbating.''

''Did you have any conversation with him about anything before he started masturbating?''

''No, we had no conversation. I don't suppose ten minutes elapsed the whole time.''

''What happened next?'' asked Boone.

''Merilyn and I went to our car parked outside. He followed us to the car and got in the passenger side and asked for all of my money.''

''Did you have any money?''

''I had twenty-three dollars in my wallet and fifty in my train case. I remarked to my daughter, 'I sure can pick them,' and she said, 'and how.' She made another remark and when I turned my head slightly to the left to hear her remark, that was it! That was the last I remember until I woke up in the hospital.

''I was in the hospital for three and a half weeks. There were five bullets in my head; four of them are still in there. The right side of my face is paralyzed and my right hand is partially paralyzed.''

''Back to the August 12 incident, Mrs. Clark. When was the next time you saw Robert Erler?''

''Today in court.''

''Did you ever have an opportunity to observe Mr. Erler

in what we call a line-up?" I could see what was coming.
The prosecutor knew a big issue would be made on cross-
examination as to Dorothy Clark's failure to identify Erler
on two separate occasions and was setting up an explanation of why she was unable to do so and thus attenuate the
cross-questioning. Mrs. Clark was thoroughly coached, and
gave the expected response:

"Frankly, I hardly remember that day. It was my first
day out of bed for longer than to go to the bathroom, and
I think it was something like two or three hours that I
waited at the police station. I was exhausted by the time I
got in the room where the line-up was."

"Mrs. Clark, I show you a photograph marked 'State's
Exhibit A' for identification and ask if you can identify
that."

"Yes," she replied, "that's my daughter."

I vehemently objected to the old prosecutor's trick of
evoking sympathy to the prejudice of the defendant.
Boone's ploy was transparent: The mother would hold the
picture of her departed daughter in her hand and break out
in tears, while testifying further.

"Apparently the prosecutor plans to put the picture of
Merilyn Clark in evidence for the purpose of identifying
the decedent," I argued. "The law is very clear that no
members of the family, and particularly the mother in this
case, may testify as to the identity of the deceased. If the
court permits this type of testimony from Mrs. Clark, I will
have to ask for a mistrial."

"I know what the law is," the judge stated gruffly.
"Someone is going to have to identify this person."

"But not the mother," I persisted, "and the principal
reason for the Supreme Court condemning this type of identification is to avoid the emotional impact upon the jury
and influence their impartiality."

The prosecutor, noting the court's vacillation, put a temporary halt to the argument by announcing, "I don't intend
to introduce the photograph at this time. I will tie it up
later."

"Yeah, later," I burned. "After you and the judge decide
how it should be done."

The prosecutor was sprawled out at the counsel table

with legs outstretched and arms behind his head, looking at his star witness and beaming smiles of confidence, announced, "You may take the witness."

A hush fell over the courtroom as I rose from the counsel table and approached Mrs. Clark with great deference. She regarded me with guarded hostility because of what she probably was told by the police officers, but in my most courteous manner, I tried to dispel Mrs. Clark's apprehension by calmly starting the cross-examination on a low key. I remembered reading somewhere that one must treat a whore like a lady, and a lady like a whore, and decided to treat Mrs. Clark like a lady.

"Mrs. Clark, just a few questions and we will be through."

Dorothy Clark lowered her head and fixed a puzzled stare at me and her face lit up with a shy smile. It was gratifying to note that Mrs. Clark was in a relaxed mood and commenced a series of mild inquiries touching generally on her testimony.

"Mrs. Clark," I began, "in response to Mr. Boone's question as to whether you saw any additional photographs of Mr. Erler, besides the one in the trailer, you told the court and jury that you 'had not'."

"Correct."

"Isn't it true that while you were recuperating in the hospital the police were constantly asking questions in order to help you get your memory, showing you pictures all the time? Weren't they?"

"No, I did identify some pictures on one occasion."

"Mrs. Clark, they were showing you pictures almost every day, weren't they?"

"No, they were not."

"How many days did they show you pictures, Mrs. Clark?"

"I looked at one group of pictures one evening, and several evenings later I looked at another group. That was the only two times."

"You are telling this court and jury that only twice you were shown pictures, is that right?"

"Right."

It was critical to establish that Mrs. Clark was indoctrinated to identify Erler in the courtroom as her assailant; particularly after she failed dismally on two occasions to make an identification in the line-up. She had to be shown pictures of Erler before she took the witness stand to make the identification. The burning and most conclusive question was: "How much prior to her taking the stand did she see Erler's picture?"

The prosecutor looked at his star witness like a professor proud of his pupil, beaming smiles of confidence while Dorothy Clark kept glancing back at Boone with every reply she would make, seeking approval or confirmation that she was doing well, seeming to enjoy the role of star witness. I realized chivalry was not quite dead, and men do not like to see a woman abused, especially one recovering from five shots to her head, but it was imperative that the jury be informed as to what methods the prosecution officials used to enable Mrs. Clark to make a positive identification of Erler. It was obvious to me that impermissive suggestibility was utilized by showing the witness Erler's photograph many times, and more recently, immediately prior to the in-court confrontation.

I handed the witness a photograph which depicted six men on a stage, with numerals over their heads, preparatory to making an inquiry about her role in the line-up session.

"Mrs. Clark, I show you a photograph that was taken at the line-up you attended on the sixth floor of the courthouse. Do you recall this scene?"

"Unless I know one of these men, how would I know if this is a photograph that I have seen before? I have looked at a lot of pictures," she added.

"When did you look at a lot of pictures?" I asked, sensing a breakthrough.

"In Officer Sweeny's office."

"When was that, Ma'am?"

"Saturday."

"How many photographs did you see?"

"Saturday? Over a dozen."

"Did you see any of these pictures today?"

"Yes."

"Where?"

"In Officer Sweeny's office."

"What time today?"

"Don't know exactly."

"Isn't it fair to say," I hastily pressed on, "that you were shown pictures just *before* you came in court today?"

"I imagine," was the hesitant response.

The jurors remained transfixed with no glimmer of perception, and I decided to set the stage to establish another vital point, that no fingerprints were available to connect Erler with the homicide.

"Mrs. Clark, did I understand you to say when you and Merilyn left the trailer, the unknown stranger followed you to your car and entered on the passenger side?" Mrs. Clark nodded her head. "In order to pull the door shut he had to grab the handle, didn't he?"

"Yes, I imagine so. He slammed the door shut."

"Did this fellow wear gloves?"

"No."

"Did you ever see him use hands? Mrs. Clark, did you see him touch the car with any part of his body?"

"Well, he managed to sit in the seat, yes. Yes, I would say he touched some part of it."

"How was the slamming of the door accomplished?"

"I do not know."

"Is it possible to slam that door without the use of hands?"

"I would say no."

I ached inwardly just to be able to inquire about the recorder at her bedside during her stay at the hospital, and agonized about "did she know a California Pete, and did she tell anyone she was shot by Pete or Carl Winkle?" but I made a solemn promise to the state's chief investigator and could not violate my oath, even to the detriment of my own client.

Always conscious of the jury's mercurial moods and since the courtroom atmosphere seemed a bit tense, it was time to inject some levity into the proceedings. Moving quickly to the end of the jury box, behind the last juror where the witness' face was in full view of the jury, I asked, "Mrs. Clark, did I understand you to say that as soon as you followed that unknown stranger into the trailer, there was no conversation but he immediately started to masturbate?''

''Yes sir, that's correct.''

''And since he was busily occupied and didn't do any talking, you kept on with a one-sided conversation?''

There were a few audible snickers from the spectators and for the first time during the proceedings some of the jurors evinced amused interest.

''Did you at least ask him his name?''

''No, I just talked about different things.''

''He didn't have any conversation with you?''

''No.''

''So he just kept on masturbating, while you continued talking?'' I asked with a blank look of disbelief on my face.

The laughter from the spectators seemed to upset the judge. His face was flushed an angry red, and his glares directed toward me went unnoticed. It was imperative that the jury witness the incongruity of Mrs. Clark's testimony; it was beyond belief that she would be prattling away, engaging in nonsensical small talk while a complete stranger was silently masturbating in her presence, and in view of her twelve-year-old daughter.

''And,'' I went on, ''he continued to masturbate without saying a word, and also holding in his hand a .38 caliber revolver?''

One of the irrepressible reporters in the press section blurted, ''Ask her which gun went off first!'' The chortles and rowdy laughter in the courtroom caused the prosecutor to charge from his seat, thundering objections. Having accomplished my purpose and desiring to end the cross-examination on a high note, I walked away from the flustered witness, tendering her back to the frowning prosecutor.

Boone took Dorothy Clark on redirect examination in a futile attempt to rehabilitate his star witness, but the damage had already been done. The rest of the morning was taken with the medical examiner's testimony as to the approximate time of death and the location of the five bullet wounds in her head. A sheriff's staff photographer produced a fiber file containing photographs taken at the crime scene, handing them over to the prosecutor who made a solemn display of extracting the pictures one by one and presenting it to the court for his inspection. Jurors love to see pictures and natural curiosity only whetted their appetite. I had already seen the pictures which depicted the dead girl's twisted body partially secluded in a sandy hammock by the side of a newly paved asphalt road, and knew Boone was going to inject a little gore to impress the jury. With a flourish, the prosecutor presented the final picture, which I knew Boone would try to get into evidence, a colored photo of little Merilyn on a morgue slab, taken after the autopsy had been completed by the pathologist, vividly showing her shaved, disfigured scalp, with the encrusted bloody bullet holes evincing mute evidence of the brutal murder.

"May we have a side-bar conference?" I asked of the court, slowly approaching the bench, with Boone doing the same. It is routine procedure to hold discussions out of the jury's hearing when matters of law are to be discussed. In some instances the defense attorney and prosecutor repair to the judge's chambers, or even excuse the jury while legal points are argued in the courtroom.

"Why?" asked the court.

I was taken aback by the judge's question.

"Your Honor," I explained, "when pictures of a decedent are proffered, the court decides which photographs are duplications or have no probative value, or are unduly inflammable. We require a conference, either side-bar or in chambers, so these photos can be examined and evaluated."

"Denied," snapped the judge. "All these can go into evidence when Mr. Boone wants them in."

"I absolutely object to the court departing from accepted procedure and vehemently object to the morgue picture as it is grossly inflammatory."

Up to this point, the jury showed signs of boredom, and the prospects of finally being permitted to see the controversial pictures seemed to resuscitate them, but their enthusiasm was short lived when the judge declared an end to the morning session as he had an "emergency sentencing" that required his immediate attention. He hastily adjourned court until 2:00 P.M.

As the courtroom slowly cleared, I perceived my investigator, Harry Long, draped over the last pew near the door. We looked at each other, but the ex-cop was the only one who laughed.

"What's so funny?" I asked.

"Don't you know about Stokely and his 'private sentencings'?" the investigator asked, with the smirk on his lips which always irritated me. I shook my head and waited for Harry's next sally. The investigator obliged, "It's better you don't know," roaring with laughter as he left me scratching my head in wonder.

32

PINKIE HARRISON, THE courtroom clerk, mounted a stool at the snack bar on the main floor of the courthouse waiting for me to touch base with Tom during the lunch recess. Anyone looking for me could always leave a message at Tom's and Pinkie knew just where to find me when not engaged in the courtroom. The lunch room began to fill up with courthouse employees, attorneys with their witnesses, litigants and trial spectators when Pinkie spotted me. "Hey, Joe," shouted the curly haired court clerk, halting me in mid-stride, "got a minute?"

"Sure, Pinkie," I smiled at my favorite court clerk, grasping his outstretched hand. "What's up?"

"Lot to talk about, Counselor," replied the clerk, "but not here."

I noted that Pinkie's thin rosy face was more pinched than usual, and I never saw him look so grim. "How about the county commission's hearing room? Should be empty now, okay?"

Pinkie nodded and slipped off the stool and we both walked up the short stairway to the empty hearing room to sit unobserved in the semi-darkness. I remained silent, sensing my friend's agitation, and waited for the clerk to unburden himself.

"You and your cop client are being shafted by the judge

and I thought you should know what is going on so you can protect your interest.''

I forced a laugh to alleviate my friend's tension and the dark shadows of the room surely obscured the lack of mirth on my face when I said, ''It's obvious that the judge hates me and my client, the way he is ruling, but I can deal with that.''

''But you don't know about his secret meetings as to how the case should be tried, or the file he keeps on you, or how he brags to his secretary how he intends to bury you.''

''Where did you get all this stuff from, Pinkie?'' I asked, peering through the darkness only to observe a serious look on the clerk's features.

''From Marcia, the judge's secretary.''

I remembered Marcia, the very efficient secretary with a voluptuous build and brooding bedroom eyes. Erler had mentioned that Marcia visited him in his cell and had wished him ''good luck.'' I also recalled how the winsome brunette appeared to confront me in the hallway on several occasions during the trial but shied away just as a conversation was imminent. I made my usual mental note to speak with Marcia the next time we met. I was consumed with curiosity as to what kind of ''file'' the judge was compiling on me. My investigator, Harry Long, was due for a new assignment: Target Judge Stokely.

''There's a hulluva lot more,'' blurted Pinkie. ''Maybe if you knew some of these things, there will still be time for you to get a different judge to sit on this case.''

''No, Pinkie,'' I explained, ''it's not possible to have a new judge in the middle of a trial and Stokely would never grant a mistrial regardless of what flagrant, prejudicial error may occur. The only protection would be to preserve all the legal errors and misconduct for an appeal in the event of a conviction.''

''Or unless the governor removes the judge from office before the trial ends,'' Pinkie said.

''Do you know something that you aren't telling me?'' I asked.

Pinkie mopped his brow. I could see that much in the obscured commission room but never expected the torrent

of words that erupted from the taciturn clerk who turned in
his seat, clutching both my hands and reported:

"A complaint about the judge to the Florida Bar Association was so serious it found its way to the governor's
office and preparations have been made for a removal hearing." I listened with shocked disbelief, but Pinkie's narrative was not to be halted. "From the very first, Stokely
would have 'special sentencings' where he called the wife
or girlfriend of the defendant into his private chambers to
fondle her bosom and make lewd proposals in exchange for
not giving the defendant jail time—placing him on probation instead."

"I can't believe it," was my reply.

"Neither did the lawyers for the defendants when it was
reported to them, except for one young Miami lawyer representing a black female named Juanita Hampton who was
on trial for manslaughter. Judge Stokely called her in chambers for a 'pre-trial conference' without her attorney and
made a deal, no jail time and probation for a blow job."

"Did it work out?" I asked, hoping my question did not
sound too naïve.

"Oh yes," answered Pinkie. "She got probation after
the jury found her guilty of manslaughter, but her lawyer
made the complaint to the Bar anyway."

It now dawned on me why Harry Long had laughed
when the court adjourned this morning for a "special sentencing." This revelation upset me for several reasons.
First, I now knew without a doubt that the judge in this
case was a real misfit. Second, I was embarrassed because
it seemed that I was the only one in town who didn't know
about Stokely's lecherous behavior—not good for an attorney who is supposed to be well-connected.

"Stokely has only been on the bench for one month," I
mused. "Are you telling me all this happened in such a
short period of time?"

"Since the first day, Counselor," answered Pinkie.
"That horny bastard never missed a chance. I know, I was
there!"

I shook my head and thanked Pinkie profusely for the
information and apologized for usurping the clerk's lunch
period during the private conference. I sat alone in the dark-

ened room after the court clerk left and ruminated as to what this new information would mean to the case. My educated guess was that there would not be enough time for the governor's office to finalize the removal proceedings in mid-trial. Looking at my wristwatch, I hastily left the county commission room to attend the afternoon trial session. The thought of lunch did not appeal to me, even if time permitted. As the information continued to sink in I became dejected at the prospect of facing a biased, emotionally unstable jurist, whose mental aberrations could conceivably result in the criminal conviction of an innocent young man.

At the afternoon session, Deputy James Rice was called to the stand to testify about the now famous *Catch Me Killer* tapes.

"Deputy Rice," intoned the prosecutor, "were you on duty in the sheriff's office the morning of August 12 of last year?"

"Yes sir," replied the deputy, settling himself comfortably in the witness chair, getting ready for a long siege.

"Tell us, please, if anything happened that morning of an unusual nature."

"The telephone rang a couple times and when I answered, a strange sounding, whimpering voice said, 'I would like to report a murder.' I was immediately on the alert and asked, 'Who is this?' "

"Did the caller give any name?"

"No sir," replied the deputy. "The caller said he had just killed three people."

"What happened next?" asked Boone, looking over his shoulder to the hushed courtroom.

"The voice answered, 'I'm serious. Please catch me before I kill more, please, please.' He seemed to be begging and crying—then the caller hung up. Deputy Sheriff Harold Lamore relieved me at 6:30 A.M. when a second call came in."

"Who answered the second call?" asked Boone, "Was it you or Lamore?"

"It was Deputy Lamore who carried on further conversation with the mysterious caller."

"Thank you, Deputy Rice. We'll just call in Deputy Lamore to tell us about the second call."

I informed the court, "The defense has no cross-examination of this witness." There was no point in questioning the deputy as to his version of what he heard. The best evidence was the actual tapes to be played before the jury in open court.

"Deputy Lamore," the prosecutor began, "were you on duty at the complaint desk on August 12 of last year?" Harold Lamore, a mature, well-built prototype of everyone's concept of the perfect police officer, looked at his interrogator with a serious gaze before replying, "Yes, sir."

"Can you please tell us what happened that morning?"

"I came on duty at 6:30 A.M. to relieve Rice, who was in the process of writing a report on a complaint sheet about a call he received from an unknown male that three murders were committed. Deputy Rice played the tape of the call back for me and I took charge at that point and waited to see if the stranger would call again. After a few moments the phone rang once more and I picked up the receiver. It was the same mysterious caller because I recognized the voice to be the one on the tape that Jim played back for me, er—pardon me, I mean Deputy Rice. The stranger said, 'Please hurry up and catch me—please, please.' 'Where are you?' I asked. 'Tell me where you are so I can come and get you.' He sounded quite emotional and wrought up."

"What else was said?" queried the prosecutor as the direct testimony of this witness drew to a close.

"He was unable to communicate any further," answered the deputy, "because he was crying and sobbing, then hung up."

"Where are the original tapes of these conversations with the stranger?" asked Boone.

"I placed them in a sealed container and put my initials and date on the box for identification and kept both recordings locked up in the evidence locker until this morning," replied the perfect cop, as the prosecutor sat down at his table, indicating the witness was tendered for cross-examination.

"No questions of this witness," I stated. It was always

good trial strategy to make announcement of "no questions" after an innocuous witness has completed his testimony, for two good reasons: First, by not asking an unimportant witness any questions, it generally conveys the impression to the jury that his testimony was not notable enough to warrant cross-examination. The second reason is, once the jury learns that an attorney does not waste time in cross-examining a witness who had nothing to offer or contribute to the issues, they will generally sit up and take notice when the lawyer does decide to go on the attack in challenging the motives or credibility of another witness of possible substance.

The state's next witness was Deputy Sheriff Wayne Madole. I recalled how Madole conducted the line-up at which Dorothy Clark was unable to identify Robert Erler, and suspected that the prosecutor had a new angle to explain Dorothy Clark's dismal failure.

"Deputy Madole, did you have occasion to arrange a line-up last September 24 where the defendant, Robert Erler, was one of the six men viewed?"

"Yes, I did. Mr. Erler was Number 5 in the line-up."

"How did Mr. Erler conduct himself in the line-up?" asked the prosecutor.

"He attempted to distort his facial appearance and puffed out his cheeks and closed his eyes so it would be difficult for Mrs. Clark to make an identification."

"What was the physical condition of Mrs. Clark, if you know?" the prosecutor continued.

"She did not appear to be very well. She was shaking and trembling."

"Thank you, Deputy Madole. I turn the witness to the defense for cross-examination."

The jurors sat up with interest as I almost ran to the witness stand and approached the deputy. There had been no cross-examination since Dorothy Clark had taken the stand, and they sensed that some significant questions would be asked.

I did not disappoint them.

"Mr. Madole," I began, "isn't it true that when Mrs. Clark was viewing the line-up, the lights were on in their full radiance?"

"In looking through the screen it appeared that they would have been on full brilliance, and I assume that they were."

"So that when Mrs. Clark was called upon to make an identification of her assailant by viewing the six men in the line-up, the lights did not present a problem to her because they were so bright."

"Guess so."

"Isn't it also true," I hammered away to the uncomfortable witness, "that the defendant Erler was one of the six men in the line-up, but Dorothy Clark told you she was unable to pick out her attacker?"

"Yes, but . . ."

"But what? Mr. Madole, Dorothy Clark was unable to point out anyone in the room, and certainly not the defendant, Robert Erler."

"But Mr. Erler had his cheeks puffed out, so maybe—"

"We'll come to that in a moment, deputy. Just answer this question: Didn't you and Mr. Boone decide to have another line-up and give Dorothy Clark a second chance to pick Mr. Erler as her attacker?"

"We did have another line-up, yes."

"And," I pursued in a relentless manner, "the lights were on in full brilliance?" Madole nodded lamely. "And," I persisted, "the positions of the six men in the line-up were changed, correct?" Madole muttered an assent.

"Now!" I raised my voice triumphantly. "Did Dorothy Clark pick Mr. Erler out of the line-up the second time?"

"No," answered Madole, "but maybe it was because Erler had his face contorted by puffing out his cheeks."

"You personally took several pictures at the line-up, did you not?"

"Yes, I did."

"Do you have a single picture that you can show to the jury with Mr. Erler's face puffed out and his eyes closed?"

"No, I don't."

"You, being in charge of the line-up, could have taken as many pictures as you wanted, is that not true?"

"Yes, sir."

"If you believed that Mr. Erler was doing anything wrong to destroy the line-up procedure, you could have taken a picture of him doing that and catch him flat-footed, isn't that true?"

"Could have."

"But you never did, did you?"

"No, sir."

I abruptly turned my back to the witness, hoping the jury noticed the lack of respect for Madole's credibility, and scornfully waved my hand in dismissal. The prosecutor made no attempt to rehabilitate his witness' sordid impression and as Madole was about to leave the stand a red-faced Judge Stokely roared to the prosecutor, "You may ask the witness, based on his experience, what the defendant's intent was in making those facial expressions at the line-up."

I angrily objected to the court's interference, complaining, "It's Mr. Boone's prerogative to raise such question and I say, most respectfully, the court has no right to take sides by injecting himself in the trial."

Stokely did not give me the courtesy of replying to my objections, but with a contemptuous sneer asked the court reporter, "Did you note his objections in the record?"

When the court reporter replied in the affirmative, the judge receded triumphantly to his chair.

The court bailiff sidled up to the bench, shielding his mouth with his hand to insure absolute secrecy and whispered something in the judge's ear that made his eyes light up.

"Ladies and gentlemen of the jury, this afternoon session is coming to a close and now is a good time to recess until tomorrow morning. The court's work is never done as I have a special sentencing that requires my immediate attention, but you good people may be excused."

I glared openly at the judge now that I knew the secret of his "special sentencing procedures." I couldn't help wonder if he knew that I knew.

33

A HUGE SHADOW enshrouded the rattling anodized glass doors of my office building catching my eye while reaching for the latest Supreme Court advance sheet neatly tucked among the sequentially numbered hardbound volumes. "It could only be Harry Long," I surmised, moving quickly across the reception room to admit the unexpected visitor. I led the investigator through the corridor to the rear of the one story building directly into my office. Opening the lower left hand drawer of my paper-strewn desk, I extracted a few Baby Ruth chocolate bars and ceremoniously placed them before the delighted Harry who pounced upon the candy with lightning speed.

"Just to prime the pump," I teased, sensing the investigator was ready to make a report of importance since his visit was unexpected.

"Where, oh where to start," sighed Harry as he wolfed down the first bar and unwrapped a second without licking the chocolate from his lips. I waited patiently, as the investigator would start in his own good time. It would be after the second Baby Ruth was devoured, or even the third. The ritual of lips and finger-licking finally ended, enabling the investigator to withdraw from his chocolate fugue and return to reality. "Oh, yes, the case."

I refused to rise to the bait and remained impassive. I steeled myself to Long's impish peccadilloes and gave him a long contemplative look. Harry grinned and knew the game had run its course. He irked me enough and decided to get down to business.

"Judge Stokely's days are numbered," he began.

"Know all about the governor's removal proceedings," I supplied, "but it will not come in time to abort the trial, and could only lend validity to our complaint of judicial misconduct on appeal in case Erler gets tagged by the jury."

Harry raised his eyebrows slightly to evince mild surprise. "Probably too many people involved to keep it secret. Chief Judge Ferris was the first to get on the problem and directed me to compile the judge's crazy actions for the hearing. Don't know what you can make of these incidents but I'll relate them and give you the names of the participants, in the event you need rebuttal testimony, or ammunition for cross-examination."

"Let's hear what you have," I asked with heightened interest.

"Start with Sergeant Joseph Portelli and Corporal William White of the Dania Police Department. They are due to testify in court tomorrow that the voice on the *Catch Me Killer* tapes is Erler's, absolutely and without question. Well, I learned these two birds were involved in a bribery rap that is under investigation by the county solicitor's office, which rejected all my inquiries and refused to discuss the matter. I got a tip they were working with Wayne Davidson who was the main culprit, and the three split up some fancy proceeds."

"Gee, Harry," I soberly responded, "that's invaluable information but can't be used to destroy their credibility unless they were convicted of the crime. Even if they were formally charged, we couldn't bring it up in court."

The investigator went through his notes, muttering to himself in barely audible tones, "Let's see. You know about the judge shooting a gun into his girlfriend's house; his judicial favors for sex, the Juanita Hampton incident." Raising his voice to a normal tone said, "Another big complaint is the judge's drinking problem."

I nodded my head. I remembered the incident about Doctor Mahoney in Fort Lauderdale telling the judge in open court during a civil trial in answer to the court's direct question, that in his professional opinion the judge was under the influence of drugs or alcohol.

"Besides the Doctor Mahoney case, were there any occasions where the judge was so intoxicated that it prevented him from fulfilling his judicial duties?"

"All the time," answered Harry. "The straw that broke the camel's back was on a particular occasion when newspaper reporters and photographers learned the judge was drunk in chambers and refused to come out. They congregated outside the door to take pictures and the corridor was filled with curious onlookers who joined the fun. You know Clyde Heath," Harry asked, "the new boss of the clerk's office?" I nodded in assent, not wishing to interrupt the investigator's report. "Well, he was so mad at Stokely ruining his efficient operation that he joined forces with Ferris to make a formal complaint for the judge's removal from the bench."

I shook my head sadly. "It's all good stuff, Harry, but everything in life is a matter of timing, and poor Bob Erler is caught in the switch." I sincerely believed Judge Stokely would be removed from judicial office, but the trial and possible consequences would be history by then. Moreover, even if Stokely appeared in court, either under the influence of drugs or roaring drunk, there could be grounds for a mistrial which would be overruled, or ignored as in the past. We were in a no-win situation and Erler was the victim.

"What else is on the agenda?" I asked in my most encouraging manner, not wanting Harry to feel he made his nocturnal trip from Fort Lauderdale in vain.

"They brought Deputy Koelsch from the Maricopa's Sheriff's Office for some character assassination and their ace in the hole, Mrs. Claire Kaufman."

"She is Erler's best friend," I groaned. "Don't tell me she drifted to the other side."

The investigator laughed out loud, holding his ample sides, exaggerating his actions for effect. Harry's antics of this nature always infuriated me, particularly on sensitive subjects and this juncture of the trial was keenly painful. "Drifting to the other side," he mimicked me. "It was more like an avalanche, and let me tell you, Counselor, that woman lured Erler into making a half-assed confession which the state will use to put this guy away."

"That telephone conversation between Mrs. Kaufman and Bob Erler was illegally procured and should be suppressed," was my hollow exclamation, without conviction. Now that I was certain of Claire's rapport with the prosecution, the chances were that even if Mrs. Kaufman were to testify the Hollywood police taped her telephone conversation without her knowledge and consent, the prejudicial trial judge would still permit the tape to be heard by the jury. Erler was doomed, which made me frustrated and angry at the same time. I was in no mood for any more of Harry's clowning. Smiling with a cheerfulness I did not feel, I thanked Harry for his extra efforts in wasting a perfectly good evening when he could be at the county morgue having fun.

Upon approaching the crowds assembled at the courtroom door there were several Dania police officers, in their well-pressed uniforms, sitting on the witness bench that lined the north corridor. Prominent among the Dania contingent was Sergeant Portelli, Erler's arch enemy, who was busily engaged in conferring with his sidekick, Officer William White. Portelli looked up as though he felt my eyes boring into him and nudged Officer White as the two left the group to seek privacy. It was obvious the Dania cops were present to give their opinion that Erler's voice and that of the 'Catch Me Killer' on the tape were identical, but Portelli and White had something else to contribute. It was bad enough that Jim Walsh of the Hollywood Police Department, who was Erler's best friend, was subpoenaed for voice comparison testimony, but White and Portelli's furtive actions worried me.

When court officially convened the fourth morning of the trial, the prosecutor rose to his feet and addressed the judge. "Your Honor, there are certain tapes which can only be played on a special transmission machine which is on the sixth floor of this building. It is so large and heavy that it cannot be moved down to this courtroom. Therefore, we request permission to send four or five witnesses up to the sixth floor to hear the tapes and come down to the court and jury and report their opinions as to voice identification."

"That's understandable," obliged the judge. "Permission granted!"

The dialogue stunned me. I could hardly believe my ears. I jumped up shouting "No—No! Absolutely Not! First of all the tapes are not in evidence; and . . ."

"Very well," interrupted the judge. "Mr. Boone, do you move the tapes into evidence?"

"Yes, Your Honor," readily answered the prosecutor taking the cue. "The state will offer the two tapes in evidence as 'State's Exhibits One and Two,' respectively."

"They will be received in evidence."

"That's not my main objection," I continued, trying to contain my rage. "The tapes must be played in open court in the presence of the jury."

"Don't you see it's impossible to do that," remarked the judge condescendingly. "Didn't you hear that the special machine could not be moved from the sixth floor?"

"Then let the jury go up to the sixth floor and hear the transmission. Your Honor is empowered to convene the court to any room in the courthouse building."

"You are not supervising this trial, I am, and I have already ruled."

"But, most respectfully, Your Honor, this is most improper. If this procedure is allowed, the jury will only hear the opinions of the witnesses, which amounts to invading the province of the jury. The jurors must hear the tapes themselves and make their own independent determination. I strongly object to this procedure. It is unorthodox, unprecedented and illegal."

The judge looked at me with a vacant stare and said, "You can go upstairs with the witnesses, if you wish." And turning to the prosecutor asked, "Who are you taking up there to make the voice identification?"

"Sergeant Joseph Portelli, Lieutenant Peter Dalziel, Officer William White, Officer Fred Caldwell of the Dania Police Department, and Officer James Walsh of Hollywood."

The police witnesses named were called into the room and herded before the judge's bench awaiting instructions from the court while I fumed with frustration and mentally made another notch on the growing list of judicial errors. Resigning myself to the fact that I was up against a stone wall of prejudice, I sat back in the chair at the counsel table, my face set in a grimace of loathing directed at the emotionally unstable individual wearing the symbolic black robe of justice.

"Gentlemen of the jury," explained Stokely to the jurors in the box, "five witnesses will be permitted to go to the sheriff's communication center on the sixth floor of the courthouse to hear the August 12 tapes that are in evidence as State's Exhibits One and Two, respectively. After they have reviewed the transmissions they will return to the courtroom and submit their testimony under oath as to their conclusions and opinions.''

"To which the defense most emphatically objects!" I reiterated.

"Objection overruled!" snapped the judge, throwing a defiant glare in the direction of the defense table. "There will be a recess of one hour, and we will reconvene in the courtroom to resume the trial."

The jurors remained in the jury box, looking at each other and in the direction of the counsel tables for some guidance regarding their function, and only when the judge swept from his chair, beckoning the clerk of the court and prosecutor to follow him, came the realization they were excluded from whatever was to occur in the communication center on the sixth floor. Boone marshalled his five witnesses and led them out of the courtroom to the elevators in the hallway. Erler remained in the courtroom with the jail guard while I made my way to the sixth floor to witness the novel procedure instigated and obviously devised by the judge and prosecutor.

The dusty quilting that lined the service elevator to the sixth floor of the courthouse made chalky imprints on the blue uniforms of the prospective police witnesses that were jammed into the close quarters. I waited for transportation until the prosecutor and judge rode up with the bailiff and court stenographer. I didn't want to be in the judge's presence any more than necessary and took the elevator to the top story where crowds of people congregated at the dimly lighted storeroom around a massive, eight-foot-high steel mechanical device with two over-sized reels, which apparently was the special transmission machine. Perhaps Erler should also have been in the musty room, as a defendant in a criminal case must be present at every stage of the proceedings, but the youthful rookie cop seemed to lapse into a lethargic state lately and I didn't need any more headaches or distractions at this juncture of the trial.

"Here is what will be done," said the judge, addressing

the assembled group, as well as the five police witnesses. "The deputy will play both tapes. You are to listen only, and not say anything to each other, or anyone. After you have heard the tapes, you will return outside the courtroom and testify as to your opinion on voice identification."

The five prospective witnesses nodded their assent, and the judge ordered Deputy Lamore to "start the transmission, and play back both tapes." Not a word was spoken by anyone as the troubled voice of the 'Catch Me Killer' crackled through the room. The two tape recordings were played back for the benefit of the silent police witnesses who listened attentively.

"Play it again, Sam," grinned the judge with ill-timed humor, emulating Humphrey Bogart in his memorable scene in the movie *Casablanca*.

"Does Your Honor wish me to repeat the transmission?" inquired the deputy.

"Repeat the recording," ordered the judge, obviously disappointed that his attempt at humor fell upon unappreciative ears. "A repetition may help the memory of these police officers."

Returning to the courtroom after the *Catch Me Killer* tapes were played in full for the second time, Robert Erler rose from his seat, looking baffled and inquired, "What is going on?" I explained the unorthodox procedure that just occurred, and told my puzzled client, "The prosecutor will now call in the five witnesses, one by one, and I expect them to say that the voice they heard on the tapes upstairs sounds like your voice."

"Impossible!" blurted Erler in a shocked tone, "I'm being framed."

"I was warned about this," was my hushed response, "so let's ride with the punches." Bob Erler had a sickly look on his face as he slowly sat down in his chair. It was not prudent to commiserate any further, as Erler would only become more disconsolate, and we resumed our seats at the counsel table, to await the crucifixion.

Portelli led the array of voice identification witnesses. Mounting the witness stand with a supercilious stare toward the press section, seeking their attention, he haughtily reminded the packed courtroom that he was the first to recognize Erler's voice on the *Catch Me Killer* tapes. Officer William White also testified as anticipated and volunteered that he had no trouble recognizing the voice on the tapes because he and "Bob Erler were good friends and they talked a lot together."

Erler gasped audibly and clutched my arm, whispering fiercely, "That's a lie! We were never friends. We hated each other and fought when I told him and the other black officer to stay away from the white barmaids in the saloon in colored town." I recalled Erler talking about that some time ago, but the subject was too risky to explore on cross-examination, and shrugged off my client's agitation.

Officer James Walsh disappointed the prosecution by testifying the voice on the tapes "sounded like Bob Erler's voice, but could not be certain." When the witness was apprehensively tendered for cross-examination, I slowly rose to my feet, stalling, while making a decision to either say, "no questions" or emphasize before the jury that Officer Walsh, Erler's good friend and co-worker at the station, "was not certain" as to the voice identification. I decided to nail down the uncertainty and perhaps impress upon the jury the distinction between speculation and absolute certainty.

"Mr. Walsh," I addressed the witness in a low-keyed confident manner, "did I understand you to say the voice on the *Catch Me Killer* tapes 'sounded' like Bob Erler's voice?"

"Yes, sir," replied Walsh.

"Using that same yardstick in the realm of speculation or guesswork, couldn't the voice on the *Catch Me Killer* tapes 'sound' like other voices you have heard?"

"Yes, sir," replied the witness, sighing with relief, having been extricated from his distasteful commitment.

"Now, Officer Walsh," I beamed, facing sideways from the witness, looking directly at the jury, "can you tell this jury with absolute, positive certainty that the voice you heard on the tapes upstairs is the same voice of Bob Erler?"

Walsh turned in his seat and looked at the assembled jurors in the box and said in a loud, clear voice, "No, I cannot!"

I fixed a direct stare on the jurors, looking for any kind

of reaction, but the blank vacuous expressions received told me nothing. Shifting my gaze to the prosecutor, it was comforting to see Boone's ears redden. With a poker-faced expression, I dismissed Walsh from the witness stand. I turned to Erler to see if he was heartened by Walsh's performance on the stand, and was immediately alarmed at Erler's unusual actions in clutching his head with both hands, his face contorted with pain.

"May the defense have a short recess?"

"Very well" agreed the court. "It's time for an early lunch break, anyway." The courtroom emptied in record time and I sat alone with Erler and his jail guard.

"What's the matter, Bob?"

"This blinding pain in my head is killing me! It comes and goes."

"Do you have any medication, or pills of some kind for relief?"

"I'll be okay in a little while," replied the stricken defendant as he stretched out prone on the hard oaken pew behind the counsel table. It concerned me that perhaps the stress of the trial was taking its toll on my client, and wondered how he would cope when his friend Claire Kaufman took her turn on the witness stand. Putting aside my fears, I left Erler supine on the bench, and went down the rear elevator to Tom's snack bar in search of sustenance and information and was not disappointed. Tom spotted me and waved for me to come to the end of the bar where he miraculously produced a stool for my comfort.

"Your boy is misbehaving," whispered Tom.

"Fighting again?" I asked.

Tom looked around to make certain he was not being observed and tapped his forefinger to his nose, looking away quickly. That gesture only meant one thing: narcotics. "It can't be," I groaned. "Not now. Not in the middle of a trial."

"Sorry Counselor, but your boy is a pill-popper and is graduating to the hard stuff."

I knew better than to ask how true this information was because Tom had never failed me. He told me about some drug smuggling going on in the jail section but only some speed and marijuana. Where did the "hard stuff" come from? No wonder Erler had a seizure that morning. I picked at the tuna fish sandwich, my appetite gone, vowing to give Erler holy hell for sabotaging his defense.

When I was certain that Bob had recovered adequately enough to weather the afternoon session which was to commence with Police Officer Caldwell, a voice identification witness, I thrust aside my disappointment with Erler and returned to the important business at hand.

Caldwell, a pleasant, balding, slim twenty-two-year veteran on the Dania force, frankly stated he was a curious person and when he learned the Hollywood Police Department had a tape of the 'Catch Me Killer' he was motivated by an urgency to go to the department and listen to it. He gave his opinion that it was Erler's voice on the tape. There was nothing on earth more maddening to me than a 'volunteer' witness in a highly publicized criminal case and I vehemently distrusted the motivation of such a person. I always believed a volunteer wanted to get into the act and become a player in the limelight of stardom. When I learned from the direct testimony that Caldwell went to the Hollywood Police Department to satisfy his curiosity about the tapes, and then declaring the voice to be that of Robert Erler, I decided this eager beaver and his testimony needed some exploratory surgery.

"Mr. Caldwell," I began the cross-examination, deliberately not calling him "Officer Caldwell" as jurors always equate more credibility and respect to a police officer than a layman, "did you ever discuss with Portelli at any time whose voice was rumored to be on the tapes?"

"The rumor was discussed with the other officers at the station."

"You were only asked about a discussion with Portelli. I must ask you again, did Portelli tell you whose voice he believed was on the tapes?"

"Yes, sir," replied Caldwell. "He said it was Robert Erler's voice on the tapes."

"And this was *before* you wanted to satisfy your curiosity to hear the tapes, is that correct?"

Caldwell nodded.

"Speak up," shouted the judge. "The court reporter

must record every word you say and moving your head up and down won't do."

"Yes," answered the witness, "but I was not influenced by what Sergeant Portelli told me."

"What about when you went to the Hollywood Police Department to hear the tapes, who did you speak to before you heard the recordings?"

Caldwell remained pensive for a moment, and replied, "Spoke with Lieutenant John Cox."

"And," I coaxed gently, "what did Detective Cox say to you and what did you say to him?"

"Asked me how well I had known Bob Erler and things like that."

"Then you went into the room where they played the tape for you?"

"Yes, sir. They asked me if I recognized the voice."

"This is right after they were talking about Bob Erler and if you knew him?"

"Yes, sir."

"And what did you say?"

"I told them it sounded like him."

"Did you say it was his voice positively?"

"I don't think I said it was positively his voice, no, sir."

"How about now? Are you saying it is positively Erler's voice?"

"No, sir."

The prosecutor's ears began to redden again and requested a short recess, which was granted by the court. I was not worried about the rehabilitation job Boone had in mind for Caldwell and when court convened, my gut reaction indicated the rosy ears on the prosecutor meant the witness would not recede from his story. The case was moving along too favorably for the defense, which made me a trifle apprehensive. It was "character assassination time," I surmised when Dania Police Officer Earl Peterman took the stand for the prosecution and professed to be a close friend and confidante of the defendant.

"He's lying," Erler whispered. "We were never friends and hardly spoke to each other."

Peterman testified that in a secretly private talk with Erler, he took him to task for making a ridiculous report to his superiors at the Hollywood Police Department on the occasion of finding Merilyn Clark's body in a field near the industrial park.

"I told Erler he was too good an officer not to take the names of the elderly couple that gave him an important clue about a body lying in a field. I even suggested that it looked like he created the incident so he could 'discover' the body."

The jurors turned to look at Erler for his reaction to this damaging testimony. It is easy to sense when a telling blow is scored by the prosecution. The jury box is generally stationed between the witness stand and the counsel table where the defendant is seated. The jurors fix their attention to the witness on the stand and when a pertinent reference is made to or about the defendant, they shift their gaze collectively to the defendant. Their attention is directed back and forth between the testifying witness and the defendant, almost like spectators at a tennis match.

On cross-examination I inquired: "Mr. Peterman, did you ever make a report of this, either written or oral, to anyone?"

"No, sir."

"You kept it locked within your breast until today?"

"Yes, sir."

"When exactly did this conversation with you and Erler take place?"

"I would say the first of December or the last of November of last year."

"Are you positive that you had this talk with Mr. Erler last November or December?"

"Absolutely," was his firm reply.

"Mr. Peterman, where was it that you had these talks with Mr. Erler last November or December?"

"I believe it was in Dania."

"Where in Dania?" I pursued.

"Somewhere near the city hall, probably in a coffee shop or restaurant," he replied nervously.

"So, Mr. Peterman, you are absolutely telling this court and jury that you had this talk with Robert Erler in a Dania coffee shop last November or December, is that true?"

"Positively," replied Peterman, his eyes darting to the prosecution table for assistance.

"Mr. Peterman," I questioned, with deliberate slowness and an accusing glare, "how do you account for the fact that the defendant, Robert Erler, has been continuously confined in jail right here in Fort Lauderdale since last September to the present time, which is January 1969?"

"I don't know," was the weak reply as he lowered his head.

The attentive jurors ceased their ping-pong antics to stare expectantly at the disappointed prosecutor who made an obvious display of nonchalance, which fooled no one. Shuffling his papers busily, Boone called for Roy Eugene Mitchell to take the stand, but the judge called a halt to the proceedings, declaring "there was some court business he had to attend to."

"A special sentencing?" I asked with a straight face. I then imitated the judge's famous rolling eyes act, and took his venomous glare in stride. I didn't care any longer and returned his malevolent stare with a wide-eyed look of innocence. It felt good to turn my back to the outraged jurist and slowly made my way back to the counsel table, floating on a cloud. All the feelings of stress and tension were gone and I was gratified that the spontaneous act of defiance against Stokely was responsible for my newly acquired serenity.

34

STILL MILDLY IRKED at my client's reported drug activities I decided to kill a little time at the snack bar until Erler was returned to his cell. I could have conferred with Erler in the jury room but feared that the room was "bugged." The conference room in the jail was much safer because of the incessant traffic of inmates and trusties who would have immediately become aware of any invasion of privacy if any tricks were attempted. Approaching the counter I looked for Tom, when a melodic gravelly voice called,

"Mr. Varon, my name is Deane Bostick, I'm a reporter covering your trial."

My attention was drawn to the speaker, a stocky, well-built, dark-bearded man and said, "Hello, Deane, I recall seeing you in the press section in the courtroom."

"Heard this was your watering hole," smiled Bostick, his even white teeth visible through his bearded visage. "Just wanted to shake your hand and have a small chat."

Bostick's gravelly southern drawl intrigued me, prompting me to politely ask, "What outfit are you reporting for?"

"I originally covered this homicide last August for *MAN*'s Magazine and am doing another piece on this trial, and frankly don't like what is going on."

"What do you mean?" I queried, sensing a new ally was found among the bevy of cynical reporters in the press box.

"I first came to the scene of the crime about four months ago with a jaded reporter's view, expecting the usual scenario, you know, run-of-the-mill homicide, manhunt, apprehension of suspect and sorting out of the clues. The deeper I explored, the rottener the case began to smell." His black eyebrows arched knowingly as he tilted his head in my direction, "and recognized a railroad job in the making."

Instinctively, I knew this new acquaintance Deane Bostick, would play an important role in the 'Catch Me Killer' case, and decided to cultivate his friendship. At dinner that evening in the picturesque Riverside Hotel between the North Fork of the New River and Las Olas Boulevard in Fort Lauderdale, I asked Deane, "What was it that made you such an Erler fan?"

"Well," smiled Bostick, his white teeth flashing, "when none of the police officers would talk to me about the case, I became curious. Detective Melrose of the Fort Lauderdale police department antagonized me no end."

"You showed him your press identification. Melrose knew you were a reporter. Why would he make you angry?"

Bostick explained that after viewing first-hand the conduct of the trial, he had some serious doubts about Erler's criminal involvement and when he further pursued the lieutenant for an interview to go over some of the disturbing details of the case, Melrose became aroused and told Bostick, "There is nothing here for you. My advice would be to let it alone."

"Can't just walk away and leave it alone, Mr. Melrose," reported Deane, holding a glass of Beaujolais up to the flickering candlelight, admiring its ruby richness. "I'm beginning to think a lot of people have something to hide in this case. Melrose looked like he wanted to strangle me and said, 'I'm not going to talk to you anymore' and turned his back on me and refused to say another word."

"What seems to disturb you about this case?" I inquired, only too eager to receive independent evaluations from an analytical source.

"A lot of things," answered Bostick, seated comfortably across the white linen covered table, cradling the wine glass in both hands, expertly savoring its bouquet, "For example, that last witness, Peterman, made up a phony story. We both know that Erler was in jail without bond ever since he was arrested and could not have met with the witness in a Dania coffee shop. But what was significant is that it was Lieutenant Goetz of the Hollywood Police Department who criticized Erler for not getting the names of the elderly couple who found the girl's body that morning."

"So, Goetz was unavailable as a witness for the prosecution," I broke in, as the light bulb flashed in my head, "and they had Peterman supply the inference that there may not have been an elderly couple, and Erler's incomplete report was deliberate!"

"Bingo!" laughed the reporter. "Here's another one," taking a large swallow of wine, "the Mickey Mouse voice identification procedure made me nauseous. Whoever heard of witnesses hearing some tapes out of the jury's view and then going into the courtroom to give their opinion?"

"That's one for the books," was my agreement. "I screamed and objected, but didn't get anywhere."

"I know there is some highly sophisticated equipment that measure voice prints. Why didn't the prosecutor go that route?"

It was my turn to take a deep draught of wine, and looked in the face of my new friend, "Have a confession to make. I know all about voice prints and decibel comparisons. The

New Jersey courts have rejected those voice tests in a criminal case because an absolute degree of accuracy was not guaranteed. If I had those tests made of Erler's voice in juxtaposition with the 'Catch Me Killer' voice, and the voices were identical, I would be duty bound to make the disclosure to the prosecution under our Reciprocal Discovery Rules."

"I see," mused the reporter, stroking his beard. "You would know your client is guilty and if you were to put him on the stand to deny the homicide, there is a matter of subornation of perjury."

"You've got that right, Deane," I said. "That's why I couldn't take the chance, even though Erler has claimed he is innocent. I never ask a client if he committed the crime. I don't want to know. All I can do is guarantee a fair trial, using all the weaponry and expertise available. If, despite all the constitutional safeguards and efforts, my defendant is found guilty, by a court or jury, so be it."

It was a combination of Bostick's hypnotic, gravelly southern drawl and the wine-laden sumptuous dinner that drained my energy. I suddenly became tired. Tomorrow was going to be a ball buster.

The fifth day of the trial. Roy Eugene Mitchell was called to the stand, a middle-aged man with tousled iron grey hair, dressed in rumpled coveralls. Mitchell, a garage mechanic, professed to have met with Erler on a previous occasion in his service station in Dania.

"Mr. Erler came into my station and wanted to know if I was interested in buying a small revolver. He showed me a small .22 caliber shot which was either a four or six cylinder pistol, which looked like a German-made gun, with white side handles."

"Are you certain the gun Mr. Erler showed you had white handles?" asked the prosecutor, looking at the jurors, hopeful they would remember that Dorothy Clark had testified that Robert Erler had a gun with white handles the night she was shot.

"Oh yes," came the expected reply, "and I told him that I wasn't interested in buying a gun."

"Did Mr. Erler say anything further?" the prosecutor inquired smugly.

"Only that he warned me not to tell anybody he was trying to sell the gun," was his sly reply.

Erler pulled on my sleeve and angrily whispered, "That's a damn lie!" The agitated comment from my client seemed somewhat out of character, as Erler appeared to have had resumed his composure. I looked at Erler's flushed face, noting something peculiar about his eyes. The prosecutor droned on with his direct examination of Mitchell but my attention was focused on the strange expression on Erler's face. It came to me in a nostalgic flash. I suddenly recalled the occasion when as a school boy, our entire sixth grade elementary class was taken on a civic visit to the stockyards on Chicago's south side and could never forget the expression in the cows' eyes as they were channeled from the pens through wooden chutes to the slaughter house, one by one, to await the crush of the sledge hammer on their skulls, benumbing them before the huge butcher knife was plunged into their throats. Erler had that same look, timorous and innocently apprehensive. Returning to reality, I attempted to pick up the threads of Mitchell's devastating testimony.

Boone was so anxious to tie Erler to the ownership of a gun with "white handles" that Dorothy Clark previously mentioned, he forgot she testified that Erler had a "large .38 caliber revolver," whereas the witness was testifying about a .22 caliber gun. Since the state did not have the murder weapon in its possession, or ballistic tests or reports as to what type of gun or caliber of missiles were used to kill Merilyn Clark, resort was made to this "back door" type of evidence. I often wondered if the prosecutor really forgot about the distinction between the small .22 caliber gun or the larger .38 caliber. Boone had been a former Florida highway trooper and would not make such a fundamental mistake when it came to handguns. I mentally saluted the good ole cracker, who was only interested in having the jury remember the "gun with the white handles." An A-plus for Boone.

There was something covert about the witness. His story was too convenient and his guarded demeanor piqued my curiosity. It was like pulling teeth to get a simple admission from the witness that his meeting with Erler took place "about a year ago." Acting on a hunch, I asked, "Have you ever been convicted of a felony?" The rationale behind this type of question was that if Roy Mitchell admitted to a felony conviction, disclosure of this fact before the jury would tend to diminish the credibility of the witness. To the surprise of everyone in the courtroom, the witness blurted out, "I refuse to answer on the ground that it might incriminate me."

The members of the press corps murmured their amazement which blanketed the rest of the courtroom with a purr of confusion. This startling revelation delighted me, particularly since Mitchell, who gave such damaging testimony against Erler, was attempting to hide under the protection of the Fifth Amendment to the United States Constitution, known in the common parlance of the street as "taking the fifth." I knew under the law Mr. Mitchell's testimony could be stricken and was just about to ask the court to nullify his entire statement when Judge Stokely actually jumped to his feet, yelling like a kid, "Let me ask him a question. Have you ever been convicted of *PERJURY?*"

"Would you please explain that?" asked Mitchell.

"Lying under oath," explained the court.

"No, sir."

"All right. The court at this time instructs the jury that this witness is a competent witness and is not disqualified by virtue of any previous conviction and you may give . . . I will instruct you later as to how much weight you may give to his testimony."

"I'm sorry, Your Honor," was my heated objection. "You are taking this entire matter out of context. No one said anything about 'perjury,' I must respectfully object to the court again interjecting himself in these proceedings. If this witness seeks to invoke the protection of the Fifth Amendment, his testimony must be stricken because the defendant cannot be precluded from a full and complete cross-examination. That's the law and I'll be glad to show the court the latest Supreme Court decisions on this point." I had to pause to keep from losing my composure. Stokely's red face was contorted with rage, but I had to make my point for the record and said, "The theory is simple: If I am prevented from cross-examining the witness because he hides behind the Fifth Amendment, then his testimony must be stricken."

"Don't you try to tell me what the law is, Counselor!" broke in the judge in a threatening tone. I looked backward over the hushed courtroom as though seeking support from someone, somewhere. If only there could be a "special sentencing" scheduled to rescue me. The prosecutor was seated comfortably at the counsel table, arms crossed on his chest, an amused smile playing about his lips. Erler sat quietly in his chair at the defense table with that peculiar look of stupefied bewilderment, coming down the wooden chute to his inexorable fate.

Stokely was on a roll. Exhibiting a shameless abuse of judicial power, he took over the role of prosecutor. On one particular occasion, when Lieutenant Melrose was tying up some loose ends for the prosecution, he opened the door to a sensitive line of inquiry that allowed me to attack Melrose in some vulnerable areas. I was peripherally questioning him on Dorothy Clark's bedside statements, gradually leading up to "tapes and recordings," when the judge loudly shouted to the prosecutor, "Why don't you object on the ground that defense counsel is exceeding the scope of the direct examination?"

My rage and frustration melted into a sick type of fatigue that I'd never experienced before. I renewed my volatile protestations to the court's conduct, until I finally realized that Stokely thrived on this type of baiting tactics, and I resolved to retrench and take the unpredictable antics of the unstable Stokely in stride.

At the noon recess, the newspaper reporters flocked around the defense table popping questions and seeking answers to the court's unusual behavior. They clamored for a comment, but I would not accommodate them, as criticism of a judge during a trial would only make the court more rabid and hostile. "Fellows," I pleaded, "I just need a few moments alone with my client before the big guns come on this afternoon. All I can tell you is that you were here and saw everything for yourselves."

The reporters pressed for an explanation of the judge's

animosity, without success, and yielded to Harry Long's bulky frame waiting patiently for an audience with me. Harry was smiling widely but I was in no mood for silly banter.

"What's up, Harry?" I asked crossly.

"They've got that Arizona deputy, Edward Koelsch," started the investigator, realizing this was not the time for fun and games, "and he's got some stuff to burn your client."

"But he's a good friend of mine!" burst in Erler. "We've been pals for years."

"So is Claire Kaufman a good friend of yours," answered Harry, "and they're saving her as the clean-up hitter, tomorrow."

"Tomorrow is Saturday. There generally is no court on Saturday."

"I guarantee you the trial will go on Saturday," answered the investigator. "Boone is shooting for the Sunday paper coverage, to give the jury members a good chance to read Mrs. Kaufman's testimony and impress it indelibly on their minds."

The jail guard interrupted the wake, "Sorry, I have to take your man upstairs now, or feeding time will be over."

"Thanks," I replied, realizing the guard would also miss his lunch, and turned to Harry, saying, "Let's go to the snack bar, for a tuna on rye for me and a dozen or so Baby Ruths for you."

The afternoon session was a disaster. Edward Koelsch, a lean, sallow-faced deputy sheriff from Phoenix, smoothed his untidy black hair from his high forehead, savoring each precious moment on the witness stand as he testified how he engineered the surrender of Robert Erler who had evaded capture from the entire Phoenix Police Department and the Maricopa County Sheriff's Department. He described in lurid detail Erler's drugged conduct at the Magistrate's hearing, how he kicked photographers and broke the judge's office window with his manacled hands, sustaining severe personal injuries, yelling, "I'm an animal and should be put away."

"Was there a time when you had a conversation with

the defendant concerning Mrs. Dorothy Clark?" asked the prosecutor.

"Mr. Erler told me he intended to blow up the portion of the hospital where Dorothy Clark was confined and boasted that she wouldn't regain consciousness."

"What else was said by the defendant as to his involvement in the matter?" asked the prosecutor.

"The defendant bragged about how he was assigned by his superior officers to stand guard over the body of Merilyn Clark, while the hunt was on for the killer and said 'and all the time it was me.' "

"You're a liar!" screamed Erler, losing his temper. "That's a lie!"

"Control your client!" shouted the judge, banging on his desk with his gravel, arousing the entire courtroom to a spontaneous wave of restrained conversation. "Any more exhibitions of this nature will be dealt with harshly by the court!"

I pulled Erler back into his seat, satisfied in a small measure that he negated in part the devastating testimony of the eager witness. Undaunted by Erler's outburst, Koelsch continued his harangue and referred to Erler as a "fugitive from justice."

"Objection," I angrily shouted. "That is an improper conclusion of law which I move to strike and ask the court to instruct the jury to disregard the witness's statement."

"Wasn't there a fugitive warrant issued against your client by the Federal Bureau of Investigation?" smirked the judge.

"Absolutely not!" I replied bitterly. "I would like the jury excused as there is an important motion to be discussed."

The judge smiled indulgently as he ordered the jury out of the courtroom promising that, "it would only be for a few minutes."

"Your Honor," I started, trying to contain my frustration, "the defense moves for a mistrial. It is impossible for the defendant to receive a fair trial at the present posture of the case. You have deliberately created prejudice by not only injecting yourself into the case, but you even compounded the misprision by testifying as a state witness. This conduct on your part is erroneous, and . . ."

"Why do you say I testified?" laughed Stokely.

"You talked about a federal warrant issued by the Federal Bureau of Investigation against my client as a 'fugitive from justice.' That was the court's own idea, and nothing like that ever occurred. Your Honor brought it out in the presence of the jury, and you had no right to do that!"

The prosecutor never said a word. He didn't have to. He knew what the court's ruling would be. "Motion for mistrial denied," snapped the judge, and directed the bailiff to ask the jurors to return to their seats in the jury box.

As the members of the jury filed back into the courtroom and resumed their seats, they collectively looked at the defense table seeming to sense the despondency of its occupants. It was always good showmanship to maintain an air of confidence in the presence of the jury so a prejudgment by the jurors in favor of the prosecution may be avoided. I would have had to have been the world's most consummate actor to portray any indicia of assurance that afternoon, and were the truth known, my true feeling was likened to a patient about to be operated upon for an inguinal hernia repair.

One of the jurors raised his hand, presumably to ask a question. I assumed the spokesman for the panel was probably the elected foreman of the jury. This was the first indication as to who was the bellwether of the flock and upon whom I would focus my most telling points. The judge noticed the juror's hand in the air and regally nodded in acknowledgment.

"Sir," asked the juror, "since tomorrow is Saturday, will we be excused from service until Monday?"

"Sorry," replied the court, forcing a toothy grin. "Saturday is business as usual in this court." Looking over the disappointed panel, he observed, "This is a good time to adjourn, so let me once again admonish you not to discuss the case with anyone and not to read the newspaper accounts of the trial. That goes for television, too."

I received permission from the bailiff to speak alone with my client when the courtroom cleared. I still did not trust the privacy of the juror's conference room fearing electronic surveillance. "Well, Bob," I opened brightly with an enthusiasm I genuinely did not feel, "it seems we are stuck with the craziest judge in the business. Don't feel too discouraged, because he is making one legal error after another, and the record is being faithfully preserved."

"Are you sure the court reporter is taking everything down?" asked Erler, a trifle concerned.

I didn't blame him for his apprehensiveness and tried to elevate his mood by jokingly saying, "As a matter of fact, I instructed the court reporter to even record the judge's breathing."

Erler smiled for the first time that afternoon and ruefully remarked, "I wish there was some way to record the judge's 'eye rolling' act, too." I was mildly surprised that Erler was so observant; he seemed so remote and disinterested during the major portion of the trial.

"I want to orient you on tomorrow's session," I continued. "Claire Kaufman will be the prosecution's final witness. Please don't harbor any illusions that her testimony will be favorable to the defense." Erler looked up at me with a puzzled expression but thought better than to make a reply. "You no doubt will be shocked and angered at the things she may say, but you are to keep your temper under control and, above all, no outbursts."

"How can I keep quiet when all these people are telling rotten lies about me?" cried Erler in an anguished tone.

"You will have your chance to make a full and complete answer to everyone when you take the stand in your own defense."

"Good!" replied Erler forcefully. "I want to tell my side of the story and am glad you decided to let me testify."

My decision to have Erler testify on his own behalf was made easier by his continued protestations of innocence. A defendant in a criminal case is not required to take the stand on his own behalf, but should he elect to do so, he is subjected to grueling and exhaustive cross-examination by the prosecutor. I was unconcerned. Bob Erler was a clean-cut, handsome young man with a polite manner of speaking that projected sincerity, and would make an excellent witness. This would be his opportunity to negate, or even overcome the incriminating innuendoes made before the jury, and could perhaps explain the context of the telephone conversation with Claire Kaufman. Another side of me said Erler would never be able to cogently explain away the intercepted telephone conversation with Mrs. Kaufman. My only hope was to have the Kaufman tape suppressed, but was certain Stokely would deny the motion to suppress and have the tape played before the jury.

The media was having a field day, referring to Claire Kaufman as the mystery woman in Erler's life and intermittently referred to as the "siren" or "lure." There were no surprises about her testimony. The state would use her telephone conversation with Erler to bury him.

35

EDDIE KAY WAS unhappy. He so much wanted to be in the courtroom to watch the action, but was barred from sitting at the defense table because he was on the witness list, scheduled to testify about Dorothy Clark's failure to identify Erler at the two lineups arranged by the prosecution officials. In a trial, either side may request the trial judge to order all witnesses to be excluded from the courtroom until called by counsel to take the witness stand to give testimony. This time-honored "rule" was designed to prevent a prospective witness from sitting in the courtroom during a trial and hearing another witness testify, thus influencing or giving him an opportunity to alter his forthcoming testimony. It is a sanitization process that preserves the integrity of the witnesses, so their testimony is spontaneous, pure and unadulterated.

Boone requested the court to invoke the "rule" against witness Eddie Kay during the second day of the trial. I immediately sprung to my feet to oppose the prosecutor's request. "Your Honor, the witness, Mr. Eddie Kay, is my assistant during this trial and since he is a qualified member of the Florida Bar should not be subject to the 'rule'."

"Denied!" snapped the judge. "Mr. Witness, you are excluded from the courtroom until it is time for you to testify," and scowling at me, added, "You, being a lawyer, know what that means, so any violation will be severely punished."

Boone had a mean streak in him which I never realized before. The prosecutor had a native cunning spawned in the backwoods of North Florida and it surprised me to see Boone stripped of his "good ole boy" image by such a cheap shot. There was no logical reason why Eddie could not sit at the defense counsel table for the past five days while the case was in progress, except for pure spite on the prosecutor's part.

Arriving at the parking lot in the rear of my office building, I could see the bright red Ford Thunderbird and knew Eddie Kay was awaiting. "Fine trial experience you're getting," I added, "sitting on your duff like a leper for four days."

"I feel like a leper, too," Eddie replied sadly, as he followed me into the library and conference room at the front of the building.

"Let me fill you in as to what's going on," I began attempting to buoy Eddie's spirits and let him know he was still considered a team player even though temporarily relegated to inactive status. "Tomorrow Mrs. Claire Kaufman will be the clean-up hitter before the state rests and Erler's half-assed confession will be heard by the jury."

"Aren't you going ahead with your motion to suppress the unlawful interception of the telephone conversation between Mrs. Kaufman and Erler?"

I sadly shook my head. "Did you ever hear the expression of 'The blind leading the blind'?" Eddie nodded, not knowing what to expect, maintained a respectful silence. "When a motion to suppress is filed, unless the facts are agreed upon, there must be an evidentiary hearing to make a factual determination as to how an arrest, or search, or as in this case, an intercepted telephone conversation occurred."

"But we never had a hearing on our motion," chimed in Eddie.

"Nor will we ever have one, even though the law mandates a hearing. Stokely decided to let Claire Kaufman testify and allow the jury to hear the tape recording of her conversation with Erler."

"And *then* the judge will make his ruling? *After* the jury has heard the tapes?'' Eddie asked, his eyes wide open with incredulity.

"Believe it or not," was the answer. "That's exactly what the judge wants to do."

"So, Stokely has us coming and going," replied the alert junior attorney. "If the judge grants your motion to suppress the tape because of unauthorized wire interception, what good will it do, because the jury would already have heard the tape?"

I chuckled indulgently, pleased that Eddie saw the picture so quickly, and said, "Sure as I'm sitting here Stokely will deny the motion to suppress, so why speculate."

"That judge is so erratic," said Eddie, pursing his lips. "Let's suppose . . ." and he held his hands up in front of his face, fingertips touching and palm together as in prayer, "just suppose that the judge *did* grant your motion to suppress. What would happen next?"

"The court would instruct the jury to disregard what they heard on the tapes as the telephone conversations were inadmissible in evidence." I had to take time out for a loud laugh. "Some scenario. Telling a jury to forget what they heard is like unringing a bell after it has chimed." That had always been one of my major gripes, when a judge would announce to a jury, "disregard that last answer" that may have been made to an incriminating question. It was like driving a huge nail into a wooden board, and when the nail was extracted, the hole in the lumber would remain, blatantly visible and glaring. The more a juror is told to forget something he heard, the more vividly would he remember.

Eddie sat in the leather chair at the highly burnished conference table, toying with his Gator tie, awaiting instructions for the following day. I watched my protégé fondly display the orange and blue school colors of his necktie, absently stroking and caressing as though he was in deep thought.

"The state will rest its case after Claire Kaufman testifies tomorrow, and you will lead off for the defense."

Eddie solemnly nodded, going over in his mind the high points of his testimony while tenderly patting his tie.

"By the way," I joked, "when you're on that witness

stand tomorrow, don't wear your school tie.''

''Why?'' asked the puzzled assistant, abruptly sitting up, ready to defend his alma mater against the whole world.

''Eddie, most of the jurors are probably not college graduates like you. They may interpret your wearing the college insignia on your tie to be a form of bragging. Just wear an ordinary tie. Get the point?''

The courthouse was deserted. It was eight o'clock in the morning and both parking areas were empty. It was pleasant to have my choice of spots but a cheerless atmosphere of gloom had a corrosive effect upon my natural enthusiasm. The overcast sky and the chilling wind—chilling for South Florida at least—sent me scurrying inside to the warmth of the snack bar where friend Tom would ply me with prune danish and small talk.

''We weren't going to open today, being Saturday, but I expect all hell to break loose and the courtroom jammed.''

''You must have heard something,'' I surmised, pouring sugar in my paper coffee cup.

''Just that the wraps are coming off the 'mystery woman' who is ready to lower the boom on her old pal Erler. Her husband is calling the shots and when she is finished testifying, they will be whisked away out of town under the protection of armed guards.''

''What could she be afraid of?'' I mused, now firmly convinced the Kaufman woman was poised to destroy Bob Erler.

''Story is that she's afraid your client will harm her. 'You know who' has been scaring the daylights out of her.''

I steeled myself for the ordeal ahead. Tom's prognosis was correct; the stools at the snack bar began to fill up and people continued to pour through the courthouse doors. As the nine o'clock witching hour drew nigh, a slow exodus to Stokely's courtroom heralded the big event, starring the ''mystery woman'' who, as Doug McQuarrie of the *Fort Lauderdale News* put it: ''would seal the fate of Robert Erler.''

Court convened in an electrified atmosphere that crackled over the crowded courtroom. The twin doors at the rear of the room remained open to accommodate the overflow of spectators unable to be seated. Television commentators and news reporters proclaimed Mrs. Claire Kaufman to be the "mystery" witness with connotations of romantic entanglements. A hush fell over the courtroom when a side door in the front was opened and a demure, striking brunette was ushered toward the witness stand. She scanned the courtroom searching for Robert Erler, who remained motionless, looking at her with a dog-like devotion, and when her eyes met his gaze, she abruptly looked away with obvious dismay. A split second by-play was a foreboding sign that portended doom to Erler's hopes that his trusted friend would come to his assistance. She nervously took the stand and the prosecutor led her through the routine preliminary questions until he came to the critical telephone call she made to Erler from the Hollywood police station, recorded by Lieutenant Cox.

"Mrs. Kaufman," gushed the prosecutor with undisguised relish, "were you aware that the telephone call you made to Robert Erler on September 17 was being taped by Officer Cox?"

"Yes, sir," was the lame reply, "but I didn't think about it at the time."

The tape was played back in the presence of the witness and the jury, presumably for authentication by the witness, but the primary purpose was to firmly imprint in the minds of the jurors the tacit confession of the defendant. When Mrs. Kaufman asked the harried and confused Erler, "Bob, did you do this thing?" Erler replied in a low, plaintive voice: "Claire, I do not know."

On cross-examination, I vainly tried to elicit from Mrs. Kaufman the fact that the police overwhelmed her by sheer dominance, and the phone call they orchestrated was designed to entrap Erler into making admissions against his interests. It was vital to the defense that Claire Kaufman establish that the telephone conversation with Erler was taped by the police without her consent.

"Mrs. Kaufman," I inquired, "can you tell this jury what period of time you spent with police officers in connection with the telephone call to Robert Erler?"

No answer from the witness. I continued, "Was it four months?"

"It's longer than that."

"Do you suppose you spoke to ten or more police officers about Mr. Erler?"

"I don't know," was the response.

"Were there more than twenty?"

"Sir, I don't know."

"Were there more than thirty."

"I don't know."

"You don't know if you talked to thirty police officers?"

"No, sir, I don't."

"How about forty?"

"I doubt that I talked to that many," was the petulant reply.

Mrs. Kaufman was alternately portraying the classic shy witness, then receding behind a coyness to mollify her interrogator, to which I ostensibly succumbed as her good will was needed. All I wanted to establish was that Claire spent lengthy periods of time with innumerable police officers in support of my contention: She acted under police psychological domination and control when the disputed telephone call to Robert Erler was made.

"Now please try to remember, Claire," I urged politely, trying to be reinstated in the witness's good grace, "the conversation we had in my office concerning your telephone call to Bob Erler you made from the Hollywood police station. Who knew the conversation was being taped?"

"I told you Bob didn't know it was taped."

"Didn't you tell me that you did not give your consent to Mr. Cox to tape that conversation?"

"I didn't tell you that I did or I didn't."

The witness was becoming evasive and it served no purpose to continue the equivocal dialogue. She was obviously not helping Erler, but the crucial question had to be asked, "Mrs. Kaufman, did you give your permission to Lieutenant Cox to tape the telephone conversation between you and Erler?"

"Yes, sir, because I didn't tell them they couldn't."

"Did you tell them they could?"

"Yes. Well, I didn't tell them anything. It didn't matter to me."

The lengthy cross-examination of the witness was of no avail. The damage was done, and the prosecution scored. With a dramatic flourish, the prosecutor announced, "Your Honor, the state rests."

The judge darted upright in his chair as the entire courtroom stirred in concert. The state's case had come to an end, and the spectators buzzed with anticipation. They eagerly awaited to see what the defense had to offer to dispel the mounting circumstantial evidence against Erler, but were temporarily thwarted when I approached the bench and said, "Your Honor, the defense requests that the jury be excused as there are two urgent motions that must be made and argued."

"The defendant has a motion to make out of the jury's presence," announced the court, "so we will be in recess for twenty minutes, when the defense will begin." The jurors marched out of the courtroom; all the others remained in their seats.

At the close of the prosecution's case the defendant's attorney is required to make a motion for dismissal of the charges, when quantum or sufficiency of the evidence is challenged, or the existence of some legal defect in the trial proceedings would require the trial judge to direct a verdict of "not guilty" should there be merit to the dismissal motion. It is known as "taking the case away from the jury" since no valid purpose would be served to carry on with a trial that lacks sufficient evidence to convict an accused "beyond a reasonable doubt," nullified because of a legal defect.

I didn't like Stokely's statement to the jury being in "recess for twenty minutes," because that meant the judge would summarily deny the defense motion for judgment of acquittal without considering or even acknowledging some novel points of law. The court also promised to hear arguments and evaluate Claire Kaufman's testimony in connection with the defense motion to suppress the intercepted telephone call between Mrs. Kaufman and Robert Erler. This aborted motion and unorthodox hearing procedure would also result in a calamity for the defendant, but an appellate record must be preserved. I was prepared to take everything the judge threw at me.

"The first matter the defense will address is the unlawful interception of the private telephone conversation between witness Claire Kaufman and the defendant Robert Erler."

"Don't waste your time on that one," answered the judge with a smirk on his florid face. "Your motion to suppress the taped conversations is denied. What else?"

"There is a valid argument to be made. The defendant moves for a judgment of acquittal as the state has not proven a prima facie case against my client, beyond a reasonable doubt, for a multitude of reasons. First is a legal reason, namely that venue has not been established. There is no proof that the homicide was committed in Broward County. There were no witnesses to the homicide, and speculation or guesswork as to where it occurred will not suffice. The law is clear that a trial can only be held in the county or jurisdiction where the criminal act took place. It is not beyond the realm of possibility that the decedent died in Dade County to the south, or Palm Beach County to the north . . ."

"As to venue, your motion is denied," ruled the judge, giving me a bored, insolent look. "What else?"

"This case is built solely upon circumstantial evidence. There is no proof tying my client to the homicide, no witnesses, no fingerprints, no murder weapon, no blood-stained clothing and all laboratory reports of all evidence gathered at the scene of the crime were negative as to my client. There has been an improper pyramiding of inferences and assumptions that do not meet the 'circumstantial evidence' test. The law on this point . . ."

"I know what the law is on circumstantial evidence," interrupted the court, looking at his wristwatch. "Your motion for a directed verdict is denied. Are you prepared to proceed with your defense?"

The court's rulings and lack of judicial finesse were to be expected. The defense motion for judgment of acquittal must be made at the close of the state's case, otherwise the sufficiency of the evidence may not be challenged on appeal. What personally irked me was the failure of the judge to require the prosecutor to make a rebuttal to the defense contentions in support of the argument for dismissal. Smoldering with anger I looked from the corner of my eye to see Boone sitting nonchalantly at his table, arms folded, and a supercilious smile on his placid features. "The cocky bastard wasn't even taking notes," I observed returning to the defense table with a forced smile.

"Would like to have a few moments before starting my defense," I knew I should have said, "Your Honor," or "May it please the court," but would only gag if I indulged in any more expressions of respect to Stokely, who now earned my eternal unremitting contempt.

"Mr. Bailiff, please bring the jury into the courtroom. They need not get into the jury box. I want to make an announcement," ordered the judge.

When the jurors were all assembled, standing in front of the box, Stokely gave them a hasty superficial smile and said, "Everyone will take a fifteen minute break, and come back on time. I want to finish this case today, even if we have to work tonight."

There was an audible groan from the jury box, and I could guess what they were thinking; "a precious Saturday night shot to hell!" The courtroom cleared giving us an opportunity to confer privately.

"Bob," I started, placing both arms on Erler's shoulders to ensure his full and undivided attention, "The rest of the morning will be taken up with two defense witnesses. You will testify this afternoon to tell your side of the story. You have a selling job to do to the jury and you can win your own case. I'm telling you this now, because during the luncheon recess we lawyers will be in the judge's chambers going over the instructions to the jury."

"What instructions?" Erler asked.

"Each side has prepared proposed instructions that the judge gives to the jury before they retire and deliberate their verdict. Each instruction is based on a proposition of law and the jury is told to apply the given law to the facts as they find them. In that manner, the jury knows the theory of the prosecution, as well as the defense theory for exoneration."

Erler nodded glumly. Recess was over and the courtroom became crowded again.

"Mr. Bailiff, please call in the jury."

The jury filed back into the courtroom in a jocular mood, some still engaged in light banter as they airily took their seats in the jury box. I always welcomed a good-humored jury panel, but loud, jovial laughter from jurors was annoying and gave me trepidations. I recalled some Lothario saying: "Laughter is the enemy of romance," and paraphrased my own rule that "Laughter in the jury room is the enemy of a defendant." I could never figure it out. The best rationale I could devise was when jurors are faced with a knotty problem, or are indecisive because of the awesome responsibility of making a judgment, they seek refuge in the stimulus of laughter. They bolster each other's courage with the mental release conceived by merriment and hilarity.

"Gentlemen of the jury," announced the court as the jurors resumed their collective sober visage, "the state's case has been completed, and we will now hear from the defense."

It was not the time to put Robert Erler on the stand. In order to lay a foundation for a proper defense, it was propitious to tender the first defense witness, Leon Gagliardi, the private investigator and photographer previously employed to take official photographs of the line-up held in the sheriff's office. Gagliardi, a short, balding, beetle-browed muscular man with a perpetual menacing stare, testified forcefully how Erler was placed in the number five position in the line-up and the entire scene was faithfully photographed from every angle.

"Were you able to ascertain whether or not Dorothy Clark or anyone else made any type of identification?"

"Mrs. Clark told the deputy sheriff she could not recognize anyone in the line-up," was the emphatic response.

"Was there a second line-up?"

"Yes, sir," frowned Gagliardi, as though the recollection was painful. "The deputy wanted Mrs. Clark to have another chance at making an identification, and you agreed to it on condition they change Mr. Erler's position."

"How was the second accomplished?"

"Mr. Erler was placed in the number four position, and once again Mrs. Clark was unable to identify anyone."

"Mr. Gagliardi, can you tell this court and jury whether or not Mr. Erler lowered his head, or puffed out his cheeks, or distorted his face at any time during either line-up?"

"No, sir!" was the firm reply.

The next defense witness was my young assistant, still smarting from being unjustly barred from participating at the trial because of the rule banning prospective witnesses from the courtroom. Eddie Kay went into detail to explain how a police officer standing next to Dorothy Clark at the line-up asked her to take her sunglasses off and see if she could recognize any person in the line-up.

"What was her reply?"

"She said, 'He's not here'."

"What happened next?"

"One of the sheriff's deputies ordered the six men in the line-up to turn sideways and then face the front. Mrs. Clark took off her sunglasses for a better look, and started to cry when she told the police officer, "I'm sorry, the man we're looking for is not here."

The prosecution's cross-examination was unproductive as Gagliardi and Kay's testimony was irrefutable. The performance of the last two witnesses was credible and convincing, certainly blunting the edge that the prosecution had forged initially, but it was manifestly evident the jury yearned to hear from the defendant. I sensed their impatience but they would have to wait.

"Lunch break time," announced the court; "We will resume at 1:30 P.M. promptly." The entire courtroom stirred and as the din mounted, Stokely shouted over the noisy crowd, "Both counsel please approach the bench."

Boone was already at the judge's bench whispering something to Stokely that I could not hear and quickened my pace to the forefront hoping to stop the private conversation between judge and prosecutor. "Please come into my chambers for a charge conference. We can agree on the jury instructions and hopefully have time for lunch."

Stokely had an elongated walnut conference table perpendicular to a plywood walnut desk, like a T-square, with three tan leather chairs on each side of the table. Opposite the entrance, under a rebel flag with crossed sabers, reposed a beige naugahyde eight-foot couch which the judge probably used for his "special sentencings." I bitterly thought to myself, "It won't be too long before the county will be rid of this depraved bastard, but the race against time was lost and poor Bob Erler would have to pay the price."

The judge seated himself at the desk while counsel took positions on opposite sides of the conference table. I noted that Stokely still wore his black robe which indicated he continued to demand the same respect in chambers that he was entitled to in the courtroom. A charge conference in chambers ordinarily is the relaxing juncture of a trial where the attorneys liberally discuss with the judge what instructions on the law should be given to the jury at the conclusion of the case before embarking upon their deliberations. Each side submits written proposed instructions to the court if any special circumstances are present, otherwise the judge reads "boiler plate" instructions from a form book.

"The defense requests two specific instructions. First, this is a purely circumstantial evidence case and the jury should be advised as to the law on circumstantial evidence."

"Denied! What's the other?"

"You must give that circumstantial evidence instruction because the law says the jury must be instructed in accordance with the defendant's theory of his defense."

"Still trying to tell me the law, are you?" sneered the judge.

"Are you going to tell the jury anything at all about circumstantial evidence?" I demanded, half raised out of my chair with a cold challenging look at Stokely.

"No," answered the judge, "go on with your next special."

"You promised the jury when Mitchell testified and took the 'Fifth' that you would explain what credence they could give to a convicted felon, so I have a special instruction on that point."

"That's out," replied Stokely. "The witness never admitted he was convicted of a crime. He just took the 'Fifth' and sidestepped the question you asked."

"That's when you pulled the rug out from under me, refusing to strike Mitchell's testimony and preventing me from cross-examining the witness,'' I angrily retorted.

"You are flirting with being in contempt of court,'' Stokely glared. "One more crack like that and the bailiff will take you upstairs.'' He waited for an apology from me, but none was forthcoming. Boone sat quietly at the table doodling on his yellow pad, with feigned disinterest in the heated discussion and appearing unconcerned. The prosecutor's deliberate air of detachment infuriated me and I angrily sat down in the chair, defiantly folding arms across my chest, signifying the end of any more discussions.

"Here is what the court will do,'' said Stokely as though he was making a considered pronouncement. "I will give the jury my usual form instructions; you know, presumption of innocence, reasonable doubt and the usual stuff. Any objections?''

"No, Your Honor, the state has no objections,'' answered Boone.

"I've already stated my objections,'' I answered, looking away.

"Very well. The court reporter has it all, so we'll convene at 1:30 P.M. for the rest of the defense.''

I gathered my papers and walked out of the judge's chambers without saying another word, and chided myself for becoming irritated over an aspect of trial procedure I personally believed was innocuous and unproductive. Reading instructions on the law to a panel of jurors was another example of foolishness as far as I was concerned. It would make me fume inwardly when a trial judge hurriedly read instructions from a form book, turning page after page, making his delivery in a boring, flat monotone without emphasis or change of inflection, knowing the jurors could not understand the complicated precepts of law, but the judicial obligation was completed. The judge had read the instructions to the jury and that is all that was required of him. They never received copies of the instructions for use and guidance in the jury room, and would have to rely upon their recollection of the court's monologue of jurisprudence.

I agonized even more than usual because I could envision the inept Stokely giving his boring soliloquy to this jury before they retired to deliberate on its verdict.

36

THE ENTIRE COURTROOM stirred to attention when it was announced Robert Erler would take the witness stand. Speculation was rife that the defendant would not testify in his own behalf because of some veiled insinuations made by the prosecutor to the press on how Erler would be drawn and quartered on cross-examination. Bob Erler rose from his chair and smiled briefly to his family seated immediately behind the counsel table. He was the embodiment of Norman Rockwell's "All American Boy," and was dressed in a blue suit, white dress shirt with starched collar and neat polka dot tie. His blondish hair was neatly combed and Erler presented a handsomely striking figure as he marched to the witness stand. Judge Stokely turned to the clerk and said, "Swear in the defendant." Erler placed his right hand on the Bible and repeated the oath administered to him with a loud and clear voice, and looked at the jury unafraid and undaunted. With a confident display of pride, I smiled at him in a manner designed to allay his nervousness, and led him through the usual preliminaries.

"Bob, please tell about your work and occupation. Did you enjoy being a police officer?"

"Very much, sir. I have always wanted to be a police officer all my life but was too young to apply for police work until after I got out of the service."

"Please tell the jury something about your home life with your wife, where you were living and if you are still married."

"My wife, Pattie, was seventeen years old when I married her in Phoenix and I have a son right now, who is approximately sixteen months old, but my wife left me and took my son away with her," he added sorrowfully.

"Please tell us about your home life, if you will."

"We were living in a house trailer in Dania and I worked for a boat company until I became a patrolman with the City of Dania Police Department. My wife tried to work but could not hold a job so we had a great deal of financial problems. We would always argue about money and she would clean out our savings account and take a plane to her mother in Kansas City, Missouri, and take the baby with her. When she felt like coming home she would return and we would fight some more because she had run up a great deal of bills and borrowed money from loan companies, signing my name without my knowledge. At one time she ran up a telephone bill of $225.00 and the telephone company called the police station where I worked and I almost lost my job because of that.''

Throughout the entire direct testimony of Robert Erler, the prosecutor made no objections to the narrative style testimony, which seemed unusual and I attributed it either to the prosecutor's inexperience or perhaps he wanted the defendant to keep talking so he could impale him with some of his statements upon cross-examination.

''Was there a time when you became a member of the Hollywood Police Department?''

''Yes. I was able to get a job with Hollywood at double my salary but still that wasn't enough for Pattie because she continued writing bad checks on accounts that were already closed. I went to every creditor and asked them to please allow me to pay a little something on account every month as I wanted to keep my job with the Hollywood Police Department. I explained my predicament to Assistant Chief of Police Carl King and begged him not to take me off the force. Chief King was sympathetic as he knew from my fellow officers that I would go without eating just to save money to pay bills. Finally, things got so bad that my wife took my son and went home to her mother. I haven't seen either of them since.''

Robert Erler was conducting himself admirably and projected sincerity in his narrative-type testimony. I glanced over to the prosecution side of the room to see why the prosecutor was not making the expected objections, and observed him furiously making copious notes on a legal pad, surmising that Erler was in for a lengthy and protracted cross-examination. I smoothly sailed the defendant over the troubled waters created by Dania Officer White's testimony about Erler, asking him to falsify a report about Mrs. Winifred Erler making an emergency call to return to Phoenix. There was a long-standing grudge between Erler and White. He also explained the personal animosity that existed between him and Officer Peterman. This was the crucial moment to destroy Peterman's credibility.

"Now Bob," I began slowly for emphasis, "do you remember Officer Peterman testifying that you had a conversation with him in a coffee shop or restaurant in Dania in November or December where it was suggested you created an incident so you could 'discover' Merilyn Clark's body back in August?"

"That is an absolute falsehood!" was the heated reply. "I never talked with Peterman about that subject. Besides, I've been in the Broward County Jail almost four months, from September to the present, and the sheriff's records will show that Mr. Peterman never visited me in jail."

Erler went into a long, uninterrupted recital of the events that transpired on August 12, leading up to his finding the body of the young woman, "heavy set" and appearing to be about twelve years of age. He narrated his call for an ambulance and the emergency report to police headquarters; the surge of police officers congregating at the scene.

"Do you remember about how long you stayed there?"

"Oh, quite a while. We made a complete search of the area and a walking search and everything."

"Prior to that time, had you ever seen this girl before?"

"No, sir, I never had."

"What about Mrs. Dorothy Clark? Did you ever see her before she walked into the courtroom earlier this week?"

"Never saw her before in my life," was his firm response.

"How about the line-up? Did you see her there?"

"No, sir," was his reply. "There were very strong lights on my face and I couldn't see a thing."

The entire courtroom was so quiet one could hear a pin drop as Erler testified in a clear, well-modulated voice. He related an occasion when he was ordered to proceed to the Tiger Tail Lounge in Dania and arrest a white male who was the main suspect in the homicide but was later released from custody. The silence of the prosecutor during the direct examination of Erler encouraged me to push forward toward the events that led to his resignation from the police force and the return to Arizona.

"Was there a time when you had a final confrontation with Assistant Chief of Police Carl King that prompted you to make an important decision?"

"Yes, sir," was the reply. "Mr. King told me that he had been receiving many complaints from the telephone company and several bill collectors that I hadn't paid any bills, and I showed him the canceled checks I was paying to my creditors $5.00 and $10.00 at a time. Mr. King told me I would have to borrow the money and pay off the bills, otherwise my job was in jeopardy. I felt that my time with the police department was limited so I resigned on September 5."

"What did you do after that?"

"I tried to settle all my affairs in Broward County. My trailer was going to be repossessed as well as my car because I was three months late in my payments and finally, around September 10, I went back to Arizona to see my mother who was very ill."

"When was the first time you ever heard about being a suspect in this case?"

"I was in my sister's apartment watching television when a special bulletin announced that I was the object of a nationwide search in connection with the shooting of these people. The bulletin stated that I was suppose to be armed with several automatic weapons, hand grenades, dynamite and various other stuff."

"Did you ever have any explosives, hand grenades or anything like that?"

"Absolutely not."

Erler recounted his trauma when his brother, Danny, advised him that his mother's house was surrounded by armed police officers and how fearful they were of his safety because the television commentator reported Erler made a statement vowing never to be taken alive. He explained he was in such a terrorized state, suffering from debilitating headaches that he took at least two bottles of tranquilizers to be able to cope with the situation. He even prevailed upon a longtime friend, Deputy Sheriff Koelsch, to arrange his safe surrender to the authorities.

"Bob, you heard Deputy Koelsch say you told him you were going to blow up part of the hospital where Dorothy Clark was confined. Did you say anything like that?"

"No, I did not. That is not true. Dave Koelsch asked me, 'Where is all the dynamite and explosives you were suppose to be armed with?' and I said, 'Dave, I don't have anything like that, only my service revolver.' "

"Now Bob, were you on Dania Beach the morning of August 12 and did you see Mrs. Clark?"

"The only time I was on Dania Beach was weeks prior to that, in the daytime, and that was the last time I ever remember being on Dania Beach."

"Did you have occasion to take that lady to your trailer?"

"No, sir. I have never seen that woman before. I have never seen the vehicle. I have seen pictures in the magazines and newspapers, but I have never seen Mrs. Clark until she walked in this courtroom."

"And you had nothing to do with the matters with which you are charged?"

"I had nothing to do except make a report on what I found, and I did that."

"And you're telling the truth?"

"I'm telling the truth, and I'm not the one that shot this woman or this girl."

"And that's the solemn truth, Bob?"

"That's the solemn truth. I did not kill anyone. I have never killed anyone in my life and never intend to."

"You may inquire."

The courtroom became alive with hushed muttering and suppressed conversation as Len Boone gathered his sheaf of yellow papers and lumbered to the rear of the jury box facing the defendant, who gazed steadily at his antagonist. The prosecutor commenced his cross-examination in a low-keyed manner and went through innocuous details as he sought to get his bearings. "Mr. Erler," the prosecutor drawled in his North Florida accent, "did you ever have a revolver with white handles?"

"Yes, sir," replied the defendant. "It was my wife's weapon and used miniature .22s. It was a German make but I cannot verify what kind."

"Pretty well fits the description of the type of gun that Mrs. Clark testified about," was the arch demand of the prosecutor.

"Yes, sir, a very common weapon."

"Do you remember Dorothy Clark testifying that she was with you that night?"

"She was never with me and she has never seen me."

"Did you hear Mrs. Clark testify about how you masturbated in front of her and Merilyn?" asked the prosecutor with great relish.

"I have never seen that woman until she came into this courtroom."

"Was Mrs. Clark telling the truth when she said she saw you masturbate in front of them?"

"I know she isn't telling the truth because I have never seen Mrs. Clark in my life. Never!"

The prosecutor attempted to be innovative and left his position at the end of the jury box from which he conducted his cross-examination, sat at the counsel table with crossed legs, assuming a "down home" and "folksy" posture, and continued to bait the defendant, trying to arouse an emotional display of anger. A cloying mantle of tedium seemed to be draped over the courtroom from the prosecutor's repetitious questions asked merely to embarrass the witness. Some of the jurors were showing signs of boredom which Boone recognized, deciding to recoup their interest with another question.

"Mr. Erler, have you ever masturbated in front of women, or just masturbated?"

"I have masturbated. I admit that. I think most males do at an early age."

"Objection overruled!" burst in the judge.

"Your Honor," I remonstrated angrily, "I never made an objection and once again I must respectfully object to the court injecting himself into these trial proceedings."

Stokely shot a look of hatred in my direction, his flushed face working to find words to censure me and burst forth with, "I can understand the prosecutor repeating all these questions because this witness rarely answers any question at all."

"Your Honor, again I must object to your making personal observation and invading the province of the jury. This is absolutely wrong!''

''It is the court's observation that this witness doesn't answer the questions asked.''

''Judge, you cannot make an observation in the presence of the jury concerning my client or any other witness.''

''Very well,'' said Stokely.''This is the last time the prosecutor will be permitted to ask this question.''

It was refreshing to receive a slight semblance of concession from my arch enemy and was taken aback when the judge asked Boone, ''Sir, how much longer will it take you to complete your cross-examination?''

The prosecutor was startled and fearing he would incur the displeasure of his ally on the bench, abruptly terminated his cross-examination. Decision time for me. It was getting late in the day and there was no point in subjecting Erler to a redirect examination because it would only give the prosecutor another turn at recross-examination which would drag on incessantly. The jury seemed restless and the muttering audible in the courtroom indicated displeasure with the monotonous atmosphere that prevailed.

''The defense rests,'' I said simply, striding back to the counsel table to await further developments.

''Gentlemen of the jury,'' said the judge to the tired jurors, ''the defense has rested and the state has an opportunity for rebuttal witness, if it so desires.''

''The state has no rebuttal witnesses,'' stated the prosecutor.

''Members of the jury,'' sighed the court, ''the case is now over and you will hear final arguments of counsel. We will have a short recess of fifteen minutes after which the state will commence its final summation. There will be forty minutes allotted to each side for final arguments. It is my desire to finish this case even if we have to work into the night.'' And addressing the jurors, the court continued, ''Some of you jurors may wish to alert your families that you may be working this evening and not to expect you home until very late.''

The jurors looked at each other with disappointment which did not pass unnoticed by the judge who remarked, ''I will have the bailiff go into the jury room with you and take your orders for sandwiches and drinks. They will arrive about supper time. Should any of you desire to use the telephone, the bailiff will also assist you in making whatever telephone calls are necessary.''

The courtroom quickly emptied and sitting in the back row was Marsha, the judge's secretary, who stared at me with an "I told you so" look. I nodded perceptively and held out my hands in prayerful supplication which she understood, and smiled. We both shared the prescience that Erler was victimized.

The closing arguments by the prosecution should have been made at an evangelical tent meeting, as he passionately exhorted the jury to hold defendant Robert John Erler, a disgraced police officer, to a higher degree of criminal responsibility by virtue of his defiling his badge of office as well as betraying a public trust. He glared at the defendant who sat there without blinking an eye, and took the calumniation of the prosecutor calmly and without expression. Boone continued shouting and thumping his table with righteous indignation, heaping abuse upon the defendant, and in a strained, hoarse voice concluded, "You have no choice but to find this man guilty of murder, as charged!"

In contrast to the wild theatrics of the prosecutor, my only recourse was to assume a low profile and cogently went through the many speculative probabilities of the circumstantial evidence case against Erler. I reminded the jurors how they were deprived of their basic duty as fact-finders by not being permitted to hear the *Catch Me Killer* tapes to make their own voice identification, rather than rely upon witnesses to tell them what they should decide. "If the apparatus on the sixth floor of the courthouse use was so unwieldy," I argued, "that the transmission equipment could not be brought into the courtroom, then the jury should have been transported en masse to the sheriff's office to hear the tapes. They brought the police witnesses up there, why not the jury?"

The major portion of my final summation was dedicated to the breakdown in the prosecution's case. Dorothy Clark was unable to make the identification of the defendant at the line-up and I called upon the jurors' sense of fair play to rationalize why Dorothy Clark entered the courtroom on the first day of the trial and identified the defendant, having been shown a photograph of the defendant merely one hour before being called upon to make a positive identification of Erler. I sincerely lamented, "This type of impermissible suggestibility was unethical and morally wrong!"

The jury's rapt attention to my final argument heartened me. I felt they were absorbing my fervent appeal to their logic and sense of fair play.

"There was not a single witness to the homicide," I reminded the jury, "so please consider the type of evidence the state could have produced in order to implicate my client, or anyone else in the homicide. If Bob Erler sat in Dorothy Clark's car that fatal night, and slammed the door shut and touched other parts of the car, his fingerprints would have been discovered. Mrs. Clark said Erler did not wear gloves that night. The police dusted the car for fingerprints—some were found—but not a single print of Erler's palm or hand was discovered. Why? Because Robert Erler was not there that night." No stone was left unturned, touching upon the circumstantial nature of the prosecution's case, lack of physical evidence against the accused, the prejudicial motives and suspicious testimony of the state's witnesses, eventually concluding with a sincere request to return a verdict of "Not Guilty!"

The entire courtroom seemed to be aroused as I wearily returned to my seat. A wave of relief coursed over the room as the emotionally charged trial came to an end. All that remained was the traditional instructions to the jury by the trial judge. When Stokely sought to discharge this judicial function his manner of delivery as prognosticated, confused the jurors which was evidenced by the puzzled looks on their faces. He read from a prepared text in a rapid nasal tone as though he wanted to complete a distasteful chore as promptly as possible. I looked over to the jurors in the box and recognized the usual vapid stares, clearly indicating they had no idea of what the judge was saying, and Stokely's occasional stuttering did little to shed light on the complex legal theorems he requested the jury to digest.

"You may now retire and consider your verdict. Select one of your number as foreman and call the bailiff when you are ready. Oh yes, I almost forgot,'' smiled the judge through tightened lips, ''your food and beverages have arrived and will be sent in.''

The jurors quickly walked to the jury room, more likely in anticipation of the libation that awaited them than the arduous task of reaching a unanimous verdict. Upon their departure, the courtroom became a maelstrom of activity, as newspaper reporters and courtroom personnel joined the spectators in flooding the corridor, rife with speculation as to what the verdict would be. Erler remained seated impassively while the courtroom emptied out. Winifred Erler left her children seated in the first row and approached me for the first time during the entire trial.

''How long do you think it will be?'' she asked.

''There's no way of telling,'' I replied. ''They will have their supper first and then start their deliberations. My educated guess is they will be anxious to get home because it has been a long day.''

The bailiff put the cuffs on Erler and whisked him through the rear exit door. I walked outside to avoid the usual senseless discussion with the various groups assembled in the proximity of the courtroom. The prosecutor invited me to his office for coffee, which was declined with thanks, preferring to be alone and settle down for the ''death watch.'' Waiting for a jury to reach a verdict is the most agonizing sensation a trial lawyer can experience. A self-appraisal of the conduct of the trial gives rise to questions. Was anything overlooked? Was everything covered? Finally, did the defense present enough evidence to create a reasonable doubt to warrant a ''Not Guilty'' verdict? Shrugging off these hypercritical thoughts, I ventured into the courtroom and encountered the court bailiff who stood guard outside the jury room.

''Anything significant going on?'' I asked.

''They are certainly having quite an argument in there,'' the bailiff replied. ''I could hear loud angry voices, so it looks like there is support for both sides.''

I'd heard this stock reply hundreds of times before and wryly volunteered, ''Maybe they're arguing over who ordered mayonnaise.''

Pinkie, the court clerk, grinned, ''It looks like a hung

jury. They've been arguing too much and from the tone of their voices I doubt if anyone will give in.''

I left the courtroom to resume my vigil and waited with the many courtroom spectators and members of the Erler family, while a thousand excruciating spurts of molten lava played havoc in my stomach. Time passed slowly and it looked as though the jury was going to continue their deliberations far into the night. After a prolonged wait the court bailiff burst through the door and announced, ''The jury has reached a verdict!'' A wave of humanity seethed through the courtroom door and filled all the seats and were lined up against the wall awaiting the judge to call the jury in. The defendant was brought down from the jail to resume his seat at the counsel table. Everyone waited expectantly until the judge made his entrance through the side door and stiffly walked up to the bench, shouting, ''Bring in the jury!''

My eyes were riveted on the jurors as they filed out of the jury room to their respective places in the jury box and noted with a heavy heart that they studiously avoided looking at me or the defendant. From experience I knew this meant an adverse verdict: Guilty!

The ritual of receiving a jury's verdict was always an agonizing ordeal. The few seconds that elapsed from the time the judge hands the verdict form to the clerk to read, until the time the clerk utters the pronouncement of guilt or innocence, seems so cruel and ruinous that it traumatized me. In the hope of minimizing the emotional impact on me, Pinkie and I concocted a ritual of our own. When Pinkie would be ordered to read the verdict, he arranged with me, since he was the only person to see the verdict besides the judge, to hold the verdict form up high to his face if the verdict was ''not guilty,'' but if the verdict was guilty, he would hold the verdict form down to his waist with stretched arms like a near-sighted person would extend his hands in order to read small print. This secret maneuver encompassed only a few split seconds but was enough of a preview to tranquilize me, when I needed solace the most.

''Has the jury reached a verdict?'' asked the court.

''We have, Your Honor,'' replied juror number one who I guessed would be the foreman.

"Please give your verdict to the clerk."

Pinkie stepped forward and received the form of verdict, and making an obvious display of not looking at the form, handed it to Stokely who took an unusually long time to peruse it. "Will the defendant rise and harken to your verdict?"

Robert Erler quickly rose to his feet, and I did the same. Satisfied that he was obeyed on all counts, the judge returned the verdict form to the clerk and bellowed, "Mr. Clerk, please publish the verdict of the jury."

Pinkie ceremoniously accepted the verdict, glancing surreptitiously to determine the result and slowly lowered his hands as far down as his arms could extend. I knew immediately what the gesture meant and placed my right arm around Erler's shoulders as if to prepare him for the electrifying shock about to be received. The clerk adjusted his glasses, and read:

"We, the jury, in Broward County, Florida, find the defendant, Robert John Erler, guilty of murder in the Second Degree." The courtroom exploded with mixed cries of triumph and disbelief. The Erler clan huddled around Mrs. Winifred Erler who reached over to embrace the defendant but the bailiff quickly intervened, "Sorry ma'am, no body contact with the prisoner."

Upon hearing the word "prisoner" Winifred lost whatever reserve she possessed, sinking down on the hard oaken bench, and sobbed. Bob was in a stupor as he watched the judge bang his gavel in an attempt to restore order. Stokely, red-faced and angry, waited until peace and quiet was restored before calling the defendant to the bar. I accompanied my client. Traditionally, a court will order a presentence investigation and set a date for imposition of sentence, but "there's no way of guessing what this crazy bastard would do," was my fear.

Turning to the clerk of the court, the judge asked, "What is the highest sentence ever given in this court for second degree murder?"

The clerk replied, "Ninety-nine years, Your Honor."

"Very well," said the judge turning to the hapless defendant and said, "The court hereby sentences you to serve a term of years in the Florida State Prison at hard labor, said number of years being ninety-nine years *and six months*!''

The bailiff quickly handcuffed the dazed Erler and led him upstairs to the jail, as I called out, ''Will be right up to see you, Bob!'' but the bailiff and his charge disappeared quickly through the rear door. It never ceased to amaze me how the attitudes of a jail guard shift toward an accused after a conviction. Erler would have an additional burden as a ''convicted cop.'' The inmates gloat when cops, always hated by most convicts, become felons. Although daily life in custody was comparatively easy in the courthouse jail awaiting trail, I shuddered to think what would happen when ''ex-cop'' Robert Erler started doing his time in maximum security at Raiford Penitentiary.

37

ERLER WENT BERSERK when his attackers pulled his trousers off, pinning him down on the mopped cell floor, the fumes of the astringent cleaner clouding his vision, unable to identify his assailants or ascertain their number. He screamed with fright as the fear of a gang rape intensified his terror, flailing wildly at his tormentors and was rewarded by the savage blow of a fire extinguisher wielded by a burly inmate flush on Erler's upraised face. A thousand flash bulbs exploded in his brain as he sank into the vortex of a bottomless pit. He was still unable to see, and tasted the warm blood gushing from his nose when he spat out his shattered front teeth.

''Fun's over! Guards are coming,'' an inmate yelled as Erler's attackers quickly fled leaving him sitting upright in the corner of his cell, dazed and tenderly trying to manipulate his left jaw which he believed to be broken. Captain Mullen pushed his short stocky bulk through the cell door and, looking with distaste at the gruesome sight, growled to a subordinate, ''Cuff this punk and take him down to the clinic.''

''I'm not a punk!'' mumbled Erler through his mangled

mouth, but it was doubtful that anyone heard as his jaws seemed to lock, and no words came out.

The doctor at the clinic gave up on the x-ray machine that was inoperative and administered a shot of morphine in Erler's gums to alleviate the pain generated by the exposed nerves in his broken teeth. The visiting dentist was not due for another five days, requiring Erler to take his place on a long waiting list.

Florida State Prison in Union County was one of the first correctional facilities for men only, designed to house approximately two thousand inmates. Within its massive seventeen foot high walls, trimmed with razor-ribboned barbed wire sits the "Disciplinary Barracks" where the dreaded "hole" awaits the rebellious con who dares to challenge the peniological system. This was Erler's first time in a real prison and his frequent guided visits to the infirmary permitted him to peek through rain-streaked windows to see two armed guards seated in front of the huge iron door with armed jailers manning a tower in the background. All he could see were steel bars, iron doors and massive forms of concrete everywhere.

The next day, Erler was ushered out of his cell to attend a meeting in the laundry room where Captain Mullen had lined up eight black inmates of assorted shapes and sizes for a confrontation to discuss the previous night's attempted gang rape. Erler wondered how the captain knew who his attackers were when he was unable to identify a single assailant, but made it a point to remember each and every face for future retribution.

"Step up here," called the captain. Erler walked casually toward the group but suddenly veered toward the black inmates standing at attention and threw a blockbusting punch at the person closest to him, then turned to the second in line, cursing and punching wildly.

"That's it!" shouted Mullen, signaling to his aides to stop the melee and grabbed Erler by the scruff of his neck and snarled, "You punk, this is my jail and I'm putting you in the hole until you learn how to behave."

"I told you before I'm no punk, and none of these black bastards are going to make me their momma."

"All you had to do," countered the captain, "was to

report to me or any of the deputy guards that they were hitting on you . . ."

"Bullshit," interrupted Erler, "and by that time I would have been raped by these animals. No, sir, I'll die fighting before they get me."

Two days in the "hole" had a sobering effect on Erler. He knew that being a former police officer would create trouble, which he expected to overcome in time, but he lost sight of the fact that he was also regarded as a child killer which doubled the hatred against him. He had been excused from attending work details due to his deteriorating physical condition and was finally notified he was eligible to receive treatment to the exposed nerves of his fractured teeth, but the fractured jaw had been ignored and finally healed in a haphazard fashion. As he was guided into the gleaming whiteness of the prison infirmary, Erler was delighted to see an old friend garbed in hospital greens.

"Hey, Jack," yelled Erler as best he could through his swollen mouth. "What in hell are you doing here?"

Jack Griffith became friendly with Erler while they were together in pre-trial detention at Broward County Courthouse Jail. He and his co-defendant, Jack Murphy, also known as "Murphy the Surf" were convicted of murdering two teenage secretaries, dumping their bodies in Whiskey Creek in Hollywood, near the Dania cut-off canal. Murphy was a flamboyant playboy with a penchant for excitement, whether it was manipulating huge waves in a raging ocean with only a surfboard under him, or stealing the precious "Star of India" sapphire from an impregnable, highly protected museum in New York City. Although he was not as famous as Murphy, Griffith was respected by the entire jail community because he was a master in the martial arts and a holder of a Red Belt in Karate, which was the highest accolade accorded to a teacher of martial arts—a Sensei.

Griffith looked at the battered face before him, and broke out in a grin as he recognized his old jail mate. "Hello, Bob," he greeted his friend. "I heard what happened to you, but didn't realize the damage."

Erler grimaced with pain. "My teeth are killing me."

"Just let me take care of things," smiled Griffith. "I'm

the head nurse here and you will have priority.''

Erler felt comfortable for the first time since coming to prison. He had always looked up to Griffith with great reverence and his hero did not disappoint him. Erler's teeth were treated and he was sent happily on his way with a generous supply of sedatives. He looked forward to the comfort of his cell, which had been outfitted with new blankets, pillow and bedding, taking a pill and drifting off in indolent languor.

Walking through the narrow corridor back to his cell, Erler smelled something burning. ''Do you smell fire or smoke?'' he asked the guard who had him in charge.

''Smells like fire,'' answered the jailer as he hurried forward, dragging Erler by his handcuffs toward the cell block only to perceive Erler's cell in flames. His bedding, clothing and personal effects were on fire and completely destroyed. Entering the cell he frantically fought to quell the conflagration, ultimately reducing the flames to smoldering black fog. As the acrid smoke engulfed the cell block, the inmates returning from the mess hall crowded around, awaiting Erler's angry reaction. There was none. Erler returned their unfriendly stares with deliberate indifference. He knew how to handle this situation.

''What happened?'' asked a senior jail guard as he pushed through the crowd.

''It was my fault, sir,'' apologized Erler. ''I shouldn't have been smoking in bed.''

Erler did not smoke cigarettes or any kind of tobacco which was apparent in his orientation records; this ruse did not escape the attention of the convicts standing in a semicircle. The senior jail guard recognized that Erler was engaged in a cover-up, rather than point to the broken glass jar in a corner that contained the alcohol-soaked rags used for the incendiary bomb which set his cell ablaze.

''Do you want another cell?'' he was asked.

''No, sir,'' Erler replied stubbornly. ''I'll clean this up,'' and bent to the task of subduing the smoldering embers.

''When you're finished,'' ordered the guard, ''go to the supply room and get a complete outfit.'' He strode away, relieved there were no inmates to be placed on report for the incident.

The cell walls were charred with soot and indelibly stained with grime, but Erler gamely bent to his task and slowly restored some semblance of order to his living quarters. It would be the first step toward rehabilitation and acceptance by Captain Mullen. He planned to request a transfer from the disciplinary barracks to the general compound, or "population" as it was called, where there were productive work assignments, school and recreational programs. Fresh bedding and blankets were obtained but the stench of the charred, watersoaked mattress remained in the tiny cell.

In the mess hall that evening, there were mixed stares in Erler's direction as he sat warily on the long hard bench, toying with the food on his tray. He knew he gained some points in the eyes of some of the inmates when he assumed responsibility for the fire in his cell, telling the senior guard he fell asleep on his cot with a lit cigarette in his mouth, but there were several frigid looks that made him feel uncomfortable.

After mess, he made the long walk back to the disciplinary barracks in the company of a jail guard and was aghast at the sight of his cell. Once again, his living quarters were set on fire and all the bedding, clothes and personal items were totally destroyed! The message was clear. Robert Erler was an unwelcome threat to the inmates in prison, and the next move was his. The only way he could personally confront his tormentors was to be transferred from the disciplinary barracks, away from the ever-present guard. A request to speak to Captain Mullen was made through the senior guard, who told Erler, "I'll tell him for ya, but don't hold your breath 'til he comes."

VI

MANHUNT AND CAPTURE

38 _____

THE CHOCOLATE-STAINED Baby Ruth wrappers on the conference table in my library were mute evidence that Harry Long, the intrepid criminal investigator was nearby, waiting to bedevil me with some cheerless news.

"What good news do you have for me this time?" I asked, not knowing what to expect. Harry's right hand drifted downward toward his pants pocket, slowly and deliberately like Wyatt Earp at the shootout at O.K. Corral, extracting a Baby Ruth bar. I groaned to myself. His actions meant I must wait until this big oaf devoured his candy before any kind of news would be forthcoming. I had been playing this game with the investigator for many years, so I remained silent, seething inwardly and not giving Harry the satisfaction of knowing my stomach was on fire.

The investigator lumbered to his feet, stretching hands outward, fluttering his pudgy fingers, said, "Goodbye, Judge Stokely. Governor Kirk removed him from office an hour ago. Get the rest of the details on your local TV." With a hearty laugh, Harry ran out of the office, while I grabbed the phone shouting excitedly to my secretary to find Eddie Kay immediately. Lucy pointed to the library where my protégé was sitting at the conference table surrounded by textbooks and annotated statutes working furiously on Robert Erler's appeal.

"Eddie," I yelled through the doorway of the library, "good news! The governor issued an order only an hour ago suspending Stokely from judicial duties."

"Great!" smiled the young attorney. "Then we're rid of that crazy judge for good?"

"Not exactly," I explained. "The governor's order of suspension is merely the first step toward Stokely's ultimate removal. There will be a hearing held before the Senate's Select Committee, who will unquestionably sustain the governor's Order of Suspension and the matter would then be referred to the entire senate for final approval and then Harris J. Stokely is history.''

"Amen,'' said Eddie with a reverent bow. ''I wonder how this political news can be incorporated in Erler's brief.''

"The main thrust of our appeal is the misconduct of the trial judge, but his ouster from the bench is not an appropriate issue in the appellate brief,'' I chided. ''Just catalogue all the prejudicial acts and statements.'' And with a hearty chuckle I speculated, ''After all, court of appeal judges are only human, and they read the newspapers and watch television, too. They will know all about Stokely and why he was suspended!''

Deep down in my heart, I did not fully subscribe to the wishful thinking statement just made to my assistant. I was experienced enough to know that seasoned jurists utilize their native human instincts and balance the equities of every case with a realistic viewpoint. There was always a possibility that the appellate court could conceivably reject Erler's appeal because of the magnitude of the crime and the publicized image of the defendant of a former police officer mandating him to be held to a higher degree of responsibility.

"Try to call Erler in Raiford and give him the news before he sees it on television,'' I ordered Eddie. ''And keep me informed. Have to get to work on that new Florida Power and Light Company murder case that just came in.''

I had been exclusively devoting my time to Erler's appeal, but the new murder case of the vice president of Florida Power & Light Company intrigued me. Fort Lauderdale resident, Kenneth Leone, had an obsession concerning the questionable relationship between his new stepdaughter, Jewel Berning, and the elderly Edward W. Smith, an FPL executive. One day Leone charged into Smith's private office in Fort Lauderdale for a personal confrontation. Smith had heard rumors that Leone was going to ''take care of him'' and when Leone ran up to Smith's desk, the FPL executive pulled out a .38 handgun from a partially opened drawer, and shot Leone twice in the chest and twice in the back, killing him instantly. What intrigued me was how I would explain away the two shots in Leone's back on a self-defense case. The prosecutor had already deduced that the two shots in the victim's back were inflicted while he was trying to run away from Smith. I had my own theory of the defense, which later proved to be successful.

That theory was this: The velocity and force from a .38 handgun is so powerful that the first two shots to Leone's chest actually forced the man's body to swivel 180 degrees in a split second, causing the victim's back to become an automatic target for Smith's final two shots. I discovered this theory during a casual conversation with a Fort Lauderdale policeman who had just recently shot himself in the leg with a .38 by accident.

39

GOSSIP TRAVELS FAST in the prison system. And the word was out about the tough child killer cop from Hollywood. A wave of hostility against Erler whet the appetites of some restless young "turks" in population determined to make a test run against the hated ex-cop. The warden and his two captains were aware of the explosive situation, justifying their decision to keep the troublesome convict in the disciplinary barracks as a "protective custody" measure. But this rationale would not be tolerated for long and it was imperative that a solution be found immediately.

In the company of a senior guard, Captain Mullen sauntered over to Erler's cell. The guard rattled his handcuffs across the iron bars, shouting "Erler, front and center!" The surprised inmate quickly approached his cell door, delighted to see the corpulent double-chinned Mullen.

"Thank you for seeing me," gulped Erler, speaking rapidly for fear the captain would rush off to more engaging business. "Please, Captain, sir, please transfer me into the population compound," he begged.

"If you were in the general population, you'd be killed in forty-eight hours."

"Please, Captain," pleaded Erler, "I have to do ninety-nine years and want to be able to make it. I'll never be able to survive living in a hole. I need a chance to exist like all the others in here.''

"I'll think it over," gruffly replied the captain, leaving a mollified Erler, holding his head in both hands, trying to squeeze away the electric flashes of light that would soon blossom into an excruciating headache.

At a top level conference in the warden's office, Captain Mullen decided to put Erler in population. One of two things can happen, he calculated. He may get killed. Or he may acclimate to prison life and become a good inmate. He also figured that Erler could be "graduated" to Belle Glade and out of his hair.

Erler was delighted to be admitted into the general prison population, even though he was assigned a cell in a remote corner where he would be minimally exposed to hostile cons. He was finally permitted an emergency telephone call from Eddie Kay and was ecstatic over the news that Stokely had been removed from the bench for misconduct in judicial office. "We've got him now!" shouted Erler. "How can the court of appeals turn us down?"

"We are not quite there yet, Bob," cautioned Eddie. "The errors we complained of at the trial are different and apart from what we know about the judge's sexual misconduct."

"In other words," cried Erler, "I was railroaded and framed by a loony judge and can't complain to the higher court about the fairness of the trial?"

Eddie knew Erler would not carry on in this fashion with me and was sorry his phone call of good tidings was met with such frustrated ravings. "Bob, I'll report this to my boss, so please be patient and behave yourself up there."

"So what you're telling me is we still have to wait for the appellate court's ruling on my case," spat out Erler, exhibiting another facet of his variable personality.

"Yes, Bob, these matters take time."

"Thank you, sir," answered Erler for forced resignation. "I'll do my level best to make time. All I have left is time."

Admission into the population compound did little to eradicate Erler's leprous image. He was the butt of cruel taunts and those taunts were sometimes emotionally harder to take than the physical beatings from the extremely hardened and ignorant criminals anxious to vent their irrational hatred against an ex-cop. I had a good grapevine but it only provided a shallow sample of what Erler was truly experiencing. I knew, for example, that the former lawman had to have his head sewed up. He was constantly under threat of being killed. The initial attack by those nine inmates with a two-by-four and other sticks resulted in a broken jaw, broken nose, broken front teeth, broken ribs, and severe cuts all over his body. He had to have plastic surgery three times on his face and nose.

And I only knew bits and pieces of what really went on behind those fortress walls. How one man could retain any kind of sanity with the pressure he was under is still hard for me to understand. His only close friend was Jack Griffith who passed the word along the steel corridors that Bob Erler was under his protection, so hands off! Most of the inmates complied out of fear of Griffith but there were still some who continued to carry out the vendetta against the former lawman. The personal physical attacks stopped only after Erler had severely beaten an ex-pro boxer in full view of about 200 inmates. The former pugilist made the mistake of sucker-punching Erler, who was no stranger to the ring. In essence, that match became Erler's last stand. However, the fighting did not completely end; later, he had to jump a death row inmate who had stabbed an acquaintance of Erler's four times with a boning knife.

Erler constantly complained that phone privileges didn't mean a thing as far as communicating with his attorney who was always "in court" or "out of the office" when he called, and we resolved our differences by progress reports sent through the mail. When an inmate corresponds with his attorney, he is required to inscribe on the face of the envelope "LEGAL MAIL" in bold letters to avoid his mail from being censored by the prison officials. U.S. postal letters between a lawyer and his client are sacrosanct and free from interception by anyone. The glowing reports about Erler's progress were a source of gratification to me. Some of the correspondence contained graphic accounts of violence and unmerciful beatings, where his nose was broken again and his facial features brutally rearranged, but with each savage encounter, Erler's stature as a good con was elevated to the degree of ultimate acceptance. He never "finked" on any of his assailants and passed the loyalty tests delineated by the "code." Erler was settling down to prison life, earning the respect of his fellow inmates, although most of the respect was acquired through fear.

Griffith played Svengali to Erler, taking command of his psyche, exercising his hypnotic powers to mold his disciple to intractable subservience. He orchestrated a spartan-like regimen that had Erler meditating at 4:30 in the morning and plunging into rigorous Karate training until 8:00 A.M. when he would reluctantly join his fellow inmates in the harsh reality of prison life.

Erler was gradually becoming a model prisoner and relished his new mental philosophy of self-discipline and seriously considered embracing the teachings of Zen Buddhism, since Griffith was a follower of that faith. He felt an inner peace and was content to await the outcome of his appeal with serene patience—much to my relief. His new demeanor curtailed all the caustic complaints about the unhurried appellate process. I was fully convinced his transformation was solely due to Griffith's tutelage. Jack Griffith was the "Sensei"—the Master, to whom Erler undeniably surrendered his soul.

Karate fever swept through the compound as a new, refreshing recreational program spearheaded by Sensei Griffith, whose standing in the compound was elevated to alarming heights. Several hours for strenuous workout sessions were openly allocated under the watchful eyes of the prison guards who reported daily to their superiors the casualties inflicted on some new untrained aspirants. There were divisional contests where some of the contenders were mismatched, resulting in a steady flow of injured inmates to the infirmary. At the warden's express direction, Captain Combs visited the newly christened DOJO the inmates venerated as their temple of martial arts, to survey and witness firsthand the type of mayhem the prisoners were inflicting upon each other in the name of Karate.

The exterior of a two-by-twelve-inch pinewood board

standing vertically against the wall in the gymnasium was
stuffed with burlap for the Jiu Jitsu and Karate students to
punch, and harden their hands, as Sensei Griffith said, "So
they would become lethal weapons of steel." Students
would attack the burlap-stuffed board until their hands
would become raw, bloody and sometimes fractured.

Captain Combs now understood why the prison clinic
ministered to a rash of maimed hands, resulting in a mounting absence from work duties. The chief would not be
happy with Combs' report on the Karate madness that fo-
mented violence and brutality. It was obvious Jack Griffith,
the Master, and his number one prize pupil, Robert Erler,
were primarily and solely responsible for the pernicious
madness that prevailed.

The warden ordered Robert Erler and Griffith transferred
to Belle Glade, a minimum security camp just sixty miles
north of Broward County, which was catalogued on the
Inmate Chart as an upgrade in behavior classification but
was utilized as a vehicle to rid a rough, tough prison like
Raiford of a rougher and tougher inmate like Erler, and his
God-like mentor.

40

IT WAS EARLY Saturday morning. I was alone in my office
ready to go through a stack of correspondence that Lucy
had neatly arranged on the left-hand corner of my desk
before she went home Friday evening. She had opened all
of the accumulated mail for my convenience except a thick
envelope from the Fourth District Court of Appeals. Lucy
had placed this unopened one on top of the stack. One look
at the return address and my stomach tightened. There it
was. The Erler decision!

I excitedly tore the envelope open and read with stunned
disbelief the appellate court's ruling affirming Erler's conviction. The court refused to pass upon any of the points
on appeal raised by the defense. One of the appellate judges
on the panel, in a comprehensive opinion, disagreed with

the other two members of the court and recommended the conviction be set aside and a new trial granted based upon the "prejudicial misconduct of the trial judge."

It was difficult to break the disappointing news to Erler who was gradually acclimating to prison life in his new surroundings in a minimum security facility. I feared the shock of the adverse ruling would send him over the edge. Erler could easily become unpredictable and unmanageable after the hell he had been through.

Eddie Kay had been aware of the unopened envelope from the court of appeals and drove by the office that Saturday. Seeing my blue Lincoln in the parking lot, he knew he could discover whether it was time for joy or commiseration.

"Good morning," Eddie cheerily called out.

"Here, read this," was my gruff reply throwing the opinion at the junior attorney.

Eddie hurriedly scanned the papers, as though he was proficient at speed reading, and asked, "What's the next step?"

Heaving a sigh I signalled him to sit down. "We, or rather you, are to file a petition for rehearing which is always denied, but must be done before we can be eligible to apply to the Supreme Court. You will then prepare a petition for certiorari, and if that is granted, the Supreme Court will take jurisdiction and examine the entire record to determine if we received a fair trial from Stokely."

"Do you think the Supreme Court will accept certiorari on this case?"

"Certainly," I explained. "The Supreme Court will be interested where there is a split decision, especially when one of the appellate judges writes a comprehensive dissenting opinion. Someone is right, or someone is wrong."

"I'll get on it right away," said Eddie, rising from his chair, halting when I beckoned him to stop.

"You better write a letter to Bob Erler telling him the results, and our plan to apply to the Supreme Court."

"Yes, sir," was the reply.

I dreaded the next telephone call from Erler after he received Eddie's report.

41 _____

FLORIDA'S BELLE GLADE Correctional Institution was a country club compared to Raiford. It nestled among long, thin scrub pine trees swaying majestically over dense floral shrubbery and bougainvillea scattered throughout open fields. The area abounded with malaleuca trees nourished by the waters of Lake Okeechobee that grew aimlessly in the warm tropical climate. There were no iron bars in the prison compound, whose only security was a light chain-link fence that enclosed intermittent portions of the camp. Erler was elated with his new quarters in the large dormitory, overlooking an olympic-sized athletic field, handball courts and oval spring track; the oppressive yoke of steel cells, handcuffs and leg irons were past history, and a new era was dawning. He would sit on a bench in the athletic field after a strenuous workout and marvel at the good fortune that seemed to be coming his way, and the fact that his good friend and confidante, Jack Griffith, was also in Belle Glade served to heighten his happiness.

Bob Erler wrote glowing reports to his family and me about his "Sensei" Jack Griffith and how the old Karate club was revived in conjunction with a special educational training program that enabled inmates to receive high school and college equivalent credits. One day Erler's brother, Paul, came to visit him and was greeted with greater warmth and affection than he ever remembered. They spoke animatedly about the family and about the appeal that was pending, as well as Bob's chances for an early release. Bob gave his brother a grand tour of the prison camp and chanced upon Jack Griffith who was casually strolling about the compound. He happily introduced Griffith to brother Paul in the most glowing and complimentary terms.

"This is my teacher and best friend I wrote you about," enthusiastically exclaimed Erler. "I could never have made it if it wasn't for Jack."

Paul Erler expressed his appreciation to Griffith for all the help given to his brother, Bob, and sincerely thanked him on behalf of his entire family. In his effusion he extended an open invitation to Griffith to come to Phoenix, Arizona whenever he was at liberty and promised to show him true western hospitality, as the family were at his disposal. Jack Griffith made an obvious impression upon Paul, who was able to understand why his brother, Bob, was so proud to be Griffith's friend and student. Griffith promised Paul that he would accept his kind offer when he was in that neighborhood and, with a parting handshake, slyly mentioned, "My visit to your family may be sooner than you think."

"Anytime at all," responded Paul. "Our house is your house. We can't thank you enough for everything you've done for Bob."

Jack Griffith leisurely strolled away as the brothers embraced and said their farewells. Bob Erler sadly looked at his brother's retreating form as he faded out of sight and sought out Griffith to explain some of the nuances he detected in Griffith's discussions with brother Paul.

"Hey, Jack," queried Erler, "what was that crack to my brother that he'd be seeing you sooner than he thinks?"

Griffith laughed and told Erler, "I will talk about that a little later on. Right now, I'm in the planning stage."

"Planning what?" asked his student.

"Getting out of here, that's what," answered Griffith, "and maybe you'd like to come with me."

Erler became alarmed. He implored Jack to abandon such foolish ideas.

"I can't go with you," apologized Erler. "I've built up a good record and my lawyer tells me my appeal is looking good. I just can't sacrifice everything for a hare-brained idea that leads to nowhere."

"Then I'll go it alone, Buddy," Jack spoke with resolution. "Just keep it under your hat."

It seemed strange that Griffith refused to confide in Erler as to his destination, and for the first time during their close friendship, Erler commenced having slight nagging doubts about Jack Griffith's eccentricities. He had a disturbing suspicion that Griffith might seek refuge in the Erler home in

Arizona, and the more Erler dwelled on this possibility, the greater his alarm of the probable consequences. The Erler family was a tightly knit group and Bob loved every member of his family dearly. He dreaded the thought that Jack Griffith would escape and force his presence on his beloved family. He never voiced his fears to his mentor and teacher and inwardly cursed the strange turn of events that threatened his new serene and tranquil—relatively speaking—lifestyle.

The adamant Sensei made good his boast and it was hours before anyone was aware that he was missing. The escape alarm blared through the compound as a bevy of guards stirred into a frantic search for the escaped convict. Two helicopters hovered over the area, beaming their strong headlights in the dense underbrush searching relentlessly for Griffith long into the night, without success. Erler's name was called on the public address system to report to the captain's office immediately. When he dutifully appeared, an angry Captain Dowling glared at him.

"You know where Griffith is, you better come clean and tell me!"

"Captain, sir," pleaded Erler, "I honestly don't know where Griffith is," but this response was met with a cold stare of wrathful disbelief.

"All right, Erler," snarled the captain. "We know what to do with a smartass like you," and turned his back on the sorrowful prisoner. Erler tried to explain that he truly did not know where Griffith went, but the retreating officer was out of range. Erler knew at that point he needlessly made an enemy and wondered when the axe would fall. The only way he could possibly heal the breach was if Griffith sent a message as to his whereabouts. Then perhaps he might summon up enough courage to inform Captain Dowling. Erler shrugged off this possibility. There was a code of honor among convicts which must be preserved at all costs.

The following Sunday Erler made a routine telephone call to his family in Phoenix and was advised by his brother, Danny, that they had a "visitor," an old friend who needed help. He went on in guarded tones to recount that the visitor said he was Bob's best friend and protector and it was only right for Bob's people to help him. Danny further reported that the visitor announced he would stay awhile until things cooled off. Erler had no advice to offer and terminated the phone conversation quickly as the subject matter obviously referred to Jack Griffith, who forced himself on the Erler family.

Robert Erler found himself in a tenuous position. Griffith's violation of propriety could justify Erler's abandoning the "code." Inasmuch as Jack imposed his presence on the Erler family, the code would have to be repudiated and Griffith's location reported to the warden. His family was in jeopardy for harboring a fugitive, which constituted a felony, punishable by a prison term. If Griffith ever knew or suspected that Bob Erler tipped the police where he was hiding, he could expect violent retribution from the arrogant, self-confessed murderer. Bob Erler was experiencing the greatest pressure he had ever known. He tried to think out what to do, but every option seemed like a no-win situation.

Mrs. Lucy Bachelor, a middle-aged, petite and comely brunette, possessing all the genteel attributes of a southern aristocrat was a dedicated social worker who taught certain orientation classes in Belle Glade. She became interested in Bob Erler.

Mrs. Bachelor was so impressed with Erler's sincerity that a special trip to Hollywood was made to interview me, and I took a liking to this remarkable lady, who devoted her entire life to assisting deserving convicts, planning and molding their existence toward ultimate rehabilitation.

"What is your opinion as to Mr. Erler's participation in the homicide?" she asked, and quickly interjected, "Not that it makes any appreciable difference since my goal is to return him to the mainstream of society as a worthwhile citizen."

"I firmly believe in his innocence," I answered and went into detail about how prejudiced witnesses went out of their way to implicate Erler in the murder of Merilyn Clark. She was surprised to learn about the line-up, where Dorothy Clark was unable to identify Erler on two separate occasions, but was able to make a positive in-court identification after being shown his picture by the police one hour prior to entering the courtroom.

"How dreadful," she softly replied and complimented me for my commitment to procure Erler's release in the face of the inequities of the trial. Encouraged by her sympathy, I related the police cover-up on the Dorothy Clark tapes which further appalled her into stating, "What you have told me makes me even more determined to help Bob through this terrible period of his life."

In turning to Mrs. Bachelor for advice, Bob Erler was told to seek out Mr. Dowling, who just became the new assistant warden, and apologized for whatever he had done to anger him, and discuss the entire Jack Griffith affair from start to finish. Erler obediently sought out Mr. Dowling, but the assistant warden refused to talk to him, stating, "There is nothing to say. I'm scheduling you to return to maximum security in Raiford penitentiary, with the rest of your kind."

"But, sir," pleaded Erler, "I have accomplished so much here with my schooling. Please don't send me back up there. I've accumulated college credits which will enable me to get my degree within a month's time. We just got off on the wrong foot. I'd like to explain . . ."

"Forget it, Erler," interrupted Dowling. "Your transportation will be available shortly, and that's it!"

A wave of nausea spread over Erler intuitively presaging the migraine headaches that would ultimately debilitate him. He had nowhere to turn and slowly made his way to the telephone booth to call his family. He was anxious to speak with any family member who could advise him what to do, or give him some manner of comfort in his time of need. Danny answered the phone and gave him the worst news he had ever received in his entire tormented life. Jack Griffith was now intimidating all segments of the Erler family. He was getting drunk and making irrational statements, such as proclaiming his love for Bob Erler's married sister. He threatened to kill her husband so he could have her for himself. Danny also told Bob that Griffith was using a lot of drugs and narcotics and the entire family was frightened of him.

"We need your help, Bob," cried Danny.

To Bob Erler, this was an understatement. He knew firsthand just what his mentor, Jack Griffith, was capable of doing. For Erler had viewed the gruesome remains of Griffith's and "Murph the Surf's" victims in the morgue while on the Hollywood Police Department. The inhumane, ghastly sight was permanently etched into Erler's memory: Two young women senselessly beaten, then stabbed and then shot. Finally, they had chunks of concrete tied around their necks to ensure their sinking in Hollywood's Whiskey Creek. Bob Erler knew precisely the danger his own family now faced with Griffith as the unwelcome house guest who would not leave.

"Let me think things over," replied Erler. After the call, he walked out into the blinding sunlight. He was the only person in the world strong and tough enough to deal with Jack Griffith. He got his family into this trouble and he would get them out of it. His mind was made up. As darkness fell over the prison camp, Erler escaped.

42

IT WAS THE first murder trial since Florida reinstated the death penalty. Circuit Judge George W. Tedder, Jr. excused the twelve male jurors and two alternates for the day, a welcome respite for me, who up to this juncture in my career had never lost a client to "the chair" but mathematically the odds were narrowing and I was more tense than usual. As the jurors filed back to their conference room, the spectators made their way out through the swinging imitation leather doors, passing me while I was pretending to be sitting at ease, leisurely stuffing legal pads and documents in my briefcase. It was always my practice not to mingle or come in contact with jurors or prospective witnesses during a courtroom exodus, preferring to wait until the corridors were clear, before making my exit. As I was about to walk out, my forward progress was abruptly halted by Doug McQuarrie, the Crime Reporter for the *Fort Lauderdale News*.

"We heard Erler escaped. Do you know anything about it?"

Shock and disbelief swept over me, "What are you talking about?"

"We got it on the teletype that Erler escaped from Belle Glade. Do you know where he is? Do you know anything about it?" persisted the reporter.

"This is an absolute surprise to me, Doug," I replied. "Please excuse me, there's a lot of work to be done," and shrugging off the reporter's restraining hand, I tore out of the courtroom and headed for my car in the parking lot.

During the eight mile drive to the office, I assessed the damage created by Erler's haphazard action. Eventually, Erler would be captured and returned to Florida's prison system, but the consequences of this untimely episode were monumental. The probability existed that a felony charge for Unlawful Escape would be filed against him, placing him in dire jeopardy just at the crucial time when his appeals looked very favorable and were about to yield some promising results. Moreover, if Erler persisted in absenting himself, all of his pending appeals would be dismissed. The law universally is that a defendant before the bar of justice who escapes from detention or custody of a penal institution is deprived of the right of appeal on the theory that he is out of the jurisdiction of the courts, and has no standing to be heard because he is "non-existent" in the eyes of the law. Our only hope was to make a concerted effort to locate him and compel his voluntary return to the authorities, which may pre-empt the formalizing of the inevitable felony charge.

"What timing!" I cursed wrathfully, barging into my office, throwing the briefcase on the oversized suede sofa, "Who needs this grief in the middle of a capital case where the state is demanding the death penalty? I can't believe it!"

All the office personnel had gone for the day. Ritually, this was the time when I would review the day's events and prepare for the next day's proceedings. But not today. I now had to figure out how to get my client back in the fold. My words for his behavior at that point are not fit for print.

The conventional telephone call to the administrative office at Belle Glade Correctional Institution was made, seeking official verification of Erler's escape.

"Yessir," drawled the warden. "Your boy Erler has flown the coop and if you know what's good for the both of you he better get back here within twenty-four hours. And you can tell him for me, Mr. Lawyer, if he isn't here by my deadline I will put a detainer on him for unlawful escape."

I thanked the warden and assured him I was aware of the seriousness of the offense. Unlawful escape from custody of a penal institution is a felony in Florida punishable by five years imprisonment, which created enough of an emergency to reluctantly call Mrs. Winifred Erler in Arizona. I didn't relish speaking with the Erler clan, but had a CYA duty to perform.

Danny Erler answered the phone and the conversation was fruitless and strangely unproductive. I seemed to sense a peculiar reluctance on Danny's part to discuss his brother's escape, nor did he venture any suggestions why Bob ran away, or where he could possibly hide.

"If Bob does get in touch with you, any of you, it is very important that he contact me immediately. Tell him to call 'collect' from wherever he may be. It is more important than any of you can realize. I'm certain he doesn't realize what a foolish thing he has done. The success of his freedom is in the balance and depends upon his coming back."

My pleas seemed to have fallen on unreceptive ears. Could it be that the Erler clan was engaging in a silent conspiracy against their own attorney? Why? Something unfathomable was occurring to which I was not privileged to know, and gradually became disenchanted with their lack of confidence.

The entire staff in the office was alerted to contact all of Erler's friends and associates for some leads or helpful information to flush him out of his hiding place. I was engrossed in a serious murder trial and my paramount duty was to keep a frightened AWOL Marine from frying in Florida's electric chair.

John Oksten, a handsome nineteen-year-old Marine from West Deptfort, New Jersey, was stationed at Bridgeport,

California. Oksten deserted because he was the butt of many pranks in the barracks from his fellow "grunts" and could not withstand the pressures of military life. One day, while on leave, he decided to desert the military service and when his leave expired, he became AWOL (Absent With Out Leave) and then a deserter wanted by the MPs—Military Police.

Young Oksten made his way to Miami and hitchhiked to Hollywood, where he was "picked up" by sixty-five-year-old John Melvin, who offered Oksten lodging for an undetermined period of time. When Curtis Padgett, Melvin's friend and neighbor, noticed Melvin's car missing for two days, he went into the neighbor's home where he found Melvin's nude, blood-soaked body, with his face smashed and battered almost beyond recognition.

The murder weapon was a heavy monkey wrench which was used to bludgeon John Melvin to death. The bloody fingerprints were identified as those of young John Oksten. A nationwide manhunt was initiated and the young Marine was ultimately spotted and arrested in St. Augustine, Florida. Because of the enormity of the crime, the state asked for the death penalty. It was apparent to me, this terrified young man had some mental aberrations, suggesting the exploration of an insanity defense.

The trial was the usual battle of the psychiatrists, with the two from the state claiming Oksten was sane and the two from the defense holding the opposite view. The issue was simple: Was Oksten temporarily insane at the time he committed this brutal murder?

Doctor Paul Jarrett, an eminent Coral Gables psychiatrist, agreed with the defense's position that Oksten lost control of his faculties and retaliated in hysterical violence when his elderly host made sexual advances towards him. The young Marine had no recollection of the incident until he found himself driving John Melvin's automobile. The jury rendered a verdict of not guilty by reason of insanity and Oksten was committed to the South Florida State Hospital for psychiatric treatment until further order of the court.

A few years later, I received a call from John Oksten proudly informing me he was a happily married man with a family in New Jersey.

Robert Erler remained a fugitive-at-large and successfully eluded the national manhunt that swept the country. The news media fanned the fires of hysteria, subtly indulging in speculation that the 'Catch Me Killer' conceivably could surface to seek vengeance upon Mrs. Dorothy Clark, or probably the prosecutor, both of whom were solely responsible for his conviction. Len Boone armed himself daily with a .45 caliber gun he retained from his service as a state highway trooper, and Dorothy Clark sought protection from the local police in Clarkston, Georgia. Boone was so genuinely concerned that he wrote a letter to his former star witness on the stationery of the Circuit Court of Broward County, Florida, addressed to "Dear Dorothy" advising of Erler's escape from prison and that he and the rest of the officers in his area were on the lookout for him. The letter further went on to say that Dorothy should not be frightened because it would be a short matter of time before Erler would be captured and suggested that if she was contacted by Erler or any of his friends or family, to communicate this information to the writer immediately. The letter was signed, "Sincerely, Len."

The intensive manhunt continued for several months but no traces of the fugitive emerged. Robert Erler never contacted me or anyone in my office. Waiting for the "other shoe to drop" the dreaded minute order arrived from the Supreme Court carrying the explanation, "An appellant who is a fugitive from penal custody has no standing in this court or any other court of appeal."

Erler's appeals on all fronts were dismissed and the case had to remain in limbo until the day when Erler would be recaptured and once again come within the jurisdiction of Florida's judicial system.

43

ENGULFED WITH THE pressure of criminal cases that demanded my immediate attention, the Erler case was placed on the "back burner." Although even on the back burner, gnawing thoughts about Erler's plight would continue to haunt me. If he were still alive, he would eventually be apprehended and complex legal maneuvers would be required to reinstate the appeals dismissed because of his escape. I personally agonized over my strange obsession to carry on the battle for Erler's freedom.

Was it my personal egocentricity that required nourishment, or was it a mulish vanity that wouldn't permit me to accept defeat? A mystifying loyalty to Erler's cause collided with the indelicate rejection displayed by Erler and his family members. Prudence dictated the entire affair should be relegated to past history, but the newspapers milked the escape story, keeping it alive.

The news media, with subliminal subtlety, depicted a vengeful Erler, using all the skills acquired in the armed forces as a commando, eluding the manhunt and foraging the area where Dorothy Clark lived, waiting for the critical moment to strike. I was impelled to vow, "This is no longer my concern; it was over, all over!"

Eight months had elapsed since Robert Erler escaped from Belle Glade Correctional Institution to Phoenix, ostensibly to relieve his family from Jack Griffith's torturous domination of the Erler household. My fleeting thoughts focused on many possibilities. "Perhaps he was killed by Griffith when he went to his family's assistance?" It was also conceivable that in his frantic efforts to elude the manhunt generated by the police in a nationwide sweep he became emotionally distraught and killed himself. I discounted that possibility, as it was logical to assume the identity of the body when found would be disclosed.

I vigorously shook my head, as if by doing so I would

rid my consciousness from the wild thoughts that raced through my fretful mind.

On March 31, 1974, all the television stations throughout the country blared the astounding news that Robert Erler, the 'Catch Me Killer' was captured in a small town in Mississippi. The following morning, April 1, April Fool's Day, the nation's newspapers carried front page headlines announcing in large, bold type, "CATCH ME KILLER CAUGHT."

The newspaper accounts that day contained only sketchy information. So I immediately assigned Harry Long, because of his police connections, to get the complete, accurate story behind the capture. Eddie Kay, who was in my office while I phoned Harry, reminded me that our primary investigator was also needed in court that afternoon as a witness.

I raised my eyebrows, fully aware that he had the priorities correct and I was somewhat puzzled at my own spontaneous order. After a few seconds of silence I said, "Harry can get all the data in a couple of hours so we're just going to have to stall a bit." Eddie recognized the slight chagrin I was experiencing by violating my own iron-clad rule against "stalling" and unnecessary delay, recalling so many times how I used to say, "There must be a continuous flow of evidence in a trial, otherwise the jury gets bored. The jurors know when you are stalling and they lose respect for you." My young assistant lost his enthusiasm for Erler's cause more than three years ago, and wondered why I clung to an ideal tarnished by ingratitude.

Were the truth known, there was no rational explanation.

When court adjourned at the close of the day, I visited Tom at the snack bar for some gossip and to replenish my supply of Baby Ruth bars in anticipation of Harry's visit that evening. Pushing a carton of the chocolate bars over the counter in my direction, Tom said, "So, they captured your ex-client? Now he'll never see the light of day."

"Why is that, Tom? What did you hear?"

"Only that in addition to the escape charges they will pile on, your boy was on a crime spree, heavy into narcotics and all that goes with it."

I quietly absorbed the news, sipping black coffee from

the last paper cup on the bar. Tom was hurriedly closing for the night, and lingered long enough to tell me, "He's headed back to the 'Rock' in max security if you want to reach him."

Harry Long was only smiling and cheerful around me when he was the courier of ominous news. I didn't mind playing "straight man" to the investigator as ultimately an unvarnished account of Erler's capture would be forthcoming. I maintained a commendable silence until three Baby Ruths vanished into the chocolate-smeared, porcine face leering at me across the desk. A low boiling point was about to belie the forced impassiveness on my face when the investigator licked his sausage-like fingers and began, "Here it is, Counselor," pulling out a four-by-eight-inch notebook from a pocket inside his loose hounds-tooth jacket, "Your man took up with some pretty bad people and lived high on the hog; girls, booze, pot, changing his looks, name, everything."

"What kind of change, Harry?"

"He let his hair grow long and dyed it black. Went under the name of Bruce Strickland. When he was captured, he even had a Social Security card and driver's license under the name of Strickland."

"Tell me about his capture. There was an item in the paper about a gunfight and Erler got wounded. How bad was it?" I asked with genuine interest.

Long reached into the carton of chocolate bars on my desk, absently removing the paper wrapper and devouring the entire morsel in a single, continuous movement. I looked on interestedly, half expecting the investigator to start choking from the excessive mouthful, and sat back in the chair, chiding myself for the unnecessary concern for Long, who was merely stoking the boiler for more energy.

"According to Bill Middleton, the sheriff of Webster County, Mississippi, your boy and his gang were operating in small towns in the south when a tip came in from an undisclosed informant that a package containing marijuana and a firearm was mailed to one Bruce Strickland, care of General Delivery, Mathiston, Mississippi. The postal inspector set up a 'controlled delivery' and waited until the addressee, who in this case was 'Mr. Bruce Strickland' would show up to claim the package. The plan was to arrest whoever picked it up for unlawful possession of narcotics and illegal transportation of firearms through the U.S. mail.'' The investigator finished his report with a suspicious "Strickland" running from the post office, leading his pursuers in a high speed chase until he was gunned down and captured.

Reading between the lines, I envisioned "Strickland" arriving at the postal station to receive the package addressed to him when he perceived something was amiss. The furtive actions of the postal clerk alarmed him, and clutching the package to his breast, ran out to his parked car and sped away, the squealing tires churning up a spray of gravel and debris.

Twisting and turning through the unfamiliar streets of the small rural town slowed down his progress and "Strickland" found himself looking into the barrel of a rifle held by Sheriff Middleton who came alongside, ordering him to stop and get out of the car. The investigator broke through my illusionary deductions and continued his narrative, "When Erler became aware that he was ambushed by squad cars, he immediately took flight and a high speed chase was initiated. The police officers were in full pursuit, pumping shotguns, disabling Erler's car, forcing a flight on foot through wilderness. A rifle shot in his backside ended the chase, forcing a surrender to his captors.''

"Tom was right," I thoughtfully said, snapping out of my reverie. "The next stop for Erler is a maximum security cell at Raiford.''

"Correction, Counselor," added the investigator. "Not only the max, but in the 'hole'.''

"Solitary confinement," I sighed, wondering how and when I again would make contact with Erler. I also asked myself "why?''

The now complete circle of Erler's imprisonment, escape and capture obviously gave me cause for bewilderment about my involvement in the case. This much was clear, however: The Federal Bureau of Investigation, acting in conjunction with Florida's state police, had the Erler home in Phoenix under strict surveillance. Jack Griffith was "street smart" enough to leave the Arizona sanctuary relieving Bob Erler of his inevitable confrontation with the man who held his family hostage, thus avoiding a murder of one or the other.

Erler had learned about Griffith no longer being a family threat and leaving for parts unknown through a surreptitious conversation with his brother Paul only after having just escaped from prison. At that point, Erler could have surrendered himself to authorities, but after experiencing a kangaroo court and receiving more than his share of physical scars and emotional abuse in prison, perhaps only a masochist would have done so. His alternative was to embark on a new career as a fugitive. For eight wonderful glorious months, the ex-cop rode on a dazzling merry-go-round of petty crime, sex, booze, and drugs.

44

WHEN THE STATE legislature was not in session, there was only a single flight available from Miami to Tallahassee, departing at 7:00 A.M. and returning at five in the afternoon. I arrived at the airport early, in order not to miss this morning's scheduled Supreme Court hearing, and browsed around the sundry store at the magazine and book counter, killing time to escape the boredom of waiting for the flight to be called, when out of the corner of my eye a familiar name seemed to jump out: Deane Bostick. There it was on a colorful paperback depicting the likeness of the bearded Fidel Castro in a background of armed, wounded soldiers, entitled *Dos Compadres*. The back cover of the book offered some data about the author who "spent three years training men to make raids to Cuba and was a public information officer for Alpha 66." I smiled with satisfaction and purchased Bostick's book. It would occupy time during the boring flight. I thought to myself, I must remember to write Deane Bostick in care of the publishing company and give him a critique on his literary effort. I warmly recalled how Deane was the only reporter at Erler's trial who openly expressed his feeling that Erler was victimized by the failure of the justice system.

It took fully three weeks before Robert Erler surfaced into prison population and was restored to an inmate's writing and telephone privileges. It proved futile for Erler to try phoning me, because I was always out of the office. So instead he wrote a lengthy letter of explanation. I received the bulky envelope marked "Legal Mail" addressed to me, "Private and Confidential," but put it aside at a bare spot on my cluttered desk. I was beset by a mixture of emotions and was just not in the mood to bother with Erler and his insurmountable problems that seemed to be pyramiding beyond control. It pained me to even begin to catalogue all the criminal acts Erler committed, starting with his escape from Belle Glade. There were no funds available for the herculean services that must be rendered in order to reinstate the Erler appeals. That was my only area of responsibility; not the escape charge or the new criminal charges involving narcotics and unlawful possession of weapons in the Mississippi caper. Shrugging off the complex vexations, I returned to the immediate pressing problem of a young girl who killed her alcoholic-crazed father. She certainly had priority over the emotionally unstable ex-cop.

Bostick was surprised when his long distance telephone call reached me without the usual secretarial interruption. He didn't know about my inviolate rule in the office, "Never ask who is calling. If I'm there, put the caller right through."

"Hello, Counselor," came the crisp announcement. I recognized the unique gravelly voice with the southern accent, and quickly replied, "Hello yourself, Deane."

"Am up here in Atlanta and want to come down to see you."

"Great!" was my elated response. "When can you fly down here?"

"Sorry," laughed the reporter. "My flying days are over."

Puzzled, I was impelled to ask, "What happened?"

Still chuckling, "It's a long story," explained Bostick. "Will tell you when I get there."

A tropical storm with gusting winds of thirty knots per hour was the reason my Sunday golf game was canceled, a good excuse to find solace in the quiet of the office. My desk looked like someone emptied all the wastebaskets on it, daring anyone to sort through the accumulation of documents and find anything. I sat comfortably in the oversized leather chair, visually surveying the debris when a casual glance subconsciously focused my attention to Erler's bulky, unopened letter resting in a relatively bare spot on the desk. It didn't take a genius to figure out what it was. Erler was sufficiently perceptive to realize his unforgivable actions placed him perilously on the verge of losing a valuable ally and this would be an explanation for his astounding conduct. With frosty indifference, I opened the bulging envelope and skimmed through the pages. The hidden anguish in the missive was a desperate plea for forgiveness, replete with factual occurrences in justification of his erratic behavior.

I read on with renewed interest. Jack Griffith was the dominant theme. Erler recounted his rookie days at the Hollywood Police Department when Griffith and his partner, "Murph the Surf" murdered two young girls. The sight of their tortured bodies always remained with him, as he recalled seeing the cement blocks tied around their necks with wire, after being stabbed, shot and unceremoniously flung into the wild mangrove bushes at Whiskey Creek. When he met Griffith in prison, his awareness of Jack's vicious propensities never diminished, even though he respected him as his mentor in the pursuit of the coveted Karate Black Belt. Griffith became Erler's protector and Sensei, exercising complete dominion and control over his devoted slave.

When they were doing time together in Belle Glade, a minimum security camp, Paul Erler came to visit his brother, who made the mistake of introducing Jack Griffith as his "best friend and protector," and impressed upon young Paul that he owed his very existence to his Sensei. Everyone in the compound knew Bob Erler and Jack Griffith were close, inseparable buddies. The untimely escape of the Sensei focused suspicion on Erler as an accomplice or participating co-conspirator, and Captain Dowling insisted on being told where Griffith was hiding. When Erler truthfully was unable to cooperate, the vengeful captain promised never to forget the lack of respect and refusal to obey the request of a superior officer. Incurring the displeasure of Captain Dowling made Erler depressed and unhappy, and his attempts to reason with the captain were coldly rebuffed, with orders to "get out of my office!"

Three weeks later, on a Sunday call to his family, Erler was informed by Danny that Jack was in Phoenix at his mother's house, receiving the red carpet treatment because of what Paul told them the fugitive did for Bob in prison. Erler excitedly warned them to get rid of the "visitor," as harboring a fugitive was a felony, and promised to call the next day to make certain Griffith was gone. A telephone call the following day was fruitless. Griffith refused to leave. He had no place to go, and nothing to lose. Erler's repeated calls to Phoenix were of no avail and the last communication with his family was the most devastating. Paul reported that Griffith confided in him that he was in love with his married sister and was going to kill her husband, Chuck, so he could have her for himself.

Bob Erler was stunned. He kept seeing the tortured bodies of the two young girls Griffith murdered, so he knew Jack's vicious nature and what his capabilities were. The idea of turning Griffith in to the police was quickly abandoned because of the danger in placing his entire family in jeopardy, should there be some of Jack's friends on the outside seeking retribution. Erler promised to call back after he made a decision. As he made his way to his cell, where he believed he could sort out his thoughts, the intercom blared out his name. He was directed to report to Captain Dowling's office immediately, where he was informed of his immediate transfer to a maximum security prison. Was it too much to ask for just one week's respite before being transferred so he could earn the fifteen credits due him from the Miami Dade Junior College courses? Captain Dowling firmly said, "You are leaving on the next bus that pulls in the gate. That is final!"

Bob knew he could never help his family with the Griffith problem if he were imprisoned in maximum security. His beloved family was tormented by a crazed killer all because of him. They were virtually held hostage, and he was the only one who could save them.

"Please try to understand, Mr. Varon, there was no other choice than to escape. I place my family above everything and felt it was the right thing to do."

I noted, reading Erler's letter that no mention was made of his confrontation with Griffith, or the wild life of crime in which he was engaged during his eight months of freedom. The explanation would probably come later when the inevitable consequences emerged. I promised myself not to become embroiled in any of the criminal charges emanating from Erler's bizarre conduct. The last line in my client's letter flung an oblique challenge, "Do you have anything to fight with now that I blew it all by leaving?"

I never realized that Deane Bostick was a writer of note, having authored several paperback novels based upon his exploits in revolutionary Cuba, and was intrigued by anecdotes of his fighting as a guerilla in the mountains against Fidel Castro's communistic hordes.

"That's why I dare not fly in a plane," explained Bostick in his gentle drawl. "There's been so many airplanes hijacked to Cuba lately, if I were a passenger on a re-routed plane that would be the end of the line for me."

"So you had to drive all the way from Atlanta just to see me?" I asked, slightly curious as to Bostick's request for a meeting. "I'm impressed."

"Don't you want to know what I was doing in Georgia?" teased the smiling reporter, white strong teeth gleaming through his neatly trimmed, dark beard. I remained silent as Bostick leaned forward, slapping both hands on the desk, and in his low gravelly voice murmured "Spending a lot of time with a nice, southern lady by the name of Dorothy Clark!"

"What?" I shouted. "Not the . . ."

"Yes, the very same Dorothy Clark in the Robert Erler case."

"Give it to me slowly," I urged, falling back in my swivel chair, simulating a swooning collapse, evoking a hearty laugh from the reporter.

"Remember the articles I wrote for *MAN*'s Magazine

where my follow-up story after conviction was *Catch Me Killer—Set Him Free*? It's my sincere belief that Erler is innocent, and was railroaded by some high-powered cover-up tactics which should be exposed. My job is investigative reporting and I'm the best candidate to exonerate Erler. The first step of my investigation was to interview Mrs. Dorothy Clark, and,'' smiled Bostick with a slight arch of his dark eyebrows, "she is all excited about the book I'm writing about the case.''

My mind worked furiously. If Deane had such a good rapport with Dorothy Clark, he could unearth some very important information in the guise of procuring background data from the state's star witness that would prove the entire trial was a farce. "That's just wonderful, Deane,'' I replied. "My entire office and staff will be at your disposal to help your cause, just remember to spell my name correctly when your book is published.''

Bostick laughed as he rose to his feet and shook hands with me, "Anything in particular you're interested in?''

"Frankly, Deane,'' was my answer, "this is as close to a breakthrough that can possibly occur. Dorothy Clark is the key. She may be persuaded to open up and tell the truth as to whether she ever laid eyes on Erler at any time before she identified him in court.''

"A piece of cake,'' laughed the reporter, gesticulating with the thumb and forefinger of his right hand in a farewell wave to me. "Will let you know when we strike pay dirt.''

VII
DILEMMAS

45

THE CALL CAME through directly from the switchboard. It was Mickey Mason, an old golfing buddy, who was a small-time gambler and a sometimes golf hustler. "Hey, Joe," he cried. "I'm at Woodlands golf course and just killed a guy."

Going along with what I believed was a joke, I replied, "Did you use a seven iron, or a sand wedge?"

"No, really," answered the excited caller. "I shot that dirty . . ." The conversation stopped and a new voice came on the phone. "Mr. Varon, your man here is in police custody on a first-degree murder charge. We're taking him to the sheriff's office for booking, in case you want to see him, sir."

"Thank you, officer, I'll be there shortly. Meanwhile, I'd appreciate it very much if you and your men would refrain from asking the suspect any questions."

"Yessir, will do," was the officer's response as he rang off.

"They all promise that," I mused and yelled for my secretary to get Eddie "on the double." My assistant strolled into my office holding a legal document. "Hello, Boss," he said brightly, "here is a detainer from Robert Erler that just came in."

"The hell with Erler," I snapped. "Were in the middle of a new homicide case, so sit down and take notes, because wait 'til you see what we've got now."

Henry Rubino was a Mafioso who came to Florida to retire from the pressure cooker of his many criminal activities and enjoy country club living at the Woodlands golfing community in Tamarac. His innate greed impelled him to engage in "shylocking" and "loan-sharking" in a comparatively small way and of necessity, he was surrounded by an accoutrement of "persuaders," a few tough thugs who would enforce loan collections that were slow coming in.

Rubino blithely played golf on the magnificent Woodlands course while his outstanding loans accumulated usurious interest at the rate of one hundred percent per month. Mickey Mason, a small-time gambler and golf hustler, borrowed some money from Rubino to cover a gambling debt and when he defaulted on his "interest" payments, his life became a living hell. He didn't mind being intimidated, or even roughed up by Henry Rubino's goons, but the threats to his lovely wife, Nancy, and his family, was of such alarming dimensions, he begged Rubino for surcease. Rubino's reply, with a vicious sneer, was, "I own you, you bastard, and I own your whole goddam family, too."

Mickey had a bad heart and became so distraught with the mounting pressures generated by Rubino and his hired mobsters, nothing mattered anymore. His family had to be saved from this beast, Rubino. One day when he knew Henry Rubino was playing golf at Woodlands, Mickey commandeered a golf cart from the bag boy at the club, drove around the course and found Rubino on the tenth hole, ready to tee off. Mason approached the tee, pulled out a gun and shot Rubino twice in the head, and as the Mafia chieftain lay dying in a pool of his own blood, Mickey stood over the twitching body and emptied his pistol, forever disposing of the mobster that threatened his life and family.

It was a tough case to defend. Why should I even care about Robert Erler's new predicament. By escaping from the authorities, he broke faith with me, and I was no longer obligated as his attorney, but yet, I firmly believed in his innocence and that the criminal justice system gave him a raw deal. Mickey Mason was facing the electric chair, but still the Erler case gnawed at my subconscious.

Eddie admittedly had trouble keeping up with my mood swings and I could understand his natural disenchantment with the Erler situation. The new murder case made me irascible and testy, but I knew there was an inexplicable, irresistible lure of the Erler dilemma that alternately challenged and mocked me.

Friday. Lunchtime at the Howard Johnson on the Boulevard with my secretary, Lucy, and Eddie. The fried clam special that was my favorite elevated my spirits to my assistant's relief, who was waiting for the propitious moment to bring up the latest tidbit on Robert Erler.

"By the way, Boss," he casually began, "Bob Erler sent me a notice of detainer addressed to the superintendent at Raiford alerting the authorities that at the conclusion of Erler's prison term he was to be detained to face escape charges in Palm Beach County. What do you want done on this?"

I munched thoughtfully on a mouthful of succulent clams, and was not quite ready to forgive Erler, fearing any further involvement would commit me to an infinite, never-ending struggle, beyond my initial responsibility. Eddie, however, was entitled to an answer. He was in training and needed the experience. "I doubt if the prosecution authorities in Palm Beach County will formalize a five-year charge against a man who is facing ninety-nine years and six months, so why don't you file a speedy trial request at your leisure and concentrate on reinstating the appeals that were dismissed because of his escape," was my reply.

It was easy for Deane Bostick to contact Dorothy Clark. The investigator made his way up to Clarkston, in Fulton County, Georgia, a sleepy little town deep in the milieu of the south, eight miles north of Atlanta at the foot of the historic Stone Mountain. Dorothy Clark lived in this post Civil War town of twelve hundred people, heralding the usual assortment of businesses: A gas station, the Starlite Motel and Bar, and the most imposing structure, the First National Bank of Clarkston. Bostick, in his folksy southern manner, infiltrated the clannish community and was able to find the residence of Dorothy Ammons Clark and was informed that she was working for the county as a typist. In late afternoon, the investigator gracefully intercepted Mrs. Clark as she walked down the courthouse steps.

"My name is Deane Bostick and I am a writer. I'm interested in a trial in which you were the star witness. I am gathering material and you are just the little lady that I hope can help me out."

"I am certainly glad to meet a writer. Do you write books?" asked Dorothy.

"Yes, ma'am," responded the investigator. "I have written many books and I am also a correspondent for several magazines." With that, Bostick showed Mrs. Clark his identifications and certificate indicating that he was a member of the Author's Guild and League, and pulled out another card showing himself to be a certified member of the Society of Magazine Writers.

"I am certainly impressed," exclaimed Dorothy Clark. "What can I do to help you?"

"Thank you for your kindness," responded Bostick, exhibiting the courtly mannerisms that were expected. They walked aimlessly together, engaging in small talk when Dorothy halted abruptly.

"There's my home." She pointed to a single-story frame house, dark grey slate tiles setting off the light blue stucco walls with the thick bougainvillea bushes trimming the picturesque border.

"It's delightful" cried Bostick, surprised to have arrived at the threshold of the Clark home so quickly. He felt he had incurred Mrs. Clark's interest, and his intuition proved correct when Dorothy invited him into the house to rest and talk a bit.

While the two were comfortably seated in the old, but clean frame house, Dorothy Clark and the investigator exchanged stories of their childhoods. A kinship developed between the two as they laughingly referred to themselves as "crackers" and southern "rebels." They exchanged mutual confidences perilously bordering on personal intimacies. Deane exulted. The floodgates were open! "Within an hour at dinner," Bostick said to himself, "he would have the true story about the Robert Erler trial from the state's ex-star witness herself."

46

THE LETTERS FROM Erler kept coming. The gunshot wound to his hip at the time of capture was almost healed, and realizing the enormous problems caused by his bizarre behavior he hardened his resolve to once again become a model prisoner. My motion to reinstate Erler's appeals was denied by the Florida Supreme Court and the legal jousting commenced at square one at a leisurely, but unerring pace.

A slim ray of hope for Erler pierced through the clouds of his despair. An innovative plan was nationally initiated for penealogical rehabilitation, whereby prisoners facing long sentences could be transferred to a penal facility in their home state to be near their immediate families, making the visitation privileges more frequent and easily accessible to the inmate. Mrs. Lucy Bachelor, Erler's friend and confidante, once again took him under her protective wing and encouraged him to make application for a transfer to the State of Arizona Penitentiary, which seemed to comfort him. This was a welcome respite for Erler who, with renewed hope, embarked upon an ambitious rehabilitation program, working prodigiously with his fellow inmates, conducting classes in Karate and the martial arts. He also pursued the genteel hobby of abstract artwork, to the gratification of the brass in the "front office," who were constantly monitoring Erler's activities, ever on the alert to some slight adversity that could trigger an abrupt emotional outburst.

Working happily on arts and crafts while awaiting negotiations for a possible transfer to the Arizona State Penitentiary, one of Erler's artistic endeavors attracted great attention in the prison compound. His new creation was a replica of an antebellum mansion painstakingly erected with ten thousand matches and household glue expending approximately seven hundred thirty hours in its construction. He was so proud of his handiwork, pictures were made of the completed structure, and circulated to friends and acquaintances. He even sent me an original painting on three foot by five foot plywood made with art materials of his own concoction, a combination of felt pens, magic markers and acrylics, the significance of which I could not fathom or comprehend, although I marvelled at the pigmentation and texture of the work with the turbulent array of incongruous shades of blue and blood red coloration. "Somewhere in this painting," I thought, studying the unusual rendition, "there is a message from a disturbed mind." Sometime soon, I would have the picture analyzed.

It was a raw, windswept afternoon in February and only Bob Erler, with a few hardy souls, ventured out in the gloomy recreation field for calisthenics, when a senior guard sauntered over with the news that Erler's application for transfer to Arizona was denied. Trying bravely to conceal his bitter disappointment he asked the guard, "Do you know why I was turned down?"

"Sure, Bob" answered the guard, genuinely sorry. "It's that detainer that was placed in your file," and observing Erler's crestfallen features, quickly added, "the warden and his entire staff were in your corner, so call your lawyer to try and get that damn detainer removed."

Erler walked back slowly to the general population area, looking for his classification officer. He needed assurance that he could reapply for a transfer to Arizona as soon as the detainer was lifted. I promised, saying, "It would be a little more time before the final order of removal was entered." Entering the empty television room Erler sat on a bench, rocking back and forth, arms tightly wound around his body, holding back tears of pent-up frustration. "Only thirty-four miles from my family."

Pressures were building up against Erler on all sides. In addition to his bitter disappointment in having his transfer request to Arizona rejected, he was beset with anxiety about his son who had been kept away from him by his ex-wife, Pattie. The more Erler thought about his son, his yearning for the boy grew into an obsession. He was periodically informed by his family that his ex-wife was considering bringing the boy to see his father. In his very next letter to me, Erler urgently demanded that the detainer for escape be dismissed. He must go to Arizona!

* * *

It was almost impossible for anyone to understand why a good-looking, pleasant matron, on the plump side, would shoot and kill her husband because, as the *Fort Lauderdale News* put it, "He took away her cigarettes." Undertaking the defense of the disoriented mother of a four-year-old boy, I knew from past experience there was a logical reason for every kind of human behavior and the administration of a battery of neurological tests, coupled with a psychiatric evaluation of the test results and discussions with the "patient" would probably unearth a clue to the rationale behind the bizarre homicide. It was necessary to learn, and understand the motivation behind the killing in order to set the stage for the defense. On a whimsical note I recalled how many times a criminal trial lawyer was equated with a Hollywood movie director, orchestrating a believable plot. For this particular scenario, as lawyer and casting director I selected a tall, handsome young doctor that set up practice in Hollywood as a cardiologist. Bernard Miloff, M.D. spent three years during World War II as Chief Psychiatrist of the United States Armed Forces in the Mediterranean area, and was an extremely capable medical doctor. He was also realistic. The community of Hollywood, Florida had geriatric overtones and the retired senior citizens were more predominant than a handful of disturbed teenagers. Miloff made his choice of medical "specialty" through economic expediency, although his training and true expertise was in the psychiatric field.

At a briefing session in my office, Dr. Miloff looked around the room and his thick dark eyebrows arched when his gaze landed on Erler's painting propped up against the wall. "What the hell is that?" thundered the doctor, straightening up in his seat.

I suddenly remembered Miloff was an art lover, and perhaps Bob Erler's rendition of Lord knows what, offended his sensibilities. "That was sent to me by a client in prison: maybe you remember the rookie cop they convicted as the 'Catch Me Killer'?"

The doctor pushed himself out of his chair and grasped the painting in both hands, placing it upright at the only window in my office for better vision. He removed his glasses and studied the rendition at close range for what seemed an interminably long period of time. No words were exchanged. Miloff solemnly returned to his chair, fixing a thoughtful gaze on me, and said, "This needs more study in conjunction with the artist in order to decipher the hidden message portrayed. The painting uniquely veils the turbulent nature of your client, which may erupt at a critical time."

"Have you any idea of what it's suppose to represent?" I asked.

"Not yet," replied the doctor, "but this abomination is full of weird surprises, so wait for the fun."

Doctor Miloff's prognostication of a "surprise" from Erler irritated me. "The whole damn law business is full of surprises," I grumbled mentally placing the Erler saga on the back burner again and returned to the newly made widow with the baffling cigarette problem.

The M and M Steak House in Clarkston provided the perfect setting for Dorothy Clark's catharsis. "You'll just love the collard greens and hush puppies," she gushed to Bostick, as they settled down at a corner table covered with a heavy white linoleum cloth, decorated with a small vase of cut flowers and red checkered napkins.

Deane and Dorothy toasted their newfound friendship from a carafe of red house wine, setting a pattern of continuous toasts throughout the entire repast. The blond waitress had cleared the dishes from the table over an hour ago and wondered how much longer this couple would dawdle over their wine glasses, talking up a blue streak, laughing and giggling.

Bostwick artfully returned the conversation to Dorothy's role as star witness in the Erler case. "Tell me," asked Deane, "was there ever a time when you were scared during this entire episode?"

Dorothy pursed her lips and frowned pensively. "My greatest fear was when this Erler person escaped from jail and no one knew where he was."

"Why should you worry about him? Did you have reason to fear that he would come after you?" asked Deane.

Mrs. Clark thought about the investigator's remarks and

said, "Well, maybe he was angry with me because of some of the things I said about him at the trial."

Bostick pounced on this like a terrier. "Was there something you said at the trial that might have made him angry with you or give him cause to seek you out?"

"It could have been things that I didn't say at the trial that could have made him mad at me," replied Dorothy.

"Do you mean that you held something back?" pursued Bostick.

"Frankly, Deane," replied Mrs. Clark, "there were a lot of things that happened to me on the beach that I was not asked to tell about. I certainly would have liked to tell my version of the true facts of the case."

"What do you mean by the 'true facts of the case,' Dorothy?" asked Bostick, trying to conceal his excitement.

"Oh, for example," related the wistful matron, "when I was on the beach that night in my car, the doors were locked and the windows were up. A man in a policeman's uniform rapped on the car window and when I saw he was a uniformed officer, I opened the window. Merilyn was with me, in the back seat trying to sleep."

"What happened after that?" asked the investigator.

"Well, the police officer, or whoever he was, reached in and pulled up the door handle and entered my car and said he wanted my money. I tried to make a joke about not having any money and Merilyn caught on right away and said, 'You must be a kook to think we have any money'."

"Please go on," encouraged Bostick. "Did the uniformed man or police officer get angry at you or Merilyn because you had no money to give up?"

"The truth of the matter is," ventured a now thoroughly pensive Dorothy Clark, "I do not remember any other details of the crime. Everything went black."

By this time Bostick could hardly contain his excitement. He knew that Dorothy Clark had testified that she had entered Erler's trailer and witnessed him committing the sexual act of masturbation. He sat back parrying for time to think of how much further he should go with Mrs. Clark at this initial meeting. He decided to take a calculated risk.

"Miss Dorothy," asked Bostick in his pleasant southern

drawl, "are you sure you blacked out and have no remembrance of anything after that?"

"That's right," Dorothy assured the investigator. "All I know about the case from then on is what I read about in the newspapers and what was told to me."

"Do you suppose, Dorothy," asked Bostick, "you would sign an affidavit as to what you just told me?"

"Certainly," answered Dorothy Clark. "Why not?"

"You see, when I write this book I have to make certain of the facts and would just like to confirm that the interview you gave me was voluntary."

47

EDDIE KAY BARGED into my office just as I was en route to the courthouse. The happy, beaming smile on his ruddy face promised a justification to excuse the sudden intrusion. "Good news, Boss. The escape detainer lodged against Erler was dismissed!"

"Great," I exclaimed, patting him on the shoulder, in silent recognition of his good work, and rushing out the back door of the office building said, "Now follow through and notify the client so he may reapply for transfer to the Arizona pen." Although I could not fathom why Mrs. Bachelor, Erler's guardian angel, was so loyally devoted to him, I knew she would set the wheels in motion for the transfer from Raiford to Arizona.

The bond hearing for the 'cigarette widow' took all morning before Judge Douglas Lambeth, who admitted her to reasonable bail, posted, to everyone's surprise, by her father-in-law. I was as much taken aback by this unusual turn of events as the newspaper reporters hounding me with questions. "Why would the father of the dead husband rally to the support of the wife who shot him?" Doug McQuarrie of the *Fort Lauderdale News* asked.

Evading further inquiries, I made my way to the snack bar in the courthouse lobby. "Sorry, guys," I called over my shoulder, "this is a strange case, but everything about this damned law business is strange, so never be surprised at anything that happens.''

Tom got up from the stool he was saving for me and went behind the counter. I recognized the signs and waited, the tuna fish sandwich on my plate untouched.

"Your ex-cop client is fouling up on drugs and misbehaving.''

"I'm shocked,'' I exploded with a trace of anger. "Bob Erler was doing so well in prison and now that little bastard pulls the dumbest stunt of all.''

"You better check into this a little deeper,'' Tom commiserated, regretting his bad tidings unsettled me. "Erler is drifting into uncharted waters . . .''

"And without a paddle,'' I supplied.

Tom gave a knowing smile and said, "I'd let him sink.''

Lucy always made it a point to place important mail for me in a spot on my desk where it stood out begging for attention. The return address on the envelope was that of the Fourth District Court of Appeals, and I nodded with approval as I avidly read its contents, then gave a whoop of triumph. The Reviewing Court, in response to my renewed motion to order the prosecution officials to produce all the tape recordings and transcripts of any statements made by Dorothy Clark while hospitalized at Broward General, granted us an evidentiary hearing. "Johnnie Melrose would be my first witness,'' I gloated, "and then the fur would fly.'' I was elated. The new hearing would definitely prove that the state willfully concealed beneficial evidence favorable to the defendant, which mandated a new trial for Erler. At last, things seemed to be fortuitous for the ex-cop in jail. I started making my usual calculations, the Palm Beach detainer was removed, and secondly, the appellate court virtually guaranteed a new trial. "Can it be, that we are seeing the light at the end of the proverbial tunnel?''

It was an easy matter to smuggle drugs into the prison. Marijuana and the mind-boggling LSD were abundant and in popular demand due to the eerie hallucinations and psychotic delusions the drugs generated. Robert Erler became a helpless participant in the drug scene, confounding the top officials in the compound who considered him a role model of rehabilitation. Educational classes and the physical fitness programs he directed were derailed, disappointing the trainees who looked up to Erler with grudging respect and admiration.

One afternoon Erler was flat on his back, his prison garb unclean and disheveled, snoring loudly as the mucus from both nostrils sprayed his lips and chin with each nasal blast, when a jail guard came into his cell to escort him to the colonel's office for an interview.

"Get up, Erler," the guard ordered. "The colonel wants to see you." The bleary-eyed inmate remained immobile on his back, unable to comprehend the blatant intrusion to a fanciful soporific dream. He stirred from his stupor with annoyance and muttered thickly, "Can't do it—don't wanna get up."

"Get your ass out of that cot!" the guard retorted angrily as he leaned over the disoriented Erler, roughly assisting him to his unsteady feet.

"I'm too high—can't you see that?" protested Erler in a slurred plaintive tone, but his complaint was ignored by the guard who, with business-like efficiency, partially held and dragged the tottering inmate down the highly polished tiled corridor, to where Colonel Hicks awaited the visitation of his most enigmatic and perplexing charge.

"Colonel, sir," respectfully began Erler, trying to stand erectly at attention and swaying drunkenly, "I'm under the influence of some strong drugs, so throw the book at me."

Colonel Hicks was dismayed at Erler's condition and closely examined him, recognizing the symptoms of drug addiction, and sadly directed the slovenly inmate to take a seat. "What is happening to you, Erler?" he asked. "What are you trying to do to yourself."

The distressed inmate looked at the kind face across the desk. His resolve to play the macho drug dealer dissolved into self-pity. His hands gripped the sides of his chair and a burning in his eyes brought forth a flood of tears. "Colonel, sir, life has no meaning for me anymore. There is no reason to go on living like an animal in a cage. All that I have ever loved has been taken away from me . . . my son . . ." he faltered, fighting bravely to stem flowing tears, "my son Bobby . . ." Erler choked, and began to sob uncontrollably; deep soul-wracking sobs that made his sturdy body tremble convulsively.

Colonel Hicks silently appraised the contrite figure who was weeping profusely, trying to dry his eyes with the sleeve of his filthy prison shirt, and said, "Crying is good relief to soothe your soul. This is a first step toward your reformation—there is no reason for you to be ashamed or embarrassed."

"I don't know why I'm acting like this," Erler apologized. "I never cried before."

"I'm glad you did, Bob," replied the colonel "because it tells me a great deal about your character. Now is the time to bare your soul." Erler tearfully obliged. The colonel's comforting indulgence had a sobering influence on the chastened inmate and was the catalyst that commenced the metamorphosis of Robert Erler.

Mrs. Bachelor, Erler's steadfast mentor, was alerted about the "new Bob Erler" and she painstakingly guided her ward to the prison chapel as well as impressing him into Bible study classes where he was warmly received by his fellow inmates who were religiously inspired. The prison chaplain presented Erler with a Bible and urged him to read the word of God. The two spent a great deal of time together and soon Erler regularly attended Bible classes, and all the revival meetings held in the prison. He would covertly kneel down and pray when he was certain he was alone and unobserved, for fear he would be ridiculed by the hardened convicts and accused of faking the "religion scam" to curry favors and receive special treatment. It was common practice for prisoners to pretend a religious awakening when their case was due for parole board review.

There were times when Erler had mixed emotions about his new religious pursuits and was assailed by doubts, but had to admit his apparent transformation made him the recipient of salutary benefits. The prison chaplain was delighted to have a strong, popular force like Erler as a bellwether to attract other inmates into his cadre of worshippers and became closely attached to his new disciple, wielding a strong influence on the new devotee of the Lord.

48

A JUBILANT DEANE Bostick telephoned from his home in Daytona Beach, Florida. "We hit the jackpot, Counselor," was his opening salutation.

"Do you have any good news?"

"Dorothy Clark admitted to me that when she met a uniformed man or police office at her car the man asked her for money, and when she said she had no money to surrender, everything went black. She also said she remembers nothing about the case from that point on except what she read in the papers," he reported proudly.

"Did you ask her about her being in the trailer and having an encounter with Erler?"

"Yes, sir," was the reply, "but she kept repeating that 'everything went black' after the uniformed man approached her while she sat in the car."

"Wonderful!" I exclaimed. "Did you have a recorder with you so we can have her taped statement?"

"No," replied Bostick. "I didn't want to do that because the first interview had to be a genteel meeting to establish a relationship. However, she promised to confirm her statements by giving me a notarized affidavit."

"By all means, Deane," I nearly exploded, my excitement mounting. "Get that affidavit. Don't let any grass grow under your feet."

"Don't worry," replied Bostick. "Give me a few more days and I'll deliver her written, sworn affidavit to you on a silver platter."

I was overwhelmed and shook my head in glowing admiration for the radiant, handsomely bearded investigative reporter, and said, "What a crazy business this is," and heard Bostick's belly laugh just before the investigator slammed down the receiver.

Ten days had elapsed, when a happy, buoyant Deane Bostick burst into my office brandishing a legal-sized single page document from his waving arms. He playfully thwarted my attempts to grab it. "Did you really get it?" I asked in genuine disbelief.

"Here's Dorothy Clark's sworn affidavit," he proudly announced, his swarthy face wreathed in smiles, "signed, sealed and now delivered. Bingo!" The two of us warmly embraced. This represented the culmination of years of travail and frustration. Bostick plumped his massive frame in an oversized chair, holding the precious affidavit ceremoniously in his hand and read with professional dignity:

> "This will confirm the fact that I have given an interview to Mr. Deane Bostick, a news writer, who interviewed me on March 26, 1974, in connection with his forthcoming novel concerning the Florida 'Catch Me Killer.'
>
> "This will further confirm that I advised Mr. Bostick that during the trial I was not asked to tell my version of the true facts of the case. For example, when I was on the beach that night in my car with doors locked and windows up a man in policeman's uniform rapped on the car window, seeing that he was a uniformed officer I opened the window. He reached in, pulled up the door handle, entered my car, said he 'wanted money.' I attempted to make a joke about not having any money. Merilyn, my late daughter, caught on right away, remarked, 'He must be a kook to think we have any money,' and everything went black for me. *I do not remember any other details of the crime.*"

"Fantastic!" I exhaled with relief.

"And . . ." the bearded writer added smugly, "signed by Dorothy Clark before a Georgia Notary Public."

My mind was at work again assessing all the legal avenues that could be pursued to fully exonerate Bob Erler. I vividly recalled how Dorothy Clark had taken the stand during the trial and electrified the entire courtroom by relating in detail how she was invited into Erler's trailer where he made a lewd proposal to her. I remembered the hush that came over the courtroom and the looks of disdain on the faces of some of the jurors when Dorothy testified that when Erler's indecent proposal was rejected, he started to masturbate in front of her and her little daughter, Merilyn. It was difficult to refrain from a vitriolic invective, as I bitterly fingered Mrs. Clark's sworn affidavit. The only eyewitness who had any direct evidence against Erler had practically confessed under oath that her testimony was "INCORRECT," to put it charitably. Someone on the prosecution team had to have orchestrated Mrs. Clark's "incorrect" testimony, but I was not interested in prosecuting anyone for subornation of perjury. I was only interested in procuring freedom for an innocent man.

The time bomb predictably erupted, not exactly as expected, but in a memorably bizarre fashion. One sunny Wednesday afternoon, preparing to leave the office for a golfing date at the club, Lucy excitedly intercepted my departure exclaiming, "Bob Erler is on the phone and wants to speak with you." Ordinarily, I would not have returned to the office to receive a telephone call, particularly when looking forward to a pleasant golf match, but since the caller apparently excited Lucy enough to thwart a sacred golf date, I retraced my steps and picked up the telephone in the library, which was adjacent to the reception room.

"How are you, Bob," I asked. "What can I do for you?"

"I'm a Christian," announced Erler. "I found Jesus Christ my Lord."

"That's wonderful, Bob," was my guarded response, wondering what was coming next. "I want to commend you very highly on your new pursuit for inner peace."

"The Bible has taught me that all sinners must own up to their deeds. I am a sinner and I want to confess my guilt," rapidly gushed Erler.

"What did you say?" I asked in disbelief.

"I am confessing that I am guilty. I don't want to fight my case any longer."

"Are you crazy, talking like this?" I shouted. "Don't you realize your telephone call is being monitored and you are talking out of your head?"

"Sorry," he replied. "I was told by God to confess my crime . . ."

"Stop talking nonsense," was my angry admonition. "You must be flipping your lid on those damn drugs you're taking. I better come up there to see you."

"It's no use. I've told my chaplain everything. I have lied to you and the courts and to all my friends. Don't waste your time coming up here. By accepting Christ, I am also accepting my responsibility."

I was crestfallen, staring with disbelief at the telephone, as though it were the culprit who delivered the astounding news. I dejectedly cradled the phone, looking back in retrospect at years of backbreaking work and untold out-of-pocket expenses. All the efforts and supreme dedication to a cause which was now drifting down the drain of oblivion. I woodenly turned to my secretary who was at my side, probably wondering why I looked vacantly around the room, as though an answer to my quandary would bounce off the walnut panelled walls.

"I refuse to believe that Erler meant what he told me on the telephone," and reported the substance of the conversation. "He is either high on drugs or has lost his mind completely. He told me not to come up there to see him, so I will at least honor his wishes at this point."

"Maybe you ought to let him cool off a few days until he comes to his senses," Lucy tactfully suggested. "It's hard to believe after maintaining his innocence all along he would make an about-face and confess he murdered that little girl."

"That's it," was my observation. "If he made a confession I must know the details of his statement and to whom he said it. I will also demand to know under what conditions he made any kind of incriminating statement. He had to be drugged out of his skull."

"Could it be that Erler might be in need of a psychiatrist at this time?" asked Lucy.

"I'm the one in need of a doctor," I lamented. "The Dorothy Clark affidavit is the key to his freedom and just as the jail doors are ready to open, he pulls this crazy stunt on me." By now I was the one holding my throbbing head in my hands. I remember thinking to myself, "How stupid can he be?"

Erler's weird telephone call occupied my thoughts for

the next few days, peevishly resenting this unwelcome in-trusion on the precious time needed for the homicide case that required all my attention. I decided to simply write Erler a letter enclosing a copy of Mrs. Clark's sworn affi-davit practically exculpating him, and, I growled, "He may act nutty as hell, but he possesses enough native intelli-gence to see his opportunity for freedom and vindication." A letter to Erler, designated "Personal and Confidential Le-gal Mail" was promptly dispatched, but that was not the last of my torments.

Another thought entered my mind which caused consid-erable annoyance. "Could it be," I asked myself, "that Erler was going along with the 'Born Again' religious scam bit?" Lately there were a rash of incidents in penal insti-tutions throughout the nation where certain convicts claimed the Lord Jesus Christ made a personal visitation into their prison cells, leading them to the path of right-eousness and became "Born Again Christians." A crafty, street smart prisoner could assume a new personality, claiming he surrendered his soul to the Lord and infiltrate the Sunday school and revival services cadre, thus attract-ing the attention of the prison authorities, ultimately leading to release on parole under the rationale that religious com-mitment and awareness precipitated complete rehabilitation. I remembered that Erler had telephoned me from his chap-lain's office, so perhaps my clever client maneuvered him-self into the charmed circle of prison politics and was playing the "Born Again" bit.

Why not? Murph the Surf, who was convicted with Jack Griffith of murdering the two young women, preached the gospel in jail and procured an early release. Perhaps that's where Erler got the idea.

49 _____

THE ONLY CONCESSION South Florida's tropical weather made in anticipation of the yuletide season was overcast, cloudy skies with the temperature dipping to the mid-fifties. The courthouse in Fort Lauderdale was gaily decorated with multicolored bunting laced with glistening silver strips of icicles. Mistletoe and holly were in abundance, tacitly reminding me and the other lawyers working in the area to distribute gifts to the employees and court attachés in appreciation for special services rendered the past year.

Everyone seemed to be radiant and happy this time of the season. So it was with me. The "cigarette widow" case was nearing its end at a most propitious time. Juries were prone to be more indulgent and compassionate during the Christmas period. The timing was perfect, and barring some unforeseen occurrence, jury deliberations would commence on the morning of December 24.

That evening, alone in the office, I made a list on the emblematic yellow legal pad of the salient points to be covered during closing arguments the following morning. While so doing, I idly looked around the room for ideas to materialize, when my secretary's handiwork became evident, especially the cleared-off space on the cluttered desk to announce an important piece of mail that required my immediate attention.

It was Erler's letter.

Dear Mr. Varon:

As I explained to you on the phone, I no longer desire to fight my conviction in court. I have become a Christian, and my appeal is to Jesus Christ. I have been so wrong in many things in life, and now I have found the way. Jesus said, 'I am the way, the truth, and the life.' I believe in Him, and I have turned my life over to Him completely. I am really at peace with myself, and it is the best thing that has ever happened to me. Praise God for it!

Whatever action you need to do to drop my appeal, please do so. If I need to do anything else, please let me know.

Have a very Merry Christmas and a Happy New Year. Remember that Christmas is the birth of our Lord Jesus Christ.

Love In Our Lord Jesus Christ,
Bob Erler

"Who needs this kind of grief at this particular time?" I groused. There was no reference or comment on the Dorothy Clark affidavit sent to him. I re-examined the letter and read each line carefully, noting it was replete with religious sayings, scrupulously avoiding all reference to the prized affidavit that proved his innocence. By her sworn statement, Mrs. Clark admitted she was never in Erler's trailer at the time of the murder of her daughter Merilyn, nor did she see the pictures on the wall where she claimed she identified Erler. Certainly the episode she recounted of Bob Erler masturbating and holding a gun on her at the same time never occurred. Someone put her up to saying that. Even though Erler had the positive proof of exoneration sent him he was no longer interested. His directions were simple,

"... Whatever action you need to drop my appeal please do so ... My appeal is to Jesus Christ."

I was not inclined to address the dilemma thrust upon me, but a decision had to be made. There was an ethical responsibility for a lawyer to comply with a client's written instructions, "but," was my rationale, "perhaps the order to quit the fight was the utterance of a beaten, disconsolate jailbird who lost touch with reality, and was clinging desperately to a newly found crutch." It seemed foolhardy to withdraw from the verge of victory on the passing whim of an emotional cripple, whose mood could change with the weather. It was a matter of judgment and I had to make the call.

* * *

In the Cutty Sark room at Joe Sonken's Gold Coast Restaurant, our annual Christmas party for the entire office staff was in full sway. Eddie Kay, now a full-fledged junior attorney, was happily ensconced between the pretty blonde receptionist and the more seasoned, attractive henna-haired bookkeeper, alternately gulping down gin fizzes and dry martinis, trying to make his mind up as to which girl he would like to wind up with. I surveyed the jubilant group from my vantage point at the head of the long table loaded with stone crab appetizers, Oysters Rockefeller, clams casino and a glittering array of partially filled wine goblets towering over shot glasses surrounding the antipasto trays. I envied the gaiety of the merrymakers and yearned to join in the fun, but the specter of the damned Erler dilemma cast a pall on my spirits. The duties as host were played out amid shrill, appreciative "goodbyes" and warm wishes for a "Merry Christmas" as the sated group joyously marched from the private dining room, waving and shouting greetings to the friendly diners who would yell back in amusement.

This display of happiness and contentment only dejected me further. I needed to have a sounding board for help in making a judgment on the Erler problem, and suddenly I knew who to see.

Early every morning, a white-haired, slim figure clad in a grey warm-up suit walks from the rear of his Emerald Hills townhouse, starting a slow measured trot which simulated jogging but realistically was a rapid walk. I waited and watched my old friend and neighbor, Doc Graditor, go through his morning constitutional and planned to intercept him for the advice sorely needed, so I also donned a sweatshirt, shorts and sneakers to create the illusion of a coincidental meeting. If the truth were known, I never jogged a day in my life.

"Good morning, Doc," was my greeting as the perspiring runner wheezed to a halt.

"Hi, Joe," announced the doctor, wiping his face and balding pate with a large bandanna he retrieved from his rear pocket. "Didn't know you exercised in the morning."

"Not really," I replied, almost ready to confess my subterfuge. "I just had to talk to you about something important, and knowing how busy you are . . ."

"Never too busy to speak with a friend," was the gracious response. "What can I do for you?"

I was slightly chagrined that my ruse worked, but I needed advice from the best. Doctor Milton Graditor, formerly the Superintendent of the South Florida State Mental Hospital conducted his specialized practice in Hollywood and enjoyed an outstanding reputation in his field. "He sure as hell is the best," was the consensus on the street and I was truly grateful that the psychiatrist would entertain my problems right on the spot.

We sat on a wooden bench at the entrance of the town house recreation building alongside the pool and the doctor listened intently while I recounted the entire Erler saga from its inception. I felt guilty for discommoding my friend who patiently sat in a perspiration-dampened sweat suit, listening to my emotional outpourings, but I needed guidance, and Doctor Graditor would help me make the right decision. The psychiatrist asked some pertinent questions, indicating to me that the doctor had his finger on the pulse of Erler's problems, and was astonished by the next inquiry. "Do you consider your client to be an alcoholic?"

"No, not an alcoholic, although he was into drugs quite a bit, pills, pot, coke and whatever else was smuggled to him in prison," I answered.

Graditor thoughtfully listened with quiet interest. "Was he addicted to drugs?"

"Not that I know of," I replied. "But I do recall that somewhere along the line Erler joined an Alcoholics Anonymous group in prison, even though he couldn't possibly be an alcoholic."

"That is not unusual," reflected the doctor pensively. "The AA ritual implicit in the rehabilitative program is steeped in religious tenets, and that may be what motivated your client to join the group."

"Then it seems that any area of religious pursuit would interest Erler enough to become a part of it, is that correct, doctor?"

"It is obvious that at this point your client is on a huge, religious kick and the sincerity of his new-found activity can only be determined through the passage of time,'' he responded.

"I'm running out of time," was my complaint. "I have to make a decision to either honor my client's request to throw in the sponge, or defy him and treat his request as another phase of his agonized mind."

The doctor thought carefully and remained silent for a long time. He turned to me and said, "It is true, as your client stated, that in order to embrace the Lord, one has to make a true revelation and admit all his sins. Sometimes certain individuals are so anxious to become a part of the new Born Again Christianity, they confess to sins which can be figments of the imagination."

"That's what I have been thinking, Doctor. Maybe Erler was reaching out for some help from somewhere and, seeking acceptance, had to admit he was a sinner. The greatest sin that he could possibly confess to is the murder of that little girl."

"Could be," mused the doctor, "and the colossal confession of killing that child would be so impressive that his status would be elevated among his peers in his Bible class."

"Do you suppose a psychiatric examination of my client would be prudent?"

"Not really," answered the psychiatrist. "It appears to me a judgment has already been made by the only person who had the right to do so."

I nodded in agreement and apologized for monopolizing precious time from the doctor's busy schedule. Dr. Graditor smiled indulgently and stiffly rising from the hard wooden bench groaned, "Just walk away from the problem. It's over for both of you."

With a weary sigh, knowing this was the end of the line, I said, "Thanks very much, Doc. I just needed someone to tell me what I already knew had to be done."

Blue Monday. I scrupulously tried to keep my calendar clear of all trial work the first few weeks in January, which was my least favorite month. The judges and jurors always seemed to be in a foul mood immediately after the Christmas and New Year holiday season. The spirit of brotherly love disappears as the reality of the harsh world emerges in the form of a physical and mental depression, not helped any when confronted with accrued bills and charges generated by the holiday season spending spree. "This is a rotten period of time," I grieved to myself. "Might as well do a little housekeeping of all distasteful matters, starting with that damned Erler and get rid of him once and for all."

My secretary was summoned to bring her book. Lucy opened the door from her adjoining office, steno pad in hand and seated herself quietly across the desk, awaiting instructions. She recognized my bad disposition and refused to initiate a conversation or make any inquiries. "Tell Eddie to dismiss all pending appeals and litigation on the Erler case immediately." I looked at my secretary for a reaction of surprise or astonishment, but Lucy maintained a poker face.

"We're closing our files on this case."

"What about your proof of his innocence?" asked Lucy. "Don't you have a responsibility to bring it to the attention of the court?"

"Technically, we're fired," I answered. "I'll always believe he was blameless, an innocent victim of an archaic criminal justice system that failed him."

"Or maybe," suggested the secretary, "even though he maintained his innocence all these years, he may have sincerely confessed his sins when he gave his soul to the Lord."

Trying not to show signs of impatience, I reached into my left-hand drawer, extracting a well-worn booklet of proverbs, and opened it to a bookmarked page and said, "This adage by Bunyon tells it all," and read aloud,

"Religion is the best armor that a man can have, but it is the worst cloak."

EPILOGUE _____

A QUARTER OF a century later, on the occasion of my retirement, the single-story building on Hollywood Boulevard
that once housed a busy law office was being evacuated for
a new occupant. Dania patrolman Wayne Davidson, who
with fellow police officers William White and Sergeant Joseph Portelli testified against Erler, was found guilty of
compounding a felony and accepting a bribe. At the trial,
White testified under oath that he, Portelli and Davidson
were accomplices splitting the proceeds of the bribe.

The prosecutor, Len Boone, went on to serve a long and
distinguished career on the Broward County Circuit bench
before his retirement.

The judge that presided over Erler's trial was removed
from judicial office by Florida's Governor Claude Kirk,
with the approval of the Senate's Select Committee on Executive Suspensions for violation of "well established
moral ethical and judicial principles" and incompetency in
office.

My protégé, Eddie Kay, became a leading criminal defense attorney with his own practice in Fort Lauderdale.

Convicted murderer and escaped convict, Jack Griffith,
remains at large to this day.

Robert Erler was transferred to the Arizona penal system
where he became a religious leader and lay preacher. He
was subsequently given his freedom to follow the Lord's
work.

It was late in the afternoon as I was about to leave my
office after a life of enough fascinating cases to fill a library
of books. In all candor, it was emotionally tough walking
out that door one last time. I kept looking around at the
walls, now void of pictures and certificates and diplomas.
The memories suddenly raced through my mind: Hundreds
of murder trials with clients in all reaches of society. Grisly
details of death. Sobbing witnesses. Ruthless individuals.

Relentless prosecutors. False testimony. Raging courtroom encounters. Many victories. Few defeats.

For a young man from the south side of Chicago, it was a hell of a life. It was a life of more adventure and more satisfaction than one has the right to ask for. Suddenly my eyes were becoming cloudy. Time to leave. Just before I walked out the back door to the parking lot, my clerk had one final set of files for me to approve for destruction. I looked at a series of four red colored folders marked "ERLER/CONFIDENTIAL." I gave the go-ahead to destroy them and then reminded myself that this was a case "closed but not solved." I could hire all the Harry Longs in the world and still never know who murdered the young girl from Georgia. More than likely the real killer is still out there.